MW00698272

The Maiden of Florence

KATHERINE MEZZACAPPA

Fairlight Books

First published by Fairlight Books 2024

Fairlight Books
Summertown Pavilion, 18–24 Middle Way, Oxford, OX2 7LG

Copyright © Katherine Mezzacappa 2024

The moral right of Katherine Mezzacappa to be identified as the author of this work has been asserted by Katherine Mezzacappa in accordance with the Copyright, Designs and Patents Act 1988.

All rights reserved. This book is copyright material and must not be copied, stored, distributed, transmitted, reproduced or otherwise made available in any form, or by any means (electronic, digital, optical, mechanical, photocopying, recording or otherwise) without the prior written permission of the publisher.

A CIP catalogue record for this book is available from the British Library

1 2 3 4 5 6 7 8 9 10

ISBN 978-1-914148-50-7

www.fairlightbooks.com

Printed and bound in Great Britain

Cover Design © Holly Ovenden

Holly Ovenden has asserted her right under the Copyright, Designs and Patents Act 1988, to be identified as Illustrator of this Work

This is a work of fiction. All characters in this publication – other than the obvious historical characters – are fictitious and any resemblance to real persons, living or dead, is purely coincidental.

For Paola Tinagli

The Gonzaga Family
(abridged)

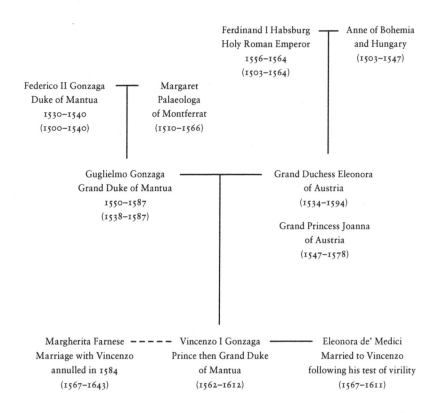

Ferdinand I Habsburg
Holy Roman Emperor
1556–1564
(1503–1564)

Anne of Bohemia
and Hungary
(1503–1547)

Federico II Gonzaga
Duke of Mantua
1530–1540
(1500–1540)

Margaret
Palaeologa
of Montferrat
(1510–1566)

Guglielmo Gonzaga
Grand Duke of Mantua
1550–1587
(1538–1587)

Grand Duchess Eleonora
of Austria
(1534–1594)

Grand Princess Joanna
of Austria
(1547–1578)

Margherita Farnese
Marriage with Vincenzo
annulled in 1584
(1567–1643)

Vincenzo I Gonzaga
Prince then Grand Duke
of Mantua
(1562–1612)

Eleonora de' Medici
Married to Vincenzo
following his test of virility
(1567–1611)

The de' Medici Family
(abridged)

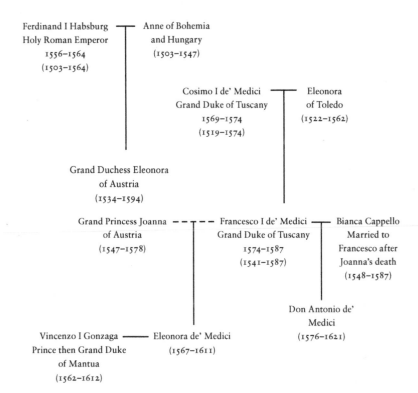

Ferdinand I Habsburg ——— Anne of Bohemia
Holy Roman Emperor   and Hungary
1556–1564   (1503–1547)
(1503–1564)

Cosimo I de' Medici ——— Eleonora
Grand Duke of Tuscany   of Toledo
1569–1574   (1522–1562)
(1519–1574)

Grand Duchess Eleonora
of Austria
(1534–1594)

Grand Princess Joanna – – ┬ – – Francesco I de' Medici ——— Bianca Cappello
of Austria   Grand Duke of Tuscany   Married to
(1547–1578)   1574–1587   Francesco after
                                     (1541–1587)   Joanna's death
                                                                   (1548–1587)

Don Antonio de'
Medici
(1576–1621)

Vincenzo I Gonzaga ——— Eleonora de' Medici
Prince then Grand Duke   (1567–1611)
of Mantua
(1562–1612)

PART I: GIULIA, AN ORPHAN OF FLORENCE

Chapter One

*No girl is to have a nickname, nor should any girl touch
another in any way, nor have any possession of her own. Nor
should she talk in church or in any place of prayer or in the
refectory, dormitory, on the stairs or in any common area;
furthermore, when she is spoken to she should respond humbly,
'Praise be to the Lord'.*

From the statutes of the orphanage of the Pietà, Florence
(25 March 1570)

My defloration was talked about in all the courts of Europe. My
hymen, which the Prioress in Florence had urged me to dedicate to a
holy bridegroom, was peered at by men, prodded, tested, certified,
then overthrown, its bloody extinction observed and written of
from Venice to Florence, to Mantua, to Ferrara, to Rome. The
Prince boasted of his prowess, of the number of times he had had
me, even as preparations were being made for his wedding, as
boldly as if he had ridden across the causeway to his Mantuan
palace with the bloodstained sheet tied to his lance.

Those events are almost thirty years old, but I remember them
as if they happened thirty days ago, though I have tried to bury
the memories. Nearly every player in that story is dead. It is only
now that what happened can be told by me, not by the men – and

woman – who decided my fate. Those who sniggered behind their hands or craned from their windows to catch a glimpse of the heir to the Gonzaga dukedom as he passed through Florence to claim his bride did not even know, or care to know, my name. I heard the fanfare of that procession while I sat in that dark house, the Prince's child growing inside me, while I sewed for my marriage chest, and wondered about the husband they would choose for me.

It was a woman who came up with that shameful plan. But, fittingly, it was another who taught me to read and write, so that I may tell whoever will listen what was done to me.

A loom stands in the corner of this room. I was put to weaving in the orphanage and cannot remember when I did not know how. For that reason I didn't want one of my own for so long. It reminded me of my slavery. When the Prioress summoned me to meet those men who told me I was to be dowered and married, she said I should learn to be a gentlewoman, and that I should never have to work again. I rejoiced. It was more than I had ever dreamed of. But now, when I am grey-haired and have children who are generous to me, I find I cannot be idle. I can sit at the loom when the light is weaker, and I do not have to strain my eyes as I now do for work with my needle. I thought I should have forgotten how to weave, but it feels as natural as walking, and the rhythm of it is comforting. That clack and whirr – it frees my thoughts. God willing, I shall have another grandchild by Pentecost. My son's wife brought nothing with her but her love for him, and it pleases me to make things for the little one, and for their home. But in daylight, I weave with ink and paper. I am not used to expressing myself this way, as I was lettered only as a grown woman. I have learned, though, to put my thoughts down just as they come to me, as memory prompts me. Perhaps what I have to say will not interest others much. However, I am a mother, and anything a child of mine does I treasure like a rare gem, so I am writing this for you, my own mother, who did not see me grow and so was deprived of moments like those that have meant so much to me.

What happened to me was no less than an affair of state. A mortal sin condoned by cardinals. To tell my story I must name those who are my betters – or consider themselves such. Vincenzo, Grand Duke of Mantua. His father-in-law Francesco, Grand Duke of Florence. Francesco's minister, Belisario Vinta, who, if he had not held that office, would be considered by honest men nothing more than a pander.

Now, there are those who would say that I was a fornicatrix, a temptress, to justify their greater sin. In Florence, the Grand Duke had absolute control even of my privy parts, though he knew no more of me than the name I had in the orphanage: Giulia Albizzi. Venice, by contrast, is a Republic – run, of course, by a small, closed clique of aristocratic men who manage things as best suits their own interests – but each is at least answerable to the others. I would like to say – or better, I hope – that what happened to me could not happen here. Yet I expect it happens daily. When a girl child leaves an orphanage to go into service, she of course enters into that little kingdom of a household where it is her master who is her absolute ruler. If he is a good man, then he will find her a husband when her indenture ends. If he is not, then she must bend to his humours, his caprices and, if he desires her, his lusts. He knows, of course, what to do with the child that is born of his tyranny. In Florence there was a wheel. Here there is the *scaffetta*, large enough only to allow a newborn to be passed through.

This story is not mine alone, however, but also my husband's – the man they found for me. He wrote his *ricordanze* regularly. He was not a Florentine, but he took on that Tuscan habit. His writings are more than a mere day book, though. Besides my memories – and my children – they are all I have left of him. They are, in part, an account of our love.

I believe I was born in Florence, though I do not know where, for I knew nothing of you, Mother, or my father, and no one has ever claimed kinship with me. Yet I bear a name, Albizzi, that I have since learned was once renowned in my native city. After I was taken from the hands of those pious, duplicitous women at my second orphanage, the Pietà, and entered the wider world I thought I should never see, it was to find that Albizzi men still held high office but had to work for a living. For many years I took it for granted therefore that my father was an Albizzi, and you, my mother, must have been a servant, and as such could count on no one for protection. Not all the girls in the Pietà were Florentines. Some came from quite far afield – Arezzo, even. A respectable family does not want to be reminded of a shameful birth, nor to encounter its likeness in the marketplace.

But unlike the other girls in the Pietà, I had been in another orphanage first. My earliest memories are of the Innocenti where I lived until I was about ten years of age, in almost exclusively feminine company. In age we girls ranged from babes at the wet nurse's breast right up to grey-haired women who had passed their entire lives within those walls. What we had in common was our abandonment, passed through an opening below the portico of the orphanage onto a cushion laid between praying statues of Our Lady and her husband Joseph. Every child, even girl infants, were thus – for a few scant moments until their cries attracted attention – at one with the King of Heaven. I have seen that opening since. There is a Latin inscription above it which my son Tino read and translated for me, for my eyes were already weakened: 'When my father and mother forsake me, the Lord will take me up.'

There were boys in there too, but we girls spied them only at Mass. They were never as numerous as us. I learned later that sometimes a man will acknowledge a male bastard but shrug off the fact that he has fathered a little girl. The only men I saw were the priests and deacons in the chapel, and the Prior – a Benedictine. Day to day we were cared for by women, and instructed by them – in spinning, weaving, embroidery. The boys, I learned later, were apprenticed to trades, for they had to make their way in the world. We had only to serve.

We orphans, I have noticed, can often find each other out, among strangers. And the hopes we all nurtured can be harder to kill than one might think. My commonest daydream when I was a very little girl was of my father coming to take me away. He would be finely dressed, a coat of arms upon his shoulder, a sword at his hip, riding upon a gleaming horse. All we girls sustained ourselves with images like that; the only singular thing about it was that our longings resembled one another's so closely. Nobody imagined her father as a workman in a greasy apron, with dirt under his nails. And no child ever said she dreamed of her mother, for it was impressed on us from the youngest age that we were the product of sin. If man was made in the image of God, then a woman's divine example was Our Lady, perpetual Virgin, and the fact that we bastards existed was proof of an offence done to the Queen of Heaven. Our parents' fault lay heavily on our shoulders, and we could only expiate it, and show gratitude for the charity shown us, by piety and hard work. Expelled from Eden, Eve span – and so did we. It was the silk merchants, those who had endowed our orphanage, who gained all the benefit of it, though.

No, nobody spoke of her mother and no more did I, though lying alongside my fidgeting companions – we were four or five to a bed – I longed for your arms. I did find a replacement mother, for sometimes it happens that as a child needs a mother there are those who also need a child, and I had Tommasa, another orphan. But only a father had the power to release any of us – and in all those years I was there, none did.

It was not that the Innocenti was a prison – or at least not in the way the Pietà was. I was sent out to beg alms. I have never told anyone of this before, except my husband. If they were fit for it, the girls of the Innocenti went out into service. I was told I would not, even though I was straight and strong, while some of the women in there were maimed, diseased or ugly with age. I thought I should become like them if I stayed all my time in the orphanage, so I wanted to go out, even to beg. They told me I was pretty, though I never saw my own face in a mirror until I was twenty years old. I would go to the doors of the churches, to the Annunziata, and to San Marco, and rattle my little box.

My husband once asked me if I had thought of running away, but where would I have gone? Tommasa, the girl I went out with, who slept beside me, could not have run anyway. She had one leg shorter than the other, so she walked with a lurch. I think now that is why they put us together: the poor maimed girl and the little one with the curls. It was the contrast we made. I loved Tommasa, and she loved me. She protected me like a she-wolf protects her cubs. There was always someone when we went begging who wanted to entice me away, you see, and even though they offered me sweet things to eat and used kind words, some instinct made me not trust them. To one man I said: 'I will come with you only if Tommasa comes too,' and he laughed and walked away. Even though I was little I knew that if a stranger really was gentle, he would show his gentleness to her too, but no one ever wanted poor Tommasa. After they had taken me to the Pietà and I realised I would never see her again, I thought I should never stop crying, even though they threatened to beat me for ingratitude. I never had an opportunity to say goodbye to her, she who was the nearest I had to a mother.

Chapter Two

Via del Mandorlo, Florence
1584

...[una] cortese, e ridente bocca... rotondo collo... petto... picciolo corpo... ellevato fianco... dritta gamba... picciolo piede...
...a courteous and smiling mouth, round neck, large breasts, small body, high hips, straight legs, small feet...
Ciro Spontone, *Hercole difensore d'Homero* (1595)

The author of this dialogue on ideal beauty in a woman was a politician and writer at one stage employed at the court of Vincenzo Gonzaga

I find that I can write of my earlier life without too much difficulty. What came later will be harder. I have to tell myself I had no choice, but I still blush with shame.

I was taken from the Innocenti to the Pietà without warning. I think I was about ten, because while I know my age, more or less, I do not know the day on which I was born. I had not been out to beg for two years or more, and I was excited at the chance of seeing a little more of the world than that rectangle of sky above the girls' courtyard. I held the matron's hand, chattering with excitement until she told me sharply to hold my peace. But she could not damp my enthusiasm. I couldn't know then that it would be another ten years before I would be able to speak so freely.

Anyone who is not an orphan and who moves from one place to another has belongings they take with them. I had none, for everything in the Innocenti was owned in common. I had no hint that I was doing anything other than going for a walk.

It was soon clear to me that the Pietà was quite a different place; not an academy for girls to be sent into service, but an anteroom to the cloister. I looked up at a sheer wall. There was no pretty colonnade with those roundels of swaddled babies as there was at the Innocenti – only small, barred windows. This place was run by pious widows, laywomen, those who did not want to submit to convent discipline so much as to impose it. I heard the clatter of looms the moment a gnarled old lay sister opened the gate to us, and smelled the pungent, bitter smell of silkworms being boiled to death to give up their precious thread. But with that, much of the resemblance to the place where I had spent my previous life ended.

The matron nudged me over the threshold. The lay sister took me by the shoulder and half pulled me inside, shutting and barring the great door behind me. The matron had gone without a word – she was not the last woman to have care of me to leave me in that way.

'You are not to look up at the windows,' whispered the lay sister, 'or you will be punished. Nor are you to talk – not at your loom, nor in the dormitory, nowhere. You may speak only if the Prioress or one of her assistants addresses you, and your answer must be as brief as her question requires.'

I soon discovered that the girls – for there were only girls in there – were for the most part older than I. I saw no men in all the years I was there save the priests, and occasionally a workman, at whom we all peeked, though he was always guarded – there is no other word for it – by two of the oldest inmates. And old they were, having passed all their lives there, a thought that makes me shiver still). In the Innocenti we could not speak to the boys, but we knew they existed and how they looked, sitting in their conical hats at

Mass on the other side of the chapel; and how they sounded, their shouts at playtime in their courtyard reaching over the roofs of the dormitories to where we played our more sedate games.

There was one crucial difference between these girls and those I had left behind. This was made to weigh on me, for every condition of life has its hierarchies, as it is part of the imperfection of being human that the most lowly among us will look to see if there is someone to despise even more than they themselves are despised. We were not all bastards. Some of my companions knew who they were. It was their fathers who had brought them there, driven by poverty. There were some, the offspring of priests, who were marked with a particular shame.

I say all of this as though we talked freely of ourselves, but of course we could not. None of us ever took a vow of silence, but silence was imposed on us in there. Yet we found ways to whisper in corners, a girl posted as look-out who would sneeze or cough to warn of coming danger, or we would mouth to each other and our mouths be read.

In my own daughters I have observed these milestones of life: the moment a child first contemplates the thought that one day she will be a woman, or when she first looks at herself in a glass and moves her face from side to side in deciding whether she is beautiful, and what it is that makes her so – or looking for defects others either would not notice or declare to be charming. I have dried the raging tears that come when a dearest friend betrays by preferring the company of another little girl. I have quietly explained what the changes in a girl's body mean – how they equip her to be a mother. In the Pietà all these thoughts and fears remained as hidden as our bodies in those shapeless tunics we all wore. That cramping pain and the blood that came with it as the moon turned were acknowledged only as a sign of our imperfection. Even simple friendship was looked upon askance, just as it is for those women who take the veil – as both a selfishness that excludes others and another manifestation of worldly wealth that it was better to renounce. There was nothing in that life that prepared me for the direction mine was to take. Nothing.

I was twenty when those two men and an older lady came, and I was called to the Prioress's parlour. I should remember the date, but do not. I can only say that it was winter still, though the days were lengthening; there was more light, each day, streaming in from those high windows to where we sat at our looms. I had by then given up dreaming of another life, for to do so had become more a torment than a delight. By then I was resigned to a choice, if it can be called that, of only two paths: to remain where I was all my life, and to be a mother at most only as an instructress in spinning or weaving to the younger slaves of that place, or to walk the short distance to the sisters at Santa Caterina in Cafaggio, closer to the Innocenti – to have my head shaved and to be vested as a Dominican sister, though I had no calling to it.

I knew myself as Giulia Albizzi in the Pietà, but I heard the Prioress with her visitors – Belisario Vinta, the doctor, the matron – call me Giulia *of the* Albizzi. I never had the surname of a foundling: Diotallievi, Diotaiuti or anything like that. I know now that it was because of my name that the Prior of the Innocenti had sent me to the Pietà instead of into service, but no mother or father stepped forward to stop those visitors from taking me away that day. They told me I was honoured, those people who came for me: they had been elsewhere – to view girls of marriageable age in the Innocenti, among others – before they came for me.

It was not the first time I had been brought to the Lady Prioress's parlour. Sometimes I had sewn there, when there were visitors who wanted to buy what we made in the orphanage. I knew whenever that was going to happen, for I would be made to wash beforehand, and the water I was given was fresh, used only by me. Because I was one of the girls regularly chosen for this kind of exhibition, I learned that I had something some of my companions did not: I was pleasing to look at. There was no other way of knowing this, for I had never seen my own face – we had no mirrors. I knew only that my skin was smooth and clear, because sometimes when no one was looking I would touch it.

That was then the loveliest chamber I had ever seen. The Prioress's parlour had tapestries around the walls, and above them, paintings of virgin martyrs: Agnes, covered in her own hair to protect her nakedness from those prying, humiliating eyes; Barbara, tortured and burned in every part of her that made her a woman; Catherine of Alexandria standing before men and countering them in argument (a thing extraordinary in itself) while in the background her executioners prepared the wheel – and Ursula. She was no poor girl, but a princess, and she was going to marry a prince, as if in a fable, only that she wanted first to go to Jerusalem on pilgrimage and the prince would have to come with her and her vast bevy of maidens. Her father must have loved her dearly to agree to all that she demanded. I never knew *my* father – and by then I thought that perhaps he had never known even of my existence – but I cannot imagine that there are many as obliging as Ursula's. Her fable did not end well (in my view), for she and her maidens were set upon by pagans in a country to the north of here – the kind where they say heretics flourish even now – yet they embraced death over dishonour. Ursula was looking towards heaven and a martyr's crown as the arrow pierced her throat. The poor young man who was to have been her husband they killed too. I thought all those saints very noble, very brave, and loved to hear their stories (the only ones we did hear, besides those in the Bible, some of which I confess frightened me, and still do). Now, of course, I can read what I like, but that does not mean I always do.

Those women were courageous defenders of their virtue. Yet that day the Prioress sat and smiled as she displayed me to her visitors – with no needlework in sight.

I recognised one of the men as a doctor because of the way he was dressed, with that wide-brimmed hat, and I trembled, for I remembered such men coming to the Innocenti sometimes, to see the older girls who had returned from service outside, and the cries and screams when they were ministered to. Doctors were not allowed in the Pietà, for when our own *medica* despaired of any girl lying sick in the infirmary, that girl was taken from her care to the hospital at Santa Maria Nuova. I do not remember anyone coming back from there. Perhaps if an orphan was to be given up for dead, the Prioress ceased to worry about the presence of men. This one they referred to as Master Cappelli.

The other man sitting there I later knew as the *cavaliere*, Belisario Vinta, minister to the Grand Duke himself. The matron's name was Giovanna Prati, she told me, but I do not remember anyone ever using it afterwards – they simply called her 'matron'. From the moment I left the Pietà, she was with me constantly – almost constantly – until one day she disappeared from my life without a word. The men were never with me unless she was present, but she always did what they told her. I came to realise that her presence was to protect them from evil tongues – not to protect me.

'A very great honour is to be bestowed on you,' began the Prioress, after presenting me to her visitors. 'His Highness Grand Duke Francesco, our patron, has in generous charity decided to dower a girl – for marriage, not for the cloister – and you are to be that girl.'

I looked from face to face, my mouth open. The cavaliere was nodding in satisfaction, the doctor commenting on the luminosity of my skin.

'He has stipulated only these conditions,' went on the Prioress. 'One is that the girl be beautiful, and capable of bearing beautiful children to the lasting honour of Florence. The other is that she should accompany this gentleman,' (the man called Vinta bowed) 'and this lady, on a journey. At the end of that journey a task will be required of her which will not be onerous, but may indeed be pleasurable, and in which she will represent her city and our rulers. She is to carry out that task with grace and diligence, in gratitude for the care that has been taken of her.'

'How will I know what to do, Lady Prioress?' I saw the two men exchange smiles.

'You will be instructed.'

'And who is to be my husband?' I whispered. I thought I must be dreaming.

'He will be chosen for you. Before you meet him, though, you must be taught the obligations as well as the joys of the married state – let us say that you must be made ready for him. We expected to keep you here in the Pietà and for that reason you have never learned what it is to be a wife, nor indeed to live in the world. Here, I think, is where we should start.' Saying that, she handed me a mirror, a little gleaming oval in which I saw what others had seen all of my life, but I never at all. I knew the colour of my skin, the darkness of my hair on those occasions when it was unwrapped to be washed, and I knew the shape of my mouth and nose to the touch, but I looked into eyes I had never yet seen and realised why I had been chosen.

The cavaliere then spoke: 'Mother Prioress, recollect that she will be meeting a prince. It is he, we might say, who will be the making of her – of her fortune, I mean. She has a natural nobility of manner as well as a beautiful face, but for our endeavour to meet with full success she must be presented to the best advantage.'

I was dizzy listening to them, and fearful. Was I too, like Ursula, to go on some strange pilgrimage, and with a prince? What would a prince want with me? Would I be martyred with him also? I said something like that, and they laughed, and the cavaliere said I had a ready wit, which was most pleasing, but that the modesty and gracefulness of my demeanour was of even greater value. He asked the Prioress how long would it take for them to make me ready, and she asked two days. No one told me what it was I was going to do, or why, only that I would bring great lustre to Florence. They said other girls had been selected, not from Florence but from some other city I had never heard of, but that though appetising, they did not fit the standard of beauty the Prince had demanded.

'You are to be married,' repeated the Prioress, 'and you will be rich enough that you need never work again.'

I stared at her, speechless, until I realised I was being very rude, and cast my eyes down, the way we had all been taught. I could not understand her words. I knew she was a widow, yet she and her assistants and our confessor had always dinned into us orphans that the married state was little else than a means of avoiding the fires of hell, as St Paul teaches, and that lifelong chastity – preferably behind convent walls as a bride of Christ himself – was the honourable choice. Furthermore, we girls had also been taught that idleness was the joy of the devil, and that the more productive we were at the loom or with our needles, the greater would be our reward in heaven (as any earthly rewards our work reaped we never saw ourselves). But after they told me I was to be married, I could barely hear anything else they said for excitement. I was to leave the Pietà. I would have a man to love me.

'Am I to marry this prince?' I asked.

They all laughed then, though I thought the Prioress's mirth was a little forced. Her laughter did not reach her eyes.

'No,' said the cavaliere, 'but he will help you understand the married state. As we have said, a husband shall be found for you.'

They asked me was I willing, and of course I said yes. I still couldn't understand what they really wanted of me, though I noticed they watched me very closely. I saw the rejoicing in their faces when I said yes, and was glad I had pleased them.

In those two days I was kept from the other girls, and never had the opportunity to say goodbye to them, any more than I had at the Innocenti. This I was not surprised at, however, for

I knew that any girl who left the Pietà and married (there were a few, collected for that purpose by parents whose course in life now ran smoother) was permitted no further contact with her old companions.

After the visitors had gone I was brought to a room where there was a bath made of marble, sunk in the floor. I had never seen it before and think it must have been the one the Prioress used, for we girls bathed standing in something like a large iron bucket, and I was never the first to use the water. Each of us entered one by one the room where that bucket was; I had never seen any of my companions unclothed nor they me. Yet this time four of the oldest women of the Pietà stripped and washed and scraped and perfumed me, but would not answer my questions about where I was to go. They puffed smoke at me too, the way the acolytes wave incense over the altar. My hair was washed also, and the animals that crept in it and made my head itch until I picked them out and cracked them with my nails were chased out of it on the point of a comb till my hair felt as though it no longer belonged to me; it was then brushed until it sparked and my head felt light with the air moving through each tendril. Before, you see, my hair had been tied and hidden beneath the caps we all wore; we girls were dressed more plainly than the nuns themselves. I learned for the first time that my hair reached to the hollow of my back, and its colour and thickness was made much of: 'autumn chestnuts,' said one of my attendants. Yet all my life I had been told that such things should not be admired, as they were occasions of sin, pride being the worst of all failings. I wondered at all this that was being done to me, thinking, *this must be how a bride is prepared.* I could barely stand still for excitement.

The Prioress inspected me after the first bath and said that my skin was merely downy and that those little hairs could lie undisturbed – neither wax nor sugar was required. Some dark hairs were torn from my big toes – I remember the pain of it still – and the hard skin of my heels was pared away. Never had anyone looked at me so minutely, but in the days to come my body was no longer my own, with all the peerings and proddings they put me to. Then they gave me a clean linen shift – it looked new to me, such a marvellous thing! – and on top of it a dark green dress in a soft, supple wool the likes of which I had never seen, much less had upon my person. They tied on the sleeves and put little soft leather slippers on my feet in place of my clogs. I cried for joy, thinking myself a queen.

'A plain perpignan becomes her,' said the matron when she came back two days later. 'We need only garland her head.'

My last night in the Pietà I barely slept, and it was not just for excitement and anticipation but because I was at last to sleep alone, in that new clean shift, in a little chamber on a low bed with a downy mattress, not a scratchy palliasse of straw. I missed the sound of the other girls turning and muttering and crying in the dark, though when I was one of them, I thought they would eventually drive me mad.

I was bewildered by the light, the noise, the smells when I left the Pietà. We hardly ever went outside, you see, only for processions like Corpus Domini where, all dressed the same, we would walk behind the cross, strewing flowers. I was always made to walk within the procession, not at its edges where the older women were. Every year, for weeks after being outside on that bright June day my thoughts would be fired by the colours and richness of what I had seen: the silks and lace of the ladies, their supercilious expressions (only now do I realise that not all of them could have been respectable), the fine features of men I could have loved, the grotesquely distorted beggars whining for alms on their pallets. When the orphanage doors closed on us again after these outings I knew I should have been reflecting on the poor broken body of our Saviour who suffered for us, but instead all I thought about were those smiling dark eyes, the sunlight glinting off swords and scabbards, the shouts and laughter beyond the droning voice of the priest and the sung responses. I was both excited by and frightened of that open space, all those people, because I was so used to the Pietà's confining walls.

And now, when they came to me with that dress, speaking to me of this unknown prince and the service I would do for one of the greatest houses in Italy, and of the man who afterwards would be my very own, I had my chance to explore that world. When the Prioress told me that even the Holy Father and all the cardinals blessed this endeavour it only added to my delirium.

The cavaliere came back for me with the matron when those women had done their work and I – marvellously! – smelled only of lavender. For as long as it is in my power, I shall always strive to be as clean as they made me then, and I have insisted (in the face of some resistance sometimes) that anyone living under the same roof as me take the same care. I was given another, simpler dress to wear, which they said had also been made for me, while the wool one was put into a leather bag they said was mine, along with more clean linen. They told me I would have other clothes in time, a proper *corredo* for a bride, something I had never thought about much less prepared for myself, believing that path in life to be closed to me. I wanted to carry my dress, not to let it out of my sight, for I had never had anything of my own, but there was a little page with them and the bag was given to him. I remember that as we walked, those two either side of me, I kept glancing behind to ensure the page was still following us.

'Stop looking back, child,' the matron reprimanded me. 'Only a hoyden fidgets like that. The boy is obedient; he won't run off.'

It was towards evening when they came, on what had been a bright cold day. They had put a wool cloak on me, with a hood, dark, but all lined with bright silk, and I remember the cavaliere saying to the matron: 'They say that Master Leonardo always advised one to walk out in the evening to observe faces, as they become more interesting and more characterful in that light than when the sun is high and our eyes dazzled. He could also have said that they become more beautiful, for such is our Giulia.' I rejoiced when I heard him, thinking of the great things my beauty would bring me. Then he said something else, which at the time puzzled me: 'She is grateful for these clothes, for she has been used to those rough tunics they are made to wear in the Pietà. This is no disadvantage to us.'

As we stood outside our destination, a house on the Arno, Vinta turned to me, and addressed me directly for the first time since we had left the Pietà.

'Did any of those pious women letter you?'

'No, sir.'

'That is good, for your presence here must be a secret.' Then he laughed and added, 'I'm forgetting myself. Who could someone like you write to? You know no one.'

Chapter Three

A house on the Arno

1584

*...vedete che sia bene instrutta ed admaestrata, et che
sappia dire minutamente tutto quel che passa...*
See to it that she is thoroughly instructed and trained,
and that she knows how to describe in the minutest detail
everything that happens.

Letter from Grand Duke Francesco de' Medici to
Belisario Vinta (26 February 1584)

Even if it no longer stood, I could tell an architect how to rebuild
the house I was taken to after I left the Pietà. It was where the
cavaliere lived, a fine tall place overlooking the river, but on the side
of the Duomo – though, depending on the direction of the breeze,
the tanneries on the opposite bank at Santo Spirito made their
presence felt. I had never yet seen what others called a home, and it
astonished me, for instead of the place of peace and intimacy that I
had imagined, this was like a marketplace. Vinta's palace – that is the
best description – rose on three floors around a stairwell. I remember
the entrance courtyard, with its well, as being as large as some of our
smaller squares in Venice. I see myself again standing at the door to
that house, looking up, until the matron pushes me forward.

Inside all was confusion, doors opening and banging shut,
servants everywhere, scurrying along the walkways. Though they

wore felt shoes, their feet thumped on the wooden treads of the stair. I have learned since that the higher a man's standing, the less he can count on privacy in his own home. Since my marriage I have had servants, it is true, but I have found I must try to make them my friends, for otherwise I cannot bear their presence.

Vinta took my hand.

'While you are under my roof, dear Giulia, you will be treated as though you were my own sister,' he said, and bent to kiss my knuckles. It was then that fear edged in on my joy for the first time; his lips and his beard touched my fingers for longer than felt right to me. That mouth was moist, too. He must have sensed my unease, for he said: 'Do not tremble, for my wife lives here too.' Yet I clung close to the matron as we were led upstairs and into a little tapestry-hung study which contained, on a table in the centre of the room as well as on the shelves, more books and papers than even the Prioress had. A sad-faced lady, a little younger than the cavaliere, rose to her feet and came forward to kiss me, and to take my hands in hers.

'My wife Camilla,' said Vinta. Then to her he said, 'You can leave us now. This matter does not concern you.'

'Indeed it does, husband. You bring a fatherless, unprotected girl under our roof. She is my responsibility, as a mother and as a Christian woman, for as long as she is here.'

Irritated, he replied, 'Remember at least that this matter must be handled with the utmost secrecy. That is the wish of the Grand Duke himself, and of his consort. Master Cappelli will be here soon to examine her. If his findings are favourable, then the girl's fortune is made.'

'Examine me?' I asked, thinking in my confusion that they meant to ask me questions on the scriptures, thus seeing if the pious ladies had instructed me well. When this Master Cappelli had seen me in the parlour at the Pietà he had seemed satisfied, so I could not imagine what more he could want of me.

Vinta looked at me in surprise, as if he had forgotten I was present. 'Yes. The doctor was pleased with your general aspect, and you meet the condition the Prince insisted on the most, that you have a beautiful countenance. But we must ensure that you are fit for our purpose, or we will have to return you to the Pietà and begin our search anew.'

That frightened me more than the cavaliere's wet mouth on my knuckles, and it showed in my face, for the last thing I wanted was to go back to that place. To avoid that fate I would have done anything they asked. The cavaliere laughed and patted my hand. 'You have nothing to fear, Giulia. If you are tractable and obliging, then you shall have your husband and a home of your own. All that is going to happen here, and in the weeks that follow, will be for your benefit, remember.'

The Lady Camilla stifled a little sound, but mastering herself said to him: 'Remember, my Lord, you are the father of daughters, soon too to be a grandfather. Think of what you would want for them.' I could not understand why her words were so bitter.

I lay a number of days at that house and the most remarkable things happened, though none as astonishing as what was done that very first night. Forgive me if I arrive at it by a tortuous path, for I shake at the prospect of writing down what was done to me, even though so many years have passed. After they had finished that first shameful examination I was put to, I was taken to a room of my own. I was trembling and crying, yet the matron offered me no comfort, telling me that I was a foolish girl who did not appreciate my good fortune, but that fortunately they had not picked me for my brains. The Lady Camilla remained downstairs. I had looked in her direction as they led me out, but her face was averted and her shoulders shaking.

The next morning tailors and hairdressers called, and I was measured and made much of: 'Half of Santo Spirito is at your disposal, Giulia!' laughed the cavaliere. You will remember, Mother, that that is the quarter of Florence where poorer men labour to dress their richer neighbours across the Arno. The Lady Camilla, who came in whenever these tradesmen were in the house, did not laugh. She was not there, though, when one of the tailors who had measured me – I remember shrinking beneath his fingers, standing there in my shift, although his touch was gentle – smiled at Vinta as he left, saying: 'I wish you joy of her, cavaliere!' I turned cold with fear, thinking all that had been done for me was for him alone – yet how could his lady permit such a thing beneath the roof they shared? Vinta, however, cursed the man for an impudent scoundrel, saying he should have a care if he wanted this work. With a hand on my shoulder a little longer than was needful, he urged me to forget the man's rudeness.

More clothes came, as I had been promised, and I started to feel happier again – what girl would not? You see, I thought after the preceding night I had endured the worst they could do to me. They returned with collars, bodices, skirts and beautiful linen, and ornaments for my hair which I was to wear loose. Can I explain to you the simple joy of moving my head from side to side, making my hair move – after all those years in the Pietà where even in bed we had to wear wimples? Once in the Lady Camilla's presence (for I needed her there to give me courage) I asked timidly if I might also have some linen which had not yet been embroidered, that I might do the work myself. She wept at that and kissed my cheek, then swept out of the room scowling at her husband. *He* said, 'By all means – whatever you desire.' I got those things and worked them. They are there in the press even now.

I hoped I might see the Lady Camilla more, but though I often heard her sad low tones elsewhere in the house I did not have her company again after the first two or three days. I think now it is because she had been too outspoken that first evening, and perhaps also in private with her husband, and so they did not permit her to see me again. I also heard a younger voice with hers – a girl of about my age, I guessed – and though I could not make out their words, instinct told me they were mother and daughter. Vinta's other surviving daughter was already wed, the matron had told me, and awaited her confinement. I wondered again what my life might have been like had I grown up with a mother and father, with a sister or a brother, in a fine house like that one.

Yet I saw nothing of it except that study, the larger room where I was examined and the room in which I slept – and where I was confined most of the time. Even my meals were brought to me there. I still grow hot with shame when I remember what I said the first time food was put before me. There was a strange, pronged implement lying on the tray beside my plate (such a pretty plate, too, all decorated in blue and yellow and gold). I had never seen such a thing before, so I asked the servant what it was. The girl stared at me and said, 'Tis a fork.' Flushing, I asked her, 'What am I to do with it?' I saw her trying not to laugh at me, but she recovered herself and said, 'For eating with, of course. You stick it in your food and bring the food to your mouth.' Then she grasped her skirts and ran out of the room.

I clasped the thing in my fist and tried so hard to get my food to my mouth, but my wrist would not bend back enough. I tried other ways to hold it and might have succeeded on my own were it not that the matron came in and saw my struggle and showed me what to do. If today I can hold a fork as daintily as any lady it is thanks to her.

In the Pietà we had always used our hands and fingers that God gave us for that purpose. The matron said, 'I can see you will have to be taught many things, not just the most urgent task that is required of you, if you are to be a lady and a wife.' She watched me eat, which I did as quickly as I could, though with that fork I was clumsy and my face burned. Then she said: 'Walk over to the door for me.'

'You move too fast,' said she. 'A lady never walks as though she is in a hurry. Nor does she ever raise her feet higher than three fingers' breadth from the ground.' She held up her hand sideways, the three longest fingers pressed together. After she left, I practised walking with my feet close to the ground, back and forth until I thought I should go mad from it, but it did not feel like a natural thing. Even now, I am fatigued only thinking about it.

Since I became a lady or at least since I have dressed as one, I have realised that our skirts are longer, and so anyway no one ever sees me lift my feet from the ground, let alone is able to say if I raise them too high. Only servants go about with ankles uncovered, and no one bothers about how they walk.

A different maid, a younger one, came in the mornings for the night soil. She avoided my eyes when I spoke to her, and would not answer me, though I was certain that she too was a foundling. There is a look we have, of a girl thrown on a merciless world, even if I am sure Lady Camilla would have been a kind mistress.

I am aware that I have gone on to tell of what happened the following day, but not that first night. I realise I am still trying to find the courage. You see, after everything that happened after it I should have lost all shame. I was examined – oh Mother! – as no woman should be; if I had been found wanting there would have been no need for dresses, clean hair, ash for my teeth.

I had been brought down to Vinta's study to await visitors. The matron stood behind my chair. Vinta was drumming his fingers on his desk. There was knocking downstairs, then a babble of voices that swelled as the visitors came up the stairwell.

'I am sure you will not disappoint us,' said Vinta, rising, indicating to me to follow. He went before me, and the matron walked behind me, but I also heard a rustle of brocade and knew that the Lady Camilla came too. I was brought into a larger chamber the other side of the stairwell. I thought at first this room was hung with rich cloth, but then realised the walls were simply painted to imitate curtains on hooks. To me this was more marvellous than the real thing. The tapers were lit and the shutters closed, for it was already dark. Master Cappelli was waiting with two women I was told were midwives, though they played no active part in what followed. They were dressed plainly but respectably, like the matron, in homespun cloth.

The cavaliere frowned when he saw his wife standing there. 'We do not require your presence,' he said, but she looked at him with her chin high and retorted, 'This young woman is under my roof and I will offer her what little protection I may,' and there was something in her manner that made her lord hesitate and then shrug. 'So be it,' he said. 'You will be a further witness that nothing we do is untoward.'

'Indeed it is untoward,' she said, 'that a marriage may only be advanced by the commission of a mortal sin, and that on the person of a defenceless orphan.' I thought she was talking about *my* marriage.

The doctor made some strange sounds which I thought might have been sniggering, but he suffocated them in his handkerchief.

'It is the will of the Grand Duke and Duchess,' said the cavaliere, 'and has the blessing of the Holy Father himself. Do not be so bold as to question what does not concern you.' Yet he let her stay. I could see he feared to contradict her further, despite his strong words.

The matron began to unlace me and put my garments to one side. By the time she reached my shift I was trembling in fear. I had been naked before the lay sisters in the Pietà so that they could cleanse me, but never before men, and I knew how shameful it was, recalling the stories of how Bathsheba tempted King David who sent her poor husband to die in battle because of the king's lust, and how Susannah might have lost her life had those palsied old men who dribbled at the sight of her as she bathed not been questioned so astutely.

'A becoming modesty and sense of shame – most appealing,' said Vinta to Master Cappelli.

'Indeed,' said the doctor, 'but I must proceed nevertheless.'

The matron unlaced my shift at the breast and pulled it from my shoulders. I cried out and tried to stop it falling to my feet but she grasped my hands. I started to weep and as soon as the matron freed my wrists I covered my sex, but the doctor told me I must put my hands on my head, so I did so, though I shut my eyes tight. I could not stop crying, nor prevent my nose from running, but my sobs were ignored. I heard Vinta murmuring huskily: 'A fine firm breast, and beautifully rounded rump. The Grand Duke can be happy with our choice.' Then I was sure they intended to whore me, that this story of the Prince, the dowry, my husband, was but a ruse.

'I need the piss-pot!' I cried, and dropped my arms, cowering.

'You could have said earlier,' the matron said. She took hold of my upper arm and led me into a corner of the room, naked as I was. I saw a door handle in the midst of those painted drapes. She half-pushed me into a tiny room and pointed me to a bench faced with pewter. Away from the fireplace of the big chamber, the place was icy cold.

The matron stood there and watched me as I pissed. Not even in the Pietà, where I had nothing of my own, had I been subjected to such an indignity.

'Wipe your face,' she said, 'and then dry yourself,' thrusting a small towel at me.

I shuffled behind the matron, back to where they waited for me, one hand over my breasts and the other over the place between my legs. I saw the Lady Camilla sitting in a corner, her hands over her face. I do not know if she was praying or weeping.

The doctor lifted my hands away as impersonally as though he unwrapped a package, then looked at my ears, my teeth, my eyes, and pinched my breast.

'Lie on the day-bed,' he said. This was a high-backed settle, pushed against the wall, and strewn with cushions over which a clean sheet had been stretched. I did so, and again protected myself with my hands. I remember they felt cold – my feet also – as though my blood laboured to reach them, for so much of it had risen to my head. The doctor loomed over me, a great crow in his black garments. I shut my eyes.

'Take care, Master Cappelli,' I heard the cavaliere say, 'for if you damage our subject then she will have to be returned to the Pietà and we shall have to start our search anew. That would not please the Grand Duke.'

'Raise your knees, and part them,' said the doctor, taking hold of my wrists and putting my arms to my sides. I opened my eyes in horrified surprise. I saw the matron standing at his shoulder, peering down at me, but at least her body provided some barrier between me and the others in the room. But she did not comfort me, no. It was the Lady Camilla who came over to me and took my hand as I lay there, and urged me, with tears in her eyes, to have courage.

'Good,' said the doctor, after I had done what he told me to. 'Now, do not move, or there will be no dowry and no husband.' He bent over the poor little sparrow cowering between my legs, opening its wings with his thumbs. I saw his head turn away. 'Bring the light closer,' he said. The matron rustled off, and I glimpsed Vinta, his eyes glittering. The matron came back, blocking him again from my view. She held the candle above my stomach and I hoped her hand was steady, to not drop hot wax on my skin. The doctor bent closer and I closed my eyes again. I felt his breath ruffle those little hairs and felt the pads of his fingers at the quick of me, and cursed silently that I was born a woman.

'She is fit for our purpose,' I heard him say eventually. 'See for yourself, cavaliere.' The doctor's fingers rested on me, a flower with its petals peeled back. 'Give me the candle,' I heard Vinta say, close by, and the matron retreated. I squeezed the Lady Camilla's hand so tightly that I must have hurt her. 'Belisario!' I heard her exclaim, with such warning force that I felt a drop of her spittle on my neck. I opened my eyes and saw Vinta step back, abashed.

'If you are satisfied, perhaps this poor child can dress,' said Vinta's lady.

The doctor straightened up and called for water. The Lady Camilla eased me upright and dried my face with her own handkerchief. I was shaking uncontrollably. I think I was also babbling some nonsense, but I could not say now what it was.

'Bring me her things, would you?' she said curtly to the matron. The Lady Camilla dressed me herself, murmuring to me that I was a beautiful girl, a good girl, and that I had been very brave. Her hands were gentle. Once my shift was over my head I could not contain myself any longer, but leaned forward and clung to her. I had embraced no one that way since Tommasa. I could tell from the vibration of her body that she wept too. I felt cold to the marrow, and utterly, utterly tired.

As my dress was eased over my head, I heard the doctor and Vinta talking about me, as though I was not there and could not hear them. I noticed in the weeks to come that the cavaliere often did that, either because it did not matter what I thought or because he didn't care.

'Poor little pullet. Those orphanage girls have no idea of what men want of them. She will have to be instructed. She has a fine, demure expression – a beautifully clear brow. But she must learn that she is to show no resistance, modest as she is. We cannot have another scene such as we have just witnessed. I will instruct the matron to train her, and if necessary, tell her myself where the devil keeps his tail.'

'Do not exceed your remit in your enthusiasm, cavaliere,' said the doctor, and they both laughed.

'We will have satisfied the demands of the Mantuan envoy, I think – and he speaks for the Prince; he stipulated a beautiful face even upon an indifferent body, but healthy – no physical impediment.'

'That girl's form would please any man, though,' said the doctor.

'Indeed. She should be given to someone even out of charity, not shut up in a convent again. Then there is the Grand Duchess. She insists that the Prince prove himself within twenty-four hours of tilting his lance.'

'Ah! That lady loses no chance to humiliate her detractors, then!'

'But what young man would fail in such an attempt, with such a subject? There is just one other thing to remember, Cappelli. Donati the Mantuan must not know the girl's identity, nor where we found her. I confess I must remind myself that I am a good servant, no more. As a man, though… had we not taken this girl from those pious ladies, she would almost certainly have taken the veil.'

'Perhaps we save her, Vinta. Had you thought of that?'

'Even so…'

'We have done our part. All we need to know is whether the Prince can do his. Even if the girl does not like him.'

'My God.'

'You will have to get her testimony after you have made your own observations. I have certified her, but remember that blood does not flow in all cases, though one would expect to see what we might call signs of conflict.'

'Very well. Your colleague Master Galletti will be accompanying the party to Venice.'

'Oh…'

'So he will certify when the task is accomplished. She will be kept there as long as is needful, and no longer. If the Prince is successful at the first attempt, then the test will be confined to one night. The hardest part will be interrogating her afterwards. She's barely seen a man, let alone understood what it is we will ask of her.'

'What have you told her?'

'Not much. No point in frightening her unnecessarily. All she knows is that she will perform a service for the Grand Duke himself, though she will never meet him. The journey to Venice will take four days, if all goes well. Our party will be well guarded. That is time enough for the matron to instruct her.'

Vinta turned round to see me staring at him. I still did not know what they spoke of, though I spent all that night and the next mulling over those strange words. How could I have known? In the Pietà even the mention of anything 'pertaining to matrimony' was severely punished. But what the doctor said about blood not always flowing even though there would be signs of conflict chilled me. I longed to ask the Lady Camilla, whose face had gone white and stiff as she heard their words. I felt I could trust her as I could not trust the matron, even though she was the wife of my captor. My captor: yes, that's what Vinta was.

I was taken back to my room and left there alone. I have not said that there was a little recess in the wall, covered by wooden doors, and below it, a prie-dieu. When I had first entered that room I had eased open those doors and found a statue of Our Lady within, carved in wood but painted to the life, her hands held out in acceptance of the message the archangel brought. I'd wished I had some offering to put in those hands – flowers, or a rosary – but having nothing, offered her only my prayers, that she might sustain me in whatever was to be asked of me. I remembered when I first saw her to thank her for my good fortune. I was to have a husband, and a home of my own. Now, after that ordeal, I knelt again on the prie-dieu and opened the doors. But in the gesture of Our Lady's hands, I now saw not acceptance, but despair.

The following day a foreign gentleman, a Mantuan, was brought to see me. He was about the same age as Vinta, but his beard was neater, his hair close-cropped, and he was soberer in his dress. They told me this Donati was also a doctor, and the trusted confidant of this Prince, and that I had to please him. Yet I did not. He looked me up and down wordlessly then turned to the cavaliere and said:

'I thought she would be more beautiful.' I feared that all they had promised me would crumble to dust. But Vinta just laughed and declared me a tender morsel. He said I did not even look my years but much younger, and that surely I met their requirements in every detail.

In the presence of the matron but without the comfort of the Lady Camilla near me I was stripped for them again, although this time my examination took place on the table in the centre of the room, a white sheet laid over it as though it were an altar. The Mantuan looked at me between the legs just as Master Cappelli had done, while the matron stood beside him like a scruffy acolyte. I cried again, but Donati told me to hold my peace as I disturbed him. At least this time Vinta kept a respectful distance, murmuring with Master Cappelli in a corner of the room. I say respectful – I mean of his visitor, not of me. The Mantuan never even looked me in the eyes. To stop myself crying I began the rosary as I traced with my eyes the swags of fruit painted in the panels of the ceiling.

'She is a virgin,' said Donati, and the matron motioned me to sit up.

After the Mantuan had gone, I was allowed to dress and was taken back to my chamber, and Vinta came to see me, accompanied by the matron. He sat opposite me and took my hand, though I longed to pull it back. His touch to me was nearly as repulsive as Donati's had been.

'Giulia, you must learn to master yourself. The Prince will not like your tears. Master Donati is only playing a role; no Mantuan can admit that a Florentine is more beautiful than the girls of that city.'

I opened my mouth to say that my tears were not because Donati had not found me beautiful, but because he too had done what Cappelli had done only the day before, yet Vinta did not seem interested in anything I might have to say.

'You will see Donati again,' he said. 'He will remain with us in Venice until our task is accomplished.'

Vinta for the next few days was sometimes absent, and I longed to see the Lady Camilla, but from then on I was kept as a prisoner. The matron was constantly with me, except when I slept, and when she went out the door was locked. She read me stories that would have caused me to be humiliated before all my sisters in the Pietà if I had spoken of them. Of course I could not read myself then, but she bade me reflect on what I had heard, which of course I did, for I had nothing else to occupy my time. Those stories tormented my dreams. Longings I had had from when my body began to change and my courses began started to take shape, and both appalled and excited me.

When I woke in the night in that house it was to wonder where I was. Yet in broad daylight I often thought I was dreaming. This Venice they spoke of. Where was it? Was it a foreign country? The Mantuan, Donati, spoke as I had heard no man speak before. Where they were taking me; would I understand anyone?

In the Pietà I was not to look out of the window, on pain of punishment. The city that had hidden me away for so long, as if I were something shameful, now wanted me to go out into the world on its behalf. I would see other people. They too would see me, though I prayed that would not be as I had been seen beneath Vinta's roof.

I wished the Lady Camilla was coming with us on that journey. There was no one in that party who loved me. There was no one I could trust.

Chapter Four

By road and water

In all innes... let him bolte or locke the door of his chamber:
let him take heed of his chamber fellows and always have his
sword by his side...

Fynes Moryson, *Precepts for Travellers*, 1617 (based on his
travels across Europe 1591–1595)

Over the next week the house was in tumult. Locked in that room
as I was, the matron holding the keys, I heard this rather than
saw it. She told me that with Donati's approval of me (grudging
though I thought it was) preparations could go ahead. She bustled
in and out of the room where I was kept, puffed up with her own
importance, to say that horses had been found and men engaged
as ostlers and guards.

'Guards?' I asked, astonished.

'Of course,' she said. 'This is an affair of state, a matter of
diplomacy, of such delicacy that it must be carried out with the
greatest discretion.'

I longed to see the Lady Camilla again, if only to thank her
for the kindness she alone had shown me. I heard her husband's
voice occasionally. Whenever he was present, the hubbub rose.
He shouted about supplies, called for messengers. The matron
packed and repacked my clothes. These grew in number. I did
not understand why there were so many of those fine linen shifts.

I wanted to take them out and admire them, but the matron slapped my hand away and locked the coffer. I could not see how looking would harm them, given that I was the person who would wear them.

I cannot say after how many days it was that we set out, only that it was early in the morning, for the servants too were sleepy-eyed, and I did not know when I lay down the night before that we would be leaving that day.

'You are not to speak to anyone at any of the places we halt at,' Vinta warned me as I stood waiting beside the matron in the courtyard of his house. I noticed that he did not wear the chain of office that had been around his neck on all the occasions I had seen him, and which he would periodically weigh in his hand as he spoke. He wore a plainer cloak, not the long one with the fur collar and squirrel lining he had had on his shoulders when I first saw him in the parlour at the Pietà.

'You are the daughter of a German mercenary in the service of Florence,' he told me, the daughter of no one. 'We are journeying north so that I can return you to your father.' He told me the man's name, but it was outlandish and I have long since forgotten it.

I walked with him and the matron through a passageway that brought us to a small square behind the house. It was thronged: there must have been twenty people there, and any number of horses. I was relieved to see that Master Cappelli was not one of them, but my relief was short-lived, for I was shown to another doctor – I cannot say that I was introduced. 'This is our subject, Master Galletti,' I heard Vinta tell him. For most of the journey, Vinta was in that man's company. When he did come to talk to me, it was only for me to wish that he had not.

I was put with the matron into a *lettiga*, a kind of box carried on shafts back and front – perhaps, Mother, you knew of such things in the households you lived in, though it was a novelty to me then. We sat inside, opposite each other, and were borne along by a horse before us and another behind. This space was curtained, but Vinta warned me that he alone would say when those curtains might be opened.

The matron seemed able to do anything on that journey, and passed hours with a cushion on her lap, making lace, or working some embroidery. I had never experienced anything like the movement of that conveyance, and thought I should not be able to keep any food in my belly for long with all that jolting; towards the end of the journey I ate nothing at all, but that was not the fault of the horses. I would have preferred to be alone with my thoughts, but the matron chattered incessantly, telling me 'as a mother' what men expect of a wife. I had little understanding of what she said then, for at that time there was nothing in my experience I could refer to. Only later did I realise that she spoke as a bawd. I have not instructed my own daughters as she did.

At the first stop we made, I noticed that a number of the men in our entourage were armed, though none wore livery or anything that marked them out as servants of a particular gentleman. I was alarmed by this, just as I was by Vinta's sober dress, and that invented German mercenary.

'You worry overmuch because you have never travelled before,' said the matron. 'All this subterfuge is for our own protection. The roads are infested by brigands, so a rich man who is also prudent will not advertise his wealth. I am reassured that we are well guarded, and so you shouldn't be anxious.'

We were not far from Bologna when I was at last told exactly what was required of me. Vinta did not tell me the name of that place, but I heard the matron say that was what it was called. I saw on that journey the towers of many fine cities whenever I was allowed to peep through the curtains, but never did we pass within any walls, so each place faded from sight as if it had been a mere mirage.

Vinta said the arrival of a score of Florentines would attract too much attention in a thronged place. I am quite sure, though, that in the inns on the road we excited a lot of comment, more than we would have done within the bustle of a town, because we were so many, and bristling with weapons. Even the men I'd first thought were simple ostlers carried arms.

Only afterwards did I wonder if instead they were there to stop me running off. But where would I have gone? I noticed the men's eyes on me, but they would turn away if I returned their gaze, as I sometimes did despite all my training in the Pietà. I heard them laughing sometimes, whispering behind their hands, and looking at me again, though they did not do this if Vinta was near. The only other woman in our caravan was the matron, and though I did not love her nor trust her, I stayed close to her at all times.

In those inns I shared a bed with her. She snored, and broke wind, and the room reeked of her feet. Whenever she went to the door to call down for something I saw that two guards stood outside. In the morning, when she called for water and breakfast, different sentries were there. Vinta grumbled about the discomfort of these places, the lack of cleanliness, the scratchy palliasses, the fleas. But then he had not been brought up as I had, and those inns were nothing like his home on the Arno.

'We shall pass by San Benedetto,' I heard Vinta say to the matron that morning. 'That way we shall avoid Ferrara.'

With the exception of one of the guards and an ostler, we had all attended Mass, though it was not a day of obligation. I had been accustomed in the Pietà to partake of the sacraments every day, so I found some peace in that simple church despite my struggle to understand the priest's speech – though the Latin words must have been the same ones I had heard scores of times.

I will remember that moment forever: I was sitting near the matron on a long stone bench on the sunny side of the church, and Vinta stood before me, black against the pale March light. He said: 'You must have wondered what all our examination of you portended.'

'You wanted to know if I could be a wife,' I said.

'In truth, the purpose of our journey is to know if the Prince you are going to meet is able to be a husband.'

'But you told me it was not him I am to marry.'

Vinta laughed. 'Of course not! If he succeeds at the test he is being set, then he will marry the Lady Eleonora, our Grand Duke's eldest child.'

'What test?'

'You, dear Giulia. He must deflower *you*, and I have been entrusted to ascertain the proof that he has done so, before the Grand Duke will accept him as a son-in-law.'

If I had not been seated I am sure I would have fallen, for my legs felt as if the bones within them had been turned to water.

'You have lied to me,' I cried. 'No husband could want me after that!'

The matron made a 'tsk' sound, as if I had merely turned my nose up at something on my plate, and shuffled closer to me.

'Keep your voice down, you foolish girl,' said Vinta. 'There are possibly some men who wouldn't want you, but I will find you one who will take you for your dowry. If you do not like that thought, then you and the money can be handed into a convent instead.'

I thought that grotesque and said so through my tears. Vinta sighed heavily, and in the tone I most resented from him, said: 'One cannot expect one such as you to understand. These are affairs of state.'

'An affair of state? To take a virgin from the care of holy women, dress her up like Jezebel in the scriptures and turn her into a whore?'

Vinta stroked the fur of his cuff and said: 'The Prince you will meet must show proof of his potency, Giulia. Without it the whole of this Catholic peninsula is at risk from the heresies fomenting beyond the Alps.'

I stared at him. What was he babbling about?

'The Prince was married three years ago in Parma – to a beautiful, accomplished and wealthy Farnese princess, though a trifle young, perhaps, and giddy. Too much given to plays and other frivolous entertainments. They might have suited each other, had things been different – they say he still harbours some affection for her. But there was an impediment within the body of that girl that meant she could never take a husband. Her family were outraged at what they saw as a slight, though eleven doctors came and examined her, just as you have been examined, but about her they shook their heads – a natural obstacle, let us say, lay across the path: an excrescence. She was made only for the convent, the doctors said, and to the Benedictine sisters she was sent, despite her protests; the child said she would submit to being flayed alive as long as she might return beneath her husband's roof. What you underwent under mine, and cried so prettily about, was nothing to what that girl had to submit to, to no avail.'

I cried out when he told me this, but Vinta went on as though he hadn't heard.

'An interfering midwife had insisted that the barrier could easily be excised and was surprised this had not already been done. The girl pinned all her hopes on this, but the priests would not allow it. Had she died under the surgeons' knives, she would have burned in hell forever, for the sin of self-murder. Some of those learned physicians also murmured that she might be barren, and as such, she was of no use to the Gonzagas. You see, Giulia, her husband – the man you are to meet – needs an heir. He will inherit the dukedom of Mantua. He has no brothers, for that hunchback Duke Guglielmo and his Duchess, after having the Prince and two mere girls, took a spiritual vow – a beautiful thing to do, no doubt, but not wise in my opinion, when one is responsible for a dukedom. The Duke's only son is a vigorous man of twenty-one years and of quite different inclinations. If the Prince's seed is not allowed to bear fruit, then his uncle's line would succeed to Mantua, but that branch of the family are French. Do you understand me, Giulia?'

I shook my head but couldn't read his expression through the blur of tears. I did not yet see what my poor maidenhead, the only wealth I had besides what I had glimpsed of my own face, had to do with any of this.

'France cannot be allowed to encroach so far into Italy. The Holy Father has said as much, for there are men of dangerous ideas in that country, who would deny the authority of the Vicar of Christ. So the Farnese girl has been shut up with the Benedictine sisters, and her marriage declared null by Cardinal Borromeo himself. And the Prince of Mantua is impatient for a wife.'

'So let him take one,' I said. 'Why must he corrupt me first?'

'Naturally, the house of Mantua has its detractors – that Farnese princess's family. They claim that the fault is not the girl's but lies with the man who was supposed to be her husband. Personally, I doubt that. I have it from a reliable source that the natural son of the lord of Ferrara, a companion of the Prince in some of his youthful adventures, was present when he deflowered a peasant girl. The Prince himself has submitted to an examination, to see if when erect he could push against the palm of a hand with force sufficient to penetrate the body of a young girl. I am convinced that he will serve you well. I hope for your sake that he can, because if he doesn't, you will go back to that place where I found you.'

'No!'

'You see, Giulia, how much you stand to gain? Florence's Grand Duchess, naturally, cannot ignore these voices and let her step-daughter wed the Mantuan Prince without being sure that he will be an adequate husband. She will not permit the marriage to go ahead without proof of his potency. He, of course, cannot refuse when all the courts of Europe laugh behind their hands. Come, do you not see that you are honoured? A feast fit for a prince.'

I stopped eating that day. I put food in my mouth and it tasted of ashes, so whenever they brought it to me I pushed the plate away.

'Nerves,' said the matron.

'Perhaps our Giulia is excited at her good fortune,' said Vinta, looking at me.

I went to bed early that night, treasuring those few moments alone, for the matron remained below, talking to Vinta. I was drifting off to sleep when she lifted the curtain and climbed into bed beside me. She gave me no peace, upbraiding me for my fasting. I don't know why she did, for she had cleaned my plate alongside hers.

'That long face will not please the Prince either,' she said. 'But I expect he will just close his eyes.'

I started crying, but all she did was complain that I was making the bed shake. That night I went over Vinta's words again and again, my chance of sleep gone, while the matron snored.

In the morning I asked her: 'What is his name?'

'The Prince? Vincenzo. Vincenzo Gonzaga.'

'Does he know mine?'

She raised her eyebrows. 'I shouldn't think so. I expect Vinta will tell him, if he wants to know.' She went on combing her long grey hair.

'And that lady in Florence – the consort of the Grand Duke.'

She stopped combing.

'What of her?'

'It was she who asked for this test?'

'That's right.'

'A woman?'

'What *is* it, child?' She dropped the comb on the bed and, fingers flicking, twisted her hair into a plait. Knotting the end, she said, 'Remember, Giulia, that you are a child of charity. The Grand Duke is guardian to everyone brought up in the Innocenti or the Pietà. It is thanks to his generosity that you live at all.'

She looked me up and down. I was still in my shift. 'If you hurry and dress, we can have something to eat. Then if you want, I shall tell you something of our Grand Duchess. But only if we are not overheard.'

The matron was Vinta's creature, you see, but she could not resist a gossip. I suppose she thought she was instructing me in the ways of the world. It was from her I learned that the woman who ruled in Florence at Grand Duke Francesco's side was a Venetian, but that was not why she was so disliked. The Grand Duke had had a wife, but a plain one. Giovanna of Austria had borne him only daughters – and a little boy who died. Even before he married, though, he had taken that Venetian girl for his concubine. Then Giovanna, with child again, had slipped and fallen on the floor of a church and never recovered.

'He married Bianca Cappello almost before Giovanna's corpse was cold,' said the matron. Her eyes glittered. Relishing her story and encouraged by my astonished look, she became reckless. 'They have a son, Antonio,' she said. 'He must be seven or eight by now, but he looks less like either of his parents with every day that passes. There are rumours regularly that she is with child, but I have seen her. She is swollen with the dropsy, that is all.'

She leaned towards me with her charnel-house breath. 'The Prince's mother and father are known for their piety, so they snubbed Bianca Cappello as a Venetian whore. The Grand Duchess of Mantua is the sister of our Grand Duke's first wife, remember, and saw his hasty remarriage as an insult to her memory – which it is. But they tried all the same to get her stepdaughter for their son, only it is said they wanted too large a dowry, so they went to

Parma instead, for that Farnese girl. Now they come begging for Eleonora again. With this test, Bianca takes her revenge. I am sure the dowry will be smaller this time than the last offer. But if you know what is good for you, you will keep your mouth shut.'

Some of our journey was by water. This too was new to me. My only sight of a boat before then had been in paintings in churches, the fishers of men casting their nets upon the waters as the Lord commanded them to do. I was handed onto the barge by a boatman; I remember his calloused palm but also his gentleness. I looked at him when I thanked him but he did not meet my eyes. I staggered when the boat began to move along the river.

The horses were left at a post-house to be collected on the return journey – as Vinta kept saying that I would be returned to Florence, though the idea seemed incredible to me. I felt as if I was going to my death, led to the scaffold rather than into a bedchamber. A few of our entourage stayed with the horses, and other men were hired. Vinta began to relax, for these men being local did not know him and showed little curiosity about him; they were satisfied with being paid. In other circumstances I might have enjoyed that journey, for the placid water was welcome after being thrown about in that stuffy box with the imperturbable matron and the clacking beads of her lacemaking always before me. I tried to ask her more about the Grand-Ducal family, but she snapped that she had already told me too much.

It was dark when we reached the sea. I could see only the reflection of our lamps in what looked like endless glittering water, yet the boatmen put out without demur. Vinta bade me look forward to where lights glimmered. 'Chioggia,' he said.

At that port, Vinta engaged a boat of a different kind, this one with eight oarsmen; it was already dark, but he refused to stop and put up at an inn. He fretted that we were already late. I had felt that dragging on my insides that comes upon me every few weeks, and with it the dampening of my spirit, though this time worse than ever before, because of the dread I felt at what was to come. My courses had come upon me; the matron told Vinta, who put his hands in his hair in frustration.

'More delays!' he cried. 'The Prince is sure to be waiting for us, kicking his heels in the city of pleasure. I just hope he is more discreet about our mission than he is generally known to be.'

To me he said, 'We will just have to wait until you are purged, and then let the doctor declare you clean again. Otherwise we will not know that the Prince has perforated you as he must.'

Perforated. Such words once made the tips of my ears burn.

If those boatmen had not been the courageous experts that they were, I would have died a virgin and Grand Duke Francesco would have had to find himself another minister. I thought we should never arrive. A boat should lie on the horizontal, not have its prow thrown up towards heaven. The sailors cursed and pulled down the sails, before they tore and left us at the mercy of Providence. Anything that was not tied down was thrown about, including us poor mortals, for though we were within an enclosed space, a little house, you might say, built on the boards of that boat, its canvas flaps blew in continuously and we were sprayed with water almost as much as if we had had no shelter at all. It penetrated everything I wore; salt rimed my mouth. I could not tell if the rags between my legs needed changing because everything about me was wet and sticky. I have always hated the way I smelled on those days – that hot, metallic stink – but even that was lost in the storm. Forgive me, Mother. I cannot believe anyone will want to read those words. I shall probably strike them through when I have done with my account.

Vinta clutched his beard as if it was about to fly off. The matron curled in a ball and blasphemed – words I had never heard before but which should not come from a Christian mouth when death is so near. I was sick, sick, retching though there was nothing left within me, my insides a cluster of glistening tripe washed clean in salt water. Our doctor, Master Galletti, alone seemed to be unscathed, though a little pale. I wonder what concoctions he brewed for himself to spare him our sufferings.

At eleven at night we arrived at that city on water, a dark shape rising out of the lagoon and shimmering with lanterns. I could not believe it was only a matter of hours that we had been on that craft, for it seemed longer than the rest of the journey combined. I was not even sure that I lived by then, and wondered if this was the place where I would shortly be judged; my companions were the ones they had always been, so I thought they must all have drowned with me.

We stopped at last below the narrow house in which I would meet the Prince, but I was too weak to take in anything other than the meanness of its aspect after the grandeur of Vinta's home. Indeed, I was unable to stand and had to be carried onto the landing stage in a litter brought from within the house. Only later did I learn that the servants had one to hand because there was a man under that roof who was like to die, but who was considered too frail, or the case too hopeless, for him to be carried to the hospital. Yet the moment I was off the water I began to feel better, though so unsteady I was sure I would have pitched into the canal had I attempted to stand up. A messenger of the Prince awaited us. He glanced at me in idle curiosity, but quickly realised which one of the party was Vinta, despite the studied modesty of his clothes, and told him that his master had already awaited us for two days, fearing some misfortune or obstacle had befallen us. 'We have had a troubled journey also,' he said. 'Near Ferrara one of the Prince's kinsmen was following at a distance, and was fired upon. Providentially, the man missed. We are trying to see this as a good omen.'

Vinta then enquired as to the occupant of the house. He named him, but if I ever remembered it I do not now: 'If the hour is not too late, I would wish to thank him for his assistance and discretion in this delicate matter – a most assiduous correspondent.'

'He is ill, sir, failing. The doctors are with him even now.'

Vinta crossed himself and muttered about evil portents. 'And the Monsignor, whose house this is?'

'I have had instructions that the Monsignor wishes no closer connection with this affair. It is a matter for you and his tenant, were his words.'

I thought we could not possibly remain in a house where a man lay dying, but we did. Despite the late hour, Vinta sent a messenger to wherever it was that the Prince lodged. It could not have been far, for before midnight the Mantuan Master Donati called. He glanced at me without speaking, but I was too tired to care. I was sent to bed yet I did not sleep. Donati and Vinta talked for two hours or more in the adjoining room – I knew this from the bells of unseen churches chiming the hours.

From the room they took me to I could hear all that happened in the rest of the house, though there were no windows in there for me to look out of; in this it resembled what I think a dungeon must be like, where there is no means of telling whether it be day or night. The chamber was much smaller than the one where I had been kept in Vinta's house, and plainer, its beamed ceiling oppressively low. Most of the space was taken up by a bed, its curtains hooked back. I looked at it and thought of those stories we had been read at mealtimes in the Pietà, from that old part of the Bible written before our Lord came: a ram, a goat, turtle doves, put on an altar and their blood spilled in sacrifice.

When the man who lay ill died the following day, I knew the moment it happened, for I heard the tread of those men of the Misericordia who came to take the body to the church; something was bumped down the stairs.

Shortly afterwards a white-faced Vinta and Master Galletti came into the bedroom, where I sat with the matron. 'We shall not move,' said Vinta. 'It would attract too much attention, and the house is ideal for our purpose; I do not believe the men of the confraternity knew who else was here.'

As he had done in the house in Florence, he spoke to the others as though I was not present. 'The girl can be confined in this room until she is fit to receive the Prince, and we witnesses can occupy the room without. That it opens out onto a terrace is an advantage to us: we can observe whoever approaches the landing stage.'

I slept – when I could sleep – alone. I was grateful for that, for it gave me time to prepare myself for what was to happen. To prepare, and to wonder. In the Pietà we had been warned to banish all thoughts of men. Now I had been told that it was my duty to think of little else.

There was a woman housekeeper there who looked at me curiously, but Vinta had warned me not to open my mouth except in his presence or that of the matron.

A young man of Lucca called at the house during those days of my purging and was shown up to where I sat in the outer chamber, where the matron was trying to get me to eat. I looked up, thinking he must be the Prince, and liked his open, honest face, his easy smile. But it turned out that he was a friend of the dead man and did not know who I was. I thought how, if my life had been different, how pleasant and natural it would have been for a young man to smile when his eyes rested on me.

'Cavaliere!' the youth exclaimed, when Vinta walked in, and I could see my gaoler's annoyance. He did not deny who he was but took the young man by the shoulder and turned him away from me. I heard him mutter something about 'a matter of the utmost secrecy, of grave importance to the honour of Tuscany. As you see, I do not appear here in my robes of office. I must be sure of your silence...' and then in a louder voice spoke of how the Grand Duke had need of 'fine young men like yourself.'

'And that young woman?' said the youth.

'Her?' said Vinta, as if I were of no account. 'The daughter of Captain Freuerberger.' The name comes back to me now. 'It was an opportunity to restore her to her father.'

The young man left soon after, promising Vinta that he would deny him 'as if I were St Peter himself,' but minutes later I heard the cavaliere on the floor above loudly abusing the servants. I had never heard him shout before. A man's voice answered him: 'How shall we know to admit the Prince?'

I began to eat again. I had given thanks to St Nicholas and all who looked down on those in troubled waters, and realised I must have been preserved for a reason. But now, all any of us could do was wait. No amount of fussing from Vinta would hasten the end of my courses. I was able to wash whenever I wanted to, a contrast with my life in the Pietà where those days of impurity had to be endured and rags scrubbed in silence and where no matter how ill I might feel my loom awaited me. Here I was cosseted, even. Though I could not explore beyond the chamber I slept in and its anteroom, I tried to imagine what my life might be were I in charge of a house like that one, with the clanging of saucepans in the kitchen above my head, messengers coming to the door with deliveries of food. I listened to the sound of bargemen, the lap of water against the landing stage. I wondered if in a city like this I would forget the clop of horses' hooves, the rattle of cart wheels on paving.

Of the Serenissima I really knew nothing more than that, for I was a prisoner in that house, just as I had been in Vinta's palace on the Arno. I was not allowed even to go to Mass, and no priest was brought to me. I know the cavaliere went, for he came back smelling of incense and sanctity though he was nothing better than a pander. In truth, he called himself such by the time we left, though I think he did not know I heard him do so.

Always at my shoulder, though, was the shadow of the Prince, this faceless man who would come to do violence to me, who would change my life. I thought of him always by candlelight or in darkness, for a sin such as we were to commit was surely a thing of the night, from which the sun would hide his face in shame.

The day we left, I saw little, for I was blinded by my own tears.

Chapter Five

The Prince's person

Ad montem duc nos
Lead us to the mountain
Motto of the Gonzaga family

It was, I think, three days before I saw the Prince. I did question whether he might come to see me earlier, given his stipulation that I should have a beautiful face. I woke each morning wondering if I might at least glimpse him that day. I hoped I might. I was sure it would make what was to come less terrifying for me, if I could at least know beforehand the lineaments of the man who would join me behind the curtains of the bed.

The matron told me, no, he would not come, and said that when the most thoroughbred stallions are brought to sire foals on the best mares, they are kept apart until the last moment so that none of their ardour should be dimmed. So I had been an orphan schooled in the scriptures and urged towards the cloister, but now I was no longer God's child, being no better than a horse. I wondered what the Prince did, with that unseen city unrolled like a great carpet to welcome him, while I was shut in with no company but my thoughts and fears of what was to come, accompanied only by the incessant clack-clack of the matron's lacemaking. It is true, though, that I preferred that sound to her speech.

Vinta complained again of the delay, frowned at me as if it was my fault, saying that Venice was an expensive place, and he was constantly in fear of discovery.

It was two in the morning when the Prince came the first time, rousing not just the house but probably the entire district with his knocking.

Moments later he stood in the doorway of my room, staring at me. Two other young men were with him, trying to look at me over his shoulder. Someone – it must have been the matron – had hooked back the bed-hangings.

The matron leaned over me and took me by the arm. She was dressed in some slatternly old undergown, and her grey plait swung. 'Get up!' she hissed.

'I am only in my shift!'

She laughed at that.

My face averted, I scrambled down the side of the bed, trying as I did so to pull the skirts of my garment over my knees. I stood on my bare feet facing my visitor, and dipped my head and bent my knee; I had seen others do this with Vinta. The matron snatched my cap from my head, loosening my hair onto my shoulders.

'Look up, girl! He wants to see your face!'

I looked. He was smiling at me now, but it wasn't the artless smile of that young man from Lucca who had so discomfited Vinta. I thought the Prince fine, as men are who have meat and comfort always, and can please themselves. He was taller than any man there and strong in the leg – I learned afterwards that he was an accomplished horseman. The day would come when I would be grateful for his interest in actual horseflesh – but I will write of that later, much later. He motioned the courtiers with him to stand back, but Vinta came forward and filled the space. The minister looked absurd, his hair sticking up wildly about his head, his clothes disarranged. Of course – he had lain down dressed every night since coming to Venice, awaiting his noble visitor's pleasure.

The Prince was fairer than the few men I had seen (and note, I had seen more of the male sex in those few weeks than I had seen in my entire life hitherto). By that I mean the colour of his hair, which was like honey, smooth and fine, and his pale skin. The soft hairs that grew on his upper lip were lighter than those of his head. But it was the blue of his eyes I noticed most, a blue I had never seen before. Vinta had told me the Prince's mother was a foreigner, sister to the poor lady that was the Grand Duke's first wife. So the marriage my deflowering was to enable was between cousins, though I know that such unions are not encouraged by Mother Church.

'You have chosen well, Vinta!' he said. He did not, then, speak to me directly, not even to ask my name nor how I did. He only did so when we were alone, for when the others were there I might have been nothing more than a picture he admired.

'We shall try her straight away and you will see how well we succeed!'

'No, Your Highness, the girl still has her courses. We need incontrovertible proof that it is you who sheds her blood, if we are to kill the rumours.'

He shrugged. 'We shall come back. We should appreciate it, cavaliere, if in the meantime you would come to visit us, that we may know you by the light of day and not shut up in this side-canal.'

'Our mission must be conducted with the greatest secrecy, if we are to succeed,' Vinta began. 'You will remember that in Ferrara—'

'Ferrara be damned,' said the Prince, frowning. I discovered later what it was that annoyed him so. He turned round in the doorway, without looking at me again. I heard him summon his courtiers. Then they clattered downstairs and out of the house. The Prince was laughing as their footsteps receded. At least, I think it was him. Perhaps a Prince's companions may only laugh if he tells them to.

'What did he mean, *we*?' I whispered to the matron.

She looked puzzled for a moment, but then her frown cleared. 'Ah, I see what you mean. That is just his way of speaking. Because he's a prince.'

Does it surprise you if I say my heart was gladdened? Well, it was. I was to be given to this stranger, but only to him. I'd thought he'd meant I was to be shared with those others with him who'd craned their necks to look at me. Yes, for that reason I was glad, but not just because I was to lie only with him. I did not like the way I saw Vinta look at me at times, when he thought he was not observed. I liked even less the feel of his lips on my fingers in his house in Florence, the brushing of his beard on my skin. But I wanted the Prince to look at me, for he was young and handsome.

When I thought my courses gone, I was examined again, lying back on the bed, though this time I was allowed to keep my shift on. Master Galletti parted my knees, patted my privates with a wad of linen and said: 'Another day. The region is still humid – impure.'

Finally they decided I was ready to receive him, but when the Prince returned, it was a Friday, and Vinta sent him away again. I did not see the Prince but heard him and Vinta talking, for the matron had bustled out of the bedroom in a hurry and had not closed the door properly. Now that I was free of my courses, I was confined to that inner chamber all the time, to await the Prince. I was still encouraged to wash regularly, and I did, but was not permitted to dress in anything other than my shift. I swear I thought my bones would go soft in that house, so little was I allowed to move about.

'Not today, Your Highness,' said Vinta. 'The Holy Father was quite specific about that. Not on a Friday. Even a husband and wife lawfully joined should abstain on that day.'

Why did they worry so much about what day it was, given the enormity of the sin we were to commit?

'Tomorrow, then?' said the Prince.

'Tomorrow,' I heard Galletti say. 'It rains today, and we shall pray for better weather for then, so that your own humours be hotter and dryer.'

'We shall return in the morning.'

'Not in the morning, Your Highness,' said Vinta. 'Congress should take place in darkness. We shall welcome you tomorrow at sundown.'

'But you will provide us with a light. I want to see what I am doing,' laughed the Prince. 'If you, Vinta, are to see, and to touch, as you tell me you have promised my future father-in-law, then you will need light too.'

Vinta hesitated. 'Very well, the chamber shall be lit.'

The hours were long in that little house. I longed to walk outside, to feel the cool March breeze on my face, but they told me that the air of Venice was not healthy, being surrounded by marshes and built upon that creeping dampness. I asked then why had the city been chosen.

'It is a place well used to keeping secrets,' said Vinta.

On that occasion they let me come out into the antechamber and look out of the window, for they saw I was fretful. I both dreaded the Prince's return and longed for it, for I wanted my task to be over, to know what would happen to me next.

Peering out, I could see the house was guarded, two armed men standing on the landing stage – just as there had been at the roadside inns.

'What do they do?' I asked. 'There are no brigands here, surely.'

'Stand back, Giulia,' said the cavaliere. 'If you see them then they can also observe you. I chose this house carefully,' he went on, and I realised he wanted praise. 'An attack from the canal can be more readily resisted than men on foot.'

'Why would anyone attack us?'

Galletti laughed and said the women of Venice were not known for their chastity, and if it got out that between my legs a citadel lay still defended then there would be many men besides the Prince who would want to attack, and to inundate. 'To inundate?' I asked. The cavaliere looked at the matron.

'Just how have you instructed her, woman?'

'I shall show you,' and she disappeared back into the bedroom and brought out the books she had been reading to me, books I had never seen in the orphanage, though she said everyone read them.

'Love poetry!' shouted Vinta. 'Boccaccio! Such books are for those who are already versed in *ars amatoria*. You foolish woman. I thought you of all people would have known what to tell her. Would you have the girl recount him bawdy stories?'

The matron merely shrugged, though I am sure he had insulted her. Yet she could not have completely failed in her task. There were indeed tales in that book that had left me perplexed, though with a certain fever in my veins at the things they hinted at. 'A fine mare's tail,' said a friar in one of them, and I thought then that a man's member might be something soft to tickle me with, and remembered the boy babies I had cared for when I was in the Innocenti. Vinta mastered his anger eventually, however, but said he would have to instruct me himself. I was sent back to lie against my pillows, and Vinta brought in a chair. The matron sat in hers on the other side of the bed, clicking away with her lacemaking, as though he spoke of nothing stranger than some relatives who intended a visit. Master Galletti came in also and stood listening by the door.

'The Prince, everyone says, is no novice in the defloration of virgins,' Vinta began, clearing his throat and looking away from me. 'So he will know what to do, but you must for your part do all that you can to please him. A modest demeanour is appropriate to the situation, so do not look on him first with desirous eyes, but downcast ones. He will embrace you, and lift your shift or cast it from you altogether. He will explore you with his eyes, his hands, and you must submit. When he puts his fingers to your sex, it would be pretty for you not to resist him exactly, but to hesitate. However, you must not let him enter you with his fingers. I shall have to ask you about that – afterwards.'

'Enter me with his fingers?'

He looked at me, sighed, and frowned at the matron, who went on working.

'Yes. The place from where your monthly blood comes. That is why we have had to wait until your courses have finished. We must know that the blood you shed is because of the destruction of your maidenhead.'

'In the orphanage we were always told we should not even think of such matters, much less talk of them. I saw a girl shorn for doing so.'

'Don't be foolish. *Your* head will not be shaved – far from it. Why do you think your hair has been washed, and combed, and perfumed and garlanded? It has had more attention in these last few weeks than it has had in your entire life, from what I observed when I saw you first. Could we please complete this instruction? Otherwise the Prince will be clamouring at the door and we will not be ready. Now, where was I?'

'His fingers on my sex, you said. And that I should hesitate.'

'Ah, yes... but only for a moment, then relax your thighs and let him explore you. A little sigh of acquiescence would please him, I think – as a small sign of tenderness and resignation – even if you do not feel it.'

I looked at him, and I realised that he did not speak of the Prince, but of his own self. I thought of the Lady Camilla holding my hand as they examined me, and of the tears in her eyes, and wondered what kind of husband Vinta would find for me. My heart beat in my breast like a little bird throwing itself helplessly against a window.

'Let me see your hands,' he said. He held them, looking at my nails. In the orphanage, they had always been cut short, for ragged ones could damage the cloth, and for the same reason our hands had always been kept clean, cleaner than the rest of us, but reddened by contact with fuller's earth. Since the orphanage gown had been taken from me, my hands had been rubbed with almond oil every day, the nails allowed to grow until sweet sickle-moons appeared on their tips.

'Good,' he said, absently, and I could see the matron was pleased at some praise at last. I eased my hands away and hid them beneath the sheet.

'When he embraces you, he may be fierce,' he went on. 'You should not be. Aim for gentleness, if you can. Trace these nails softly on his skin, not to hurt him but—'

Then he stopped, as though a new thought had occurred to him. 'Giulia,' he said, and I was attentive, for there was a sudden intensity in his voice. 'When you are in your bed, before he comes, run your fingers gently over your flesh – but do not, I warn you, stray to your sex, even if you might find you wish to. Touch yourself to find where it pleases you the most: your stomach, the softer skin of your sides, under your arms, the back of your neck – your breasts. Think on what you feel when you do that, and then you will know better what to do to please him. He may also touch you that way, and you will find that his touch is more welcome than anything you can do by yourself.'

I looked him in the face then, for his voice was strange and he breathed as though he climbed a stair. 'You will find your way. If he gasps gently, or catches his breath, or his breathing quickens as your hands pass over him, you will know that you have done right.' Vinta's eyes were dark pools, and his face flushed, as though the blood mounted to his head. 'The nipple of a man is particularly susceptible,' he said. 'It is for that reason we men must have them, for they are no use to a sucking infant. Caress his, for he will caress yours. Caress his manhood – he will want you to do that.'

'His manhood? Such as boy babies have?'

Vinta glared at the matron in exasperation. I saw him think for a moment, and then he said: 'I shall show you what I mean.' He left the room; Galletti put a hand on his arm as he did so, but Vinta muttered something – 'I know what to do', I think it was – and brushed him off. He came back a few minutes later with something done up in sacking which he unwrapped carefully. He held out a little bronze statuette, its back turned to me. I looked at it and put my hand over my mouth so that I might not cry out. Yet the image was small: no higher than the length of my forearm.

'Is this how men are – like devils?' Indeed, the thing had shaggy haunches, a tail that curled upwards, and it went on hooves.

'Not a devil – a satyr. A mythological beast. I brought this because the Prince, I am told, is pleased by such curiosities. This came from Padua, where they delight in imitating ancient art. No, Giulia, men have legs and feet like yours, though hairier, as our faces are. But in this they are different, men from women,' he said, and turned the little figure around. I gasped; the matron laughed. The tiny, bearded face leered at me and its hands reached out as though to clasp me. But it wasn't its expression that alarmed me, nor the little horns poking through the curling hair, nor the pointed ears that grew high on its head. It was what it carried proud between its legs.

'This is what the Prince must have, if he is to be a husband,' said Vinta.

'And how does one become a wife, then?' I said, transfixed by the statuette.

'Our creator has made us, men and women, as opposites that, in coming together, fit perfectly. Man's humours are hot, and dry, whereas a woman's are cool, and wet. This he carries outside his body that it not overheat, yet it is still the warmest part of him, whereas womankind is made as its antithesis – hollow, where he protrudes. Think of yourself as a finger of a glove, Giulia, of the finest, softest kid. That glove lies limp, within a press. Yet put your hand into it, and it takes shape, is animated. Its purpose is fulfilled. It cannot be a glove without a hand. You cannot be a woman without a man. That is what you were made for.'

'And the nuns?'

'They speak of a holy bridegroom, do they not?' He pointed at the statuette. 'These sacs contain a man's seed. We know this, for deprived of them, man cannot attain this state,' his finger hovered over the creature's – oh, what must I call it? Member? – 'and can never be a father.'

'I remember them... on those tiny babies – but not like this. Are all grown men in this state, always?' I whispered.

Vinta smiled, without mirth. 'That depends on the man. No, not all, but many – often. It happens when they are tempted, when they think of salacious matters, look at certain images – or immodestly dressed women. Younger ones are prone to it more, but older and wiser ones are not safe from it.' He fidgeted in his chair.

'An honest wife, a chaste one,' he said, 'is timid, yielding. She defers to her husband in all things. She keeps to her home most of all, and if she ventures out, does not do so unaccompanied, and does not look into the faces of the strangers she encounters. Yet she must seek to please her husband, while not being forward with him. If she were, he would only suspect her, for that is how whores behave. That is the wife you must be, and I confess I chose you with that in mind, not only for this congress with the Prince. You do not only have a beautiful face, Giulia. You are gentle, modest in manner, noble in your bearing.' His voice shook. 'I pray you do not lose any of those qualities in the days that follow. Yet it is crucial to our purpose that you please the Prince.'

Already my fears were lessening. I had dreaded something monstrous, searingly painful. I looked at the rampant little satyr and thought of the Prince crying out in my embrace. I thought I should love him for that. 'I hope indeed I shall please him,' I offered.

Vinta looked straight at me then as though he had just recollected who I was, and said in a firmer voice: 'Endearments are practised by the fondest lover. If he indulges in them and encourages you to do so, you are both of you fortunate. He may not, of course. Sooner or later, whether he does this with affection and sweet words or no, he will come to you and the front of his body will be as hard as this bronze though clothed in flesh, and he will push that between your legs and into you till neither of you can see it any more. It will hurt you, and you will bleed, and with that blood, and with the evidence I shall see, and touch with my own hand, our undertaking will have been successful. If he repeats his attack, then it will not pain you so much, and you may even be blessed to feel pleasure in it.'

I stared at him, appalled at the violence he described, and started to tremble. Galletti stepped forward then, and said: 'As a physician, I can tell you that he probably will wish to give you pleasure. We know that a woman's soil is not receptive to a man's seed unless she too experiences enjoyment. Indeed, those who have studied the matter in detail are of the opinion that hers is greater than his. Without her pleasure, her own seed is not shed.'

'Thank you, Master Galletti,' said Vinta. 'Yes, I have heard that some women do feel pleasure in the act – and some of course will say they do if you reward them well enough.' He walked out of the room, and I heard him march down the stairs, Master Galletti following, and I sat there shaking, feeling that I had been sentenced to the fires of hell, that Eve would never be forgiven and that all women must pay for that fall. The beads on the matron's lacemaking cushion danced and clicked.

After that I was bathed again from head to foot and my hair washed with vinegar and thyme water, and left to hang down my back as far as what Vinta was pleased to call my croup (though he didn't use that word before the Prince). Then the matron brushed it until the comb caught no more. I am sure I was bathed more in those few days between my selection and my submitting to the Prince than I had been bathed in my entire life until then. Almond oil was rubbed into my soles and heels. The few hairs stripped away so painfully from my toes had not yet grown back.

The Prince never looked at my feet.

Chapter Six

Test

...et una incorrotta fede in riferirle la verità di quello che udirò e vederò, et che m'ingegnerò anche di toccar con la mano, se poterò.

[I will] in absolute faith report to you the truth of what I will hear and see, and I will undertake also to touch with my hand, if I can.

Belisario Vinta, to Francesco, Grand Duke of Tuscany, Florence (25 February 1584)

The Prince returned, not at sundown on Saturday, but when Friday had barely died. It was 4am, but by then I had lost all sense of what was day and what was night, and barely knew what meals I took. Vinta looked at me again when he heard the knock and said to the matron, 'I see you have washed her and prepared her well. Only a man made of clay could fail to be pleased with her.'

The Prince's courtier carried sheets, though those on the bed were clean. From the way they addressed each other, I think this man must have been a kinsman of the Prince's.

'We shall place them on the bed ourselves, if you will observe us, cavaliere, so that you may see for yourself our good faith – no subterfuge, nothing introduced that should not be there. I shall be armed only with myself,' laughed the Prince. In fact he did none of the work, watching the others from the doorway, while I stood silently by the bed, barefoot in my shift and linen cap. I trembled, though for March the room was warm, my heart beating so fast I thought it would choke me.

'Hurry, gentlemen. We should not keep the damsel waiting,' said the Prince, and glancing at me, added, 'I trust I shall serve you well.' I dropped my head, feeling the blood rise to my face.

Once the bed was ready, the matron helped me up onto it, turning back the sheets for me. When I was lying there, she looked me over one more time, then took the cap from my head, unwound my braids and loosed them. She spread my hair about the pillow and then she leaned in and kissed me, the first and only sign of affection that she ever showed me. I thought she did it because the others stood in the doorway and observed her. I lay straight, my ankles together, and crossed my hands on my breast: it was the way I had been taught to go to sleep in the Pietà. I heard the Prince laugh, and say, 'Gentlemen, she looks as though she lies in her tomb,' and they laughed in reply, but I was too mortified to change my position, and merely shut my eyes. The room was crowded by then: besides the Prince and his courtier, there was Vinta, Master Galletti, the Mantuan Donati, the Prince's manservant and the matron. Did they all expect to stay and watch?

I heard Vinta say, 'Your Highness, there is one last thing we must be sure of before you enter the lists.' I opened my eyes. What other indignities did they want to subject me to now?

None, at least not then. The Prince was unhooking his doublet, tossing it to his manservant, stripping himself of shoes, of britches, of hose, discarding them on the floor for others to gather up. In the midst of this despoiling he belched loudly. When only his shirt remained I closed my eyes.

'Don't look away now!' he cried. 'Don't you want to see and remember for always the fine stallion who will break you in, sweet Florentine filly?' I heard the rustle of his shirt as he shed that too, and then I did look from beneath my lashes, and saw him standing with his back to me, and I marvelled that all men are made to the same model, yet some have cloth of gold to cover their nakedness and others only rags. I had nothing to compare his figure to but the statues I saw in Florence on feast day processions, and, God forgive me, the poor lacerated Christ hanging on the cross, but he, however humiliated and ill used, at least was granted a strip of linen. The Prince was more beautiful and terrifying than those still figures I had seen. The two doctors were examining him, as he stood there looking down at them, his hands on his hips. Vinta watched them, his head on one side.

'We trust you will give us a good report, cavaliere,' he said, 'though if you would see this lance at its finest then it would be better you come to my lodgings just as I wake, for it is then that I can give the best account of myself. *Then* I am as straight and hard as a spindle!'

'I shall put my trust in Master Galletti, for I have no expertise in these matters,' said Vinta stiffly.

The Mantuan – Donati – said: 'You see, cavaliere, that the report put abroad by the Farnese faction was nothing more than calumny.'

'Indeed,' answered Vinta, 'His Highness is neither too mighty nor too pitiful, though both have been said of him.'

My courage failed me then, and I shut my eyes again. The bed heaved: the Prince lay beside me. Though he wasn't touching me I could feel his warmth. I opened my eyes again, not to look at him but to take one last look at the door before it closed on us.

The others had gone but the matron and Vinta were still there. He was writing in a little notebook. He spent much of the ensuing days scratching away like that, noting everything he saw and then writing endless letters and calling for sealing wax.

'Leave a light behind, and wait beyond the door,' said the Prince. 'When I have taken aim and unleashed my arrow then I shall call for you, that you all may bear witness to it quivering in its target.'

'I kiss your hands,' said Vinta, backing out of the door. Out of the corner of my eye I saw the matron turn to look at me, but I do not know what expression she wore, for my ravisher then took my face in his hands. He leaned over me and kissed me, stroking my neck, opening my mouth with his tongue – a relentless, darting serpent. I tasted wine, then his hands groped at me through my shift. He pulled away, smiled, then turned his face to one side and belched again.

'Let me see the gift my uncle has made me,' he said and, putting my arms up either side of my face, lifted my shift. I prayed silently, but I didn't know what for. For the house to collapse around our ears?

'Do stop trembling... hmm... I asked for a beautiful face but your person does not disappoint. Whoever made you, my Florentine filly, has endowed you generously.' He must know I am a bastard, I thought. I felt his hand between my legs and remembered Vinta's admonition: 'Do not let him enter you with his fingers.' Then something flared in me, a pleasure that was like an exquisite pain, and barely realising I did so, I cried out. But those fingers stilled, and the Prince's body lay heavily against my side. A moment later he slept, and the air that came noisily from his open mouth was foul, though I could see his teeth were sound, and I wondered why my breath had been sweetened with cloves and parsley if it was to be mingled with such a stench.

He had eaten too well and upset the delicate humours of his body. I lay there, too fearful to even pull down my shift, but when I felt sure he was not going to wake, I tugged the covers over us both. The candle guttered out and I lay a long time listening to the Prince's snoring, wondering what would happen next. If it was true after all what they had said of him, and he was not potent, what would my fate be? If I was returned entire to Florence it could only be to the cloister.

I woke from a dream in which I was once more on the road to Venice, but our conveyance was being thrown from side to side as though the driver had lost control of the horses. I opened my eyes as the Prince kissed me; daylight showed round the edges of the door, making the room greyly visible. Then he groaned and, throwing the bed into a commotion, he pulled away from me, clutching his stomach and crying out for a clyster. I was mortally afraid then, for he looked fit to die, and I might be accused of his death, for it is certain that none of those without would take the blame. The door opened and Vinta came in, fully dressed, his face nearly as pale as the Prince's, but the Prince swore and pushed past him, shouting for his clothes. He was still roaring when he left the house, for someone unlocked the casement to follow what was happening without, and I heard him blaspheming at the boatmen and then the sound of him vomiting into the canal.

They all came in to where I sat up in bed and Vinta shouted: 'Well?'

I pulled the sheet around me and said, 'Nothing! I am as I was.'

Vinta swore, he who was normally so precise in his speech. He and the two doctors and the matron hunted beneath the bed, among the curtains.

'Get down,' Vinta commanded. I did so, and watched as they turned everything uppermost, though the bed was clean.

'There is nowhere she could have hidden it,' said Donati.

'Hidden what?' I asked, but no one answered me.

'How could she have had anything about her?' said the matron. 'I made sure of that myself.'

They were looking for venom, I realised, some little phial. I felt calmer then, for they could not find what was not there. But they went on searching, and talking, as though I wasn't there. I could not read any of those scribblings that Vinta was forever making, nor the little volume that lay on a table beside the bed though the matron said it was a breviary; she had put away those other books after Vinta scoffed at them. That did not mean, though, that I could not reason.

'What are you saying?' I cried, so that at last they looked at me, for I made so much noise. 'I have no reason to murder the poor Prince. Who could wish harm to such a fine-made man? I know my duty.'

The matron stopped flapping the sheet she had in her hands and said to them: 'Why indeed would she do such a thing? The child knows that she will lose her dowry and her husband if our enterprise does not succeed, and that she would be returned not to the Pietà but to the Bargello, and that only for the shortest time.'

Vinta calmed down a bit and got out his notebook. 'Lie down again and lift your shift,' he ordered. 'Gentlemen?'

The two doctors examined me.

'A virgin still,' said Galletti, straightening up.

Then Vinta asked me had the Prince mounted me at all, and I said no.

'Was his tail stiff or soft?'

'I could not even say.'

'Did he say anything to you?'

'No, nothing. He didn't care if I lived or died,' I said, and started to cry. 'He went off without even bidding me goodbye. I'd thought he liked me, and you all said he was pleased with me, and now you and he will be angry with me. He was like one stunned, only that he snored.'

At this they nodded, as they could not have failed to hear him themselves.

'Don't worry,' said Vinta. 'He was only sick.'

I looked at him and stretched my lips in a bitter smile but said nothing.

'He'll come back tonight and do what he is supposed to do.'

'I don't want to see him again!' I cried. 'What good is all this to me?'

'Poor girl,' said Vinta, wetting his lips, and turning to the matron, 'brought up to this pitch only to be disappointed. I really don't understand it – so well made as he is. Well, we are still within the twenty-four hours prescribed. Let us hope he can raise his standard at the second attempt.'

They went off, murmuring something about a colic, and as none present were Venetian there were some hard comments made about the food of the city, though I confess I had no complaints and since my fasting on the journey indeed had never eaten such delightful things in my entire life: all the eggs I could want, a bird they called a partridge, and all manner of fish and strange creeping creatures that lived in the lagoon – with wine, though mine was always mixed with water.

'It was nothing we gave him, at any rate,' said Vinta. 'The fault is not ours.'

But the Prince did not come back that day. That was a Saturday; I did not see him until Tuesday. Vinta came in and out, muttering to Galletti, about the condition the Grand Duchess had set, that the Prince must succeed within twenty-four hours of the commencement of the test. I heard the doctor say something about how an exception could surely be made for the Prince's indisposition.

'I have written to tell them this. But I daren't say yet how much this stay has cost. Nor did I mention the rumours abroad of a party of Florentines, with a young woman in their midst. I fear that young man of Lucca must have talked, for all the promises he made.'

I think it was soon after twelve the day the Prince returned, for I had just been given something to eat – yes, I remember the Angelus bells. He was full of bravado, keen to show off to all of them there his new clothes, 'in the Venetian fashion'. He was thinner in the face, fully purged no doubt, and clean: he smelled sweeter. I do not know why I had had to be stripped, and scrubbed, and perfumed, when he, prince as he was, that first time could come to me reeking of sweat and drink.

'I shall come tonight and I shall not disappoint,' he said to Vinta, turning to look at me. 'Nothing like this has ever happened to me before and I can assure all present it will not happen again!'

'Oysters,' said Donati. 'Our Prince has always had a good appetite, only this disruption to his normal habits has meant he did not digest so well.'

I don't know what his normal habits might have been, for when he came again, it was a little after four of the morning on the Wednesday, the same time as he came on Saturday. I know this because I counted the strikes of a church bell. I could not read and write then, but that much I could do, by use of my fingers.

He was in the highest of spirits, and caught me up and spun me round, his hand on my bottom pushing me against him so that I felt his arousal. He kissed my neck. The matron came forward, officious as always, to prepare me for bed, but he batted her away and began to unlace my shift and pull off my cap himself, all this before the eyes of Vinta, the doctors – even the Prince's own servant, who acted as though nothing was amiss. Perhaps he had been present at many such jousts.

'Do as you would in your own home, Your Highness,' babbled Vinta, but he got no answer. I stood shivering in my shift, my hair loosed, when the Prince said, 'Get into bed, while I satisfy these gentlemen,' and with the help of his barber again stripped and paraded himself before them, this time facing the bed; I, in the same state, would have been fit to die of shame. He held up his hands to show that he had no weapon but that which his own body provided – it stood erect, just like the satyr's, and he spoke of it as if it were not part of him but some uncaged beast. I looked away, my heart pounding.

'Cavaliere, I shall call you when the lion is caged!'

He climbed in beside me and the others bowed out of the room, pulling the door to, though I felt the silence seep through it, and knew they all stood there holding their breath.

'You are worth the wait,' he murmured. He pulled back the sheet and lifted my shift. It was another new one, of the finest muslin, the most delicate thing I had ever worn, and I was afraid of it getting torn, but he seemed not to care. He kissed and nibbled me until my poor flesh was on fire for him, and I thought I could endure even the torments of hell if I had this to remember.

'Hold me,' he said, and took my hand, and guided it to where he wanted it to go, to that butting weapon, but I pulled away from shame, though I remembered Vinta's instructions. I thought the Prince might be angered with me, but he just laughed and said, 'Very well, we shall wait no longer,' and he went blindly forward, pushing at me. I wished he had gone on caressing me. He hurt me, I felt resistance, and I cried out, but in an instant was bathed with his effusion, and I knew this was not right, for the cavaliere had told me the Prince's member had to disappear from sight. But the Prince merely laughed and said he had not moved quickly enough. That subdued tail damp against my thigh, he nuzzled and kissed and murmured in my neck, in my armpits, at my paps, my belly, until he was as he had been before, and this time he drove at me with determination and I thought I would burst for now he was in me and how could my poor body hold such a force – and he thrust, and thrust, as if he would break down a door, as if he would reach into my bowels and draw them out of me. I have forgotten the pangs of childbirth, as they say all women have, but I have never forgotten that pain. He was pitiless, his face above mine flushed, distorted, yet proud, and cruel, although he had his arms about me as though I was the tenderest thing in the world to him.

Then he called out, even as he panted: 'Cavaliere! Cavaliere! Come back here – touch and feel with your hand.' The door opened at once and Vinta rustled in. I saw him through my lashes lean over us, hesitating, his right hand trembling in the air above our entwined legs. Finally he pushed it between our bellies. I felt the cool air between us as the Prince raised himself on his hands, and I could hear Vinta's breathing, and felt his fingers exploring my secret pelt, he frowning in concentration. Then I looked down my body, past my shift ruckled up to my armpits, and saw those fingers close around the root of the Prince's member, and felt the pads of Vinta's fingers warm against my most delicate parts. The cavaliere grunted with what sounded like satisfaction, and I thought, 'Now it is over. Now I will be taken back to Florence and I will see if they will keep their promises, and if I shall have another man who will do this to me, and he will be the only one for the rest of my life,' and I tried to imagine that man's face. I saw Vinta now touch the Prince's pelt too, as though to check there was no counterfeit, and only then did he turn his head and look me in the face, so I shut my eyes, and cried from shame that he saw me like that, and let the tears seep from their corners.

'That is good,' muttered Vinta. 'A seemly combination of pain and desire.' Then I heard the Prince speak, and opening my eyes saw the movement of his chest above me as he did so: 'So now you've seen, and touched, leave me to get on with my business!' Vinta backed out of the room, bowing as he did so. When he opened the door I glimpsed other faces there: the matron, Galletti, Donati, trying to peer over each other's shoulders to see in. Mercifully, the door banged shut.

The Prince thrust at me I think only seconds more, before he flung his head back and gave a loud, grating cry, followed by a long sigh. I wished with all my heart that in that moment he could at least have looked at me. Instead the Prince eased off me, giving my body only a cursory glance. I wanted to put my hands down to myself and touch where it hurt, but I was afraid to do so – not to cause more pain than I felt already, but because Vinta had been so emphatic that I should not explore my own body in that way. My very person was evidence, you see.

What astonished me the most, thinking about this afterwards, as I did again and again, was how fast this act had been – after all that preparation, all those fears, all that subterfuge.

The Prince was oblivious to all this. He rolled onto his back and started talking, but it was more to himself than to me.

'I wish they'd all come in this minute, all my detractors, and see me now!'

For myself, enough people had seen me and I wanted no one else to do so ever again. I didn't know how to answer him, but I don't think he expected me to. I lay there with that smart between my legs, and some warm liquid cooling on the sheet beneath me, blood or his effusion, or both. I longed for him to comfort me, to hold me the way he had when his need had been so urgent. If he had noticed my tears, he didn't care. He scratched his armpit, and then those sacks that lay between his legs and that had hit against me so hard I was sure it must have hurt him. Then he asked me, 'What is it the Grand Duke will give you for this night's work?'

'Three thousand *scudi* and a husband.'

He laughed. 'And I will get a hundred times that, and a princess! But not all at once, you understand. She will have to do what you have just done first, before the full balance will be paid. And if she does not live long, I will have to give something back, and go searching again.'

'Will you need me again, then?' I asked.

'No, you goose! Your job is done. No one will doubt Vincenzo Gonzaga now. So, what will you do with your three thousand scudi, then?'

'It won't be mine. It will be my husband's. But if he is kind, I will not have to sit at a loom again. I will have a house of my own, and clothes I can choose to wear, that are not the same as the other girls'. I will have my own hearth, and maybe even a servant – a girl from an orphanage, for that is how all Florence is served. My children will sleep each in his own cot, and not four or five to a bed as I had to do, until I was taken to the Pietà and they told me that sleeping huddled together was an occasion of sin. I will bathe in water scented with lavender and wash my hair with vinegar and thyme and braid it and dress it as they did in readiness for this occasion.'

I stopped then, thinking I had never spoken so much in my entire life, and was afraid my babbling had displeased him. But he was silent; all I could hear was his breathing. I turned to look at him. He was asleep.

Some time later, in darkness, he came at me again, wordless in his attack. I tensed, expecting more pain, but it was easier. I confess also, and have learned not to blush when I think this, that it was pleasurable, only that he finished too soon. I wanted him to put his fingers or his mouth to me again, but he did not and I did not dare to ask him. But I stroked his body, the way Vinta had told me to, and he rewarded me with happy murmurs and by stretching like a cat. He complimented me on the gentleness of my touch. I wish that is all he had said.

'Why don't you stay in Venice? A girl like you with such a pretty way about her could sell her maidenhead again and again. There are women in this city practised in those arts: some astringent to tighten the passage, a little bladder of pig's blood, a modest expression and some regretful tears, and one of your dupes would want to keep you, in recompense for having dishonoured you.'

I do not think he could have hurt me more if he had struck me across the face.

'I want to go back to Florence. I want my dowry. I want a husband,' I said, fighting the tears. I shifted away from him on the bed; I hated him – the touch, the smell of him, but most of all those cruel words.

'Ah yes, the dowry! That will be the sixth one paid out over this matter – an expensive business, getting me wed!'

'*The sixth!*' I exclaimed.

'Ssh! Let old Vinta and the others sleep. There were four in Parma, I believe.'

I listened to him in a kind of horrified delirium.

'Yes, when they examined poor Margherita – that was my first wife, who was malformed, as you, lovely maiden, are not! – they didn't know quite what they were looking for, those doctors. They could have asked me. Probably the only maidenheads any of them had encountered had been owned by their virtuous wives, and the desires of a young husband trump the curiosity of the doctor, so they never stopped to look first, and there is but one eye in the head of a penis, even if it weeps when it is happy, and that eye is blind. The only women they ever got to anatomise were hanged whores, you see. Virtuous girls and chaste wives may go to their graves unmolested. Four peasant girls were brought to them, all of an age with Margherita, so that they could see how a normal girl was made. I wish I'd been there; what a winsome parade that must have been! I'm told Cardinal Borromeo – it was he who signed the annulment that made me a free man – lived on bread and water for days in expiation. I don't know why – those girls were all paid off with dowries, so they could make better marriages than they would have dreamed of.'

'Who was the other?'

'Oh, I never saw her either.'

He had one arm behind his head as he said this, and with the other played idly with his member, which was stirring again. I could see him now, for outside it had to be day, and a sliver of light was visible around the closed door, so that gradually the details of the room, and of the Prince himself, became visible. I remember the hair of his body, dense to the top of his thighs, where it stopped as though a line had been drawn across, only for it to blaze out again around his sex, and to shade that little well in his stomach that all of us have, that once connected every one of us to a mother.

'That girl was in Ferrara and had been prepared just as you were. I wanted to see her beforehand, but they wouldn't let me. I couldn't stand their hand-wringing, their orders, their insistence, and most of all I couldn't abide the Medici ambassador, dull old fool! At least Vinta one can reason with. So I left for Mantua.'

'And the girl?'

'Got her dowry, and it paid her way into the convent... ah, I see this talk has pleased him. Look, Giulia, he has raised his head in your honour. Let us oblige him once more.'

After he had joined himself to me that time, he did not sleep, but instead spoke of himself. He described a childhood unimaginable to me, in which he ran laughing from his tutors through endless long galleries hung with tapestries and portraits of people he could name, for they were his forebears – and, horrible to relate even now, the mummified corpse of a former lord of his city, vanquished by the Gonzaga, displayed in a sort of cabinet of curiosities along with a unicorn and those strange armoured crawling creatures they call crocodiles, such as St Teodoro stands upon on his column looking out from Piazza San Marco.

'You have a mother and father,' I said, tentative. That was what I wanted him to speak of. Remember, I had encountered no family until I heard Vinta's lady speaking with her daughter, save the paintings of Our Lady with her gentle husband and the Christ Child.

He laughed then, not a happy sound.

'I barely see them. It has always been so, but now it is by choice. My father is a pious, hand-wringing hunchback; when he bathes, it is in cold water. I do not know if it is not my mother that makes him so – apart from his crookback, of course. She was some years older than I when she deigned to marry, having refused the King of Denmark and a Saxon prince merely because they were Protestants.'

I shivered at his flippancy. Were we two not mired in mortal sin so that he might wed the Medici princess and not some heretic foreigner?

'You're cold,' he said. 'Let me warm you.'

He did warm me. Later, I tried again. 'Your mother and father must love you, surely?'

'What, them again?' he said, scratching his armpit. 'They do nothing but complain of me. I think they would rather I were someone else. My father had a courtier he loved more than me, a foreign youth. But then he spoke twelve languages and had a fine voice for both singing and oratory.'

'Do you have brothers and sisters?'

'Two sisters. I cannot think why they could be of interest to you.'

'Forgive me. It is only that I have never met anyone who had sisters or brothers.'

'They are younger than I. Margherita has been Duchess of Ferrara since she was fifteen years old. Anna is Archduchess of Austria. I have not seen her since she left for Innsbruck. They tell me the poor thing longed to be a nun, but I cannot say how true that is, for I barely knew her.'

'Oh. And what happened to the courtier?'

'He had to be silenced.'

I thought if I did not ask more I could cling to the belief that the young foreigner had merely been expelled from court.

The heaviness of the Prince's own chill silence frightened me. To my relief, he spoke again, but as though to himself. He talked of that wife who was no wife, with a tenderness he expressed at no other time. He said he would never forget her screams, this thirteen-year-old girl whom God had fashioned only to be a nun, and how he had rolled away from her in despair, lying on his back as his hand worked, his eyes wet. 'Since that night,' he said, 'I have never been able to tolerate a woman who yells when she is aroused. I would have kept my Margherita by me had they let me, and met my carnal needs elsewhere, only that I must have a son. I think of her every day, shut away in her cell. We could have been happy. I do not know that I ever shall be, so I must be content with amusing myself.'

That was when he turned to kiss me, as if only then remembering I was there. I wanted to fight him. I wanted to find that girl in the Ferrarese convent and ask her to pray for me – her and poor Margherita with her obstinate maidenhead. I struggled, and though he persisted for a while and could have overcome me if he had wanted to, he laughed, as if it mattered little to him.

'I see the filly has not quite been broken in after all,' he said. Then he yawned and turned his back on me. I cried myself to sleep but he never stirred.

When he woke he woke me also, with the force of his bouncing off the bed. I watched his slender back through my lashes, and wondered if he would turn and look at me. He did turn round, but it was only to pull the piss-pot out from under the bed. He used it, not caring whether I looked at him or no, and I did look, even when he shook the drops from that shrivelled piece of flesh, unrecognisable as that terrible bar that had caused me so much pain. I saw that he was smeared with my blood, but he either did not notice or did not care, carrying those marks like a warrior does his scars.

Then he rummaged among the clothes tumbled on the chair and pulled out a soft leather bag.

'Here,' he said, throwing something onto the bed. 'Another *scudo* to add to your hoard – a Mantuan one this time!'

I picked up the coin, the first piece of gold I had ever handled, and thought about how long an honest poor man must toil and never see such a thing.

*

'Come in!' the Prince shouted. The door opened, and Vinta was the first to enter, dishevelled and grey from lack of sleep, in the clothes he had worn when he had come in and touched us.

'Virgin no more, Vinta!' said the Prince, hilariously. 'We have worked well, have we not? See for yourself.'

'I see the signs of conflict,' said Vinta, looking at him and those smears of blood. 'You have indeed worked long and well, for it is two o'clock in the afternoon!' Then the Prince's barber came in, carrying a clean white shirt, and helped him into it. Without looking round at me where I lay under a rumpled sheet, the Prince went into the antechamber, leaving the door open, in just that shirt, and I heard him joking, laughing – boasting – with those assembled there, while the barber gathered up his clothes, avoiding my eyes. Vinta stood by the bed. He had his notebook in his hand. There was no sign of the matron, but now, of course, I did not need to be guarded.

'It's cold, Your Highness,' I heard Donati the Mantuan say. 'I shall close those windows, for your head is uncovered.'

'Don't fuss, Donati! I've had a warm night and could use some fresh air to cool my ardour.' But he allowed the servant to put a waistcoat on him, and finally a fur-lined cloak.

'I didn't call you the first time, Vinta,' he said over his shoulder. 'My bucket was full to the brim and I spilled the lot on the doorstep.'

Vinta told me to lie there just as I was, with the sheet pulled up to my chin, and my hands above it, crossed on my breast. But one hand was a fist, hiding the coin. 'I shall need to ask you some questions, once I have spoken to the Prince. I'll tell the matron you are not to wash for the moment.'

'Where's Galletti?' called the Prince. 'Doesn't he need to examine me too?'

'I shall send for him,' said Vinta, but then he turned back to me, and seizing my uppermost hand, pressed my fingers to his lips. Then he left, and I heard him say to the Prince: 'You're in fine fettle, Your Highness. Last night's work has not tired you, but rather replenished your energy.' The latch of the door clicked shut on their laughter, and I was alone.

I cried, looking at the coin he had tossed at me. On one side was the figure of a man dressed like a Roman statue. I turned it over, and saw a short-armed cross, and in each of its quadrants a bird, I know not what kind, all of them with their wings raised not in flight but in threat, as if all four were going to descend on me and pluck out my eyes and tear out my heart.

Chapter Seven

Proof

sì che mio ti vo' dir,
chè mio pur sei,
benché t'involi, ahi crudo!
a gli occhi miei.

I still want to call you mine, cruel one, even though you flee
from my eyes.

From Claudio Monteverdi's *L'Arianna*, first performed for
Vincenzo Gonzaga, translation by Iain Fenlon, *Music and*
Patronage in Sixteenth-century Mantua (1980)

After a while the voices in the next room ceased, and I heard steps
descending the stairs, the door opening and closing below.

It was about an hour after the Prince had left me when there was
a soft knock at the door – the first time any of them had announced
their presence to me – and Vinta came in with Master Galletti, Donati
and the matron.

'I will ask you some questions, Giulia,' said Vinta, 'as I have
asked the Prince – no, do not rise. It is important that you remain
lying down. But first we will examine you.'

'No!' I said, huddling up under the sheet. 'Leave me alone!'

'It'll be for the last time, we promise. I was satisfied with my
observations last night, but it is only correct that we reassure our
Mantuan friend.'

'Leave me in peace!' I cried. 'He has done nothing to me. I am still a virgin.'

Vinta stared. 'Come, this is absurd. Help me, will you?' he said to the others, taking hold of the sheet.

They held me down, the matron at my shoulders, Galletti and Donati holding an ankle each though I struggled. Vinta himself put his hands on me, saying: 'She is damp, her lips here are swollen as if they have been lately handled, and the mouth has been opened, but I am no expert.'

'Let me be!'

'Let me see,' said Galletti, ignoring me. He changed places with Vinta, and handled me, talking all the time to Vinta. 'You have seen yourself, cavaliere, that the Prince himself is properly made. I have had his testicles in my hand, and they are the correct weight. You should also know, and should tell the Grand Duke this, that of his own volition he has shown me a fistula on his left buttock, close to the organs of procreation but not so close as to impinge on them in any way. I also yesterday followed through on his suggestion that I examine him upon waking, and in company with my Mantuan colleague I can testify that his lance stands up.' He paused. 'I see that the girl has not suffered any lesions in the assault. But let's put a clean piece of linen under her, that she may sit on it.'

They let go of me then, and I sat as instructed on one of the cloths brought for me to wash myself, while they examined the sheets where I had been lying.

'These were clean when the Prince himself had them put on the bed,' said Vinta. 'Now they are bloodstained, and here is the Prince's seed and the girl's own tribute mixed. Matron, I told her not to wash, but let us see also the cloths in case she has—'

'I didn't use them,' I said, for it was obvious to everyone there that my feeble lie had failed. I sat on that cloth, in the disorder of those fouled sheets, and finally made them listen.

'The Prince went inside me where he was meant to go. I would have him another time if I could, and I hope only that he has got me with child, for he is food and drink, blood of my blood, and the source of every comfort to me, and the girl who gets him as a husband must be the luckiest alive.'

Anyone who reads this must wonder why I spoke that way. The Prince had caused me pain in mind and body, suggested a whore's career for me, tossed a coin onto the bed where I lay, and had gone away boasting of his prowess without even a word of farewell to me. But remember that I am an orphan, denied the company, even the thought, of men, though in scripture itself it says we women were made to be their companions. How many girls have been walled up within convents who longed only for a hearth, a crib to rock? How many have never been shown love, and can barely imagine what a wondrous thing it can be, and so, like me, cling to the first man who tells them they are beautiful, who finds pleasure in plundering those treasures they have been told since infancy to deny even themselves the sight of? And I pitied the Prince too, for all he wore fine clothes that he barely needed to put on himself, having others to do even that for him. I pitied the child who barely knew his parents, for might that not be worse even than to have never had a mother and father at all? I thought of his sister, who had yearned to be a nun but was a wife, and of poor Margherita, loved by him still. I feared him too, his coldness when he spoke of that courtier, who must surely be dead. Though he had made light of my feelings, and made me weep, that night I loved the Prince. All I wanted was to see him again.

All Vinta did was laugh. 'I think,' he said to Donati, 'we have no cause for alarm – the Prince has passed the test, and well.'

'I shall write to Mantua forthwith.'

'I admit I was anxious after the first failure,' continued Vinta. 'Perhaps he isn't one of those men who is erect at any hour of the day or night, but he has acquitted himself as well as any woman could want.'

'His opening is not so wide that he spills all his seed at once,' put in Galletti, 'and that is better, for men made like that cannot so quickly return to the joust.'

Then Donati said something that lifted my heart and halted my tears. 'The Prince told me on his way out that he would like to give the girl something for her trouble. Some money, or jewellery.'

'There is no need,' said Vinta. 'The Grand Duke will give her a dowry and a husband.'

'But surely if the Prince wants to give her something as well, why prevent him?' asked Donati.

'I will take her back to Florence shortly, now that our business here is concluded; if he wants to give her anything he should do so quickly.'

'The Prince is also keenly aware of the trouble you have gone to on his behalf,' said Donati, 'and would like as well to make *you* a gesture of his appreciation—'

'With respect, we will not talk of that further. I have done no more than serve Their Highnesses, and, I trust, your Prince. And now, as the girl seems a little more composed, I have questions to ask her.'

'Perhaps, sir,' said the matron, who had not spoken until then, 'we can put the room to rights, and let her wash and dress.'

I was still in my crumpled shift when a male servant came to change the sheets. I saw the man look at me curiously where I stood, and he did not look away when I stared back at him for his insolence. But the matron saw what he did and upbraided him, telling him not to dawdle. He shrugged and tugged the corner of the soiled undersheet out from under the mattress. The other edges were already free, for the bedlinen was not just stained but ridged and tangled from our fight. My blood was on the mattress beneath.

'I shall bring you salt water,' the matron said to me, and I felt doubly humiliated. Only when she went out, with that man trailing the bedlinen, she took with her the ewer and basin by which I had washed myself when I was still a virgin. She returned some minutes later and it was filled with fresh water that had been warmed over the kitchen fire. Hooked to a finger she carried a little pewter flagon, and a clean white cloth was over her arm. I asked her with what rag should I clean the mattress, and she smiled and said, 'No, child, you are not to do that work. When all this is done you shall be a rich woman and will never need to coarsen your hands again. This is for you to wash where it pains you. Put some of this salt in the water. It will sting, but you will heal more quickly. Then dress decently and come out to me in the antechamber, and I shall send for that oaf to scrub and turn the mattress.'

Chapter Eight

Interrogation

*...after defloration... she is a little downcast and remorseful;
her eyes are sad, lacklustre and diffident; she blushes readily in
the presence of those dear to her.*

Lorenzo Gioberti (Laurent Joubert), from
Popular Errors (1578)

Medical treatise for laypeople, published in Italian in 1592

I ached between my legs, but it was a comfort to me to splash
myself with that warm salty water. Ever since then, I have found
some solace in clean water whenever I am grieved or melancholy,
even in washing things other than my own flesh. Are we not reborn,
made whole, cleansed by water in baptism? I dressed slowly, as if
afraid my clothes would not fit the new person I was. It was a relief
at least to wear something more than just my shift. I walked stiffly
to the outer chamber, where the matron had told me Vinta would
be waiting for me.

She looked up from where she sat with her incessant lacemaking
and patted the chair beside her. Vinta was sitting at a little desk,
scratching away on paper as usual.

'May I look out of the window?' I asked timidly.

The matron glanced at Vinta, who said without looking up, 'Very well.'

I looked down at the landing stage, at the water lapping against it, heard the thump of the hull of the boat moored there, and saw that the guards who had been posted below were gone. There was no need for them now, for I had nothing left that was precious to any of them in that house. I heard Vinta cough, and went and sat down. He lifted his chair and came over, placing it opposite me. He had another of his notebooks in his hand. The matron made as if to leave the room, but he stopped her, and said, 'I need you to witness this, and perhaps you could cease that clicking for a moment.' She sat back down.

'I have to ask you some questions,' he said to me. He cleared his throat. 'Did the Prince have with him any instrument made of iron or glass with which he could have opened you, other than by his person?'

'No.'

Scratch, scratch.

'Are you speaking the truth?'

'Yes.'

Scratch, scratch.

'Did he open you with his fingers, or make the opening wider by that means?'

'No. He only put his... his...'

'Member,' murmured the matron.

'Yes, he only put his member in there, nothing else.'

Scratch, scratch, scratch.

'Did he at any point offer you or make a present to you of jewellery or money, or anything else that might either persuade you to remain silent or speak of other things than what you both did, as might suit his purpose?'

'He neither gave nor offered me anything, and nor did he speak of any such thing.'

Scratch, scratch.

'How many times did he have relations with you?'

'I can certainly remember three times, but perhaps it was four times.'

I did not know what counted. The first time when he had spilled outside, the last when he had desisted? Vinta stopped writing and said: 'Yes, the Prince said that on the fourth occasion you would not lie still.' Then he asked: 'Did you cry that first time?'

'I did not.'

He turned back two or three leaves in his notebook, read what was written there, and said: 'The Prince himself says that for excess of ardour or impatience that first time he merely spent his seed on you but did not penetrate you. He said that on the second occasion he did succeed, and that you cried then, and that was when he called out to me.'

'Yes.'

'Let me just confirm this, if I may. When I was called was on the second occasion?'

'It was the second. But what difference does this make, first, second or third? You were there, sir. You saw.'

Vinta rested his pen on the page. 'Please confine yourself to answering my questions, Giulia. Do so, and we will be finished all the sooner. You must realise that I am obliged to reassure the bride's father that the Prince is not only capable of consummating his marriage with the Lady Eleonora, but that he be consistently capable thereafter.'

I bowed my head.

'Did you feel it when I put my hand between your pubic hair and that of the Prince?'

I wanted to say to him that I would feel his touch there for the rest of my life, as though he had branded me.

'Well?'

'Yes.'

'So was he inside you then?' Vinta leaned forward. I could hear the quickness of his breath. I nodded and shrank back in my chair. When he spoke again, his voice was hoarse.

'You were crying – was that for shame or because he was hurting you?'

'He was hurting me.'

Vinta cleared his throat and shifted back in his chair. I breathed a little more freely, though my heart thumped. 'Did you hurt inside your body or because he was blocked trying to enter you?' he asked, this time looking down at his notes. 'Giulia?' he prompted.

'It hurt inside, sir.'

'Was he hard and firm?' The matron shifted on her chair. She still held her lacemaking cushion and the beads shivered.

'He was. He hurt me because of it.'

Scratch, scratch.

His questions went on, relentless. I closed my eyes to not see his, for they glittered, only that in not looking at him, I heard the heaviness of his breathing, that catch in his throat, all the more clearly. More than that, I saw and felt again what the Prince did, with every question Vinta asked. He wanted to know if when the Prince entered me, he held himself erect by means of his fingers. I remembered that he did so only to guide his way, but not after-wards, for he embraced me then with both arms. I started to weep again, for in that moment I had thought, *this might be what it feels like to be loved, to have a man's arms around me, and to hear him sighing into my hair.*

'Did you hear me, Giulia?' Vinta was irritated with me now, or with my tears, but that was better than that breathing of his.

'Sorry?'

'I was asking you did he use his fingers—'

'No.'

Then he wanted to know had I felt the Prince spend. But what did it matter what I felt or didn't, if the fact that my heart was broken was of no account? I told him yes, the Prince had done so twice, wishing Vinta's questioning would end, but he went on. Was the Prince's seed spilled within me or on the sheet? The Prince had already told him all of this – had he not read his notes to me only a minute ago? What could my testimony add?

I opened my eyes to see Vinta turn a page in his notebook. I had stopped crying; all I felt was a great weariness. He asked me then about the condition of my shift, the bedding. The matron made to speak here but with an impatient gesture he waved her to silence.

I thought of that strange sliding dampness that so quickly turned cold, and how I knew because of its strange smell that it could not only be blood, but I merely said my shift was smeared at the back.

'I have nearly finished with my questions. Tell me, was it pleasurable for you when he put his seed in you?'

I was silent.

'Please answer me, Giulia.'

'Yes.'

'Tell me, Giulia,' asked Vinta, looking at me directly, 'would any girl who got him for a husband be happy with the Prince?'

I started to cry again. 'I cannot speak for any girl – only for what I know myself. But I think he could not fail to please any woman.'

'Would you like it if the Prince came to you again?'

I said nothing. I could not look at him.

'Well?'

'Yes, I should like that.'

'This is my last question. Do you believe that you have been deflowered?'

'Yes, but the first time it did not seem to me that he put it into me far enough.'

'Is there anything else you saw which you have yet to tell?'

'Only, that he did not pause for long...'

'Do you mean that he obtained his erection again speedily?'

'Yes.'

'Once more, Giulia. Do you believe you have been deflowered or not?'

'How can I know? All your questions! You have looked, and poked, and scribbled there in your book. You must know better than I!' I dropped my head to my breast and begged him to leave me in peace.

The following morning, at around three, we were all woken by hammering downstairs. I did not mind – of course I didn't – I just hoped my face was not too creased with sleep. Through the closed door Vinta cursed loudly and wished himself at home in his own bed. Then I heard voices: Donati, the Prince's barber, and I think another man's, a Mantuan's. But not the Prince's.

Vinta opened the door. 'Get up,' he said.

'It is the Prince's pleasure that the girl be brought to his palace, that she may pass the rest of the night there with him,' I heard Donati say.

Then Vinta almost dashed my hopes.

'I cannot allow that and know that the Prince, if he were in my place, would not yield her either. In fairness to the girl herself, it would not be right that he show her too much affection. Nevertheless, I'm glad that she has pleased him so much that he wants her still… it would not be right to repulse him. If it is not such an inconvenience to His Highness, he can come to her again under this roof.'

An hour later I was crying for joy in his arms, and he took me on three more occasions, and didn't hurt me at all.

He left at midday, after passing a hand over my sweating skin, and kissing me.

'I love you,' I said.

He laughed and turned away.

Vinta came back with his notebook and asked his questions again. Had I cried this time, he asked, and I said, 'Not from pain.' Had I felt pleasure? I looked at his wagging beard, his pleading eyes, and said, 'Yes.'

He said, half to himself: 'I think you love him.' I said nothing to that, for it was true.

He and the matron looked at the sheets, and at my sticky shift, and the cloths they gave me to wash myself, and he said to her: 'That other night he opened out his path and I see he has worked well. Our task here is finished. He has gone to dine, and then takes the road to Mantua.'

When I heard that, I said: 'You mean, I will not see the Prince again?'

I wept then, as I had not wept since the loss of Tommasa. The cavaliere tried to comfort me with talk of my husband, the care he would take in his selection, the home I would have.

'Leave me alone!'

He sighed and left me, but not before he had stroked my cheek, and seen me recoil at his touch. I washed the Prince off me for the last time, dressed myself in the dark green perpignan, my favourite, and sat down by the bed. The door was open to the antechamber but I did not want to leave that room. I sat in silence, my fingers caressing the Mantuan coin, and I thought my heart would break.

I had hoped he would keep me. I thought of what he had told me of his palace, a small city in itself, with its uncountable rooms, endless corridors, and secret staircases, with its courtiers, chaplains, secretaries, ostlers, scullions numbering near to a thousand, all in the service of three mere mortals. He joked when he told me that, saying he hoped the bride they had promised him would be fecund, to fill the halls of his home. He had talked to me of that shimmering pleasure palace where his grandfather had installed the woman he loved and had her painted as the naked goddess of love on a couch. I saw myself in that place and thought I could bear the times he would pass in his wife's arms, for he was obliged to unite with her, whereas he would come to me by choice.

On the road back to Florence I was to think of him again and again, twisting in pain when I imagined the women he would encounter in the inns where he spent his nights, and how he would turn his blue gaze on them and they would think him the finest man they had ever seen.

Yes, I had wanted him to keep me. I thought that if Vinta had allowed them to bring me to him in his palace on the Grand Canal, he might never have let me go again.

A little while later the Prince's kinsman called, bringing his compliments to the cavaliere. My gaoler's voice was confident now. 'Ours was a delicate mission,' he said. 'The Grand Duke and Her Highness will be pleased at our success.'

'All those stories of impediments have been proved false,' was the reply.

'And his coming back for another night. That should lay to rest any doubt as to his stamina,' said Vinta. 'I believe you have letters for me.'

There were letters, but there was nothing for me. The Prince had forgotten he had spoken of money, and jewellery. I rubbed my thumb on that coin.

I sat opposite the matron, my hands folded in my lap, as she sought to divert me with those stories she had earlier used to try to instruct me. Though they had both puzzled me and sometimes made me laugh, now I struggled to hear them. The people in the stories, the friars and nuns, the faithless wives and comely apprentices, coupled as freely and joyfully as if there was to be no tomorrow, no day of reckoning. As I sat there darkness descended on me, and I knew the Prince did not care for me any more than he cared for the fate of the Ferrarese nun, or those four girls lined up to be fumbled by the doctors in Parma. I let her drone on just as I did nothing to stop my tears.

When she at last paused I said, 'The Prince told me there are ladies in this city who keep themselves by having lovers, and that they live well and are richly attired. He said with my face and modest manners I could have much success here and be wealthy and esteemed.'

The matron narrowed her eyes. 'Child, it is true that there are such women, and also true that some of them influence government without ever setting foot in any council chamber. They not only have sonnets written about them, but compose them in turn; they debate with prelates and philosophers, are painted by artists and have music dedicated to them. But you, you cannot even write your name. The Prince does not advise you well, for you do not have the heart of a whore.'

She did not mean that kindly. I could see from her face she thought me a fool.

Chapter Nine

Absolution

Con l'assunzione in cielo della sua santa madre noi miriamo qui gli Apostoli, uomini grandi, semplici, potenti, scelti da Gesù fra i pescatori... mentre la Vergine sale in cielo... gli Apostoli orfani piangono e implorano...

With the assumption of his holy mother into heaven, we below admire the apostles, great, simple, powerful men, chosen by Jesus from among the fishermen... as the Virgin ascends, the orphaned apostles weep and plead...

Frate Germano di Casale (1518)

Germano di Casale, Prior of the Franciscan convent of the 'Frari', describes Titian's *Assunta*, that he had commissioned

As they prepared to leave the house, I rebelled for the first time, but perhaps it was only a little rebellion, one they could hardly refuse me.

'I want to go to confession,' I said. 'I will not leave here without it.'

The matron laughed. 'You have found scruples *now*, have you?'

'I am fearful,' I said. 'One of the Prince's men was fired upon on the way here. We almost drowned coming from Chioggia and arrived to find a man dying under this roof. Those marshy flats we crossed to get here reek with ague, and it is cold today. Besides,' I added, dropping my glance, 'I still feel pain,' though this was no longer true and I knew I should have to confess that lie, if I could remember it after all I had to tell.

'We will bring you a confessor,' said Vinta.

'No,' I said, reddening. 'I would not trust the one you would bring. Is not the owner of this house where you have made me commit a mortal sin a Monsignor? Yet he knew what use you would put it to.' The truth of it was that I did not want to be closeted in a room with any man, even a priest, where I could see in his face and in the movement of his mouth his reaction to my story.

'Let me go to a church, as any Christian woman should, and not give scandal by meeting my confessor behind a closed door.'

Vinta shuffled his papers impatiently. 'Very well,' he said. 'That would be better than wasting any more time *here*. You must go veiled, though.'

'I would anyway,' I said, offended.

'It had better be somewhere discreet,' muttered Vinta to the matron. 'Nowhere I have been seen already... call one of the servants, would you?'

The matron got up and called upstairs to the kitchen. A moment later the same manservant who had taken away the dirty sheets walked in.

'You, fellow, do you go to confession?'

'Yes, sir. I know my Lenten obligations as well as you.'

'Don't be insolent. Where do people of your class go?'

I saw the man's resentment, and also his cunning. However, Vinta was anxious and preoccupied, and appeared not to notice.

'I can take you,' said the servant.

'It would be better if it were not far, and a quiet place,' said Vinta, 'but you may take the less public route even if it makes the journey a little longer.'

The servant went ahead, and Vinta and the matron walked either side of me, just as they had done when they had escorted me from the Pietà. The cavaliere grew more and more irritable, for we were led through innumerable alleyways, some of them foul-smelling, and over countless little bridges that looked identical – Vinta must have known as well as I that we could not have found our way back unaccompanied. I am sure that at least once we covered the same ground, but every time Vinta enquired, the servant merely said, 'Not long now,' without bothering to turn his head.

I looked about me everywhere, but it wasn't for curiosity about a city I'd not been permitted to know. I nursed one last feeble hope that I might glimpse the Prince again, that he might have decided, now his work was done, to disport himself a little in this strange and wonderful place before returning home to prepare for his wedding. I didn't see him, of course, but I remembered to confess that last longing (while Vinta fretted at the time I was taking).

We were brought at last to a church of the Franciscans, and it was hardly the discreet place Vinta had hoped for. In that soaring, incense-filled place, vibrating with the music of a great organ, its brick walls bare of the paintings on plaster which in Florence had both comforted me and haunted my darkest hours, I made them wait. The hour tolled, and then the half-hour, and I was still there telling all through a grille to a gentle friar.

'I love him,' I said at last, sure that this would cast out any hope of grace.

'Of course you do, child. That man embraced you as a husband does, and a girl who is not called to the cloister is called to love a husband's arms. It is the Prince who has sinned, and all those who advanced and connived at what was done to you. You, poor innocent, responded in the way you were designed to do. I will pray that when you are found a husband, he be worthy of you, and you find the happiness you deserve before you and he are gathered up to a greater joy. Are there other sins you have on your conscience?'

I unpacked my little store of grievances and petty jealousies against my companions in the Pietà; I had been so used to the practice of regular confession that they came readily to hand, but as I recounted them, I felt that I spoke of matters now as remote as the pale moon, though they had consumed my life only a matter of days ago.

I was absolved, washed clean, and my penance was light.

'Pray for me, Giulia,' said the friar, 'as I shall pray for you every day that remains to me. Pray also for those who did this to you, for they are all guilty of the same turpitude as if they had followed the Prince onto those fouled sheets.'

I got up from my knees renewed, strong enough to let Vinta's scolding words slide off me. Above the altar in that place was a great painting of the most holy and powerful woman who ever walked the earth, yet she was as weightless as a cloud, borne up into heaven, far beyond the reach of men. She was clad in a startling crimson dress – plain, but as a Florentine I know that to be the most expensive dye.

Vinta plucked at my sleeve but I shrugged him off. I felt invincible – that now he could do me no more harm.

How wrong I was – but that is not the fault of Our Lady.

Chapter Ten

Payment

*Do not so much as let a man touch your hand. A woman's
flesh is like wax, and every touch leaves an impression.*

Girolamo Savonarola

We were a smaller party on the way home, fewer servants, fewer
guards. I was allowed to travel with the curtains of the lettiga tied
back, that I might observe the landscape we travelled through. I
was grateful for that: the sight of spring and the land awakening
was balm to my suffering, and a source of wonder, as the most
green I had seen in my life up to then had been the Pietà's physick
garden. I thought the world might yet be a beautiful one for me.
I would have liked to have climbed down and walked a little, but
feared that I would ruin my slippers, so I asked the matron if she
had pattens she could lend me.

'Only a hoyden would want to walk,' she said. 'I have been
doing my best to make you into a lady.'

My face burned at this rebuke, but looking down at my idle
hands I remembered that she had said I would not make a whore.

'When I am a lady,' I asked, 'who is to be my lord?'

'The minister will decide,' she said, adjusting her embroidery
without looking at me.

'Were you a wife?' I stammered.

'The world knows me as a widow,' she said, glancing up with a frown.

'Do you... have you children?'

'If they live, I do not know it. You ask too many questions about what does not concern you.'

Where had Vinta found this woman, and what qualified her to teach me to be a lady? I looked away and held my peace.

As we got down at the first stopping place she said, 'I will have care of you until you are wed,' and then scuttled off behind some foliage to relieve herself.

Vinta's agitation had disappeared. At that first inn I noticed that he did not get out his notebooks, or fret at the time we took, or worry who might observe us. The matron made to sit by me at our bench, as she had done on our voyage out, but he sent her to the end of the table and took the place she'd occupied beside me. I didn't feel hungry, but I kept my eyes on my plate and would not look at him. I felt as I did when he made me sit and answer all his questions, on and on, making me tell him all that had been done to me, as his breathing deepened and he twitched in his chair. I had wanted to keep those thoughts to myself, to treasure them, but Vinta had turned them into a slab of meat left to congeal in the sun and attract flies. I hated him too for denying the Prince's request that I be brought to his palace, instead making him come to me under Vinta's nose. I'd spent the journey until that moment remembering every word, every caress of the Prince's, trying to imagine the palace he had inhabited in Venice. I did not have much to go by, so in my mind's eye saw a place much like Vinta's in Florence, only larger.

'I have two tasks to fulfil on my return, Giulia,' said Vinta. 'One is to forward the negotiations for the Prince's marriage. The contract will be signed any day, now that there is no impediment, and then the Grand Duke will seek the permission of Philip of Spain – a formality, for this marriage is desired by all. The Prince will be coming to Florence to meet his bride. My other task is to find you your husband.' I heard him swallow. Then he murmured, 'A man I confess I envy.'

I barely heard what he said about my husband, nor his attempt at a compliment. All I thought was that the Prince and I would be in the same city. 'Thank you,' I said, and tore a hunk of bread to pieces.

At the inn we stayed in that night – we stopped at no place where we had been on the outward journey – I had had to find my own voice to ask one of the servants to bring me water to wash with, for no one thought to do that for me, though on the way to Venice they had been most assiduous that I should wash myself at every opportunity. The woman obeyed me without turning a hair, as if it was the most natural thing in the world, and I thought about how my life was going to be, how I should have servants myself. I was sure, though, that I should be afraid of them, that they would find me out because I wanted to walk when I could be carried, and because I did not know how to impress men with wit and learning so that they would shower me with riches. How long would it be before they realised I had been sold for a dowry and was only married because my husband had been bribed?

It was on the afternoon of the second day of our journey that Vinta took me aside. We had paused on the road to water the horses. I told the matron I wanted to make water. She nodded towards the trees and I walked into that little wood.

Vinta met me as I came back. I wondered how long he had been there: later, if he had watched me. He stood as immobile and silent as one of the oaks themselves. First, I thought he merely wanted to tell me to hurry. I looked beyond him expecting to see the matron.

'Sit here a moment, Giulia,' he said, indicating a fallen trunk. His voice was odd, as though someone held him around the throat. I did as I was told, only to see him kneel before me, and pull off the velvet cap he wore. He bowed his head so that I looked down on grizzled hair, wearing away on the crown.

'Cavaliere…'

He did not answer me but put his hands gently around my ankles and stroked his thumbs up the back of my calves. The day was mild and I wore no stockings, so it was my skin he touched. I tried to pull away.

'Giulia, for the love of God, unbolt your door tonight that I may come to you.'

I felt the backs of my knees melt like wax. 'The matron,' I said.

'That bawd will do as I tell her.'

'You told me I was to have a husband, not that I was to be made a whore of.'

'You'll have your husband – when I choose him.' He reached up and put his hands about my waist and pulled me down and tried to kiss me. I went rigid, holding my elbows against his chest, bending my neck back to keep his face from touching mine.

'Giulia!' he cried. 'Do not be cruel to one who is as your slave! I promise you I shall find the best husband for you the Grand Duke will allow, if you will only have pity on me. I have wanted you since the moment I saw you. All I have done has been for your benefit – though it went against every nerve in my body to deliver such a peerless bloom to be crushed and trodden on by that man. Can you not show me some gratitude?'

I stared at this man who asked me to pity him for *his* suffering. His eyes were wet. He looked like a kicked dog.

'Just sometimes… remember that I chose you, Giulia, that you owe your good fortune to me.'

'You want to keep me and cuckold my husband. You, whose lady is the only person who has shown me kindness since that day you came to the Pietà!'

I could see he did not like it when I spoke of the Lady Camilla, but he ceased mauling me, instead grasping my hands in both of his.

'Everyone does this, you innocent,' he said. 'Even the Grand Duke and his Duchess were married to others.'

'Her husband, then, must have had the good fortune to die rather than carry his horns for longer, or she were no Grand Duchess.'

'Her husband, Giulia, was set upon in the street and died from his wounds.'

'And his assassins?'

'I am sure you have more wit than your question suggests, Giulia. They have never been found.'

'*You?*'

'No, that bit of business does not weigh on my conscience. But I should be whipped at a cart's tail from Florence back to Volterra if I were to question it. In my own way I am as powerless as you.'

I pulled my hands away.

'Remember that you cannot go back to the Pietà.'

'I don't wish to,' I said.

'But there is always the Convertite,' said Vinta.

'What's that?' I asked, though I guessed.

'The convent of the penitent prostitutes.'

'*No!*'

'Open your door to me tonight, then, and you shall have your husband. I promise you.'

In the inn I was given a room to myself. But I did not sleep. I paced the room, sometimes going to the door and bolting it, only to strain my ears for footsteps and to slide back the bolt a minute later. I did not trust Vinta. How could I? He hadn't told me the real reason for our journey to Venice before it was too late. But what choice had I had then? The alternative was to stay in the Pietà having incurred the rage of the Prioress for going against the express wish of our patron. I had only Vinta's word that he would find me a husband, but no idea who that husband would be. Yet I did believe him when he threatened me with the Convertite. I wished I had the counsel of that unseen friar in Venice to guide me. Would God pardon me if I left the door unbarred, in doing so rejecting a life of cloistered penitence?

Heaven forgive me, but I could not give my life up to God. Leaving the door unbolted, I knelt by the edge of the bed and prayed to the Magdalen for her help to get me through that night. My face was resting against the sheet made sodden with my tears when I heard him scuffling at the latch.

'Giulia! We are alone at last!' I heard Vinta whisper, but I didn't move. Though he saw me there on my knees, sending a last anguished plea to heaven, I felt his hands on my shoulders, clammy even through my shift. He raised me up, turned me around, and pushed me back across the bed. No, I did not resist him – how could I? I lay there as stiff as a wooden doll – would that I had had no more feelings than one! But I could not stop the tears. I lay looking up at the ceiling, just as I had when Donati examined me on that table. I could describe the knots in the beams even now. Vinta abandoned his nightshirt beside the bed, and I caught a glimpse only of his fleshy, pale shoulders before I shut my eyes. His breath was hot on my ears, on my neck. The soft grey hair of his chin against my skin was as repugnant as a marching horde of ants. Even now I shudder and want to look away at the sight of a man with a full beard. He pressed his mouth on mine, and I felt the tip of his tongue trying to force an entry, but I clenched my teeth – at least that I would not grant him. He licked my earlobes then. I have never liked being touched there since, not even by my husband, though I never told him why – I would just move my head so he kissed my mouth instead.

'At least put out the candle!' I begged.

'No... I want to see you as he saw you.'

He pushed up my shift and kissed my breasts and mumbled over them, and felt my fig while I screamed inside. Vinta did not force himself on me. He did not have to. He knew I could do nothing, though all my will strained against him. His touch was nothing like the Prince's, his flesh cool and yielding, like something not long dead – yet I felt that touch impersonally, as if I looked at what he did from a distance, and, bringing my knuckles to my teeth, I silently recited a decade of the Rosary. He was greasy with sweat; I thought he smelled of something dead, like rotting fruit. He took much longer than the Prince; his cry, at the end, was a whimper of surprise, his mouth wet against my neck. Vinta hurt me, more even than the Prince had done that first time, for though I barely moved, every muscle and sinew rebelled against him.

The moment he slipped out of me, with a ghastly sucking sound as of boots in a mire, he started to murmur endearments, told me how beautiful I was, said again how when he saw me that first time in the Prioress's parlour he knew he must have me. He made to kiss me in all the tenderest places in my body, where he had soiled me the most, but then I could hold back no longer. 'Not that too!' I cried, tugging fists of his hair to force his head away, and pulling down my dirtied shift. The bed heaved as he climbed down; I heard his feet slap the floor. Then he stood there, a revolting, flabby, pitiable figure. I put my hand over my eyes and rolled away from him.

God forgive me, I wished myself dead.

'I wanted you so much,' he cried, 'when I saw your lovely face on your pillow in that room, your lips parted in an exquisite marriage of pleasure and pain, your eyes deep dark pools in the candlelight—'

'Don't! Don't ruin even that for me!' I cried.

'You love him, that tom-cat, don't you? You love him though he will never think of you again, nor speak of you except to boast of what he did with you in some low tavern, with men who are as vicious, spoiled and lascivious as he. Do not envy the girl he will marry within days, Giulia. She'll be his Duchess but he will care for her as little as he cared for you – less so, for she is no beauty. His compliments to her will be all form, and in proportion only to the size of her dowry. But you'll never love me, will you, though I want you so much it unmans me.'

'I left the door unbolted only because I had no choice,' I said.

'Have mercy!' he cried.

I turned round then. His legs looked too thin for the body they supported. Acid rose in my throat; he was holding his member, shaking it, trying to awaken it, but it lay inert and shrivelled as a piece of offal two days old. I screamed. The old Vinta, the agitated, fussing Vinta who feared discovery, flapped his other hand at me for silence.

'I will be quiet only if you will leave me,' I said. 'I want to wash. At least grant me that privacy.' I did not care who knew he was there. My skin itched as if it was diseased. I thought I should never rid myself of the smell of him.

'You'll have your dowry, and your husband, Giulia,' he said, pulling his shirt over his head. 'Just stop making that noise.'

As soon as he had gone, I tore off my shift, bundled it up and flung it into the farthest corner. I had treasured all those new things that had been given me, but that garment I left for who-ever came into that room next. I bolted the door and then washed myself in all the places where Vinta's skin had touched mine. I pulled the sheets from the bed, and turned them about face, so that at least I would not be lying where he had lain. The place he'd made wet I covered with one of the wash-cloths. Then I lay down and cried, and again begged the Magdalen for help. I thought I should not sleep, but I must have done, for I remember waking and thinking about who my husband might be. A terrible thought then seized me, that this husband would be some creature of Vinta's, or someone over whom he had absolute power, and that though I was his wife he would be compelled to share me with the cavaliere. Could the Convertite be as cruel a place as the Pietà?

When dawn broke I called for the servant, and asked for clean water. When she returned with a fresh ewer, I said I wanted my breakfast in the chamber, for I did not wish to eat with them in the room below.

The matron treated me with greater respect than I had ever had from her before and was solicitous to my every need. She thought me her master's concubine, you see. All that day and the next I felt his eyes on me, but I stayed as close to that woman as if I loved her.

It was not until the dome of Florence came into view that I asked the matron where we were going.

'To an address in Santo Spirito,' she said.

'When will I have my husband?'

'That depends,' she said. 'If you are not with child, then you will be married in a month's time.'

'And if I am?' I asked, my mouth dry.

'Then he will be found for you after your confinement.'

'Would it not be best straight away?' I ventured. 'So that he may think the child his?'

She looked at me, incredulous. 'I said you had not the heart of a whore, yet you reason like one! You would enter that holy state with a lie? If there is a child, do you truly think you would be permitted to keep it?'

'So what would become of him?'

'You have a face the colour of milk, child. Don't fret. You may not be with child, and even if you are, not every babe lives to see the light outside his mother's womb. If yours does, you of all people know where such a child would go.'

'Wouldn't my husband...?'

The matron laughed. 'You are still a green girl, I see, for all that the Prince might have taught you. Find me the man who would take in his wife's bastard! There are some wives who accept those of their husbands, as well they might, for they must have failed as wives if their men seek the embraces of other women. Consider what you are saying, child. Would *you* want to be the wife of a gentleman who cares so little for his own honour that he would play the father to some nameless creature?'

'Will he be told? I mean, if I become a mother?'

The matron raised her eyebrows briefly. 'That is a pertinent question, and one which we must refer to the cavaliere, I think, as it is he who will find you your husband, not I. Personally, if that proves to be the case, I think he should be told. He would know he was not getting a virgin, so it might at least be some comfort to know that you were not barren.'

I was taken to a small house in a narrow street, the far side of the Arno, where I had never set foot before. Here the buildings were tall and crowded up against that dwelling, so that inside was a perpetual dusk. Vinta helped me down from the lettiga, leaving the matron to make shift for herself. He took his leave of me as he would of a lady, bowing and forcing my hand to his lips.

'You have done great honour to Florence, and your loyalty will be rewarded,' he said.

The matron's chamber adjoined mine, and I could not reach the staircase without passing through it. A scruffy, barefoot woman brought us our first meal there. The wine tasted strange to me and I pushed it away. I realised later that it was only because it had not been watered down.

I wondered were they wishing to poison me, now that I had served my purpose, and stared into my broth without tasting it, only to see that the matron was making short work of hers, and she had been served from the same tureen.

'What will happen now?' I asked.

'I told you. In the meantime you must prepare your marriage chest.'

My room was as plain as a cell, the only decoration on the walls a small crucifix, an ivory Christ pinned to dark stained wood; my unadorned bed and a prie-dieu were the only furniture. But at least I was alone.

I woke to the sound of familiar bells I thought I had not heard for months, though my absence had been far less than that. The next day, though, as I broke my morning bread, I heard a sound rising up beyond the usual noise of people shouting, calling, laughing in the street below, the rattle of carts, the striking of hooves on pavement. A distant drum roll, then a burst of trumpets.

'He is come,' said the matron.

'Who?' I said, though I knew.

'He is come to meet his bride.'

'Oh.'

'There will be fireworks tonight, and feasting. The bishop is to present her with a golden rose, sent to her by the Holy Father himself. Then the Prince will return to Mantua, and she will follow him two days later, that he may be ready to meet her. So they say. They say too that he is pleased with her.'

'She must be very beautiful.' I thought my heart would break. A golden rose, but for me not so much as a petal, only a coin tossed upon a bed.

'I have seen her. She has intelligent eyes, and a fine carriage. She wears her clothes well. She does not need to be beautiful. She brings him a fine dowry, and a healthy womb. She is seventeen.'

I went to the window, though I knew I would see nothing from that dark alleyway. I just wanted to be closer to the noise.

He had come, and he had gone. The matron and I sat either side of the fireplace. I was hemming linen sheets, while she embroidered a cushion with gold thread, the kind that is used to embellish the garments the priests wear at the altar. In the orphanage we were watched closely as we worked those things, for fear of theft of that costly thread – though where we could have hidden anything, or how we could have done anything with it, I do not know. Sometimes we were searched before we left the workroom. And now this embarrassment of riches: drapes, cushions, fine linen – a reward for sin. I felt weary, yet the matron observed me closely, and said how well I looked.

One morning I woke to bile rising in my throat, and I scrabbled beneath the bed for the pail. I had barely time to make sure my hair was still contained in the nightcap before I leaned over and was sick until I could be sick no more. The matron came in without knocking.

So I was not barren. But whose child did I carry?

Vinta called to congratulate me on my maternity, holding both my hands with tears standing in his eyes. The matron sat in the corner of the room, and I was afraid he would send her away, but it was as if he had forgotten her presence.

'I have postponed the immediate search for your husband, Giulia. The delay, though, allows me a wider choice,' he said.

'What about my child?' I said.

'That will depend,' he said, smiling, 'on what countenance he shows us.'

I put my hand over my mouth and ran from the room. I thought I should spew up my very soul. When I came back, pale and shaking, Vinta had gone.

'They know that you are with child,' said the matron.

'*He* knows?'

'I believe so. No reason why not. It is a good omen. The Grand Duke knows his son-in-law can give him grandchildren. There are no more doubts. Sit down, Giulia.'

I did so.

'You will not even have to see your child. I will bind you so that your milk does not come, and give you almond oil to anoint your stomach, and wind cloth around you so that you will be as you were before. And then you will be dressed as a bride.'

'And my baby?'

'The Innocenti. We told you that. You will have new children who have your husband's face, for if you bear this one you will bear others.'

I had always known that was what they intended. The matron said I would be as I was before – a feat no more possible than an apple tree bearing pears. I ran to my bedroom and flung myself down, curling on my side. The doctors say a woman's humours are cold and damp, and that is why we produce more tears than men. But my tears were hot, and there were so many that I thought my body would be drained and my baby and I would both die.

At midday the matron came in to me and sat on the bed. I have pondered many times what moved her to say to me what she did, but I think she saved my life. I thought I should cry myself to death. Was it – belatedly – a fear of the reckoning that would be made of her wretched life before the most powerful judge of all, or fear that Vinta would punish her for the loss of his concubine?

'There is one thing you can do, Giulia. A token.'

I sat up and turned my smarting face to her.

'You might one day be able to claim your child – perhaps as your servant...'

'Go on.'

'You should prepare something by which your child, if still living, could be identified. Something no other person could know about.'

I remembered what she'd said to me once of her own children. 'If they live, I do not know it.'

'I have that token,' I said.

'This will not do,' said the matron, the Mantuan scudo shining in her palm.

'But my child's grandfather is on it.'

'Give them that coin and it will disappear, melted down with the excuse that the orphans are needy, the donations sparse. I have a better idea,' she said. 'Bring me a candle and sealing wax.'

Twenty intent minutes later, the matron held up her work for me to see: two circles of hardening wax attached to a strip of linen.

'You see how the letter U is worn, and that there is a nick taken out of this edge here? Now look at the impression in the wax.' I peered at the still warm reddish blob, afraid to breathe on it in case I marred the image.

The matron pointed at the other lump of wax and said, 'And here, on the other side, do you see how the hand is separate from the wrist, as if a tiny piece of gold was missing in the pressing, and how there is a scratch just here by the left leg?' I compared the coin with the impression; the mirror image was perfect.

'Only you have the exact match. So if one day you go to the Prior of the Innocenti with this coin, there will be no doubt that you are the child's mother.'

'Thank you,' I said and, bursting into tears, fell into the arms of the matron. I knew she had no love for me, but there was no one else.

Chapter Eleven

Gravida

Avoid eating dough, dairy products, goose and duck, and for now, drink white wine... don't get cold, and avoid your legs getting cold. Rule out fish...

Sperone Speroni, letter to his pregnant daughter (1561), translation by Paola Tinagli

The new house in Santo Spirito was just another prison. It was meaner than Vinta's house, of course, but its ceilings higher than those in Venice. Here were no wall-paintings, nor any panelling, only distempered walls and plain, ancient furniture thirsty for wax. Except for its silence, for we were attended only by one maidservant who I think must have been told not to look at me, we could have been in the Pietà. I call it a prison, though I know that there were no dungeons there, nor fetters, nor cries of poor wretches in the toils of the rackmaster. I never knew whose house it was, nor what it had been used for before I was brought there. I asked the matron but she shrugged. Perhaps she truly didn't know.

Sometimes, though, it was pleasant to sit by the window as my belly grew, with food brought to me. I had my sewing in my lap and the matron nearby, but she made no comment if my head nodded and I slept in my chair; at nights I sometimes got little rest, for the burning in my throat was worse when I lay down. When

I did sleep, I regularly woke myself with my own snoring (something I had never done before – girls who did so in the Pietà were prodded until they woke and turned onto their sides).

When I opened my eyes I would find my work placed on my *cassone*, my marriage chest, which sat between me and the matron. I have that chest still, for it is simply and sturdily made. She and I worked those months to fill it, to make up, as she said, for lost time. Lost time? All my years in the orphanage and then in the Pietà. Years which for other girls would have been spent with their mothers, laying aside linens, sheets, hangings, overdresses, collars, hose – and finally a wedding dress.

I wondered often in those months how you, Mother, spent the time as I grew quietly beneath your breast. Were you cared for, secretly, as I was, or did you go in fear of discovery, day after day, until there was no more disguising your predicament? Did you wish – I will not reproach you for this – that I would be one of those innocents who would give up the fight for life even in the womb? There is so much I want to ask you and still do, here or in heaven.

The only person who called was Vinta, and that was not often. He would always send the matron away and speak to me alone. The first time this happened, I was almost sick with fear, until he said: 'Rest assured, Giulia, I shall not embrace you. The enjoyment of a woman with child is a sin against God's law.' But the enjoyment of a terrified and helpless girl was not?

'What will happen to me?' I asked, every time.

'We shall see, when your child is born,' he invariably said.

'And my husband?'

'I shall choose carefully.'

Before he left each time, he would kneel at my feet, and take them in his hands, and caress and kiss them, while I stared at the wall, waiting for him to finish, my knees locked, my hands pressing down on my thighs. Afterwards I would ask the servant to bring warm water, and cloths.

It was on the second of his visits, though, when he asked me, 'When was it you felt yourself conceive?'

I laid down my work – I always had it with me on his visits. It felt like a shield. I looked straight at him.

'I did not feel it, but it happened in that house in Venice,' I said. 'You told me yourself, you and Master Galletti, that a woman does not spill her seed to unite with a man's unless she too feels pleasure. The Prince gave me that.'

I clung to that belief because I didn't want my child to be Vinta's. Many times, though, lying on my back in my bed and raising my shift, looking at the smooth white globe of my stomach, its surface rippling with the movements of my child, I wondered if I could be wrong. I asked the matron about it once, as I sat stitching a shirt for my unknown husband.

'They do say we women must feel pleasure if we are to be mothers,' she said. 'I do not believe it, though. When a town is besieged, and capitulates, the victorious soldiers always celebrate on the bodies of the women they have captured, no matter how much they scream and beg for mercy. Yet their bellies fill all the same. It happened in this city, some thirty years before you were born. German mercenaries. The orphanages struggled to cope with the damage they left behind.'

I did not dare ask her more, for in that moment I felt some pity for her.

'Pray that your child is a boy, and that he looks like the cavaliere,' she said. 'The Lady Camilla has given him only daughters. He would take the boy and bring him up in his own home – make him his heir. You would not need your token, then.'

'That would be a base coin to reward that lady's kindness to me,' I whispered.

'It's what he hopes, I am sure. That is why he has not troubled you again, child. And why he has not told me to feed you pennyroyal. Be grateful – that herb can kill more than a child.'

I have heard that there are cities where if a woman with child is condemned to die, she is spared until her baby is delivered – but then die she must. It was like that, being in that house, feeling and watching every lurch of my belly, every twitch and kick, seeing my child take charge of my body in everything, and marvelling in it, but knowing that as he or she grew the sands ran out for my life. No, I was not condemned to death, unless that was to come in childbed. It was the prospect of losing my child that was a kind of death to me, because the poor little creature would be taken from me, no matter who the father proved to be. It was as if I saw the shadow of a noose always out of the corner of my eye. Just as the condemned wretch must hope that someone, some rich man whom she does not know and who knows little of her sufferings, will lift a pen and with a swift movement mercifully cancel the rope, the block, so I hoped that someone or something – I knew not what – would intervene and I should keep my baby.

About two months before my confinement, Vinta came again, and after greeting me and asking courteously after my health, took the matron aside for a private conference. He went away without speaking to me again.

'It is the cavaliere's wish that you make a pilgrimage to ask Saint Margaret for a safe birth,' she said, coming back to where I sat.

'A pilgrimage?' I said. 'So close to my time?'

'It will not be so far – a short distance across the river. The cavaliere has already arranged the date you should go and will send a lettiga for you.'

It was October, and still warm, though the shadows lengthened earlier in the afternoons. I had not been out for so long, and the blare and crash of the city had been muffled in that side street. I had grown unused to the shouts, the smells. I felt sure even the horses that carried us were agitated.

They stopped, and I pulled down my veil.

The church was ancient, with bare walls and no side-chapels, a simple hall of a building. Yet on the high altar shimmered a vision of gold and blue and red and green, of shot silk fabrics, gilded finials. There was the Christ Child enthroned forever amid a company of saints. St Margaret was one, standing in silent witness, holding the cross with which she defended herself in the fiery belly of the dragon, until that cross grew and grew and split the creature asunder, and she stepped out unharmed. This is why expectant mothers pray to her – why I have done so, all my life, every time childbed approached. Later, I went back to that church on many occasions; I could still tell you now exactly how it was ordered, and what paintings adorned the side-altars.

The only other people in the church were two men, an older and a younger. They stood murmuring beneath the statue of St Sebastian but fell silent as we passed near them. I supposed them to be father and son. The matron genuflected in the direction of the light on the altar and then I did the same, though I had to hold her arm or I should not have got up again.

'Lift your veil,' she whispered. 'The saint will want to see your face.'

We sank onto a bench nearby, and the matron made the sign of the cross and creaked to her knees. I made to follow her, but she stopped me.

'Pray where you are, seated. And keep your head up, or you may feel sick again.'

I obeyed her, shutting my eyes. I don't know how long we sat there in that blessed silence. I heard footsteps, soft leather on the paved floor, but did not hear the door open, so those men were still there with us. I prayed for them too, and for the older one's wife and the son's mother, thinking that she must already have gone from them. In childbed, perhaps? I sighed, trying to swallow my fear. The matron touched my arm. 'We can go now,' she said.

I got up, my hand to the small of my back, and turned around. Those men stood near the door, and they were watching me. The elder, I noticed, was dressed more richly than the younger. His doublet was padded velvet, despite the warmth of the day, and the cloth that protruded at the collar and where his sleeves were tied on was of the finest linen. The man stared at me, looking me up and down with frank curiosity. Offended, I turned my eyes to his companion. No, they could not be father and son. Master and servant perhaps; yet that did not fit the confidential way in which they had been talking. The younger man also had a fine linen shirt – I remember how dazzlingly white it was – yet he wore a worn leather tunic without sleeves, and plain perpignan hose. I saw dark curling hair, an olive-skinned face, cleanly shaven, and an expression of utter contempt and loathing – directed at me.

The matron held my arm or I would have hung back. She was chattering now about how we must go home, how the days were shortening, how we would not want to catch an evening chill. I did not want to pass near those men, but evidently they did not wish it either, for the elder touched the younger's sleeve, and motioned him away. I put down my veil, but I could feel their eyes on my back.

'Who were they?' I said, as soon as we were outside.

'I have never seen them before,' said the matron, not looking at me.

Chapter Twelve

Partum

If the baby is a boy, it will push harder, making things easier... other difficulties may arise if the mother is young and has a narrow vaginal canal...

Michele Savonarola, *Ad mulieres ferrarienses* (1385–1468)

This Savonarola (grandfather of the Dominican friar Girolamo) taught medicine in his native Padua before becoming court physician in Ferrara

Two weeks or so later a wagon with two porters drew up in front of the house. The matron called me, and I came down, and saw what they had brought.

It was a chair. To me it looked like an instrument of torture.

'You are a very lucky woman,' the matron told me, not for the first time. 'A mother of your class usually has only the knees of a stronger sister to rest on.'

I stared at it, sitting on its plinth. Of smooth, strong, unadorned wood, it had high sides and arm rests. I expected there to be manacles for my wrists, so uninviting did the thing look.

'Why is the seat cut away like that at the front?'

The matron looked at me as if she thought me foolish.

'So that midwife can kneel in front of you. Why don't you try it, just now, as you are?'

I thought of some holy monks I had been told about in the Pietà, who every night instead of lying on beds slept in their own coffins.

'No... it is too early.'

'It is not. The year is almost out, and with it nine months since Venice.'

I turned my face away from her, because I was afraid of dying. I didn't know then who had sent me this chair. If I had, I should not have feared it as I did.

I was standing up after evening prayers when it happened. A pop, sounding so clear in my body I was sure it must have been audible to others, and suddenly, beneath my skirts, I was drenched. My child heaved within me, as though he gave a great sigh. I looked down and saw the water spreading dark across the red tiles.

The matron clapped her hands and scurried off. I heard her issuing instructions; someone went out the front door. She returned with the maid of all work, holding a pail and rags. I wanted to mop up myself, but the matron just laughed.

'Silly girl! You can't even bend in the middle.'

She was right. For the next ten hours I was helpless in the hands of others.

Or to be more exact, I was in the hands of one particular person. Those hands were glistening with linseed oil and camomile. Their nails were cut short and square, with one exception: an index finger ended in a long, curved talon, sharpened to a point. I stared at that claw open-mouthed, and its owner laughed, saying: 'You have saved my nail one task, at least, for you have broken your waters without its help.'

I liked her, though. I liked her because the matron obeyed her and seemed afraid of her. I was afraid too, but not of her.

'Help her undress,' said the midwife. That done, I was laid upon the bed and examined. Was my life outside the Pietà to begin and end with people I didn't know probing me in my most secret places?

'Narrow, but not too narrow,' murmured the woman, looking down at my helpless white mass. She squeezed a breast and nodded approvingly. Yet she knew my child was to be denied my milk.

'A clyster first,' she said, turning to the matron.

I thought I should die of the pain. The midwife was unperturbed, I thought indifferent. Later, the matron told me that she had been in no fear of losing her patient, but all she said to me in those shortening pauses before those pangs racked me again, naked and sweating in that chair, was that 'screaming helps bring out the babe'.

Later I did not just think I should die, but I wished it. Anything to bring the agony to an end. Then I feared to do so, because I had wanted it, and that was a mortal sin. I sobbed and asked, 'How much longer?' and all she said was, 'That is in God's hands... you suffer because he wills it, for of all the female creatures who walk the earth and carry their young within them, only a woman brings forth her babe in pain. The Bible says it must be so.'

I didn't know why I should be punished for doing only what I had been told I must. Yet when my child at last slithered into the world to be caught in the midwife's greased hands, I was astonished at how this tiny, squirming creature had been the cause of so much torment. And I marvelled that all of us are born as helpless and puling as he, yet once clothes are put upon a babe his station in life is marked out, unmistakeably.

The pain stopped, as though by the hand of heaven, and I slumped in the chair. I shut my eyes, and I laughed for the joy of it. I had looked at that tiny, secretive face, the radiant blue of those puzzled, barely seeing eyes, and knew whose child he was.

It was a long time after that before I laughed again.

When I opened my eyes I looked around but the child was no longer in the room, and nor was the matron. 'Where has she taken him?' I asked.

'To be washed,' said the midwife. 'As you will be shortly. You will have many more children; I counted the nodes on the cord that bound him to you. Now, a little more patience, for I have not finished with you yet.'

She knelt in front of me and put her fingers into that space made wide by my child and tugged. Something slipped from me and into the pail she had ready. She took this to the window and opened the shutter on a cold but cloudless day. I saw her poke what was in the bucket with that terrifying nail of hers, but she turned and smiled. 'Entire, and healthy. Your supple young bones helped.'

I heard the outer door close below, and steps swiftly retreating up the alley – then a thin cry, like a cat's, fading away. A moment later the matron returned but did not look at me. She carried more linens, and a basin of warm water. I lay on the bed as they told me to do, and they washed me with great tenderness, as if I might break, from the soles of my feet to my navel. Yet now that the pain had stopped I felt stronger than I had ever done. They worked in silence, drying me afterwards and then anointing me with sweet-scented oils, and at last covered my lower body with a sheet. Then they washed the rest of me likewise, and the matron promised me that she would wash my hair.

'Now we will bind your breasts,' said the midwife. 'The milk will not come down and they will be as firm and fresh as a maiden's for your husband.'

'But what about my baby?'

'Tsch!' said the matron. 'Haven't I told you that ladies do not suckle their own babes?' She hadn't, and later I discovered that what she said was not true, or not always.

'I should like to see him now.'

The matron looked me full in the face and said: 'You have always known you couldn't keep him. But he has gone with the impress of your coin.'

It was then that my agony began, far greater than what had torn my body that night, for I knew it should have no end. There was no respite either, none of those shortening minutes between one roll of thunder and another, gasping for breath before the next contraction. I screamed unceasingly, trying to drown out in noise the terror that engulfed me. I wanted to rise from the bed, to go downstairs and to follow those swiftly retreating feet, though I didn't know where they had gone with the baby they had not even let me hold. In a rattling carriage on the road to Mantua, where his presence would offend the heart of the Prince's bride? Handed through that dark aperture at the Innocenti as I must have been? Or his neck cleanly broken before his poor little body was taken from the house, and thrown into the nearest drain?

'*What have you done with him?*' I shrieked, but they pushed me down on the bed, the matron and the midwife.

'He'll be cared for,' spluttered the matron, her knee on my chest, for in that moment I found strength I didn't know I had ever possessed, despite the work of that night. A page came in without knocking, wide-eyed but speechless. I had never seen the boy before, but realised straight away that he was the matron's creature and that he had been waiting only to be sent on an errand by her.

'Get Master…' I could not make out the name she said and did not recognise the man who came.

It could not have been more than ten minutes before the doctor entered the chamber. He took a philtre from the leather bag he carried on his shoulder and held it up to the light of the window, shook it a few times and unstoppered it. I had not ceased to struggle, though I grew tired. He poured that mixture into my mouth through my screams. I spluttered, coughed, thought I was about to choke, then took a great gulp of air and saw the man's face recede as though he was being pulled back by no human force through a long tunnel. I gasped for breath, as I was lifted into the air and looked down on the heads of the people in the room. I don't know how long I floated up there. I thought perhaps I was dead.

I have never had an experience like that since and hope I never shall again. Later, I spoke of it to the doctor who attended us here in Venice, when I felt I knew him well enough. 'Henbane,' he said. 'They could have killed you.'

Afterwards, I found myself lying in near darkness, but I didn't know if it was still that day, or the day after, or many days hence. I thought I was in a church, hearing voices babbling around me, for though we orphans were always trained, on pain of punishment, to behave with the utmost decorum in holy places, I had always noticed that those who were free, and supposedly our betters, had no such compunction – but the echoes were wrong. It was not a church. Was I dead, and in some anteroom to wherever God judged fit to throw me next? I could smell vomit, and the taste of it filmed my mouth and burned my throat. My heart was racing as though I had been running. I saw also, against the shutters of my eyelids, that room in Venice, hearing the voices of those thronging the chamber beyond. I even thought I could hear Vinta's voice.

I could.

The doctor was speaking. 'The delicate balance of her mind has been overturned. Woman is weak, and closer to the animals than we are – than we men, I mean – for in the dampness and cool-ness of her humours she, like them, is nearer to the earth. Think of a hound deprived of her whelps, a sheep of her lamb. There is no reasoning with such a beast: she will call out for her young even if she has seen them slaughtered before her eyes. Her womb, her breasts, have been denied.'

'What do you advise, Master?' That was Vinta.

'There are three courses of action open, as I see it. I know as a physician which I would take, but given the delicacy of the case you must also decide according to your own exigencies. One: she could be returned to the Pietà. It might be that within familiar surroundings, faces she knows, the blessed rhythm and discipline of the cloistered life, she finds some quiet—'

'Out of the question!' A woman; I flickered an eyelid hoping they would not see it, and they didn't, caught up in their discussion as they were. It was the Prioress – perfidious, scheming snake in female form.

'Giulia was tractable and obedient when she was with us. But now she would be only a source of corruption to the other girls. A virgin was taken from us, debauched and delivered of a bastard. The carnal longings of a maiden find little sustenance in her imagination, but she who has tasted that forbidden fruit cannot but long for it again, and that longing occupy her thoughts to the exclusion of all else. You might consider the Convertite—'

'She is hardly a whore,' interrupted Vinta – the man who had threatened me with that very same fate!

'Whatever she may or may not have become, she has a tongue in her head, and I am sure, cavaliere, you do not wish her to use it,' said the doctor. 'It is not my area of expertise, but it would not be hard to declare that she has lost her reason. She may well have done. In which case there is the Stinche. She can scream herself to death in one of their dungeons and no one will marvel at it, nor pay heed to anything a poor mad girl says. If that is your choice for her, it would be appropriate, out of Christian charity, to offer some support. A friendless woman will have nothing to eat in that place unless she finds some way of supporting herself, and I am sure no one wants to provide an occasion of sin.'

'We have already done that,' said Vinta wearily. 'You said you would give us your opinion as a physician. What would that be?'

'The third, and recommended course of action... that the fertile soil of her womb be again seeded. So many maladies of the female have their seat there. She was promised a husband, was she not? Let him be found and let them be wedded as soon as her milk has dried up and her membranes are once again firm, and let him give her another child.'

'A husband,' I murmured. I had to repeat it, more loudly, before they turned to the bed. 'You said I could have a husband.'

Vinta came over first, and took my hand, looking down into my face. I saw him again as he gazed at me that time in Venice, the Prince embedded in me. I shut my eyes, and opened them, to dispel that vision.

'You shall have him, dear Giulia. I have already identified someone I think will be worthy of you.'

But I cared not at all for who he might be. I only knew that if I lived, and was not imprisoned in a convent or a dungeon, then there was some hope I would find my child again.

Chapter Thirteen

Finery

...il viso bellissimo ferma li viandanti, e non gli loro ricchi ornamenti... non hai tu visto le montanare involte ne gl'inculti e povere panni acquistare maggior bellezza, che quelle che sono ornate?

...it is a very beautiful face and not rich ornaments that stops passers-by... have you never seen peasant women wrapped in plain and poor cloths possessing greater beauty than those who are adorned?

Leonardo da Vinci

'The base is of the finest velvet, and the stones sewn to it are not rare, but valuable nevertheless – it drapes beautifully,' said the *rigattiere*, letting the garment slip heavily over his arm. The second-hand clothes dealer pinched the burdened fabric between finger and thumb. 'Worn by a noble lady at her own wedding twenty years ago and stored in sweet-smelling herbs ever since. My colleague here will rework it, so that it is your very own – you have, if I may be permitted to say so, a most beautiful bust, and so that you and this cloth may complement each other he suggests recutting the neckline – to make space for a softer ruff that shows more of your neck. When the Princess Eleonora was brought out and displayed in *her* finery last year, *she* could barely turn her head.'

'There will be no procession, no display,' said the matron, sitting in her corner. 'The bride will put a cloak over her dress, and pull up her hood, and none of this will be seen until she is inside the church.'

The two men in the room exchanged glances. 'What a pity!' said the rigattiere. The tailor – I remembered him as the man who had supplied me with the clothes I wore to Venice, the first that had ever been mine – said nothing but went on pinning and tacking the coarsely woven cotton pieces that formed the *toile* to which that fine dress would be refashioned. I felt his breath fan my cheek.

I stood barefoot, gazing at that noblewoman's old bridal finery. 'No, stop, both of you.'

The tailor stared at me. The rigattiere looked around as though he hadn't understood who had spoken. The velvet dress hung from his arm as stiffly as a vast dead bird. The matron rose from her chair.

'Take this off me. Please.' I pulled at the pieces of cotton, grazing my hand on a pin. 'I don't want that dress, nor anything like it. Second-hand finery for a second-hand bride!' I was crying by then.

'Giulia—' said the matron.

'No! Enough of this monstrous pretence! You, sir, compliment me on my breasts – you are not the first. Those breasts should be feeding my child, but instead they mourn him, dried up and the milk squeezed out of them! I was barely allowed to see his face, and struggle to remember him, but I feel his loss, here, and here—' and I struck myself in the belly, over the heart. 'But you would have me smile and laugh and look at baubles and fine stuff. No! I shall stand by God's altar in my plain perpignan – the first dress I ever owned that had only ever been mine – and a dark veil on my head. The man who gets me has been bought, but he buys only my sorrow.'

I was introduced to that man just once before we were married, when I was taken to Vinta's house and the contract signed. In that entire proceeding I uttered never a word. I did not need to – nobody asked me anything. My husband already had the habit of writing; within a few pages, Mother, you will come across his hand. It is right that his story too should be told. He, like me, was the pawn of men more powerful than either of us.

'Are you ready?' asked the matron.

'Yes,' I said. Why would I not have been? I had gathered my few belongings into a leather bag and pulled its strings tight. There wasn't much: the clothes that had been made for me to go to Venice, along with some underlinen, and at the bottom where I could not see them but knew they were there, a pair of loose overdresses that I had worn in pregnancy. In sorrow I had wanted to give these away, except that the matron stopped me and said I would need them again. I could not, though, imagine myself being with child once more. I could not imagine ever being happy enough to con- ceive. It was my wedding day, and I was full of gall. I pulled down my veil and huddled in my cloak, for the day was cold.

'Don't forget your bag,' she said.

'Am I not coming back here?'

'Of course not. You will go to your husband's home.'

I looked around the room for the last time. I had not loved this place, but I wanted to remember every stone of it. My child had grown within me here and torn his way out into the light in the room above.

'My marriage chest!' I said.

'It has gone ahead. It is in your husband's home.'

My husband. 'You said he was a foreigner. Does he not talk like you and I?'

'He's from Rome.'

'Of course,' I said. 'No Florentine would want me. What does he do here? Apart from find himself a dowry?'

'He is a musician. In the pay of the Grand Duke.'

'We are all in the pay of the Grand Duke.'

PART II: A POOR MAN, AND A FOREIGNER

Chapter Fourteen

From the ricordanze of Giuliano Sperati

*Husbands must love their wives as they love their own
bodies; for a man to love his wife is for him to love himself*
Ephesians, 5:28

Every Florentine of note, if he be head of a household, and even more
if he be a father, writes his ricordanze. Why does he do this? Who
will want to read his remembrances? I do not wish to draw attention to myself, not only because of my marriage, but because I am a
foreigner, and a poor man in my soul, though tradesmen smile at me.
Vinta thinks I make too much of this; he is not poor, but being from
Volterra, he is a foreigner too, though his speech is not as outlandish
to the Florentines as is mine, and he has tempered it over the years,
just as he has tempered his thoughts and acts to the prevailing winds.
He loses no opportunity, though, to point out that he was made a
Florentine citizen for his loyal service to the first Grand Duke.

Anyway, I write these ricordanze. I think I write them for
myself. My wife knows I write, though of course she cannot read.

'You are a poor man, and a foreigner.' Those were Vinta's words
first, up there in the musicians' gallery at San Lorenzo. He saw the
blood rush to my face and my fist clench. Cristofano – my *maestro
di cappella* – put his hand on my arm. That time I mastered myself.
I had to – a poor man, and a foreigner, can do nothing else.

'If you wish it,' said Vinta, 'the Grand Duke will make you too a Florentine, in recognition of the service you render him. If you do not wish this, then you may with his blessing return to Rome with your wife and a post will be found for you once more with his brother the cardinal. You would return there wealthy – His Highness has provided a considerable dowry – and with a beautiful woman on your arm.'

'She's beautiful, then, even if she is not chaste?'

'I do not think I have seen so fair a girl, in all sincerity. The Mantuans demanded nothing less. Any man would be glad of her – slender without being bony, with the clearest skin, delicately shaped hands and feet, an elegant neck, a noble manner though her beginnings were of the humblest: an orphan, a foundling, though it is said of good blood.'

'You speak as though you were as intimately acquainted with her as her seducer.'

Vinta hesitated at that, then said: 'It was my duty, in company with the Grand Duke's doctor, to ensure that the girl fitted our purpose. She did, most admirably, and furthermore, is fecund.'

'Good God! She is with child?'

'A good omen, don't you think? You need not concern yourself with that. As soon as the child is born it will be consigned to the Innocenti. Her next you can make in *your* image.'

I turned away from the two of them, Vinta and my master, and looked over the balustrade into the nave of the church. I had been there so many times, taking my place alongside my fellow musicians, holding my viol ready in expectation of the trumpet blast that announced the arrival at Mass of Florence's ruling family, yet I had never glanced down until that day. It is true that I have an instinctive fear of heights, one that seems worse looking down into the well of a building than when I look outward. I know this because when I was newly arrived in this city, Cristofano took me up the bell tower of the cathedral to see the entire city laid out before me. When I looked to the surrounding hills the confusion in my eyes steadied, for I saw how insignificant I was – yet, how small Florence had seemed to me then, compared with teeming Rome; too small for secrets to remain secrets for long.

I turned back to their expectant faces.

'What has she been told of me?'

'Nothing but what I have just said to you,' said Vinta. 'The girl yearns for a husband, and trusts you are willing.'

I had no choice. And of course she yearned. Some other man had taught her to. I glanced at my maestro di cappella. He was close enough that I could smell a mixture of sweat and some strange spice, and with a shiver of horror imagined that dark cheek scrape against his wife's soft skin. Cristofano said nothing, but his gaze was as unrelenting as a hawk's.

'I accept, cavaliere,' I said to Vinta.

'A wise choice. I shall inform His Highness immediately.'

'I should like to see her, at least.'

'That can be arranged, of course – when the notary comes with the betrothal papers.'

'Before then. Without her knowing it.'

Vinta paused. 'As you wish. At present she is in her eighth month.'

'That does not matter,' I said. Then I added (and remembering it now, I flush for the shame of it): 'If the girl dies in childbed?'

Vinta raised his eyebrows, but he looked at me for the first time with something like respect.

'In that case, some sign of appreciation, I think, could be made, for your willingness to second the Grand Duke's plans. You would not go empty-handed. Let us pray that she does not perish. It would be a great pity, for she is quite lovely.' He glanced at Cristofano. 'Gentlemen, I thank you for your time, and trust the arrangements I make will meet with your approval.' Looking at me he said: 'I will manage things so that you may see the girl.' He bowed and left us. I did not speak until his footsteps had faded.

'Many whores are beautiful,' I said to Cristofano. 'In Rome a condemned man can escape his punishment if, on the scaffold, one of them will take him for a husband. But I am no criminal.'

'The girl is hardly a whore – and may I remind you that adultery is a crime,' said Cristofano. 'At the very least you'd be fined more than you could pay, and so would be imprisoned.'

'I never touched your wife but the once—'

'So she told me, through her tears. You unlaced her bodice and pressed her breast through her shift. Is that really how it was or what you agreed you would both say? I could have you dragged to the Bargello, to that dungeon where even the walls sweat fear, where you'd be stripped and your arms bound behind you. Then you'd be hoisted on their rope and dropped until your arms were nearly pulled from their sockets. That's why they call it the *strappato*, for you would indeed be torn. You are slender – they would need to hang weights on your feet for the stretching to do its worst. Then we might hear the truth, Giuliano, though what kind of musician you'd be afterwards is anyone's guess.' He shrugged. 'Whatever you truly did or didn't do matters little, perhaps, for you sin with my wife in your heart even now. And who do you think would be believed, strappato or no strappato? You, a Roman, or me, master of ceremonial music for the Medici, a Florentine who can trace his family back four centuries in this city, the man who brought you here, nurtured you, looked after you as a father? Or if not the strappato, I could have you whipped in public, branded, expelled.'

'You wouldn't. You couldn't bear the scandal,' I said, but my voice shook. I remembered seeing a youth flogged on that platform at the corner of the old market not for adultery but for sodomy; I had been in Florence just a year then. His cries were piteous, but the crowd jeered him. A tanner standing near me told me that the boy had been made to witness his lover hanged from a window of the Bargello before being carted across the city for his own punishment. 'Because he is the younger, and the woman of the pair, they have let him live,' said my companion. I was sure that no rich man guilty of the same sin would be punished in this way.

Cristofano smiled and looked at his fingernails. I stood stiff as a mouse waiting helplessly for the cat to pounce again.

'You're right,' said Cristofano, looking up. 'That noise would not help me at all.'

'Let me marry, then, and I promise to forget Donna Lucia,' I said. 'But I wish it was anyone but that debauched girl.'

'She has passed three nights in the arms of one man only. And she comes richly dowered. Three thousand scudi, no less.'

'*What?* You play with me. You mean thirty at most.'

'I do not. The money comes from the Grand Duke's own coffers – not that he is likely to miss it, for it is no more than he would spend on a joust, or a banquet. Three thousand, Giuliano, paid over to you the day you wed that damsel.'

'This has little to do with your wife, then,' I said.

'Indeed. But it is a rather neat way of resolving that problem too, you must admit, and to everyone's advantage – though most of all your own.'

I clutched the balustrade, feeling that the church below was rushing up to meet me.

'Sit down, Giuliano. Remember that the girl was selected with care. If you'd taken her virginity yourself, that pleasure would have lasted only seconds – and thereafter she would have been like all other women.'

I shivered, though my palms were damp. 'What is her name?'

'Giulia. Giuliano and Giulia has a certain ring to it, does it not?'

'What does she know of me?'

'I don't know. Vinta says he intends to tell her your name, and your profession, and that you are no richer than your talent. In his view, a poor man with your gifts is an unstoppable thing, for when a man is merely poor he is likely to remain so: he will never see himself as anything else, spending what comes to his hands without thought, since he has no direction in which he wants to go. He says that she is a good-hearted girl who will be grateful to be the means of advancing your art without the constant nagging anxiety of how you might eat – she will enable the divine plan God had for you when he gave you your ear and your hands.'

They had me, those two, where they wanted me, from my own foolishness. Donna Lucia was seventeen when she was married to Cristofano, a widower of forty, and was glad to accept him, for it was him or the veil, and it would have been an offence against the Almighty to shadow the sun that was her face in a cloister. Cristofano was so taken with her that he overlooked the pitiful dowry she brought, barely what the nuns would have accepted for her – that and a cassone full of linen embroidered by her dead mother.

It was her voice he had heard first. Lucia was educated, you see, by those aristocratic nuns at San Pier Maggiore, and they had taken her to board there at a pittance, because of the sweetness of her singing. Hers was ancient and noble blood, but in Florence it takes only one wrong turning, one mistaken alliance in the eyes of those who rule here, for a once great family to be reduced to near penury. And yet, Lucia had a gift that could not be bought. There was no instrument that could compare with the sounds that came from her throat. Her husband wanted that for himself, and desired her to learn to write music that he might dictate to her, and to play the spinet so that she could accompany her own voice. The day Cristofano brought me to his home that I might teach her – her previous instructor having recently died – he must have thought her safe, a doting mother of three small children who esteemed her husband, though did not love him. She bowed before me and extended her hand. Then she looked up at me.

It is true: I am a poor man, for only the prostitution of Giulia to that prince has made me wealthy. I will probably be able to dower my daughters respectably, but my sons will have to work for their living, though honourably. What is the Grand Duke himself, for all his pomp, but the descendant of bankers and merchants?

I am a butcher's son from Trastevere. I sang in the choir in Sant'Agata and was fed and clothed by the charity of the Confraternity of that virgin martyr. I believed then that music was the closest one could come to heaven while walking on the earth – now I think there are other means too, if a man is fortunate enough to find love at his own hearth. My childish voice was so fine that there were those who wanted me to go to the Papal Court, only that my father stood in their way.

I raged against him for that, for I was only a little boy and did not understand his obstinacy. Another father would have beaten me for my insolence, but that simple and good man, butcher that he was, merely said that no gelding knife should be used on his son. So I stayed in Trastevere, and in time my voice deepened and was not noticeably different from any other man's; instead I learned the organ in the church from the choirmaster, and my father asked a musician who was his customer to try me as a pupil, in exchange for quantities of meat the man could not have eaten otherwise. From him I learned the lute, the viol and the harpsichord. But it was hard for us: we were many, and my lessons meant there was less for our mouths.

It was through the choirmaster that I was put on the road to what a musician would consider fortune, though a merchant might scoff at it: a post as an organist at the Papal Court – if this sounds grand, remember that I was one of many, called to play across the city. I do not believe I ever played for the Holy Father himself. Yet one Sunday I was sent to serve for the Mass at Santa Maria in Domnica, the titular church of Cardinal Ferdinando de' Medici – a youth little older than I was, who had nevertheless received the purple without ever having become a priest. I pleased him. But men such as I do not control our fates, any more than do house slaves.

It suited the cardinal, in one of his rare moments of rapprochement with his elder brother the Grand Duke of Florence, to send me north as a peace offering. He tapped my knee and said, 'Fear not, Giuliano, you and I shall meet again. My brother's poor wife gave him only daughters, and that fat whore who shares his bed now is barren, whatever either of them say to the contrary.' It was the fat whore, of course (I merely imitate the talk of all Florence, here in my private writings), who marked out my path for me, when she ordered that shameful Congress of Venice, thus pushing that poor used girl onto me.

My mother was already dead, and my father ailing. I clasped him tight and wet his greasy shoulder with my tears, for I was sure I would not see him again.

The night before I left I went one last time to little Veronica's lodgings. I was fond of her, and she, poor child, loved me. One can be fond of a drab. When one cannot afford a wife, one takes comfort with honest women like her. I took her a shirt of mine, for she had asked for a keepsake – 'bring it just as it is, unlaundered, so that I remember you better' – and left her crying over it. I do not know if she still wears the yellow scarf of her profession, or if she even lives at all.

Vinta was as good as his word. He had the girl brought to the church of St Margaret, on the pretext of praying to that saint for a safe delivery, and I spied on her there. I frightened her, a thing I should never have done, for they say that if a woman with child looks on a fearful thing, that fearfulness stamps itself on the creature growing in her womb – and that poor innocent had intended me no harm. I told Giulia much later that the hatred she saw in my face was not directed at her. It was directed at myself, for having been so readily bought.

Chapter Fifteen

Betrothal

*If any one saith, that matrimony is not truly and properly one
of the seven sacraments of the evangelic law, instituted by Christ
the Lord; but that it has been invented by men in the Church;
and that it does not confer grace; let him be anathema.*

Council of Trent

It was about three months after that when Vinta sent word that the
papers had been drawn up for my betrothal. I know now that it is
customary here in Florence for a bridegroom to go the house of his
bride, supported by his father or uncle. I had no one, for I had not
had the courage to send word to my poor father of the shameful
match I was about to make. I never did tell him all, and he went to
his quiet grave believing that the money I sent him was because I
had succeeded as a musician beyond my wildest dreams, and that
my marriage was no different from any other man's. It was better
so, though a lie, for I am sure it comforted him to think that the
sacrifices he had made for me were not in vain.

Cristofano came, of course, but we did not go to the house of
the bride, for she was fatherless. We went to Vinta's.

We were brought up to a quiet wood-panelled room to the rear
of the house, far from the bustle of the street. My first reaction,

I remember, was one of envy. I wanted a chamber like that one, and moments of leisure in which to enjoy it. Two walls were given over to shelves, but on the wall opposite the window there was a high-backed day-bed of some expensive, inlaid wood – walnut perhaps – strewn with cushions. I imagined myself lying on that bed of a summer afternoon, while everything outside was hot and still, with one of Vinta's creamy vellum-bound books in my hands. A soft cough, and I remembered where I was, and why. A dusty, dark-clad little gnome of a notary unfurled himself from a cross-framed chair by the casement and bowed to us.

'You are Giuliano Sperati, sir?'

Never in my life before I had agreed to that marriage had I been treated with such deference. Then Vinta joined us, his hands fluttering, touching my sleeve, telling us refreshment would be brought. The notary handed me a document. I untied it and read: a draft for three thousand scudi to be paid by the Medici treasury on consummation of my marriage to the girl known as Giulia Albizzi, ward of His Highness Francesco de' Medici. Only by a great effort of will could I still the tremor in my hands. Wordlessly, the notary held out his quill, and pointed where I should sign. Vinta watched me, then put his own hand to the document. Finally the notary signed. Then almost as an afterthought, as he waved the parchment to dry the ink, he said: 'The girl can be brought in now.'

A servant came in just then, carrying a tray of chased silver cups filled with warm red wine, and a plate of little cakes, placing it on the table under the window. Vinta nodded to the man, casting his eyes upwards, and the fellow went out. The door reopened almost instantly; those two women must have been right outside.

What shall I say of Giulia, when she was at last face to face with me and knew who I was? She was accompanied by that woman who had been with her in the church – from her manner then and now I could see she was more a gaoler than a companion. Giulia was veiled, but the veil fluttered with the agitation of her breath. She wore a plain, dark wool overdress, covering her flesh up to the base of her neck, where it met a stiff, plainish ruff. I thought her garments would have suited a widow better than a bride. The older woman took her elbow, and nudged her forward – without tenderness, I thought.

'Couldn't you at least lift your veil?' I said. Those were the first words I spoke to my wife. Her anxiety had infected me; I wish they had been kinder. With pale, trembling hands, she showed her face to me. It was wet. I saw her eyes flare wider for a moment; she had recognised me. She made the slightest of sounds – a tiny moan of despair.

That face was also thinner than when I had seen her in Santa Margherita. Of course it was – she was no longer with child. She was young, yet older than I remembered. I saw sorrow, a beautiful face, but one that had lived beyond its years, and recognised a fellow sufferer.

The notary shuffled over. I could smell him: the mustiness of badly aired clothes and ink and parchment. 'Your right hand,' he said, looking at Giulia. She stared at him, until I heard the other woman mutter: 'That one!', tugging at her sleeve, and I wondered if they were marrying me to a fool. The notary pulled the girl's hand towards me and said, 'The ring?'

The ring. It was I who was the fool, then, to come to a betrothal empty-handed. Cristofano, who had not spoken since our arrival, beyond the necessary greetings, muttered 'Here,' and pulling a plain silver ring from his own hand placed it warm into my damp left palm. With the fingers of his left hand, the notary tapped where I should place the ring, and put Giulia's hand in mine. Cold, it lay there inert, though not limp – the first time I had touched her. I slipped on the ring with ease. It would need to be tightened, I thought, or she would lose it. I looked into her face then, but her eyes were downcast, the lashes still wet. To myself I said, *I do not know that I can love you, but I will strive to protect you, and cause you no further hurt.* I vowed that when we went before the priest, she should have a ring that was not Cristofano's.

An awkward silence followed; I stood there before them, holding her hand. What was I supposed to do now? Kiss her? There was nothing in her expression that said she would have welcomed that. Eventually the notary said, 'Well, gentlemen, I think that concludes our business satisfactorily.'

The older woman took Giulia's elbow, and only then did she slip her hand from mine – though I felt the memory of its cool presence in mine for hours afterwards. Without a word they both left the room.

'I assume you will be making the necessary arrangements, sir?' said the notary, looking at Cristofano.

'Certainly.'

'Is – are we now married?' I asked.

The notary turned back to me. 'You are betrothed, handfasted. You must marry her now or incur the displeasure of her guardian.'

'But the girl said nothing.'

That man glanced at Vinta, then back at me. 'Why should she? Her presence is enough. Silence and modestly downcast eyes are becoming in a woman – a chaste one.' He gathered up his papers. 'When I was a young man, all you would have needed to do now was to take her to your home and bed her. These days you must call the banns on three successive Sundays and then ask a priest's blessing, before two witnesses. How much noise you wish to make about all that is your decision.'

'A quiet and decorous ceremony is best in my view,' murmured Vinta.

'Quite,' said the notary. 'Call on me when the marriage has been celebrated, and the dowry will be yours.'

I remember thinking that 'celebrated' was not the right word. I could not break a pledge to the ward of the Grand Duke himself, but I still did not know the sound of her voice.

The priest was both impatient and bored. 'Perhaps she will not come,' he said, for the third time. I was standing by the altar of the church where I had seen her first. As then, Cristofano was with me, and a sacristan as the second witness, but there was no one else present, save an old woman muttering over her beads in the shadows. I said nothing: the hour could only have struck five minutes ago. It was then that the sound of hooves distinguished themselves from the babble of voices outside – and stopped.

My bride wore the plain dark dress she had worn the last time I had seen her. I wondered if she had any other. The old woman who had been with her at Vinta's house accompanied her, but it was Giulia who shouldered a bulging leather bag. The priest coughed, and began to intone, as Giulia stood beside me, letting her bag drop to the floor. I knew the words I was expected to say, and said them, but it was as if I was hearing them for the first time, as if they had some meaning I had not until that moment grasped. Her responses were so faint as to be almost inaudible, and I could not have described then the voice of the woman the priest was binding me to, but he didn't seem to care.

He wrapped our clasped hands momentarily in his stole, and I pressed her fingers gently in that darkness, seeing a fleeting image of the curtained bed she and I would lie in that night, in the house that had been made ready for us, the first I would live in that I could really call my own.

Then it was over, and I was putting coins into the priest's hand, and he nodded and strode away. Cristofano patted my arm and said something conventional: 'I wish you both joy,' I think it was. I picked up Giulia's bag, but I have no recollection of leaving the church, only of standing facing her outside, as she looked about in confusion.

'They've gone,' she said. Her voice was high, almost childish with anxiety.

'Who?'

'The matron. The driver. The horse.' She looked me full in the face for the first time.

'Don't be frightened,' I said. 'Come home with me.'

Hearing the front door, the maidservant came down from the kitchen, drying her hands on her apron.

'This is your mistress,' I told her. The girl gaped at Giulia for a moment, and then both women looked up at me.

'So it *was* a marriage chest, sir?'

'You've had it moved, I see.'

'It's in your bedchamber, sir. The bedlinen has been changed, as you asked.'

'That is good. Now bring us some food, would you, and wine. I believe my wife is hungry.'

Giulia nodded, but it must have been to please me, for she ate little enough of what was put before her. Yet when the servant came to take the plates, my wife put a hand on her arm and said: 'What will happen to this?'

'I shall eat it, lady,' the girl stammered.

'That is good,' said Giulia. 'It must not be wasted.'

When the girl was out of earshot, I said: 'Perhaps you should not be so familiar with the servant. A mistress should be a little haughty, should she not, if she is to be respected?'

Giulia crimsoned and looked as if she might cry.

'Not that I have the greatest experience,' I said. 'Until this... this fortune, I have always served more than been served. I have lodged in places where those who were meant to wait on me and my companions were sharp-tongued and lazy.'

'I do not know what I should do, sir,' she said, staring at the boards of the table. 'It was on the road – and in Venice – that I was waited on for the first time in my life. And those servants worked for those who took me there, not for me.'

'Do not call me sir,' I said, 'at least not while we are at home. Call me by my name, or husband, if you prefer.'

'Husband,' she said, as if testing the word on her tongue.

'What did they tell you of me?' I asked.

'They said: "He is good-looking, and not foolishly young. In his thirtieth year. A Roman, an accomplished musician, and penniless." I was told I should be grateful.'

'And were you?'

She met my eyes. 'I was crying. They had taken my baby. I told them anyone could have me, for all he would want was my dowry.'

'Giulia, I am glad to hear your voice at last – but not so loud.'

She dropped her head and whispered. 'I am sorry. I have displeased you. I beg you, do not send me back to them.'

'I won't.' I stretched my hand across the table and covered hers. It trembled. 'What did they say then?'

'The matron gave a bitter little laugh and asked me why I thought the Prince had taken the Lady Eleonora, for it was certainly not for her face, and said there was no difference between that transaction and this, except for the sums involved. I took some comfort from this – except because she'd said the bride was not beautiful. I didn't want her to be.'

'Your matron was right. She isn't.'

'You have seen her?'

I marvelled at the eagerness of her question. This innocent, taken from an orphanage and subjected to every humiliation and indignity, her child torn from her breast, a stranger bribed to take her – yet she asked me a young girl's question. This gave me a way forward, a means by which I might convince my wife to trust me. I wanted her to know I took her part, not that of those powerful men – and one woman – who had thrust us together. The words I chose might seem exaggerated, to please Giulia, but I spoke nothing more than the truth.

'I have indeed seen her, when the Prince came to claim her. I was performing there in the cathedral when she was given the golden rose that came from the Holy Father himself. I have seen them both – so stiffly attired that I do not know how either moved or spoke. The Princess wore her hair upon her shoulders, and an elaborate diadem above, but her locks were sparse and not very long and they would have been better veiled. The girl takes after her mother, I believe. Her jaw is pointed, from what I could see, for her face was embedded in her ruff, and longer than it should be by half the length of my thumb. Her lower lip is fleshy and protruding. You see that indentation you have, between lip and chin...' I lifted my hand and touched her gently there. 'She has none. It is as if she has folded a piece of linen and placed it between gum and lip, so that mouth joins chin directly and both seem larger.'

Giulia listened, fascinated. 'And her eyes?'

'Grey, and they bulge a little.' I saw my stratagem was working, for she looked pleased, and so I added: 'She has the stare of a dead fish.' To my delight and surprise, Giulia laughed. I thought I should like to hear her do that again.

'The Grand Duchess was with her, of course, but though she was splendidly dressed nothing could disguise that she is bloated with the dropsy.'

A frown flickered across Giulia's face. 'I hope I shall never see her.'

'The Grand Duke is her dupe still, they say, though her beauty is gone. He is not loved by his people, because of her. You see, Giulia, that a marriage based on love may not be the wisest thing? Or if a man has a mistress, perhaps she should remain only that, the joy of his private hours.'

There was a pause, until she said, 'Do *you* love, husband?'

I started as though she had struck me, though her tone was the gentlest. The way she looked at me, I knew I could not lie to her.

'I do not know if it was love, Giulia, or pity for a lonely and neglected woman.'

That first afternoon of our marriage I told her everything. I told her how I sat by Cristofano's wife at the spinet, admiring first the way she placed her white hands on the keys, and then the delicate curve of her neck, the sound of her breathing, her frown of concentration. I said that my heart lurched when I saw her bend down and embrace her little children, and wished her arms around me instead, though it is no honour to a man to be jealous of innocents. I told her of Lucia's expression when she turned to me, smiling, when she had mastered a difficult passage, and how her mouth opened just enough for me to see those pearls of teeth and the tip of her tongue. I urged my wife to believe that my desire for Lucia had never been consummated, though I was sure the priests would condemn me just the same for all the times I made love to her in my dreams.

Giulia sat opposite me by the window as the light waned, looking down silently at her clasped hands. It was restful to my soul to talk to her, and I thought that if nothing else, we might find some companionship. Then I remembered how I once talked to poor Veronica. I nearly gasped, seeing my future before me like a dark, yawning chasm of the unknown. Veronica I had walked away from, because I could. This young woman would be under my roof always, obedient to my will.

'What is it, husband?' she murmured, and I realised I had fallen silent.

'I forget myself. I have not even shown you your home.'

I did not touch my wife that night. I wished her a good night, snuffed the candle, and laid down beside her in the darkness. She answered, 'Good night, husband,' and I could tell from her breathing that she was awake, waiting. I wondered how they had instructed her. How would a poor innocent know that a wife should not be the first to offer a caress, for such is the action of a whore? To my relief she did nothing, and eventually I slept, fitfully, aware that I had disquieting dreams, though I could recall nothing of them.

When I woke, I was alone.

It took me some moments to realise that I should not have been. I turned to where she had lain and touched her pillow. It was cool, though it still held the dent of her head. I had by then not even seen her hair properly, for by day it had been covered by a dark veil and at night she had bound it into a coif.

I pushed at the hangings and swung my legs over the side of the bed. Giulia was sitting by the window, her head bowed, her lips moving. She looked up at the pad of my feet, and crossed herself rapidly, so I knew she had ceased praying and that I might speak.

'What prayers do you send up this morning, Giulia?'

'To Saint Cecilia, husband, that your music may always bring joy.'

I was delighted, then, and said so. Only later did I remember that the holy protectress of every musician was a married woman, yes, but one who lived with her husband as do brother and sister.

That morning I went to the notary and arranged for the payment of Giulia's dowry. 'You look tired, Master Giuliano,' he said. 'I congratulate you.'

I woke in pitch darkness. Giulia was weeping softly. I put my hand on her shaking shoulder.

'I do not please you, husband,' she cried.

'Not so. It is only that I do not know you yet.'

A sob. 'You think of her.'

'Sometimes. I pray that she is not suffering.'

A small silence, then, 'In the darkness you might think me her, sir. I should not mind.'

It was on the tip of my tongue then to ask her whom she might think of, but I swallowed the thought. 'That would not be fair,' I said, 'and I should still be sinning.'

'And I would be an occasion of sin.'

That was the first time she astonished me with her natural piety. I was to learn that she had an instinct that would confound – or even shame – the most learned of theologians. This, from an illiterate who did not know her right hand from her left.

'Giulia,' I said, 'try to rest. I think you did not sleep last night, and you do not sleep now. Turn on your side, will you, away from me.' She did so, curling up like a cat does.

I put my arm over her, reaching up to stroke her cheek. She let out a small sound of satisfaction.

'No one has put an arm around me like that since the Innocenti,' she told me. 'At the Pietà I had my own cot, though in a room full of girls. But when I was little my friend Tommasa lay behind me like you do. She was a mother to me, in a place where there were no mothers.'

She was asleep within minutes. I lay awake, thinking about that place, about those children abandoned to God's mercy and the city's charity. Then I remembered that her child, the Prince's child, had gone there too.

It was not long before my colleagues knew, for they are not foolish. A musician is not held in great esteem, though he must be a learned man, able not only to read and write the vernacular, but also Latin if he is to have any career advancement – and for that skill I must be eternally grateful to the priests at Sant'Agata. He must be conversant not only with words, but also with the notes that hang upon lines so that he knows what he sees is a madrigal, or the Magnificat. He must always appear decently, though he is at least helped in this, for in performing he is dressed in the colours of his employer. That way he does his patron honour, but he knows himself that this is because he is owned. Some among us are aristocratic or think themselves such, men who compose and have thus some means of perpetuating themselves. But I am no Peri, no Caccini, for no matter how well I play the organ, the viol, the lute or the harpsichord, the sounds I make last only as long as those live who have heard me play.

I had left the lodgings I shared with Agostino and the others when the announcement was made that I was to be organist at San Lorenzo – my acceptance of Giulia brought more than that dowry, you see. There were mutterings about that, of course, for why had that place gone to a foreigner? Surely the church of Florence's ruling family should be served by a Florentine? I did not tell them of the house that had been made ready for me, nor of the room that I would share not with their snores but with this woman I had been paid to take.

Florence is a small place, and the court proportionately smaller despite all its magnificence. I never proclaimed my newfound wealth as a Florentine would, in finery and display. To placate their murmurs and their questions I told my colleagues eventually that I had a secret life, but that it should be secret no longer. I said I had married quietly – that much is true – and that I had done so for love. It was a mistake, to tell them that. I could have told them I had married some ugly old childless widow for her dowry and her late husband's house, and they would have commiserated or congratulated. and then left me alone. No, they spied on my wife, going to see her at Mass just as I had gone to see her that day in the church of St Margaret.

About a week after my marriage, I came home late in the evening, for I had been engaged at Vespers at San Lorenzo, and was waylaid as I descended from the organ loft. I was thinking how pleasant it was to return to that quiet house, and to find food put politely before me. I preferred not to remember that it was Vinta who had put all of this my way, providing even Deodata, a maidservant of about fifteen years of age.

I did not miss the crowded, greasy lodgings I had occupied, with four or five other men in the same chamber, grunting and sweating their way through the night. I was sorry only for Agostino, in the cot next to mine, a lutenist from somewhere near Pisa with an aged mother to support, the only real friend I had there – nay, the only real friend I had in Florence. Vinta, fussing about keeping things quiet, had told me not to tell anyone I was leaving that place.

It was Agostino who was waiting for me when I came down the stairs. 'Giuliano!' he exclaimed, reproachfully. I didn't know what to say, so I embraced him, called him my dear friend. He was stiff, and edged out of my arms, but when he saw my face said: 'What is it? Where have you gone?' and I saw that he still loved me.

'Let us go to the tavern and I shall tell you.'

I asked for a private room. Agostino saw the coin I pressed into the man's hand and looked questioningly at me, but said nothing until we were seated and wine was brought to us.

'You've money,' he said.

'I have a wife.'

'With a fine dowry, evidently!'

I had no intention of telling him quite how fine a sum it was, money he would not see in years.

'You said nothing, Giuliano. I thought – we all thought – that you loved.'

'I did. I think I do.'

'Then—'

'How does Donna Lucia? You are the only man I trust to ask.'

'I have not seen her, Giuliano, but I know Bartolo goes to her now.'

Of course, Bartolo. A poor hunchback with thin, sandy hair and a squeaking voice, but whose long fingers produced sounds that brought tears to the eyes. A man with a heart as beautiful as his body was pitiful, whose ugly face was transfigured by gentleness as he played.

'They say that Donna Lucia can bear no more children,' said Agostino, 'for she nearly died bringing forth the last.' He looked into his cup. 'I expect you knew that, though.'

'Yes,' I said faintly. 'So beholding a hunchback is no danger to her.'

We sat in silence for a moment. Then Agostino took a long swig of his wine, as if he sought courage.

'Your wife, Giuliano?'

'Our acquaintance is very short.' What could I tell him of her? Another man knew my wife better than I did.

'Is she beautiful, then?'

'Yes – she is very beautiful.'

'Her carriage, her voice, her eyes?'

'I would have said she is noble, only she is not. I would say from her face and her downcast glance, that she was pure, but she is not.'

'*Giuliano!*'

'She is a good needlewoman, they told me. And I am discovering that she has a fine intelligence, though she is utterly without instruction. And modest, despite...'

'Who is she?'

'An orphan.'

'But dowered? Some charitable citizen—'

'I would hardly say that. Plucked from the Pietà and decked out as a sacrifice, and after the act – I was bribed to take her, to ease their consciences.'

I saw the moment that truth dawned. '*That* girl.' Vinta's anxiety to keep the matter secret was wasted effort. Those men he had hired to take Giulia to Venice – what need had they to hold their tongues once they were back home and out of his employ? The more secrecy Vinta exercised the more they realised there was a tale worth telling in the taverns. Thus it was that all of Florence hung out of the windows to see Vincenzo Gonzaga riding by, craning to see the size of his codpiece.

'I'm a poor man, and a foreigner,' I said, echoing Vinta. 'What Florentine would have her?'

'When did you marry?'

'A week ago.'

'Poor girl,' he said, and got up. 'Go home, Giuliano, and count your blessings. A beautiful girl, good with her hands, pure in heart though sullied by others. Teach her to love you. And grant me the honour of calling on you both.'

When I came home, I could not at first find her. For a heart-jolting moment I wondered if she had gone, or even if Vinta or someone sent by him had come to take her away. It shames me even now to confess that I felt a momentary surge of relief. Pity as quickly took its place, for I imagined her wandering like a faithful dog turned out of doors, pleading for scraps at other men's houses – or worse. God knows there are women in Florence, as everywhere, forced to sacrifice all if they are to live. Everyone knows where to find them, for their clothing is marked and they must live in prescribed areas of the city where they give the least offence – and never within a stone's throw of a church or convent, as though misery and degradation were as catching as plague. These were my thoughts as I climbed the stairs, wondering where she was. It was then that I heard a burst of feminine laughter I did not recognise – from further up, where the kitchen was, beneath the roof.

The laughter stopped the moment they saw me. Giulia's laugh froze on her face, a rictus, and her hands stilled – she had been plucking a fowl. She stood up, and bowed her head, a child awaiting chastisement. The servant turned round from where she stirred the pot over the fire and rolled her hands in her apron.

'Husband...' stammered my wife. Merciful God, she was afraid of me. I lifted a hand, wanting to reassure her; she saw the gesture from beneath her lashes, and flinched.

'My wife knows how to cook, I see,' I said gently.

'I do not… That is, I can learn – I have never been taught. Other girls worked in the kitchens. I took care of the worms… and spinning… and embroidery.' I saw she was on the edge of tears.

'Giulia, Giulia. It's all right. If you want our servant to teach you, you may. Though I would still have her wait on us at table, rather than you. I would only ask that if others come to the house – my colleagues, for instance – you do not tell them that you spend your time up here. They would think less of me.'

She looked up at me, her eyes wide in alarm. 'If others come here, they will not want to see *me*, surely?'

I saw then what they had done, Vinta, the matron, those pious women at the Pietà, those prelates who steepled their fingers and talked of the greater good. Greater men than I would not call Giulia chaste, yet her innocence was intact. She was not a lady – she did not know how – nor nun, nor whore. She was wax in my hands, for me to mould and shape – and keep from the flames.

'Have you supped?' I asked.

She nodded.

'Bring us water to wash with to our chamber,' I said to the servant.

Giulia searched in her cassone, bringing out an embroidered nightgown, shaking out its folds. From the way she stroked the linen, and the expression on her face, I could see it was new, and her own work – the Prince had not sullied it. Then she moved behind the bed, where I could not see her for the hangings. I heard rustling as she undressed, and then her furtive washing, as I peeled off my own clothing and pulled on my nightshirt. The bed creaked as she settled into it. I lifted the curtain. She was still wearing her coif.

'Giulia, I have yet to see your head bared.'

She sat up and fumbled with the strings tied under her chin.

'Oh… I have done this too tight—'

'Let me.'

My wife's brows were dark, soft arched plumes on her clear brow. Her hair was lighter, but with a reddish tinge, and shiny – the colour of chestnuts freshly burst from their burrs in autumn, and rich, heavy. I weighed it in my hands and spread it over her shoulders. I saw her face pink with pleasure in the light of the candle.

'This is beautiful,' I said. Then I let go of it and unlaced the top of her nightgown. She looked down and I saw she no longer smiled.

'Don't be frightened,' I said, and turned to snuff the candle, leaving her sitting in the darkness. I did not want to see her yet. Too many men had looked at her already.

I reached for her and felt her shoulder. I crawled over, the mattress heaving like a ship in a storm, and eased myself into the space between her back and the bolster. I opened my legs around her, pulling her to rest against my chest, making a cradle for her of my body. She could not have failed to feel my desire nudging her, but gave no sign, save some tenseness in her shoulders as she moulded to me. Her hair smelled sweet against my face – she must have washed it with rosemary.

I am a musician. The most complicated piece must be learned slowly, each phrase perfected before moving to the next. Anyone can make loud, discordant sounds, and perhaps even find pleasure in so doing – I do not. I have patience.

When I woke, the first thing I saw was her sleeping face, a sweet pale oval surrounded by the pleasing disorder of her hair. I kissed her mouth for the first time, and her eyes smiled straight into mine.

'What were you laughing about last night, you and Deodata?' I asked.

My wife put down her spoon carefully.

'She was telling me about the time a mouse ran across the altar during a sermon and the Prior could do nothing about it, though the little creature sat up and washed its whiskers.'

'What Prior?'

'At the Innocenti.'

'Deodata is an orphan?'

She looked startled. 'Except those that are slaves, nearly every servant in Florence is, sir.'

'I had not even thought to ask how she came here, I confess. The girl came with the house. I thought she must have been with the last tenant.'

'No, Vinta sent her here. She is his.'

'Ah. But of course she is,' I said bitterly, remembering how I came to be there myself. 'Like everything else under this roof. Ourselves included.'

Giulia looked stricken. 'She was in his household, she told me.'

My stomach went cold.

'She's his spy, then! What does she know?'

Giulia paled. 'Nothing. I was in that house – Vinta's – taken there from the Pietà. I didn't see Deodata; another woman attended me.'

'But she must have been aware you were kept there?'

'If she was, she has not said.'

'She would know that a woman was harboured under that roof. What servant would not? What have you told her, Giulia?'

'I have told her only that I was an orphan too – do not look at me so, husband! We orphans know each other everywhere – in our aspect, in the words we use, in our ignorance of the world. I said that I had been dowered, out of the charity of the Grand Duke. Exactly what they said to me when I was chosen – that, and only that.' My wife was weeping; she pushed her bowl away. I stood up and went round to her and held her shoulders.

'Vinta pays her, yet she is here,' I said, half to myself. 'Well, we must make the best of it and lead a quiet life that will be of no interest to him. Perhaps he may forget us in time.'

'I pray that he does,' said Giulia, with a force that surprised me. 'Deodata is indentured to him, she told me. She keeps the document behind the flour-barrel, though she cannot read it any more than I, until the day he presents her with her husband and pays her dowry.'

'I wonder what report she has already made of us?' I muttered.

'Husband,' she said gently. 'If a girl has no father, no brothers, no uncles, then who else will find her a mate if not her master? It is that, or the cloister.' She twisted round to look up at me. 'I have no friends, sir, no one I can trust. Deodata is not wicked – if you had lived as long as I did in a community of women, you would know how to judge. I shall make her my friend, and thus she will continue to send word to the cavaliere – telling him whatever we wish he should know, nothing more.'

I bent down and kissed her rapidly, seeing hope kindled in her eyes. 'You can trust *me*,' I said. 'I see I have not only a beautiful wife, but an astute one,' I added, though in truth, I thought her dangerously innocent.

Chapter Sixteen

et quo coniuges fiunt una caro
and by which the spouses become one flesh
Canon Law 1061/1

Of the harmony between breasts and womb we have plentiful
evidence and many convincing arguments... when the nipples
are caressed, the uterus takes pleasure in it...
Lorenzo Gioberti

As she was undressing that night on the other side of the bed, I asked her to go beneath the sheet naked. 'And with your hair loose,' I added. There was a tiny pause, and she said yes so quietly that I could not tell if she was pleased or fearful.

In the darkness I ran my fingers over her face, insinuating them into her unresisting mouth until my nails clicked on her teeth. I nuzzled her beneath her ear, kissed her throat. Her breathing deepened, but still I did not know if it was from pleasure or dread, even when I laid my ear against the chamber of her heart and felt its incessant, quickening thud. Only when I heard her sigh – a long soft 'oh!' – and felt her hand, tentative against my hair, was I reassured my caresses were welcome.

I raised my head. 'Hold me, Giulia, kiss me.'

*

When I was a very little child, no more than eight at most, I had been frightened by an itinerant Dominican preaching in the open air, promising the torments of hell to godless men who did not pray. I went to the altar of my patron saint in the church where I sang on feast days, where one of the priests of the *agatanesi* found me crying. Between my sobs, I told him that often I prayed and nothing happened. My mother was still ill and my father's customers perpetually late in paying their bills, and I was sure it must be so because all I did was kneel and close my eyes and say the words and feel nothing.

'Then you must go on doing so,' he said, 'for God sees your efforts and is pleased by them. If you try to pray, and reverently make all the actions of one who does, then in time you will find that indeed you do pray. You will learn to see the signs of his grace, and they may take a form you do not expect, and when you least expect them.'

I have thought of his comforting words many times since, and they have brought me through the darkest of times. I think of them now and wonder whether, if I behave like a man who loves, in time I shall find that I do, in fact, love.

I have read again the words I wrote yesterday and realise that the world would say no decent woman should see them. Yet these same people would say Giulia is *not* decent, pointing at the mote and ignoring the beam. For now I shall leave what I have written, for, I swear, I wrote in praise of her.

Agostino tells me in this city it is the custom that a husband makes a gift to his new wife, the morning after he has bedded her. 'It's his tribute to her for the sacrifice of her maidenhead,' he said, and then blushed as he realised his mistake. I thanked him, for I know the spirit in which my friend spoke.

In the district of Ognissanti there is a ceramicist, an Umbrian, so a foreigner like myself. He will paint for me on a plate the marriage of the Count of Saluzzo and the peasant girl Griselda, stripped of her clothes and revested in finery worthy of a princess. I was told I should take a wife, like the count in Boccaccio's last tale, for without one I was like to burn. I pray, though, that I do not misuse this poor woman as the count did. He tore her children from her and told her they were dead. About the child torn from Giulia I have not yet had the courage to ask, for I see that she begins to be happy.

'What do you find to talk about, you and Deodata?' I asked her, a few days after surprising them together in the kitchen.

'Our histories. No one can understand what it is to be nameless, to exist only because of the bounty of others, unless she has walked that stony road herself.'

'You said you were a child of the Innocenti. Yet you were plucked from the Pietà.'

'I have never understood why I was sent there, except that someone must have decided that I was to take the veil rather than to serve. I know of no other Innocenti girl who took that path.'

We will not know until we are dead if it is really true that the meek will inherit the earth. Men more learned and more powerful than I know they must not oppress the widow, nor the fatherless, nor the stranger, nor the poor, yet they do so just the same – the world goes on with its business regardless.

'I know I must have been wet-nursed,' said Giulia, 'or I should not be here to tell you so. Some of the babies were sent to wet nurses in the country. It was worse for them, for they were two years old or more when they were brought back, crying bitterly because they had been torn from the only mothers they had ever known. There was also a room in the orphanage for the babies who had not been sent out. It was high up and had windows looking down into the chapel. We could always see the wet nurses, from where we sat listening to those endless sermons, pale silent faces looking down on us like the saints in heaven. It was whispered that some of those who came to suckle within the Innocenti were the babes' own mothers, too poor to keep them, but able to offer their milk for pay. I wondered then if they knew when they nursed their own.'

She looked straight at me and said: 'I should know my own child.' Then her face crumpled and she cried against my nightshirt until she was exhausted and it clung damply to my skin. I would not let her bring me another, but snuffed the light and held her just as I was. In the morning she asked my pardon, eyes downcast as I pulled on my hose. I leaned over and kissed her forehead.

'I and the other girls washed and dressed those nursing infants,' she told me. 'We rocked them when they cried, sang to them. I learned very young how it is that men are different from us women, but those little curly snails did not prepare me for what... for what they made me do.' She stopped and looked at me. I said nothing, but stroked her arm. 'I thought how much I should like a baby of my own – more than I thought about my mother.'

'And your father?'

'Whoever he was, he had not cared for me, nor for her, or I would not have been in that place. They put us to work there. I embroidered and sewed from when I was, oh, I'm not sure, six years old. Firstly simple things, shifts for the younger girls, like me, then when I was in the Pietà, veils and habits for nuns, altar cloths, lace sleeves for the priests to wear on feast days, then altar frontals, copes, those stiff garments shaped like your viol—'

'Chasubles.'

'Is that what they are called? I learned to spin in the Pietà, and to weave – wool and silk.'

'I would not have any child of ours slave in that way,' I said. She turned her face away at that and I saw my mistake immediately. The baby they had taken from her would in time be taught to work too, though his father was the son-in-law of the most powerful man in Florence. I tried to distract her, speaking of my own childhood, for though the agatanesi kept us at our lessons, sometimes telling us that a beating would sharpen up what musical talent we had, I also remember one younger priest who would join in our joyful ball games. And of course I had a father who loved me, though I feared we would never meet again. Giulia listened, and sometimes she smiled, but I could see she wanted to tell me more about her life behind those walls, the privations, the silences, the cruelty. She had never been able to tell anyone.

'If a piece of cloth was spoiled,' she said, 'the girl who did it would not eat that day. She would stand instead in the corner of the refectory with the damaged material draped about her neck. Any girl who felt sorry for her and tried to take food to her would be punished too.'

'Were you?'

'Punished? No, though just being there was a punishment. I was too careful, too fearful. The worst for me was not having anything of my own, not ever. Our clothes were all the same: plain white garments, unmarked, so I'd have to wear whatever shapeless old sack came back from laundering, with a rope like a friar's tied around the waist.'

She hesitated. 'There was a young priest all of us girls loved, though he never spoke to us, and to my delight I saw him wearing one of those...'

'Chasubles?'

'Yes. One I had made, I with three companions.'

To my surprise I felt the smallest twinge of jealousy at the mention of this first man my wife had loved.

'I don't suppose he ever spared a thought for the unknown girls whose fingers were pricked and calloused from those stiff filaments – our eyes ached with the strain. We went to Mass every morning and were confessed three times a week, but it was always the palsied old chaplain who heard us – Don Alessandro. He would pinch us just here...' she said, passing her hand fleetingly over her breast, 'whenever he thought the Prioress was not looking – we hated him.'

'Confession three times a week? What on earth did you find to say, shut up in there?'

'I spoke of my longing to be outside, to walk the streets freely – even the begging I had done with Tommasa felt like freedom by then – to have something that was my own. I don't even mean fine things, but a room all to myself, with a door, without having to hear other girls snoring, weeping, farting in their sleep. I think making us sleep in that dormitory was one of the ways they encouraged vocations – not a spiritual longing, but the longing for a cell to sleep in undisturbed.'

I understood this, thinking of where I had lodged before our marriage. How could such small things be considered sins?

'Of course the pious women who ran that place thought Don Alessandro a man of great Christian charity. When a girl called Anna complained of him, it was she who was punished.' Giulia shivered. 'She was brought into the refectory where we were all standing waiting to say grace, and was made to kneel before the Prioress's table, and we were told to turn and face her. The old sister in charge of the habits pulled the veil and wimple and linen cap from her head, and her black hair fell down in great matted hanks. We were only able to wash our heads, and our bodies, once every two months, though we were in trouble if our clothes were not clean, white though they were. It was unavoidable then, but I can no longer bear the reek of unwashed flesh.'

I smiled. 'I know! I heard Deodata exclaiming to the baker that you expected her to bathe from top to toe every Saturday evening, and that she was afraid she would catch her death of it.'

'She will become accustomed to it.'

'And your companion?'

'Anna? The Prioress said that she was to be punished for "speaking of matters that pertain only to the married state, and for having spoken ill of a good and holy man". The sewing sister brought her shears and hacked the hair from Anna's head in great uneven lumps. Anna knelt there crying with those black locks strewn around her. We owned nothing in that place, not so much as a pin, but a girl's hair was her own, the one gift – other than chastity – that each one might hope to bring to a man as his bride. We always ate in silence, but our silence was different that evening – a hundred and fifty girls stiff with horror and shame at what we had witnessed, while Anna sobbed and snuffled unceasingly – the very smallest ones cried with her. I longed to go and wipe her poor face, clean the mess that coursed from her nose. I could eat little and was cuffed for it. She was not to eat at all. She was taken from the refectory before we were dismissed, and we found her in her cot in the dormitory when we went up, still crying in the darkness. During the night I crept to her and stroked her face, and I was not the only one, but if we had been seen by the Prioress's assistants, we too would have been punished, for we were not allowed to touch each other. Even in the Innocenti there had been hugs: Tommasa was always embracing me.

'When he was at last in his coffin we were made to kiss the old goat who had cost Anna her hair. We were told to shed tears over the corpse's hands and feet. I screwed up my eyes but could not force tears to come, though spit gathered in my mouth. I leaned over the dead body without touching it, holding my breath. I whispered: "You are not worth even my curse."'

Listening to her, I saw where my duty lay, yet it was not onerous. This woman deserved to be loved; she had been starved too long of kindness.

That night I made her my wife. I do not believe there is any virgin, no matter how gently born, who could have received my embraces as artlessly, as lovingly as Giulia did – for Agostino was right: whatever had been done to her had not sullied her soul. I wish I had a way of committing to paper the little sounds she made, but I am a poor writer. Yet as long as I live and have my wits, I shall not forget them.

In the morning I got out of bed, and just as I was, went to open the shutter, convinced that the day I would see would be brighter and lovelier than the one just gone. I believe it was. I heard a rustling behind me, and turned to see Giulia peeping through the hangings, looking at me. I seized a garment that I'd abandoned on a chair, to cover myself, for I was still sticky with love, but she smiled at me and said: 'You are golden, my husband.'

The friars tell us that husband and wife should never behold each other as God created them, for sin taught the first man and woman shame. They say also that one act of coitus weakens a man more than ten blood-lettings. They can say what they wish, but I left the shutter ajar, so light streamed across the floor, and went back into her arms.

Afterwards she said, tracing the line of my left eye socket, 'You are tired, my husband. There are little lines here. They tell me you are wiser than me.'

'No. I have only lived longer.'

'Your brow is as dark as the wing of the blackbird.'

'But I cannot sing as sweetly as he.'

'When I look into your brown eyes, I fancy I can see into your soul.'

'You can – except when I kiss you between your legs.'

Her eyes widened, but I saw her delight.

'I love the sounds you make,' I said.

She hid her face in the pillows then, like a bird tucking her head under her wing.

Some weeks after that I discovered our idyll was observed. Deodata had just left us at table, having served our broth with unsteady hands. My wife waited until the sound of footsteps receded before she spoke.

'She went to that house on the Arno this morning,' she said.

I reached for her hand. 'How do you know?'

'She was too long away to have only gone for vegetables. So I asked her.'

'Asked her what, Giulia?' My poor innocent.

'What they talk about – she and Vinta. "He asks me shameful things," she said. She wouldn't look me in the eye.'

'Go on.'

'He asked her who comes to the house. She said only Agostino.' Giulia hesitated.

'That is true. What can be so remarkable in that?'

'He asked if he comes when I am alone...'

'*Ah!*'

'She swore to him that Agostino comes here only in your company, Giuliano. Even though she feared his anger, she told him that it was unjust of him even to think of such questions. But all he did was smile. He asked about you too, Giuliano.'

'About me?'

'He asked about your habits – were you overfond of wine, or did you go out to gamble...'

'And?'

'Deodata told him what is true – that you are a man of very ordered ways, who drinks wine only with his meat... that you are very clean about your person and particular as to the state of your linen, but she said that was all she could say, given that you leave the house to go to work, and sometimes your hours are late because you have been required to perform.'

'He must know that,' I said, 'for the last few times this has happened have been for great feast days, when he was present at the celebrations himself, and either saw me or could easily have enquired to know if I was up there in the organ loft or in the musicians' gallery.'

'He wanted to know if you ever returned with clothes disordered or with any scent of drink about you. She told him, no, and that if ever you looked tired it was only because of the hour. But most of all, he asked Deodata about me. And there, there was nothing to tell that would excite the imagination, except—'

'Except what, Giulia?'

She avoided my eyes, this woman whose every thought can be read in her face.

'Deodata said he wanted to know what she and I do when we go out to market together – to whom we speak. He wanted to know also what I would be doing in that moment, left alone in the house while she was with him, and she said I would be sewing, or preparing food – exactly what I *was* doing this morning. Apparently he raised his eyebrows at that, but Deodata explained how I liked to work with her in the kitchen, for it was still a novelty to me and so not such a chore.'

'A bit impertinent of her.'

'Not really. I never could do those things in the Pietà.'

'This isn't all, though, is it?'

'Not quite.' Giulia looked at her plate. 'He wanted to know if Deodata had ever returned to the house where I had been alone and seen signs of the presence of another person. She said not, and took my hands, for she saw I had turned pale. Does Vinta think me a whore, husband?'

'He cannot – but perhaps he wishes you one.'

'I remember this about him – in Venice, I mean. He would ask questions, and I would answer, but he would keep coming back to the same point – as if he meant to catch me out. And not only that.' She paused. 'He took pleasure in it, husband. I know that from the way he breathed, the way his eyes darkened, he imagined himself in the Prince's place.'

Bile rose in my throat. I put down my fork.

'Vinta was doing exactly that with Deodata,' she went on. 'It's as if he is not content until he has stripped me bare and knows everything about me.'

'Not everything, at least!' I said, trying to smile. 'He cannot know what we did last night, you and I.' But I did not feel as confident as my words. Giulia looked down and grasped fistfuls of her dress.

'He knows something... that way.'

'*What*?'

'Don't blame Deodata, husband! If she is truthful with me then she was as discreet with him as she dared be. He started by asking her how you were with me. She told him that you were always respectful, affectionate, that you show in many ways your esteem for me – those little gestures you make at table, always insisting I am served first, and offering me the best of the meat. She said that you never tire of my company, and that you revere my good sense.'

'That is true.'

'She said that when she told him these things, Vinta looked discomfited, disappointed almost – as if he did not want me to be happy.'

'I do not like all of this interest in us. Have we not served our purpose?'

'He also asked her about how we sleep – did she hear us at night?'

'Merciful heaven!'

'She said she did not, and how could she, for she sleeps up there by the kitchen, and cannot hear anything unless you or I were to stand on the staircase and call her.'

'You're crying – look at me!'

'Then he wanted to know: "Do they lie abed on days when they need not rise?" She said his flabby old cheeks shook when he said that – she can imitate his expression so well, you know.'

I wiped my palms on my thighs.

'She said, "Yes, sometimes, but there are few days like that, for neither of them are idle people." Then he asked about the bedlinen, whether she had the changing and laundering of it, and when she said yes, he leaned in close and said: "Tell me of the marks upon it!"'

'Scoundrel!'

'Poor Deodata said she would do no such thing and told him he offended her in asking it. She said the sweat was gleaming on his brow, and that beard of his waggled. She said how much she hated that beard and started to cry. He debauches her, I am sure of it. Husband, I want never to be alone here. Vinta knows too much of my movements. I have taken to barring the door when Deodata goes out.'

'Does anyone come?' I croaked.

'No one has, but I should not answer them if they did.'

I did not know what to say, for I was too angry for words. I feared Deodata's presence in our home not just because I thought her Vinta's spy but because she might also collude with him in his desire for my wife, if only to distract Vinta's attention from herself. But all I did was to get out of my chair and onto my knees beside Giulia to lay my head in her lap so that she might not see my expression.

Giulia stroked my hair.

'I have told her to go to Vinta again soon, and to tell him that I am blessed in my marriage, for my husband is the best of men. I said: "Tell him I am with child."'

That night I kissed the skin which sheltered my babe. An hour later I woke and found my wife weeping. My fingers on her cheek, I asked her why.

'Don't take this one from me!' she cried. I could not tell her the boy was in a happy place, for she knows that cannot be true. That is, if he lives.

It took me some time to convince her to tell me about the night of her first lying-in, for they had impressed on her never to speak of it to the husband they would find for her, as, they said, it would surely displease him. Then she told me where she kept the Mantuan coin. I asked her how often she thought of the child.

'It would be easier to say when I do not,' she said.

She slept after that. I did not, and the next day I played many wrong notes.

Chapter Seventeen

Melancholy
Florence: November 1585

*Every physician should know that God has placed a great
arcanum in the herb, just for the spirits and mad fantasies
that drive people to despair.*

Paracelsus (1525), writing of hypericum perforatum
(St John's wort), translation by Lindsey Merrison

'Help me,' I said. 'I don't know what to do for her.'

'The problem lies not in your wife's body, Messer Sperati, but
in her mind,' said the doctor. 'There is no surgeon alive, not even
the best of my colleagues brought from Padua, who would venture
there. Bleeding might restore the humours, but that she is still pale
from the birth. Her constitution is sound. Her breasts are full, and
your daughter suckles.'

'While her mother drenches her head with her tears.'

'This troubles me, for the child's sake too. Your wife's milk
may be embittered, and that could stunt your daughter body and
soul. Will you not consider a wet nurse?'

'She will not countenance it,' said the midwife, 'and you
would do well not to press her on that matter, as she is convinced
the child would not be returned to her. She is sleeping now; she
has worn herself out. And the child too – shaken on her breast
by her sobs. She said she wished death had come to her in her

travails, that you, sir, might be free, and her child not know her unhappy mother.'

I named my daughter Elisabetta after my mother, and Agostino stood godfather to her. She was baptised in the room she was born in, for she came puny and shrivelled into the world, though I saw the promise of beauty in her puckered little face. I had prayed that the shadows engulfing her mother as her belly swelled might be banished once the child was laid on her breast, but if anything they deepened.

Three days after the birth an unliveried page called at the house and delivered to me a purse of money as 'a gift for your child' but fled without telling me our benefactor's name. It contained a sum of money that my father would toil ten years to earn. I had a dowry for my daughter.

This did not cheer her mother. She looked at the money and looked at me. 'Vinta believes anyone can be bought.'

Giulia defended our child like a lioness and would not let her out of her sight for an instant. I pinned all my hopes on that, but three weeks later they were trampled in the dust. I paid for tall white candles for the altar in Ognissanti, and four to stand each side of the tiny casket. The members of my confraternity swelled the little funeral party. Yet, faced with the disintegration of my wife, I was barely able to think of the frail scrap of flesh we had made now lying in that dark and terrible hole beneath the north aisle of the church. *Laus deo.*

Our benefactor must have known of our loss just as he'd known of Elisabetta's birth. But as his gift was anonymous, I could not go back to Vinta with it.

Agostino came to live under our roof in that time of tears. Men who think themselves wiser than he would have counselled me differently, but only by listening to him did I save my wife's reason.

Yet when we set out on our errand, I still did not know if I wanted my quest to succeed, or to fail.

'You are the child's father?'

'I am his mother's husband. I intend to recognise him,' I said.

The Prior raised his eyebrows.

'Only once, sir, in the last two years, has someone come to claim his child.' He sat back. 'An unusual case. The man had been punished in the Stinche for his defilement of the girl, and fined. Yet while he had been imprisoned, his wife had died, and on his release he had petitioned his lover's father to marry her. By then she was into the second year of her Benedictine novitiate, and there was the question of the dowry that the nuns had already received. The man got the girl, in no more than the clothes she had relinquished on entering the convent – and then they came for the child.'

He dabbed at his eyes, though I had seen no tears, and I wondered if he'd told me this tale to encourage me to tell mine.

'I cannot afford to be emotional,' he said, though I had made no comment. 'I see the blameless fruit of so much folly pass through the grille into this institution, day after day, or rather night after night. Some fifteen hundred at least in the last year alone. If it were not for the Grand Duke's patronage, and the generosity of the silk guild...' He tailed off, and I could see him eyeing my clothing. I am a wealthy man now compared to what I was, but I have never been able to shake off the habit of poverty. My clothes are decent, unfashionable, and show the marks of my wife's careful mending.

'And this gentleman? Your brother?'

'No. I am Agostino of Pontedera, like my colleague a musician in the service of the Grand Duke.'

'Ah! Does our patron and yours know your errand, gentlemen?'

I hesitated. 'He will know – by now.'

'It will take a matter of days, of course,' said the Prior, as I fidgeted. 'There are so many mouths here. We wet-nurse a few infants here at the Innocenti, but it is probable that he is in the country, with a peasant's wife, as is our usual custom for the first two years. Boys, the doctors tell us, relinquish the breast less easily. It would be better if he were weaned first, for the sake of the child's health. And you will of course know that we cannot hand over the children entrusted to our care without following proper procedure.'

'His mother has milk.'

'Ah, well... Was any token left with the child?'

'Yes,' I said. 'The two faces of a Mantuan scudo impressed in sealing wax, attached to a strip of plain linen. I have the original coin here, and you will see that the impressions you have will match it exactly.'

'I do not think we will need to confirm that, sir,' said the Prior, staring at the coin. 'If you can tell me the date when the child was brought here, then I am sure the matter can be resolved as soon as possible.'

'I can only be vague about the date. My wife is unlettered. But it must be that child and no other,' I said, placing the coin by his hand. 'Please go and find out where he is, and if we have him by sundown tomorrow at the latest, we will leave more than this to the orphanage as a sign of our appreciation of your charity towards him and his companions.'

The Prior rose, jolted out of his caution. 'I shall deal with this matter personally. If you would be pleased to await me here, I shall have refreshments brought.'

I hated the thought of leaving that place empty-handed, even though it seemed the boy lived, and that I should see him the very next day. But my hand was on the door before I remembered.

'Tommasa,' I said. 'Do you have a girl called Tommasa – a cripple?'

The Prior stared at me, more astonished at this request even than at my other. 'Old Tommasa? You can't want her. She's beyond thirty and beyond help. Useless as a servant, although we did try – ugly to look at and clumsy. Not the woman's fault, of course, but she cannot hold a plate straight. A fine needlewoman, though, and a good and pious soul.'

'I want Tommasa.'

The door closed behind us and was bolted, and Agostino and I stood outside speechlessly regarding our new servant. Tommasa had barely spoken since being brought to the Prior's office and asked to confirm her name, which she did in the mumble of those who lack teeth. The pity I had felt on first seeing her – the greyish skin, the gapped mouth, the look of resignation in the face of constant pain – gave way now to embarrassment. It is easy to feel compassion for such as Tommasa when seen in her natural surroundings, when one can walk away and count oneself lucky, but to have her walk – if one could call her movements that – alongside me to my own door?

I thought of my wife, and how I had left her, weeping and pressing the milk from her engorged breasts into a bowl held by Deodata. 'Come home,' I said.

Tommasa lurched grotesquely from side to side: her right leg was shorter than her left by the length of my hand at least. Surely there was a clog-maker who could make her some built-up contraption that would level out that horrible flinging of her entire body? His artistry could be then disguised beneath a longer hem than servants commonly wear. Yes, I thought, I must act on that tomorrow. After Giulia had seen her old friend. Which would be the greater shock: to be reunited with Tommasa, or later, with the child? I looked sideways at my new acquisition, thinking that I should never need to provide her with a dowry, at any rate. This woman would be with us until she died. I was sure even Deodata would think I had taken leave of my senses, and that Agostino would make his excuses and find another lodging, rather than stay any longer under the same roof as a madman. I did not mean to, but found myself walking three paces ahead of Tommasa, and without a word she fell into a stumbling rhythm behind me. I looked round for Agostino, and saw that he walked alongside her, talking quietly, ignoring the curious glances, the tittering. Hearing one man say loudly to his companion: 'Ah, marriage is a great institution!' I wanted to correct him but did not know what I should say. Shamed, I took my place the other side of Tommasa.

On the Ponte Santa Trinità she paused in her lurching progress, transfixed by the grey wintry flow of the Arno.

'Have you never seen the river before?' I asked.

'No, sir. I have never been this far. I didn't know the city was so big. When I was little I was regularly sent out of the orphanage to beg—'

'I know. It is not my intention that you should beg any longer,' I interrupted.

'No, sir, thank you, sir. I meant only that I took my little box no further than San Marco. I am grateful. I hated begging.'

'You went with Giulia.'

The ravaged mouth gaped.

'You know my Giulia?'

'Yes. As I know myself.'

'She lives!'

'Yes. You will see her. Tommasa, ask me nothing more now.' I was sweating despite the cold, fearing an outburst of emotion to add to the spectacle we already presented. The woman grasped my sleeve; I wanted to shake her off but saw in her face a transfiguring happiness I had never seen in any human countenance. I cannot say that she was made beautiful by it, but in that moment Tommasa was as one with the angels.

At the foot of the stairs, I asked her: 'Tommasa, what did they tell you about Giulia?'

'They told me only that she had gone to be a nun, and I cried so much that I thought I should die, because they said I should never see her again. I have thought about her every day since and prayed for her. She is the person dearest to me on earth.'

'I need your help. Giulia has undergone many trials since she was taken from the orphanage. I feared – I still do – that she might lose her mind.'

'Who are you, sir, that you have care of my Giulia?'

'I am her husband.'

That woman kissed my hands and pressed them to her tearful face.

'Wait here,' I said, outside the door. I tiptoed into the bedchamber. I heard some rustling, then a dull voice: 'It's all right. I'm not sleeping. I do not sleep.'

'I know, Giulia.'

How well I knew that. I slept myself only from sheer exhaustion, and when I woke, felt guilty for doing so, looking at her stiff, pale face on the pillow beside me. I at least could find some relief placing my hands on the keys of the organ in San Lorenzo, or in picking up my lute. What could *she* do? Look at the baby clothes she had spent those quiet months stitching?

'I have brought you a new maidservant,' I began.

'Oh? Why?'

'I thought… To help you, and Deodata. She is not young, and not lovely to look upon, but she needs the place. Hers is a good heart; I am sure she will be most capable.'

To my horror, Giulia began to cry, and through great gulping sobs, railed at me: 'Because I am not! Because my milk curdles in my breast! Because I could not keep your daughter alive!'

'Our daughter,' I said, reaching for her hand. She pushed mine away and sank back on the pillows; looking at her, I saw a face drowning in the depths of a well. I left her, dropping the bed curtain, and went to the door. Tommasa thumped and dragged across the floor and lifted the drape.

'Giulia! My Giulia!'

I hope it's true after all what the evangelist recorded, that the meek will inherit the earth. The light she brought to Giulia's face, that no doctor and no words of mine could, tells me that it must be so.

Agostino had gone out for a walk; he has always been a tactful man. I went upstairs and told Deodata to heat water for a bath.

'But my lady washed this morning, sir.'

'It's not for her, Deodata. It's for your new colleague. She's in my wife's chamber and will sleep beside her tonight. I shall make shift on the day-bed in the parlour if you will bring some bedding. Tomorrow we can decide where she is to be housed. Come on – I shall draw the water for you if you will do the rest.'

'I haven't given satisfaction?'

'No, it's not that. I don't know what practical help she will give us, but you will see that we need her. Tommasa is crippled, ugly, not young. My wife loves her, and we must learn to also. I am told she is good with a needle. Which reminds me – she will need clothes, underlinen, everything.'

'That Tommasa!' exclaimed Deodata. 'You've been to the Innocenti?'

'And I shall return there tomorrow.'

'Nobody ever wanted *her*, poor soul. There are some old things of the mistress's – she must have had them in the Pietà.'

'I would have wished her not to have seen them again... All right, they will do, for the present. They can't be worse than what covers the woman now.'

I pushed open the door gently, lifting my candle high. The murmuring voices had stopped. In the silence all I could hear was the regular breathing of the sleepers. I lifted the curtain and peered in at the two unconscious heads, seeing the gentle bubbling of Giulia's mouth that always made her look like a child, hearing Tommasa's heavier whistling rhythm. I let the curtain drop and went to join Agostino who had come back quietly and awaited me downstairs.

'She sleeps,' I told him.

'There isn't one man in fifty who would have done what you did this evening.'

'Apart from you, dear Agostino. But this part was easy. The real test is tomorrow.'

'Have you told her?'

'No. I cannot. What if something happened between now and then? What if – and there is nothing I can do about this – they give me the wrong child?'

'She will know. He will look like – whoever it is he looks like.'

'I fear I shall resent him, Agostino – as if the Prince himself shoulders his way past me into my own bedchamber.'

'He's a child, Giuliano. A child his father didn't want.'

'I wanted mine, yet she is dead.'

'Then you must make another.'

After an early breakfast I went to a clog-maker. I was not required until the midday Mass, but needed an errand, and a brisk walk, to calm my jumping nerves at the thought of the next meeting with the Prior. I persuaded the man to leave his workshop in his apprentice's hands, and to come home with me. The fellow raised his eyebrows at the sight of Tommasa.

'I need to measure your legs, lady,' he said. 'It is best if you lie on a hard surface, off the ground. A table.'

I stood near the window as Tommasa, with Deodata present to ensure that propriety was observed, was helped onto the dining table.

'Raise her skirts to the other foot,' said the man to Deodata. The girl folded up the hem of Giulia's old Pietà gown until Tommasa's gnarled right toes were revealed. I looked away quickly, for Tommasa's longer leg looked like a pale shrivelled root. He took a piece of string from one pocket and measured the difference.

'It is a bad case,' he said to me, 'and the wood will not be light, but it will help her.' In a louder voice he said to Tommasa: 'It will take you time to get used to it, but you must persist. You will not quite be as other women, for your back has been unnaturally forced for so long, but it will be better. A hour each day to start with. You will think you are to be thrown over, but it will not be so. A stout stick will reassure you, though you will not need it for long.'

'I want you to come with me to the orphanage, Tommasa,' I said. I was too abrupt, of course, for to my horror she threw herself to the floor and scrabbled at my ankles.

'Oh sir, do not take me back! I will do anything you wish – eat bread and water and pigswill for the rest of my days if you will let me remain here!'

'Get up, Tommasa; of course you're staying here. And you'll eat what we eat, for that matter. You and I and Agostino are going to fetch a baby.'

A girl of about fifteen, dressed in the grey tunic of the orphanage, a white cap covering her hair, padded silently in behind the Prior. In her arms, his hands around her neck and his head resting against her shoulder so that his face was hidden, was a year-old child.

'This is the boy known as Filippo Nocentino,' began the Prior. The child looked round, as though he had recognised his name, and frowning, tried to focus vivid blue eyes on the strangers.

'Oh, he is like her!' I exclaimed.

'He is like *himself*,' murmured the girl.

Frowning, the Prior opened his mouth again, but I held up a hand.

'She is right,' I said.

The orphan said: 'He is just starting to walk. They have kept him in a *girello*, so he doesn't hurt himself, but I have tried him out of it this afternoon, and he nearly manages on his own. Bianca – my friend – and I get him to walk from one of us to the other. He's more confident when he sees somebody holding their arms out to him.'

She lowered the baby to the floor. He was wearing simply constructed chamois slippers, tied round his ankles with drawstrings. I guessed these were made within the orphanage from offcuts from one of the tanneries that lined the Arno. His white tunic of rough woven wool was a little too big for him. It nearly touched the floor, and there had been some attempt to shorten the sleeves as well as the length, the new hems made with long, sloping stitches that could be readily pulled out again. He wore an odd little hat of the same coarse material, pointed and with a brim, tied under the chin, and from under this protruded tufts of reddish-brown hair, damp and spiky from washing. *He has been cleaned up*, I thought, *just as his mother was*. Intimidated by the visitors, Filippo Nocentino showed no desire to walk, but subsided onto the tiles and started to cry. To the accompaniment of that strident wail, I signed the papers that would deliver the boy into my care, aware that my hands were trembling. I heard the Prior say: 'We would appreciate the return of his clothing in due course.' Tommasa looked at me, as if asking permission, and then silently handed over the bundle of her own orphanage clothes. I saw the blood flood her face as she did so: she knew for certain now that she was not going back.

'I changed his breechcloth,' said the orphan.

*

I picked up the Prince's son. His face was close to my own, and I felt his breath on my cheek. He was more passive in my arms than yielding. His garment smelled musty, but his skin of milk. He wore nothing on his legs beneath that tunic, and his thighs resting on my hand were taut and smooth, as though his plump flesh would burst out of his skin. He was heavier than I expected. Of course he was – I was remembering the weight of my daughter as I placed her in her casket, lighter in death even than she had been in life. Why did that man's child live, and mine not?

By the time we reached the river, the boy's head was heavy on my shoulder. Was he just tired, or was he simply accepting me as he accepted all adults, because he must?

Plato tells us that children never love their fathers and mothers so much as when those fathers have carried them in their arms and their mothers nursed them at the breast. I vowed then to defeat the Prince and cast his shadow from my thoughts by making his child love me. Would he make me love him?

'My little man, don't be afraid. Don't be afraid...' said Tommasa.

I heard Giulia sit up in the bed. 'Do you mock me, all of you? Who is there?'

Frightened by the voice that came from behind the bed curtains, Filippo Sperati – for as such the world would know him now – made an inarticulate sound and hid his face in Tommasa's skirts.

I said nothing, but with my heart pounding, I hooked back the bed curtain.

'Look, Filippo, look at the lady,' said Tommasa. The child peeked out, only his blue eyes visible, and with that movement the absurd little hat fell back and hung by its strings. He looked at his mother, up there in our bed.

Giulia started to laugh uncontrollably. It was an unnatural, high-pitched laugh that chilled my blood. I saw her shaking, and realised this was not laughter but tears. Filippo started to cry too, and, abandoning his hold on Tommasa's skirts, sat down heavily on the floor. My wife held out her arms.

'Come in, Tommasa. Quietly, if you can – leave your clogs outside the door. She sleeps. They both do.'

Tommasa followed me into the bedchamber. Filippo was stretched sleeping against his mother. A burst of jealousy left me almost breathless. The Prince's bastard was alive, thriving, in the place where my tiny, sickly daughter should have been, she who had not lived long enough even to smile. Giulia lay on her side, her nightgown unlaced, her right nipple close to the boy's slack mouth. Milk had dribbled a patch onto the sheet. I was aware of Tommasa standing at my shoulder – she still had that stale smell, as though it would take many baths to wash the orphanage out of her skin. She stifled a sob.

'Let me stay here, master. You are tired. Let me sit in that chair and watch over her.'

That night I lay not in the parlour but in Agostino's attic room on a mattress that needed restuffing, and we talked until late. Yet afterwards I slept better than I had in weeks.

May God forgive me for the sin of pride, but the following day I played as I hope that one day I may be allowed to play in heaven, far from the austere grey and white planes and arches of San Lorenzo, in a place drenched in gold and celestial blue. When I came down after the Mass, Cristofano signalled that he wished to speak to me. For a moment I thought he meant to compliment me, but the secretiveness of his expression dispelled that thought.

'You have taken the Prince's child into your home,' he said without preamble. I had told him nothing.

'I have.'

'For what motive?'

'My wife's sanity,' I said, holding his gaze.

Momentarily abashed, he said, 'I know the loss of your daughter was a terrible blow. But do you not intend to make another?'

'Yes, when my wife is well enough. A new child would console us, but not replace Elisabetta – just as Elisabetta was not a replacement for the boy.'

'The Mantuans may be told.'

In that same morning I had thought myself transported to heaven, but now Cristofano hurled me into the depths of hell. It was not the place of fire and torment the old paintings show us, but dark, bitterly cold – a dungeon where the silence was broken only by the sound of sobbing. It is true that I didn't yet love Filippo, but I saw then with absolute clarity that this drear place, this hell on earth, was where Giulia had languished until that child, and a crippled orphan, had led her out between them into the daylight. I would do anything to save her from returning to that darkness.

Though he had put me in it, it was Cristofano himself who broke down the door of that prison. I saw it even in the set of his shoulders, the moment when he ceased being Vinta's messenger and became again my master.

'Of course, there is no real need. The Prince's lady is with child.' He touched my shoulder to reassure me, and I seized his hand.

'You intend to recognise the child, Giuliano?'

'I do.'

'You look for no gain from the transaction?'

'None – only Giulia's happiness, and thus mine.'

'Your happiness is important to us too,' he said, 'if it enables you to play as you did this morning.' He smiled.

PART III: A CIRCLE CLOSED

Chapter Eighteen

Domesticity

Virtue must be preserved in the souls of children neither with beatings, nor with fear.

Bermardo Tasso (1493–1569), letter to his wife, translation by Paola Tinagli

Some might consider this heresy, but when my husband restored Filippo to me, I felt I shared the joy of Our Lady when she learned that her son had risen from the dead. But sorrows and joys are the common lot of mothers, I believe, and even when my child lay in my arms, I worried if the Mantuans might decide they did want him after all, though in fact I never knew if they were ever told that he had left the orphanage. Yet there was always a part of me that resented their silence, however much I prayed it would continue. Did they care so little? Giuliano said that sometimes he saw us both as though we were ants toiling beneath wide skies. Then someone would crouch between us and heaven, and hold a magnifying glass over our inconsequential lives, and from caprice, or rage, or even boredom, he who observed us so intently could with a small movement of the wrist redouble the heat of the sun through his lens, causing us to shrivel up and die.

Filippo moved quickly to the wearing of loose skirts, with no breechcloth. He learned swiftly to use the piss-pot, though Giuliano joked that it took longer to teach him not to bring the contents to show him whenever he entered the house. Though he spoke with my Florentine tongue and Giuliano said he had my smile, my laugh, my glance, I knew that nothing would change those blue German eyes nor his red-gold hair. The shape of his hands and feet were another man's too. Brought to us in the mornings, he would bounce between us, and throw himself on my paps, but more for the embrace of it, for Tommasa and Deodata vied with each other in finding him things he liked to eat. His back grew muscular and straight. There was no sign of the twisted spine that tainted the Gonzaga line, though I found myself watching for any indication that one shoulder began to sit higher than the other.

I will remember always the day when Filippo tugged Giuliano's sleeve and called him 'Father'. My husband turned to me and said, 'He is the first creature on God's earth ever to call me so.'

My beloved Tommasa was also a source of joy. After a few months with us, I saw contentment in her eyes. The curve of her cheek was fuller; she had lost that grey tinge, her orphanage pallor. She worked hard at mastering what she called her new leg; I would hear her clogs going back and forth in the kitchen above, practising. Before long she put aside her stick. Observing she and I playing with Filippo one evening, Giuliano said, 'For this I could be denounced for the sin of pride and idolatry, but when I look on you and Tommasa with him, I think of St Anne with Our Lady, the Child Jesus on her lap.'

But I blush with pleasure remembering that Giuliano was no chaste St Joseph. Because I nourished my son with the milk that had first been made for our poor Elisabetta, my flowers took some time to return, but my husband knew me again in those happy months of Filippo's restoration. As Giuliano said, 'The friars tell us that the way we do this is sinful, that we should only have congress face to face, you the earth and I the sky, but the men of

God cannot know how beautiful is this viol that is my own wife's back and buttocks.' Then he added, 'Nor do I want to crush your breasts when they are swollen with milk.'

I don't know if scripture says anything about connection with a woman who nurses, though some doctors frown upon it, saying it disturbs the flow of blood north from her womb, to be distilled as milk for her child. Yet it seemed in those days that neither I, nor Giuliano – nor Filippo – were to be punished for our incontinence. I knew also that Giuliano longed to see my belly swell again with his own seed.

Filippo understood enough to know that he was to be a brother. As he was only little, I do not think he understood that my child would not emerge as a fully formed playmate from his mother's womb, as armed Minerva from the head of Jupiter, for like all children, I believe, he found it hard to wait for anything.

Giuliano enquired of the Prior at the Innocenti who stood godfather for Filippo when he was taken to the Baptistery and his soul saved. The man looked at him oddly, he told me, then said that it was the City of Florence in the person of Grand Duke Francesco, though by long-standing arrangement he, the Prior, acted for His Highness by proxy. I wondered how far Giuliano's question might travel.

On the anniversary of Elisabetta's death my husband gave Vinta's gift to his confraternity. It will provide funerals for those who die without means.

I learned much later, reading his ricordanze, that Giuliano made one more visit to the Prior of the Innocenti. Agostino accompanied him, though he had counselled against going at all.

What my husband learned was that I was handed to the Innocenti in the days of Prior Borghini, now several years dead.

The present holder of that office told Giuliano that the register held only a brief description of me and the date they took me in. He did ask the name I went by, but though Vinta had told me it was an illustrious one, the man merely shrugged, telling Giuliano: 'The Albizzi are no different from any other noble family. Their sons err too, and their servants pay for it. That family may not have the standing they once did but are still a power to be reckoned with.' He warned my husband that as faithful servants to the Grand Duke, the family would not welcome an approach, and pointed out that as most babies come to the orphanage under cover of darkness, their parents should be left with the anonymity they clearly wanted or perhaps even deserved.

But when Giuliano asked him why I was removed at ten years of age to the Pietà, the Prior was momentarily silenced.

Eventually he said, 'I do not know. Nothing like that has ever happened in my time here. We keep our children here until in the case of the boys they are apprenticed, and the girls until they go into service. The Pietà takes in girl children who are indigent, but not infants. If you insist on knowing more, then in view of your generosity to us, I will see what I can find, but you will need to give me time.'

Giuliano gave him time, and some more money too, but ten days later the Prior tried to return his offering. All he was able to tell him was the date I was baptised in the vast font of the Baptistery, along with other foundlings who were given up to the orphanage that same week. The Prior could not or would not tell him why I bore such a notable surname, but said that I was called Giulia only because it was the next name on their list. My parents had given me none.

Giuliano pushed back the gold coin. The Prior again refused it, urging my husband to have Masses said for my mother and father instead.

'You are a priest,' Giuliano told him. 'Let them be said here.'

The Prior took the coin finally, saying that the gift would go the way of the orphans. Then he dismissed my husband with the words, 'Love the woman and children under your roof. Abandon this quest.'

On the way home, my husband wrote, Agostino asked him why he had disturbed these waters.

Reading Giuliano's answer made me weep. He told his friend that he had wanted to tell me I was as noble as my bearing suggested to him I was – more noble than the people who had used me. He wanted me to know that I honoured him by being his wife, and that he was humble beside me.

Agostino said: 'You know her qualities without all of that.' But he added, 'What I cannot fathom is why she was sent to those Dominican women in the Pietà and not into service. And, Giuliano, it is my belief that our visit this morning will not go unobserved.'

Chapter Nineteen

Illustrious corpses
Florence: 1587–1589

...learned women are commonly thought suspect... because
an artificial malice is added to the malice natural in women. If
you wish to see how rarely learning and chastity go together,
look at the example of Sappho... learned but unchaste women
were infinite.

Bartolomeo Taegio, *La Villa* (1559), translation by Paola Tinagli

Our new son was named for Giuliano's father: Matteo. I could see my husband was glad he had a son and thought this must be because every father wishes one over a girl, until he told me that otherwise we might have felt compelled to give the name Elisabetta, as the custom is – as if that little lost one can simply be remade. I asked my husband if his father knew he was married, or if he knew my name. He looked shamefaced then, and said, 'I would dearly wish him to know the boy in person, his namesake, but I have been foolish, and not mentioned Filippo. I should have told him I had married a widow, but that would have heaped another lie upon the tower of falsehoods I have already built. I don't think he would have believed me in any case. A young widow's child goes to her dead husband's family, if she accepts another man, and thus to all the bawdy jokes made at her expense is added the taint of being a heartless mother. You deserve none of this, Giulia. Nor does Filippo. So I have kept silent.'

I knew that he continued to remit funds to Rome via the clerks in the Michelozzi and Ricci bank. Giuliano shared all that with me. They were not sums large enough to excite suspicion.

Another purse arrived, of the same value and in the same manner as before. Though I liked it no more than I did the first, I learned to daydream of what Matteo might become thanks to that money: a lawyer, a surgeon, a priest? Or perhaps simply a musician.

Our son was a month old and Giuliano had just entered the bedroom where I lay resting against the bolster, Matteo in my arms, when there was a knock below. We heard the shuffle and thump of Tommasa descending the stairs – she was quick by then, on her built-up shoe, and she had gained some dignity from being able to gaze directly into the face of whomever she spoke to, without peering up at them sideways.

The feet ascended again and paused outside our door. 'Come in, Tommasa,' I called out, before she could knock. 'Everyone's awake.'

'There's a package for you, my Giulia,' she said. 'A page has just come with it, but he isn't expecting an answer. He asked only confirmation that he had the right address.'

'Was he wearing any sign?' I asked.

'Yes, something red, with a gold bar – up, and down, like that,' and Tommasa sketched an upended V with her finger, 'three little gold things in each of the spaces, trees or flowers perhaps they were... a blue strip above... I can't remember anything else, it was so quick.'

'Vinta,' I whispered.

Giuliano fumbled with the knots of the package but was too impatient. 'Help me unwrap this,' he said to Tommasa.

She, a better needlewoman than I, schooled for longer in the repetitive boredom of the orphanage, deftly unpicked the cords tied around the coarse cloth. Out tumbled baby clothes of the finest linen, and finer embroidery, and beneath them, a note. I snatched it up.

'I can't read this. But it doesn't look like the scratchings I saw him make in Venice. I'd recognise them again until the day I die.' I held the note out to Giuliano.

Hearing that you have been safely delivered of your son, I send you these things made by my own hand and worn by my own daughters with the humble wish that all God's blessings may rain upon you, your husband, and upon every child beneath your roof.

If your child has yet to be baptised, and you and your husband have not already asked someone else, I would consider it a great honour if you would let me stand godmother.

I think of you often, and as often hang my head in shame.

Camilla Bartolini, spouse of Cavaliere Belisario Vinta

After Tommasa had brought us our supper, and Matteo slept, Giuliano wrote my reply, with my words. He sat close to me on the side of the bed and read it back to me; I asked him if I was not being presumptuous.

'Perhaps she didn't really mean what she said about being godmother. Perhaps she was simply being polite, believing that we have already chosen someone, and I am meant to refuse?'

'No,' Giuliano said, 'for that lady wrote to you from her heart.' Then, almost without a pause, he asked, 'Giulia, would you like to learn to read?'

'In the orphanage they said that girls should not read, that temptation and danger lay that way. They said a woman should have no use for reading, for she can never be a man.'

'They said lots of things to you that were not true, I think.'

'They said things they didn't mean.'

'You haven't answered me. Would you like to?'

'If you wish it.'

'I do.'

'But how should this be done?'

'Someone will come here. A learned man, but a poor one. A friar, perhaps.'

'Not a Dominican!'

'Not a Dominican. Perhaps a woman, then; a gently born widow. Someone who has instructed her own daughters.'

'Could Tommasa…? She is always with me. I would not shut her out.' I had an image of the two of us, side by side in the little panelled parlour, intently writing at the little table.

'Yes,' said Giuliano. I put my hand to his cheek.

The Lady Camilla came herself to the font as godmother; we had expected a proxy. She embraced me as though I were her own daughter, but later I cried. I thought the poor woman thin and pale.

In the summer of 1587 the hunchbacked Duke of Mantua, so derided by his handsome son, died. When Giuliano told me, I nodded, but said nothing, though later I went to peer into the little bed where his grandson lay asleep on his back, his reddish hair slightly damp, his cheeks flushed, his mouth open. So the man who sired him had come into his inheritance. But Filippo did not even know nor care that Vincenzo existed. And by then, my belly was again swollen.

I overheard Giuliano and Agostino in the parlour, speaking of Vincenzo. Some of their companions had been to Mantua to perform for the Princess Eleonora.

'Cristofano says that the new Duke is so enamoured of music, and so restless in his soul, that he will be comforted only by the best players, the best composers, and that he lures them to his court on the Mincio not only from across Italy but from much further afield – Flanders even. In sound he intends to eclipse Ferrara, and in magnificence even the Papal Court. Cristofano frets that the Grand Duke will dismiss us all for sounding like nothing more than a procession of feast day peasants, capable only of making a row with their monotonous *zampogne* pipes and clacking like bird scarers.'

Neither spoke of the Prince with regard to me, though later Giuliano said they'd known I listened.

The threat of dismissal died in October that year at Poggio a Caiano. The Grand Duke expired first, his dropsical wife following him within a matter of hours. Cardinal Ferdinando – his brother and successor – was at table with them, they say, but suffered no ill-effects.

'There is a rumour that the servants are to be interrogated, in the ways best known to those who hold the keys to the Bargello – ways that draw no blood, yet inflict exquisite pain,' said Giuliano. 'We musicians are to prepare for Francesco's funeral.'

The citizens of this city would as gladly have sung madrigals for the occasion as hear a dirge, for he was not loved.

No one was to see Bianca Cappello's coffin, though. Giuliano learned that her brother-in-law the cardinal did not permit her corpse to return to Florence, and so the Grand Duke was laid to rest beside his unloved first wife rather than his second. Deodata said that the talk of the marketplace was that the Venetian woman had been buried beneath the floor of the nearest church, while others claimed that she was flung into a pauper's pit. Giuliano said to me, 'Live long enough, and you will see your enemy carried past your door.'

Giuliano remembered the cardinal as being wise, but not saintly.

He told me that his relations with his maestro di cappella had become cordial, but distant. 'I regret this,' said my husband, 'for he was a father to me, albeit a severe and demanding one, when I came to Florence. Agostino tells me to remember that I came to Florence by recommendation of the cardinal, and that his star is now in the ascendant, and so I should feel safe.'

No servant was thrown into the Bargello, not even a cook. Deodata heard that all who had worked for Francesco, with the exception of some of his favourites, would serve Ferdinando, for he never returned to Rome. I wondered if one of those deprived of their posts would be Vinta, but Deodata said not, for there were rumours he had been despatched to France, as the new Grand Duke, having cast off his cardinal's hat, required a wife. I thought Deodata remarkably well informed for a kitchen wench, but then she always enjoyed gossip.

We named our new daughter Camilla.

In the days after her birth, the surgeon was called and I was given willow bark and yarrow, and bathed with warm water and vinegar. I do not remember much of this, for I was feverish, but Giuliano said, and Tommasa confirmed it, that I would not hear of our daughter being wet-nursed. When I was recovered, I was told that our unseen benefactor had already delivered Camilla's dowry. I accepted this, being too exhausted to complain.

Our new Grand Duke wanted the arrival of his French bride to be celebrated with a sumptuousness such as this city has never seen. For much of the spring of 1589 Giuliano would slip into our bed in darkness and would often be gone before I woke. Every artist, musician, scene painter, architect, engineer, actor, singer, must have abandoned whatever commission he was engaged on to dedicate himself to masques, madrigals, plays, dances – even a sea battle to be staged in the flooded courtyard of the Pitti Palace for which Giuliano was one of those who provided the musical accompaniment – designed to drown any memory of the former Grand Duke and his solitary alchemy. What I still do not understand is why it was now fit that an Italian prince should unite himself to a Frenchwoman, whereas five years earlier it was not.

I thought our lives would follow their tranquil course, now that there was a new Grand Duke and stability restored. But Nicolò Martelli put paid to that.

*

That day, Giuliano came home barely able to speak for rage. Agostino was with him, trying to calm him.

'Every group of musicians includes a man one wishes was not there,' said Agostino. 'Each one of us is relied upon by his companions to produce the right sound at the right moment, or the result is cacophony, yet the moment our instruments are laid down that harmony is in jeopardy.'

I looked from one to the other. My husband's face twitched, but eventually he mastered himself enough to tell me, 'Agostino is right, as he usually is. But it makes this no better. He speaks of our lutenist, Nicolò Martelli. He picks quarrels with others besides myself, for he assuages his bitterness at the decline of what he keeps reminding us is his noble blood by diluting it with too much rough wine. I am the only foreigner up there in the musicians' gallery, so I am an easy target, and Nicolò thinks any favours should be reserved for Florentines.'

'What happened?' I said faintly.

'Cristofano was introducing into rehearsals a new piece of music to be played in honour of that new French bride. Nicolò turned to me in front of everyone and said, "Not quite the nuptials *you* had, even if you too got a wife fit for a Prince."'

'Oh, Giuliano, no.' What he said next surprised me not at all.

'I hit him, Giulia. I punched him in the mouth.'

I began to cry.

'There is more,' said Giuliano.

'Of course there is...'

'Cristofano summoned us both. I had burst Nicolò's lip, but not damaged his teeth – they were already rotten beyond repair. "Giuliano's lady is deserving of your respect," Cristofano told him. "I would be honoured to be married to her myself."'

I thought Giuliano might have added these words to reassure me, but he swore Cristofano had spoken them. And though Nicolò bowed low, Giuliano had seen that he smirked. To my husband

Cristofano said, 'Your behaviour was better suited to a tavern than the musicians' gallery of the Grand-Ducal church. Any more like it, and you will grace it no longer.'

My courses did not come when I expected them and I thought it was from fear of what would happen next. The incident with Martelli, I was sure, would be recounted to Vinta. But that was not the reason for my unmarked linen; I was again with child.

Chapter Twenty

Giulia writes

We've had enough exhortations to be silent! Cry out with a thousand tongues – I see the world is rotten because of silence.

St Catherine of Siena

I realise I have not written of Maddalena, the beloved lady my husband found to letter me. God rest her soul, best and kindest of women. She was what is commonly called a *pinzochera*, a laywoman consecrated to God, often the butt of cruel jokes, for what else is a woman who is alone, no longer young, and for the world of no use to anyone? A professed nun is deserving of respect, carrying her atrophied virginity to the grave like a talisman. But a woman who has known love – or at least a husband – and has nothing now to show for it?

Maddalena's children are all dead, all seven of them, some of the smallpox, some of a putrid fever in which she held them while blood gushed in a river from their mouths. Her eldest boy lived until he was twenty. She lies with them now, and with her husband, beneath the north aisle of Santa Croce. I look at my children, straight and strong, but with them see the shadows of their dead sister Elisabetta and my little boy Taddeo who followed her a decade later. They grow, year by year, in my thoughts. In my prayers I talk to them, and at other times when I am alone.

So how did Maddalena live with her loss?

She took what remained of her dowry into a little house on the Ponte Vecchio which she shared with five other women, living on what each had brought from her former life, and on alms. I don't know if anyone still carries their light, for women like them are looked on askance by some priests, as they are subject to no rule but such as they decide for themselves – or more accurately, I would say, God's rule as they discern it to be. Therein, say some tonsured men, lies the taint of heresy.

She told me what a joy it was to enter a house like mine where there was the babble of children, but I am sure the greatest child there was me, for I did not know even how to hold a pen, any more than I knew that day under Vinta's roof what I should do with a fork.

The first thing she taught Tommasa and I was to write our own names. 'Gi-u-li-a.' Each sound was a fragment, a brightly coloured tile with which to begin putting together the mosaic of my life. It seems extraordinary to me now, to look back on that first task she set me, to copy my name again and again, saying it aloud as I did so, following the example she so fluidly scribed at the top of the paper. Most of the time we worked on slates, but Maddalena told me I should want to keep that first page. My effort was so clumsy, but now I look at it again and marvel at how far I have come. It is for me as extraordinary as seeing a helpless babe find his feet, his voice, his soul, when as a mother you think he will be dependent on you forever.

There is not just this world, then, that we see and touch. There are other worlds, to be found in books, in words written by people long dead, but who speak on the page. When I was starting to feel at ease in my native Florentine, Maddalena started me on Latin too, but said I should never snub the vernacular, as some learned men will do; after all, Dante wrote in our Tuscan tongue. I never said this to Maddalena, but I remembered the sermons preached daily to us in the Pietà and I marvelled at the learning of the priests. Now that I can read and write, I know they are as mortal as I and not gifted with special powers – and I also know that this is why some of them would resent the pen now in my hand.

The first letter I wrote was to the Lady Camilla, asking her to forgive me for my mistakes and the clumsy way in which I expressed myself, and for having taken so long to thank her for all her kindness to me. Giuliano had had to write for me, you see. She wrote back almost straight away and told me how much my words cheered her. Her hand was less certain than it had been, and I am sure those blots were tears.

When I could, after a fashion, read and write, Giuliano took my hand and said, 'Now you can help *me*.' Then he taught me that the lines and blocks on the pages he kept in the chest beside his spinet could also be read, though they did not fill my head with words but with sounds, sounds that he and I could hear with our eyes, though the room be so silent that you might hear someone peel an onion through the wall. This is a wonder indeed. I learned to copy for him, and he complimented me on the neatness of my transcription. Oh, Giuliano!

Tommasa did not like, as I do, to read for the mere pleasure of it, though she would sit enthralled when I read to her. Her gift was more practical: she learned to add, and subtract, and to compute the costs of things, to hold her own with any market trader. And when Filippo squirmed at the table trying to do the calculations that his tutor set him, it was Tommasa who helped him make sense of them, using pulses and rice grains.

Chapter Twenty-One

Paterfamilias
February 1590

Thy wife shall be as a fruitful vine by the sides of thine house:
thy children like olive plants round about thy table.

Psalm 128:3

We lived by then in a house full of noise and movement. Agostino still inhabited his attic room at this time; one of our four living children, his namesake, was in his cradle. But our dear friend was preparing to leave us, to wed. I am grateful that he was still with us in the catastrophe that was to come; in the end it was us who would leave him, not the other way about.

Filippo went to abacus school. His tutor told Giuliano he was an intelligent but over-lively pupil, and he had had cause to thrash him. I know this was an unpleasant surprise to the boy, for Giuliano never raised his hand to him, nor to any of our children, but he said he would not interfere with Messer Adriano's work – though my husband called himself twice a coward, once for not striking Filippo and then for not preventing another man from doing so. There is much in scripture that says a wilful child will bring shame on his parents, yet Giuliano said that as a child is neither a dog, a horse nor a lion, reason should be used with him, not a whip. Giuliano also had pupils at home by this date, for though he knew he was no longer a poor man, he still had a poor man's fears. Any man should, I think, whose family grows at the rate ours did. Giuliano also tried to teach Filippo, but the boy succeeded only in breaking the strings of his lute.

Filippo's brother Matteo was by then three years old and waited always for his father's homecoming at the top of the stairs, though Tommasa restrained his exuberance lest he fall down and break his neck. Giuliano would always go up to him and hold him tight while he prattled his day into his father's ear.

Vinta's lady stood godmother to Camilla as she had to Matteo, though she looked frail, as though gnawed at from within. The gifts she brought were those a woman would choose – a birth cup, for instance, with on its lid an image of the childbed of St Anne. I was glad of this – I feared her husband's generosity. I remember that lady in my prayers and teach my children to remember her also.

In the days when Agostino courted his bride, we had made another child, to bear his name. The midwife frowned when she saw him – his birth was protracted and this little Agostino was feeble. His godfather, who was in the house, was called to the room at once so that he might be baptised then and there.

We have always called our child Tino, to save confusion. No purse arrived for him. I thought this meant that Vinta meant to leave us alone at last. Not so.

I knew something was wrong as soon as I saw Giuliano, but it took some time for me to wrest from him what had happened; he only told me in the end because I said I would not sleep if he did not, which was true. It was late, but I knew he had had an evening performance. It had not been a good one, for he said that Nicolò Martelli had come dishevelled, the smell of coarse wine on his breath, and Giuliano and the other musicians had had to play louder to cover his mistakes. Giuliano knew Nicolò had never forgiven him for that blow to his mouth.

It wouldn't have happened if Cristofano had not congratulated my husband on Tino's birth. He was about to go, pulling on his gloves, when his maestro di cappella said, 'Your quiver is full,' clapping him on the shoulder.

'Maybe some are even his!' called Nicolò. Giuliano ran after him, pulling off his left glove as he did so, spun him round, and struck him with it on the cheek. Martelli muttered an oath and seized my husband, making to throw him to the ground (he was bigger and stronger, and fortified with drink), but Giuliano made to trip him.

'You were only defending yourself,' I cried.

'No,' said Giuliano, shaking his head. 'My intention was to pitch him backwards into the opening of the spiral staircase, not caring if he cracked his head – but Cristofano and Alfonso the viol player pulled us apart.'

I thank heaven still that they did so, or my husband would have thrashed the air below the windows of the Bargello, for killing a worthless man. Cristofano dismissed Nicolò on the spot, leaving Alfonso to bundle him downstairs, amid oaths that should not have been uttered in a church, nor indeed in any decent place.

Cristofano then forced Giuliano into a chair and gave him a warning. 'I shall say that Martelli's poor musicianship risked shaming the Ducal family in public,' he said. 'But if Nicolò harms you, then stranglings in the Stinche would surely follow, only that would be too late for you. Look over your shoulder always, Giuliano. I must speak to Vinta.'

Giuliano woke himself shouting in the small hours, also waking Tino, who had to be pacified with the breast. I was awake in any case. I feared Martelli more now that he had less to lose.

I put my arms around my husband. 'Oh, Giuliano, let them say what they like of me! But what are we to do now?'

Giuliano didn't see Nicolò again. But he must have known every move my husband made.

As Agostino and Giuliano were often engaged together, they made company for each other to and from our home. We only discovered later that even Agostino had armed himself, though by God's mercy he never needed to make use of his dagger. For weeks, Giuliano told me – not then, but later – he walked glancing behind, jumping at every shadow. The evenings were getting lighter, and we hoped that Martelli's rage was cooling.

But Giuliano was watched. Agostino caught a fever and sweated it out in his attic, Tommasa muffling him in blankets and feeding him broth. On Giuliano's third evening of returning alone – on a fine, cloudless night beneath an almost full moon – he was three strides from our door when two pairs of footsteps quickened behind him. Before he had time to fully turn around, those men were upon him, slamming him against the wall. The cracking of his head against stone stunned him; he told me that in that moment, sure he was about to die, he saw me as I looked up at him outside the church we had just been married in, bewildered and utterly unprotected, and said he knew he had to live. So he shouted and put his arms before his face as one of them pushed against him. He heard the cloth of his sleeve tear. In that moment the front door opened – Deodata was on her way to the apothecary for a draught for our sick friend. I don't think they even saw her: the sudden noise close by was enough to frighten them off, and to save Giuliano's life.

Only when Deodata had got him indoors did he complain of the pain in his right arm. The sleeve of his doublet was not torn but had been cut, as had the shirt beneath, and the linen was seeping blood.

I held his hand while the apothecary cut the wound wider and deeper, until the blood flowed into a bowl. After he had at last bound the wound, he made Giuliano walk up and down the room, faint as he was, and pinched his fingers and feet to see if they were becoming numb. Bless that man – he stayed with us another four hours and would not let my husband sleep. Only then was he satisfied that the dagger was merely a dagger – that it had not been steeped in poison.

Two days later, Cristofano came. Giuliano was lying on the day-bed in the parlour, for in that way he could reconcile the apothecary's instruction that he keep to his bed with his impatience to be nearer recovery.

Cristofano glanced at me. I wondered if he wanted me to leave, but I stayed, holding my husband's hand. 'I have seen Vinta,' he began.

'I see from your face that you are going to tell me nothing is to be done about those ruffians,' said Giuliano.

'You have said yourself that you wouldn't recognise them again.'

'So what did Vinta say?'

'Some advice, which you must take. Not advice, perhaps – an instruction. Nothing can be proved against Martelli,' he began.

We were to leave Florence. To go somewhere where we were not known. Giuliano had been found another post. An orphanage... he was to be their organist and choirmaster. There would not be much of a stipend, and only a room for him within the orphanage walls should he require it. A house – our home – would have to be found and paid for. But as he said, 'I will have to take it, Giulia, or we shall have nothing.'

This orphanage, Cristofano told us, was supported by the greatest families of the city, governed only by noblewomen and a charitable confraternity. 'So respected a place it is that the boys assist even in government, when the city fathers are balloted; the girls are dowried,' he said. 'It is called the Pietà.'

I flinched; Cristofano saw it. Giuliano's fingers tightened around mine.

'Vinta himself found it,' said Cristofano. 'Grand Duke Ferdinando might have denied his sister-in-law an honourable grave, but his minister maintains his old contacts there just the same. You are to go to Venice.'

By the end of that month, as soon as the doctors had said Giuliano was fit to be moved, the wagon stood at our door.

PART IV:
SERENISSIMA

Chapter Twenty-Two

Campo San Giobbe

Venice... yeeldeth the most heavenly and glorious shew upon the water that ever any mortal eye beheld...

Thomas Coryat, *Coryat's Crudities* (1611)

I never imagined, when I was taken away from this water-bound city after the Prince had finished with me, that I should rest my head here again. I listen to the slap and suck of water at the canal edge as though no time has passed since I was imprisoned, guards pacing outside, awaiting my ravisher. I do not think I could find that house again, and do not wish to, nor does Giuliano ask about it, though I can see he looks, and wonders, and his handsome face darkens. Vinta always told me I should be grateful for what happened here, but my gratitude instead is to my husband, to Tommasa, to Agostino. I have learned to forgive the Prince even, for in his own way he was the tool of others too, and without that gold coin so carelessly thrown onto that soiled bed, I would not have Filippo back in my arms. Without him I would not have Filippo at all.

I can never forgive Vinta.

Men like him I am sure consider my life humdrum. I have served the purpose of those who wield power, but now am of no further use to them. At least, I hope it will be so. My children, a man who loves me – these, Mother, are what count for me, for I thought I would never have them. That is why I continue to write, not just because writing has become a habit, but because it gives me immeasurable pleasure to put down on paper the happiness my quiet life with them gives me.

Our house lies almost at the edge of the city, as if we were about to slide into the lagoon, and unlike most of those who live in the burrowing streets of this place, I can look out on a little apron of a square – they call it a *campo* here, not a *piazza* – a church to one side, a canal to another. No one of note lives here; five minutes' walk over their little bridges to the east the Jews are penned in at night in their teetering buildings, behind sheer windowless walls, for they may not look out on their Christian neighbours, nor we look in on them.

I still struggle sometimes to understand the speech of the people here, though they have always been civil. From my window I can see the hospice adjoining the church, that the friars keep for the old and indigent, and those who end their days here have a little garden to till. They give me vegetables they have grown, that the children may grow bright-eyed and strong.

I find solace also at Mass for the priest must use the same Latin words as I have heard all my life, though they are strange in his mouth.

This church is named for poor suffering Job, as though he were a saint – even the Church, it seems, does things as the Venetians wish, as though all the edicts of Rome were nothing but a mirage vanishing where the water meets the sky. But there were Florentines here once: someone built a chapel in this church and set in its vault those unfading, gleaming images in blue and white and green and gold such as can be seen on nearly every corner in Florence – in this case of the Evangelists writing their gospels within wreaths of fruit and leaves. I wonder if they were fired in the same oven as those babes, arms wide in silent appeal, that gaze out from the façade of the Innocenti, the first home I ever knew. Will this one be my last?

*

When we left Florence, Vinta came to bid us farewell. We had little enough to go on the cart in the end. He'd provided that house, and every stool, fork or bed hanging within it. We took from it only my cassone, Giuliano's spinet, lute and viol, the birthing chair and the things I had made, I and the matron, as we waited for Filippo to be born. Vinta smiled inside that soft beard of his, and looked me straight in the eye when he said: 'You will be far from Florence but Florence will never be far from you. It was before my time, of course, but there was a Medici once, a murderer, who fled to the lagoon city for sanctuary. He must have felt safe there, for more than ten years passed, but vengeance caught up with him – darkness and knives. That was my esteemed father's work, of course. Forgive me, my dear – stories to frighten naughty children with!' He kissed my hand; as was his habit, his lips lingered too long.

After he had gone, Giuliano said: 'The hiring of assassins and the procuring of virgins... that is how to make a career in Florence.'

I hushed him – the children were milling about us.

Vinta took my Deodata with him. I wonder if he will dower her, for she is already beyond the age for marriage, and without me to spy on, perhaps he will have no further use for her. I went into the kitchen and looked on the shelf where she kept her indenture, but it too was gone. I shall never see her again.

Giuliano must each day descend into the warren of lanes that is Venice to reach his orphans. When the days are short and he works late, I urge him to stay where he is, and not come home in darkness. At Easter he is always busy, so the children and I go across to the church we see from our windows, holding our candles, and await the resurrection of our Lord without him.

One early memory of our days here stands out. It was 6 December, the feast of St Nicholas, he who stealthily by night dowered the three daughters of a poor man, that they might not be compelled to earn their bread in dishonourable ways. It was fitting, then, that this saint's bounty might be invoked for the poor orphans of the Pietà – I mean of course Giuliano's Pietà, here in Venice – by a high Mass where my husband played and his little charges sang, and alms were collected for them. Leaving Tino at home with Tommasa, Filippo, Matteo and I were sculled to the Zattere. Filippo, of course, wetted his cuff, for though I told him not to, the temptation to trail his hand in the water was too strong for him. I wrung it out at the landing stage and urged him to fold the cuff back against his sleeve, for fear he would catch a chill – we live a long way from the dryer air of Florence.

The swell of the organ and the purity of those young voices lifted me closer to heaven, as beautiful music must always. I could read the blocks and lines and dashes by then, though I have never forgotten my dismay when, having learned to read words on a page, I found that I was still blind before a page of music. But after mastering one language, it was not such a burden to master another, and it was a joy to me that I could help my husband and that he trusted me above any other to transcribe for him.

My children showed some aptitude for music, and even Tino responded to it; his father played his lute to help him go to sleep. There was only one exception: Filippo. He loved to hear it, and would close his eyes and ask for something he liked to be played again and dance to it, too, but despite all urgings, he would not lift an instrument, though in our home they were to be found in every corner. Indeed, he became mulish, awkward with an instrument in his hands, and was like to break it not from wickedness but sheer clumsiness. Yet in the churches he would stand in front of a painting with his blue eyes wide and describe it to me afterwards in the minutest detail, and when I went back to look at it again, I saw that his memory was accurate. He would draw with any materials that came to hand, including in flour spilled on the kitchen table.

I was not surprised at this, for it was the pull of his blood. I wondered, looking at my son intent on a scrap of paper in a corner, how the Prince used his gifts.

I learned early that my meeting with the Prince of Mantua was already common knowledge here. I had just come out of Mass at San Giobbe, with the children gathered around me. Giuliano was not there, for he was of course required at the Pietà, on the other side of the city, but when he came home and saw my face he at once asked me what the matter was. It was only a gossiping woman who told me the story – reassuringly wrong in a number of details (according to her everything took place in the Prince's palace, which I had been denied). She had not seen me before and so asked, as is the nature of an inquisitive though friendly stranger, where I had come from, and on hearing Florence, could not hold back. Seeing my sudden pallor, the woman apologised for telling 'a decent wife and mother like yourself' such an indelicate tale. It would appear, though, that it was merely the story itself that was talked about – nobody knew the name of the girl. Why should they indeed? She was of little account.

You can bribe a servant, but once the briber has gone, that servant opens his pocket and his mouth to his friends in the nearest tavern. I thought of the man who had come in to pull the sheets from the bed – who had led me to my confessor – and the way he had stared at me. I wondered sometimes if I ever passed him on my way to the Pietà or if I might encounter him buying fish from a barge, he for his master, I for my family.

Vinta, you see, was so agitated about keeping his mission secret that he only drew attention to it. That story about my being the daughter of a German officer – why would such a girl merit so large an entourage, or guards posted at the landing stage? The promises made to that boy from Lucca were so exaggerated that he must have known something was being hidden. But even if he had been silenced, or that servant's tongue stopped with a knife, who could have prevented the Prince from bragging?

I went to confession regularly; not so frequently as I did in the Pietà, because I had to, but at least once a month. It is a habit I have been unable to break, though Giuliano smiled and said he wondered what dark secrets I hid from him.

In truth there was only one, for I wish I could hide that secret from myself. He never knew what happened on the journey away from Venice.

I did not go to San Giobbe, for the priests there knew me and would recognise my Tuscan tongue through the grille after three words. They were good men, and would not break the seal of the confessional, but I preferred to be unknown. I went at first to different places, seeking out larger churches frequented not only by Venetians. The Dominicans I avoided, though they have a fine church and the people speak well of them. Eventually, though, I found the courage to go to that church where I had insisted I be allowed to confess before I was put, wounded in my poor body and in my soul, back in the lettiga for Florence.

Our Lady was still there above the altar, her face turned up to heaven, her glory undimmed. It was on my third visit there, when I had knelt and crossed myself and told the shadowy form listening to me through the grille that I had once again sinned, that I heard the words, 'God bless you, daughter, for I have prayed for you always, that your life might be a happy one after all you have suffered.'

Not always did that unknown friar hear me, but regularly, yes. I say unknown, for I did not want to know who he was. I never waited for him to step out of that box, and nor did I go to Mass there because I did not want to hear his voice on the altar and give him a face. It was enough for me to know he was there, and that we recognised each other through our words, though we would not know each other if we were to pass shoulder by shoulder in a *calle*. 'For now we see through a glass, darkly; but then face to face: now I know in part; but then shall I know even as also I am known.' Well, that we shall know when all of this is over. So be it.

Chapter Twenty-Three

Inheritance

*Ogni famiglia ha di bisogno del padre, che la governi, e la
conduca al suo fine conveniente per li debiti mezzi...*

Every family needs a father to govern and guide it, to the most
appropriate ends

Francesco Tommasi, *Reggimento del padre di famiglia* (1590)

If any of my children were ever remotely important to those who
consider themselves my betters, it was Filippo, for the manner
in which he came to be conceived. Not then, nor since, have I
had any difficulty in getting with child. Some women would call
this a joy and others a curse. Just as the Joys and Sorrows of Our
Blessed Lady depend wholly on the life of her son, our Saviour, so
for me have my children brought me the greatest happiness and,
when they have been taken from me, dragged me down to the
profoundest depths of despair. Not one of them have I ever put
above another, and nor has Giuliano – not all men would have
accepted and loved Filippo as if he were his own. As their mother,
I write of them all.

On the feast of St Martin, in 1592, my daughter Tommasa entered
the world, to the delight and incredulity of her humble namesake.
We knew her at home as Masina. She was a beautiful child of

graceful proportions and grew ever more lovely; I do not believe only her father and I thought this.

Two years afterwards, on the feast of St Christina, Taddeo came into the world. I had a long and difficult travail and he was a puny child who showed little zest for life, and so was baptised at home within hours, with Zuan Trevisan of the Pietà standing godfather. I held him, caressed him, talked to him constantly, but this was not enough to keep him with me. Four days later, on the feast of St Martha, he died in my arms. *Laus deo.*

On the feast of St Margaret in 1595, I lost a life I was carrying within me, despite my prayers to that holy helper who protects women in childbirth. I had felt the child quicken, so he or she must have had a soul, but after there had been no movement for some days Master Marinello the doctor came, told me to carry a lump of clay at all times and to eat shrimp, but to no avail. Tommasa gathered up the traces of what was all too mortal in a pewter dish but would not let me see what she saw. With the help of one of the old men of the hospice, Giuliano buried what had been ours in the shade of his rosemary bush. They said prayers, and afterwards he laid pebbles in the sign of the cross. That is all.

24 August 1596

This is not the date of another child entering the world, but the day Filippo learned how he came to be born. He would be twelve years old before that year ended, old enough to be apprenticed and also, as he insisted, to be taken up the bell tower of San Marco. Giuliano put off this adventure as long as he could for, unlike Filippo, he has no head for heights. When the two of them returned, my husband was still pale, but my child ran to me and held me as though terrified he was going to lose me. I looked over his shoulder to where Giuliano hesitated in the doorway. Something had happened when they were out and I confess I did something ignoble because I wanted to know what. Only afterwards my husband came looking for me and told me he knew I had been listening the entire time.

They were in the little parlour with the door closed, but with the heat of summer the casement was open and they sat by it, in search of air. Masina napped upstairs. The others had gone out to play, so apart from muffled thumps and bangings from Tommasa up in the kitchen, the house was unusually quiet. I slipped outside in felted shoes to lean sweating against the wall. There was no one about in that shimmering heat but a rootling dog. He came up to me, but I stilled him with a hand on his nose.

'I am used to climbing cramped and steep stairs to reach organ lofts and musicians' galleries,' I heard my husband say, 'but you could almost ride a pony up that bell tower.'

I listened for Filippo's response but heard only obstinate silence. When eventually he spoke, I thought my son's voice more like a man's, not from its pitch, which was still a boy's, but for its tone.

'You still haven't answered the question I asked you when we were up there,' he said. 'About what Matteo said – about me sneezing differently from the others. I am not foolish, Father. You pretended not to hear me – and you a musician! I know you were trying to distract me when you asked me the names of the other bell towers. My sneeze is not the only way I am different from them, is it?'

'We are each one of us different, Filippo. Each of us unique in the sight of heaven.'

'Well, *you* are. You do not sound like us. Does everyone in Rome speak as you do?'

'I don't know. I have not been there for many years, so the Romans might not think I sound like one of them now.'

'Where was *I* born?'

'Florence.'

'Was Mother in labour long?' I heard Filippo ask. 'The way she was with Taddeo?'

Giuliano muttered something I couldn't catch. I moved closer to the window, dislodging a pebble. I held my breath, fearful I was going to be discovered.

'You weren't there, were you?' said Filippo.

'I am proud to call you son,' I heard Giuliano say, above the pounding of my heart.

'Though I look nothing like you, and what I have in common with the others is only what we all have from our mother.'

'You are my son because I have recognised you as my own, you bear my name and I love you as I love your brothers and sisters. That is what being a father means, to me. No, please, don't pull away like that, Filippo. Not if you love me at all.' That is when I started to weep.

'I have wondered about this a long time,' Giuliano went on. 'I didn't know if I should tell you, or if your mother should, and so I did nothing. And you have guessed.'

'I like to look into men's faces,' Filippo said, 'to see what it is they give of themselves to their sons and daughters. A nose? The shape of a lip? Or a glance? It is something I think about a lot. You know what made me first wonder? It was that time Camilla said to me that I laugh in a funny way – she meant differently to everyone else.'

'I remember. So does your mother. She warned me then not to speak, that it was too early. She said – hoped – you'd think nothing of that comment.'

'I thought everything of it – ever since. It opened my eyes to other things. I knew about the sneeze even before Matteo said anything. I looked at all the things my brothers and sisters did, whether it was holding a fork or brushing their hair, and then watched myself to see how I was different.'

'You are your mother's son. I saw her just once – from a distance – when she was with child; with you. I married her after you were born and given to the Innocenti.'

'The Innocenti? What is that, an orphanage?'

'The greatest in Florence.'

'Mother didn't want me?'

It took everything I had not to run inside and embrace my son.

'She did want you. Losing you, Filippo, nearly destroyed her reason. It was when Elisabetta was born that the loss of you finally overwhelmed her. And then she lost Elisabetta too. That was when I went to fetch you, to bring you back to her – you came at the same time as Tommasa.'

'Why couldn't she keep me before? What about my father – her husband...?' I heard my child's voice crack and knew he was on the edge of tears, so hard for a boy who thinks himself on the brink of manhood to show.

'Who am I? Who is *he*?' he asked.

'One of the richest men in all Italy.' I heard the love in Giuliano's voice, even as he at last admitted the truth. 'You have his blue eyes, his pale hair and skin – his sneeze and his laugh, too, it would seem. Your poor mother was given to him, a pure girl, an innocent, an orphan, living in what was an antechamber to a convent. They told her she would have a husband, a dowry, a home of her own – a family. The kind of thing Camilla and Masina play at with their friends. She did not understand at first what they wanted her to do, but they said her sacrifice would be to the glory of Florence.'

The silence could only have lasted two heartbeats, but standing out there it felt like an hour.

'So my father is a violator of virgins...' Where had our child learned such words? How did he *know*?

'Don't call him your father, Filippo. I am the one who loves you.'

There was silence, followed by rustling, and finally the muffled sound of sobbing. Giuliano was murmuring, too low for me to make out the words, but I knew that he was comforting Filippo, just as he had when he was a very little boy. But then Filippo shouted so loudly that I jumped.

'They whored my mother!'

I could not hear what happened next, for the belfry of San Giobbe sounded the hour. As the last reverberation ebbed away, I heard Filippo ask: 'Does he know of me?'

'He knows your mother was with child, that is all.'

'And I was abandoned...'

Giuliano told Filippo everything – or not quite everything. He spoke of the token, and how I never gave up hope. He spoke of the marriage of two strangers, but did not mention their bribe. He described households he knew of in Florence where a natural child lived in the same house as his father, usually because the man's wife was barren and he had no other heir, but that he had never known one to stay with his mother. I heard him explain that if even a widow's children are taken from her by her dead husband's family, what chance would a woman alone have? Gently but clearly Giuliano told our son that both he and I would have starved had I kept him, unless I had taken up a way of life that would surely have destroyed me utterly and would probably made a criminal of him. And finally, he said that I had been given no choice, deprived of my baby before I was even able to rise from childbed.

After that, it wasn't just Filippo's tears I heard, though I knew that Giuliano thought no son should see his father weep save at a graveside.

Eventually I heard Giuliano say, 'You are my son. I too comforted you, when you cried with the pain of your teeth breaking through. My heart turned to wax when you first smiled at me. And your mother is the purest and noblest of women.'

I pressed my hands against the wall for support, though the heat almost burned my palms, and closed my eyes. I could not remember ever feeling so tired. But then Filippo said, 'I love you too, Father. Forgive me, but I want to be alone for a while. Please tell my mother I know but let everything be as it was before.'

'I will go and find her now. Stay in here as long as you like. I will keep your brothers and sisters away.'

'No need. I want to go for a walk.'

Then of course I had to flee. There was only one door Filippo could come out of and I did not want him to find me there. I hid in the church. Giuliano knew me well enough that it was the first place he looked for me. He found me in the chapel of the Florentines, beneath the gaze of our Eternal Father and the Four Evangelists, in gleaming blue and white majolica.

'I knew you were there,' he said, lifting my face so I had to look at him. 'I always know when you are close.' Then he dried my tears.

That night after Giuliano loved me I cried in his arms. Afterwards, he told me that the Prince of Mantua and his duchess had come to Venice two months earlier, honoured by the Council of Ten. 'I recognised those terrible birds on the livery of the entourage I saw milling about before San Marco. I couldn't bring myself to tell you.'

I thought of that gold scudo tossed so negligently onto the bed where I lay, as though I were a whore. 'It matters to me not at all. I would not have wanted to see him.'

I lay awake that night until after the bell at San Giobbe chimed twice, wondering what it was that *you* had given me, Mother. Do I look like you, or like my father? Whose sneeze do *I* have? Whose eyes? Whose hands?

Chapter Twenty-Four

Vinta

My desire to learn my art, or better, my natural talent for it...
was so overwhelming that in a mere matter of months I rivalled
not just the good but the best young craftsmen in the field...
Autobiography of Benvenuto Cellini (1558)

Despite my contentment, I felt as though a shadow had pursued me
ever since we came to this city. There were times when I sensed it
as a physical presence, a quick sliding into a doorway as I looked
round, a feeling in my shoulders that someone watched me. And
then it entered my home. Filippo was fourteen years old when
Vinta's letter came – he was two years into his apprenticeship with
Master Jacopo di Palma. I knew the hand, of course, the moment
that paper rested in mine. The messenger called not long after
breakfast, but Giuliano was already walking across the city, and
as he was engaged for a Mass that evening, he would eat in the
Pietà's kitchen. So I had all day to face that folded paper, the smug
face of the Grand-Ducal seal. That lump of wax told me just how
dangerous a missive this was – it wasn't written in the cavaliere's
study, but in the Grand Duke's presence, perhaps by his dictation.

I was still a Florentine citizen.

Tommasa watched me in alarm as I beat carpets out of the
windows despite the coldness of the day, as I rubbed beeswax into

furniture that was already greasy with it and boiled water to scald the pots clean. The children were all out, Filippo at his master's studio, the boys with their tutor, the girls in the convent classroom.

We had learned to be happy here.

Standing in the pool of light by the candle to read the letter, Giuliano became very still. As I watched him, my heart beat so hard that my breast ached. At last he turned to me – though it couldn't have taken him long, for he always read quickly, and I realised he must have gone through the letter at least twice, an age while I stood waiting. He held it out to me, and by a trick of the light his eyes were huge dark wells.

I took it with shaking hands. 'Just tell me, Giuliano.'

'He wants Filippo. Read it.'

My dear Giuliano,

Now, as always, I take great interest in you and your family, for, as you might say, I have had a hand in creating it. I hear good reports of your eldest boy – I mean Filippo; that his natural high spirits have found some vent in the workshop of Master Jacopo. I have had a lifelong interest in fine painting – you may not have known this, but to forget myself in the study of a painting has been a regular solace for me, an escape, one might say, from the burden of the office I fulfil. I know that you have done the best you could for Filippo by apprenticing him to the most flourishing workshop your adopted city offers. Far be it from me to criticise, as a mere connoisseur who has never held a brush or ground colours in his entire existence, but my observation is that the painters of the Serenissima, while outstanding in their use of colour and tone and for their bravura, lack some of the discipline of the more classical canons of Tuscany – or indeed of Rome. The human body, as we know, is built on a foundation of bone, then muscle, then flesh, and one cannot have the latter without the careful articulation of the former. It is my humble opinion that in Venice, God's highest creation is sometimes depicted even by the greatest artists with all the slippery bonelessness of the fish that swim in the lagoon. Furthermore, the artist who trains in a workshop in Venice must confine himself to an easel, for in such a damp city as yours, your churches, though marvellous for their rich colours of stone and marble, gilt and oil paintings, are somewhat lacking when it comes to those paintings on plaster, that permit even the humblest illiterate worshipper to understand all the richness of scripture.

There is a painter here of considerable renown, in stature a little fellow but of immense energy, the most prolific of his class. He cannot accept all the commissions that are offered to him, for there is no public building or church or convent that does not seek him. My own coat of arms graces his work in the Annunziata, a favour granted me by the Grand Duke himself. Master Bernardino seeks a talented boy whom he can teach all his art and make his heir, for he and his wife had but one child, and he did not live. He has not yet found such a pupil, but I think I see a way to help him, and you.

Filippo must be fourteen now – ah, how time rushes past our ears! – and is making his way in the world. I am sure you would not wish to pass up this exceptional opportunity for him. He would be fed and clothed and housed and would work on the greatest commissions in Florence, both noble and ecclesiastical – I have, of course, always been aware of the financial sacrifice you had to make, the father of a growing family, in leaving our city in the way you were compelled to do. I will instruct our envoy in the Serenissima to settle with Master Jacopo directly for any disadvantage he and you may have in the breaking of the boy's indenture.

Please remember me to your most gracious lady, daughter of Florence. While the boy would lodge with his master, it would be a great honour to me if his parents would sleep beneath my humble roof when they bring Master Bernardino his pupil, and on any visits afterwards. Sadly my home is not the happy place it once was, for my dear wife has already gone to her eternal rest.

I kiss your hands,

Cavaliere Belisario Vinta

Giuliano caught me in his arms, or I would have sunk to the floor.

'How does he know all this?' I cried into his shoulder.

'He will have informers everywhere, Giulia. It would not be hard to come by that knowledge. What I do not understand is why we matter to him that much, that he wants us to be so beholden to him, after all this time.'

I could not look at him. 'He writes as though there is no question of our not accepting. But Filippo is too young!'

'He's not, you know. I was younger than he when I entered Cardinal Ferdinando's service. If *he* remembers me, then he may prove a good friend to our boy. I think we must consider this, Giulia, for his sake, though it would pain me as much as you to lose him.'

'What if we say no?'

My husband sighed. 'Vinta got me my engagement here. I am sure he could deprive me of it too. I don't think we really have a choice.'

'I will never, never, set foot in Vinta's house again!'

'Ssh – don't wake the whole house. You won't. I am sure we can lodge with Agostino.'

'Let us speak to Filippo, at least,' I said, clutching at threads. 'We must write to thank the cavaliere.'

'He is right about one thing, at any rate.'

'Oh?'

'Master Jacopo's figures *are* rather boneless.'

Have you ever heard the desperate wail of a mother cat whose kittens have been taken from her to be drowned? She will not be comforted and flashes her claws at anyone who comes near her. Yet within days she has forgotten and seeks out a patch of sunlight where she can warm herself and wash her whiskers as though nothing has happened.

I was as inconsolable as that wailing cat, but could not forget as she can. I felt as though I had been punished by the lopping off of a limb. I pulled my other sons and daughters to me and held them tight, one after the other, until each one wriggled out of my grasp. Yet Filippo's eyes danced with excitement.

Giuliano took Filippo to Florence himself and came back with comforting words about little Master Bernardino Barbatelli – or Poccetti as they call him, for his fondness for the tavern – and about the motherly old dame who is his wife. Agostino also promised to keep a fatherly eye on our boy. I tried to feel reassured.

My husband and my son lit candles in the church where my first daughter lies.

Filippo promised he would write, and he did, quite frequently at first. When his letters began to tail off, Giuliano strove to reassure me. 'That is a good sign. He needs us less.'

I still needed him. I'm his mother.

Chapter Twenty-Five

Dusk
Venice, 1604

Pray for us sinners, now and at the hour of our death
The Hail Mary

The story of a contented family is of no interest to anyone but its members, or, at most, those to whom it pays its taxes. Giuliano became active in the confraternity nearest to us. It was not a fashionable or wealthy *scuola* (as they call them here), but a modest community not long established, which quietly carried out its charitable intentions. It too was called the Pietà!

The confraternity was very kind to me and to my children.

Thanks to the interest of a fellow member, Matteo obtained a post in the lowest rungs of government. He writes a good hand and is diligent, so for at least one of my children I need not feel anxious.

Camilla has the most beautiful oval face, large grey eyes and my high forehead, the child who most resembles me, Giuliano always said. She would flush and cast her eyes down when men looked at her, which I saw them do often, but that only made them want to gaze on her even more. By sixteen she was assiduous in her prayers, and I wondered even if she might take the veil, though I would never suggest it. She was tractable to a fault, and I feared that she would say yes, only because I asked her about it, thinking that she pleased me.

All of my children, save Filippo, made music, but only Tino wished to follow his father. With the agreement of the orphanage, he became Giuliano's apprentice.

Masina was my prettiest, merriest child, the one who made the most noise beneath this roof. She was also the naughtiest, the thief of the last egg, the child who broke things and then pretended she hadn't. While she was quick to learn, she squirmed over her books. At Mass she would sigh, and fidget, and I would wish the homily was not quite so long.

I watched my husband waste before my eyes. First it was a cough that would not leave him, no matter how many tinctures I made for him, or how many inhalations. He seemed perpetually tired, and though he would sleep for as long as his cough allowed him, when he woke he was not restored. He begged me to get my rest somewhere else, for later he became so agitated at night that I was awake also. I heaped pillows against the bolster, for in the end he was only comfortable if he was almost sitting upright in the bed.

I resisted sleeping elsewhere. I had a day-bed brought into the room, but I would lie awake there listening to his laboured breathing, or that rattling cough. He asked, shamefacedly, for a spittoon, but I woke one night to find him sluicing it with water from the ewer and tipping the contents out at the casement. He didn't want me to see the splashes of his bright blood, but I had already found the stains on the linen, on his nightshirt.

His beautiful golden skin became grey, papery. Below his eyes it looked as if one could poke holes through to the darkness within.

To begin with, Giuliano insisted on still going to the Pietà, though he agreed to being sculled there. His illness had hobbled at last that loping stride with which he had crossed and recrossed Venice morning and evening. It was only at the direction of Trevisan, my poor Taddeo's godfather, that he eventually remained at home, and though that good man insisted on this for Giuliano's benefit, I saw the light of hope fade from my husband's eyes. Trevisan, or other of his colleagues, called regularly. Masses were said for his recovery. I found gifts of herbs from the hospice garden at my door. The orphans remembered their teacher in their prayers.

In the end, I slept in another chamber. I regret that still, leaving my poor husband alone to cough his life away. I only did so because the surgeon – Dr Marinello, who treated Giuliano without charge for the regard he had for him – said that I must, that I might not fall ill too, and leave my children undefended. I am ashamed to confess that there were some nights I did sleep, though I did not always. I was as faithless as the apostles at Gethsemane. I wrote to Filippo in Florence, copying my letters to Agostino in case my messages to my son went astray.

Afterwards, the doctor told me that he had sent me from the room not because he feared contagion, for, as he said, 'You survived all those years in those orphanages, huddled together with those other girls, unwashed, in those airless spaces.' No, he had feared that I would become so overset that I should die of exhaustion. Can one not also die of grief?

I called the priest to Giuliano on a day when he was so tranquil – though exhausted and pale from his endless fight for breath – that I thought there might be hope. I remember the oil glistening on his forehead, at the base of his throat, on his hands and feet, and he was able to swallow the Host without coughing.

Thanks be to God in his mercy.

That evening he asked that the shutters be opened, so that he might see that square of sunset above the houses of the Campo. I hastened to unlatch them, but as I turned round to him again his eyes widened in surprise and his mouth opened as though he would speak, and a great flow of blood gushed forth. Yet I thank Our Lady and all the saints that I was holding him when his poor head lolled and sagged, and he was still.

I don't know if I should write this to a mother, or how I would feel if one of my own daughters said it to me one day, but it comforts me to put it down. My husband was the only man who embraced me as I was made – those other two merely pushed up my shift. I did not want him to see me so to begin with, for those men who had prodded me and looked at me with glistening eyes while I grasped the hand of the Lady Camilla had made me feel like a beast in the marketplace. And I thought perhaps it was what whores did, but Giuliano said that he and I were like Adam and Eve in the garden before sin came between them. I was not sure he should speak that way. Then he said that our bed, with its hangings, was the tranquil sea of our life where we sported like dolphins in the waves. That was a happy image; I smile even now thinking of it.

He even liked those silvery marks that were left on my belly and breasts with each child. He traced them with a fingertip and said they were like the rings of an oak tree, with our sons and daughters like branches unfurling their leaves in the sunshine.

I wanted to keep his bloodstained nightshirt, a last memorial of his suffering, but the surgeon shook his head and gave it to Tommasa to burn.

Filippo was already travelling with the post when his father died. Three days later he stood by his coffin.

I don't know that the church of the Pietà has ever seen such a funeral, nor that any Medici or Gonzaga soul has ever been lifted up on such sweet voices, voices he trained. But when those orphans are gone – and I long gone – will others step respectfully around his grave slab, or stop to read the name carved there, or will their tread wear away the name of Giuliano Sperati into oblivion?

After he was buried, I began to go often to the Pietà, and not only to be close to him. I instruct the little girls in their red dresses in embroidery. Most of all, though, I hope I show them some love – and teach them that they are worthy of being loved.

*

Dear Lady Giulia,

I learned of your sad news from Master Bernardino and wish that I could find the right words to comfort you in your loss: I have written countless letters in my career but find with this one that my pen does not scurry across the page as it is accustomed to do. If my beloved Camilla was still at my side I know she would find more fitting words to use than mine. I am sure that you, like myself, feel keenly the loss of the beloved's presence in the dark hours of the night. One sleeps less well the more years have passed, don't you find? Since I learned of the departure of our dear Giuliano it is most often your face that comes to my mind as I restlessly turn my pillow.

Your son Filippo may be too modest to say this to you himself, so let me be the person to tell you that he is held in the greatest esteem by all who know him. Master Bernardino advances in years, and he and his lady are considering how best to prepare for their old age. The old painter is likely to go into the Innocenti, not because he is an orphan or ever has been, but so that he may work there for the good of the children and those who care for them, beautifying their surroundings with his brush in exchange for bed and board. His workshop, which already has more work than it can handle, will then be handed over to your son.

Dear Giulia, if you wish now to return to your native city, then please be aware that though old I am not without influence, and would be at your disposal to assist you in any way. Perhaps I might thus, in some small fashion, be able to make redress to you for the precipitate manner in which you left us? That did no honour to Florence, but at the time it seemed the only wise solution – forgive me. Consider my house to be yours should you need it; so clearly do I remember your virginal protests, your tears, when you submitted to the necessity of our examinations, that sometimes I feel you have never left it.

Too much time has passed since I last set eyes on you, but it is no exaggeration to say that you have been in my thoughts and prayers every day since. My contacts in your city have kept a paternal eye on you all these years, as they do with all Florentine citizens living there, and they keep me informed (you see that the habits of the loyal Grand-Ducal servant die hard, sweet lady). They tell me that the years have not dimmed the beacon of your beauty.

I kiss your hands.

Your humble servant,

Belisario Vinta

I knew I had to reply to his letter, but Matteo wrote for me, signing himself as the head of the household, which is what he was, with Filippo back in Florence. He thanked Vinta fulsomely and formally, but wrote that 'as I have become a Venetian citizen, though without rank, and have a modest career as a tax official, I believe I will, by the grace of God, be able to shelter my widowed mother in the house my father bought for us to live in. She wishes to be excused for not having responded herself to your kind letter, which gave her much comfort, but she is still prostrated by this cruel recent loss, though she recommends herself to you with tears of gratitude in her eyes.'

We went out together, not to find the next courier for Florence, as we did when writing to Filippo, but straight to the study of the Florentine envoy. He only had time to rise from his chair before I handed him our response myself, saying, 'This is for your master.'

Chapter Twenty-Six

Vendetta
January 1612

> *Await the time and place to take your revenge, for it is never*
> *well done in a hurry.*
>
> Italian proverb

I had thought that I would quietly spin my widowhood out to the end of its thread. Camilla had gone from the house, taken to the altar by Matteo and married to a merchant's son – one who did not stare like the others, but who sought out her brother at his place of work and asked if she was spoken for. Masina was still at home, refusing to countenance marriage. But there were still those, greater than me in the eyes of the world, who wanted to make sport with an undefended woman. In the pale early weeks of that momentous year I received a letter from Florence, and though I knew it was not Filippo's writing, I opened it with joy, for I recognised the hand of Agostino, now serving Grand Duke Cosimo II – his third Medici master.

I wish I had not been alone when I broke that seal.

Dear Lady Giulia,

I do not know how to write these words and hope to follow them soon with better. Your son whom I promised to look after has been arrested and has been taken I know not where.

The Podestà's men came for him – while he was at work in, of all places, the Prior's lodging at the Innocenti. Old Poccetti was out at the tavern, so he was up on the scaffolding alone, and they took him despite the Prior's protests. The Prior was able to tell me only that Filippo was not simply bound and carried off by these men, so that all who passed him on the street would know he had been arrested, but instead was blindfolded as well as pinioned, and forced into a covered wagon harnessed to two speedy horses.

I do not know how often Filippo writes to you – he is a young man, and a busy one – but I think you know he no longer lodges with his master. I have been to Filippo's rooms, searched his things, and questioned his landlord, but found no clues to either implicate or exonerate him. A little maidservant said she believed she had seen Filippo at the time he is supposed to have committed his crime, but when faced with the prospect of giving evidence quailed and said she could not be certain.

The charge is a serious one, of lewd and licentious behaviour with a nun of San Pier Maggiore, and for this the Podestà has the right to use whatever methods of interrogation he chooses to establish the truth. I have found a lawyer for Filippo and have gone with that gentleman to the Signoria to read the case against him. Two other sisters had gone to the Abbess with a description of the man they had seen, and a watchman claimed to have seen someone climb down from the roof and recognised him as someone he had seen in Poccetti's company – and all these descriptions fit Filippo, though each deposition fits each other so closely that the lawyer says that this in itself is suspicious. I need hardly tell you I believe not a word of this accusation.

The lawyer's task and mine is made almost impossible by the fact that neither of us know where Filippo is. We went firstly to the Stinche, carrying food and clothing and blankets, and though we eventually, by means of a bribe, got to see the captain, he would neither confirm nor deny that Filippo was within – though I could see that our visit was not a complete surprise to him. From there we went to the Bargello, but to worse treatment. One of the guards sent me sprawling in the gutter and would have served the lawyer the same way had not Messer Dardanelli, the governor, come back to his post to bawl out the guard and try, ineffectually, to clean the stink off my cloak. He was at least able to tell us that Filippo is not within his walls and we have reason to believe him, for he and the lawyer belong to the same confraternity. Our search for the witnesses is inconclusive, for we have been unable to find the watchman so far, and the nuns of course we are not allowed to see. The one whom he allegedly had relations with risks perpetual imprisonment within her convent, but we do not even know her name. They say, though, that one of the witnesses is a girl of the Martelli family, a cousin of that Martelli who caused so much offence that he was dismissed from his post. I fear that we are not looking at the administration of justice but are in the coils of a vendetta – a plan that has been hatched and nourished for years.

Your humble servant
Agostino of Pontedera

My son was to be tried for debauching a nun. I never believed that he had done such a thing, though I had a flicker of a thought that the Prince of Mantua would not have balked at a crime of that nature. Now I look back at those terrible days and ask myself why it had been deemed a fit thing to divert me, all unknowing, from the path that led to the veil of St Catherine, and deliver me defenceless into the embrace of the Prince, there to commit a mortal sin – but when the finger was pointed at his son and mine, that same sin was a crime for which Filippo might be put to death.

I tried to imagine Filippo clambering across the roof of the convent – in darkness! I know he is the only one of my children who doesn't fear heights, just another thing that marked him as being different. He had written to me before about the exhilaration he felt high up on scaffolding, painting onto wet plaster images which others would afterwards crane their necks to admire – until my fear meant the pads of my fingers dampened the pages he sent me.

My instinct was to run to Florence, to beat my fists on every door, and bathe the Grand Duke's shoes with my tears – but who would let one such as I get so close to him? There was, though, one man in that city who never missed anything, who had followed the coffins of three Grand Dukes and now served the fourth. If anyone knew where my son was, or if he was even still alive, that man was Belisario Vinta.

Chapter Twenty-Seven

Mantua
1612

Forse che sì, forse che no

Maybe yes, maybe no

The cryptic motto that appears ten times within the labyrinth design of the wooden ceiling of the Hall of the Labyrinth in Vincenzo Gonzaga's apartments in the Ducal Palace, Mantua, placed there in 1601 on his return from his third crusade against the Turks

My letter to Vinta was written straight away, and I indicated that I should follow it. When Tino and I scurried across Venice to the Florentine envoy, the man looked at me this time with barely a word; I could see he had expected my visit. For the shortest time I felt something like relief that I had acted swiftly, before I was again overwhelmed by the question: what next? Or better, where next? Tino voiced my thoughts before I did, thus reassuring me that my idea was not mere foolishness.

'Mother, should his father not be told?' And then he took my two hands between his, and said: 'If you wish it, then I shall accompany you.' And so he and I took the same road that the Prince had taken when he left me and Venice all those years ago.

As the wagon bringing us into Mantua lurched on the cobbles Tino took my hand. In that moment the mist that hung like a pall over us for most of our wearisome journey cleared and the sun shone on the calm waters of the Mincio girdling that city.

In the lodgings I paced up and down like a madwoman, until Tino held me by my upper arms and told me gently that if I didn't stop, others in the house would complain. He sent downstairs for something to eat, but I had to force it down. Then he made me lie down, though I did not sleep, but watched him sitting at the table until the candle guttered. I felt weary of life, but knew I had to go on, for I would have been giving up on my own child.

Twenty-eight years had passed since I met him, Mother, but I thought heaven must have been smiling on every woman who shared that title, for the very next day was the one when the Prince granted audiences to his petitioners. I took a great risk, for I didn't tell them at the palace the real reason for my visit, but said I wished to ask for a place for my son as a musician, given that he had a widowed mother and an unmarried sister to support. The young man who received my petition clearly heard many of this kind and showed no surprise.

I could think of no better stratagem to reach that man whose child, for all I knew, lay in a dungeon in Florence where he could not know what time it was or if the sun shone or hid his face in shame.

The palace was a city in itself, a labyrinth of passageways opening out into chambers so high that I hurt my neck just looking upwards, but I was led forward so quickly that I didn't have time to gaze, only hoping that I would also be escorted out afterwards for otherwise I might have wandered there forever. The functionary I followed had spoken to Tino, not to me, and raised his eyebrows when I answered him instead, saying that the petition was mine alone.

'Then he must wait here,' said the man. I opened my mouth to say something to Tino but the Mantuan was already five strides away.

Those vast spaces were cold, and no fires burned in the grates.

At last we arrived in an antechamber, and the servant who brought me there motioned me to wait, and then disappeared. Far above me the room at first appeared open to the heavens, and then I realised that the expanse of blue and the clouds were the work not of God but of a talented artist. Below that ceiling, all around the room, were corbels, painted as heads of beings grimacing with the effort of holding up the sky. I saw an eagle, an angry man, a woman I knew was a woman for her breasts were displayed. And between them hung curtains which were not curtains but were also painted, and beyond them I glimpsed the hooves of animals – horses, but not only horses, fantastical creatures I didn't recognise, standing in the painted open air. Was that palace not big enough but that these tricks must be used to make it appear greater still?

Then I looked down, mortified, for I saw the room was full of guards, young men who stared at me insolently, though I was of an age to be their mother. I shifted against the wall at my back, but it was hung with a tapestry, and it moved with me and startled me. I took out my rosary and passed it through my fingers, looking at it, rather than at those soldiers, or at the other silent supplicants.

Without the tolling of the hour at Sant'Andrea, I would have lost count of how long I stood in that antechamber.

Others were brought up to that room after me, but I saw them first only as a blur of faces, as separate as trees and as indistinguishable, though I noted that I was the only woman, and hence the only mother. I wondered how I would know it was my turn, and rather than challenge anyone there, resigned myself to waiting even if everyone else was called before me. Indeed, I thought that might be better, for if there was no petitioner after me, the Prince perhaps would be more likely to bring the audience to an end by accepting my plea. I had completed the entire rosary, but held the beads in my hand for support, though when I looked down at them later I saw that I had wound them around my hands so that they chained me.

To divert myself, I furtively observed the standing figures through my veil, wondering what it was they could have to ask, and then of course saw that each was simply a person with his own anxieties and burdens. One of them looked like an artisan; he seemed not to know what to do with his large, calloused hands, for without tools to handle, they fidgeted constantly, clenching and unclenching. I wondered if he had not been paid. Another, from his profile and some oddities of dress, I recognised as a brother to the men I saw going in and out of the sheer walls of the ghetto in Venice. My legs ached; I longed to sit down, but didn't know if I should – did one not have to remain standing in such close proximity to a prince? No one had availed himself of the stone seats in the window embrasures, and there was nowhere else to sit. Nor could I go back the way I had come, even had I wished to, for I didn't know the way, and to pass back through the double doors to this chamber, I would have had to pass two guards with crossed pikes. The doors in the far wall, leading to the room beyond where my quarry sat, were similarly guarded.

I thought of the guards outside that little house in Venice, whose faces I had never seen, for I had glimpsed only the crowns of their heads. I wondered if they still lived, and if they ever spoke of that strange vigil. Then I realised I must have made a sound, for three or four faces turned to stare at me.

I turned my back on them, my face burning – let them think what they would. I murmured a prayer to St Ivo, patron of widows and orphans.

I was torn from that comfort by the crash of steel as the crossed pikes separated. Looking round I saw a tall young man, slightly stooped, and pale with working indoors. He was standing on the threshold of the further room, smaller than this one. This appeared to be empty save for an enormous, curtained box, something like a bed.

'Moisè of Ancona,' he called out. The summoned man bent his head in acknowledgement and disappeared into the chamber. The doors were closed from within, and the pikes crashed back into position. Sant'Andrea gave out the half-hour before the doors reopened. He did not reappear; I supposed he must have been ushered out through doors into rooms beyond, brought down another staircase in this endless rambling building, so that he might not confer with anyone still waiting here. Or what if instead he was confined somewhere at the Prince's pleasure? I was engulfed suddenly in a wave of heat despite the chill of that chamber, its fireplace empty even of fire-irons. There was nothing to do but wait. Other names were called, others rustled away. The pikes clashed again and again.

Finally, my own name, spoken as it if were a question. Then, 'My lady?' and I realised that the young functionary was standing in front of me, looking at me curiously.

'Are you unwell? I have been repeating your name.'

'No... no.'

'Well, follow me, then. The Prince has had a tiring morning, and he is not well. His gout... We should not keep him waiting any longer.'

Gout. But of course, so many years had gone by. It was impossible that he was still the man I remembered – I was no longer that girl. I trembled and caught at the young man's sleeve. He looked in astonishment first at my face, then at my clutching fingers. 'Forgive me my impertinence,' I said, feeling the heat creep up my throat. I uttered a silent prayer: *May God grant that this young man looks at me as he would at his own mother and pardons my foolishness.*

And then at last I was in the ducal presence. Or was I? The doors closed behind me, and the guards clashed their weapons again. But here within was silence. I looked upwards, and into a labyrinth of blue and gilt which filled the ceiling, in which the words 'perhaps yes, perhaps no' repeated themselves along each arm of the maze. Perhaps yes, perhaps no. What would the Prince say?

The young man swished quickly past me and lifted a curtain into that strange catafalque.

'Your Highness?'

'Is the woman young?'

'She is veiled. But I think not.'

'Bring her into our presence.'

It was his voice, and not his voice. Deeper, more tired – bored, evidently. I thought, *He won't remember me. I must be much changed.*

The young man pulled back the curtain fully and motioned me forward. In that stuffy twilight I could make out the bulk of a man but could not bring myself to look in his face. I saw puffy ankles pushed into tight, jewelled shoes, silk hose, a doublet so encrusted it looked as stiff and uncomfortable as chainmail. I curtsied low, grateful to my plain, enveloping widow's dress as if it instead were a suit of armour, and put my lips forward to kiss the beringed fingers held languidly out to me. I remember that I held my breath for I did not wish to smell him. The hand was fat, slightly spotted, sparsely haired, but what I noticed most were the knuckles, inflamed and swollen. Those rings evidently did not come off. With a spurt of horror, I wondered if he would be buried with them, so embedded were they – or if they would be cut free.

'Look at me, lady,' he said.

I raised my eyes but could not swallow my gasp of surprise. Vincenzo frowned slightly, as if trying to remember something. From behind the safety of my veil I observed him. His face was swollen, florid: his eyes looked smaller, embedded in cushions of flesh, his forehead higher than I remembered for that tawny hair, faded to sand, was sparse, retreating into a tuft on the crown of his head like the crest of a cockerel, and into a ring of limp tow growing just above his ears. I remembered how silky his head once was, but his hair had not been plentiful even then. That crest was stiffened with something – flour and water, perhaps. He looked ridiculous, an ageing popinjay, but the worst was his skin, inflamed and scaly around his eyes and across his nose, angrily reddening his cheeks. There was something odd about that nose. I remembered its fleshy tip, slightly upturned to give him a look of arrogance. That tip looked larger now, not only because of that dry redness, but because the nose above had somehow retreated, sunk back into his face. Vincenzo Gonzaga looked like a man who carried all his sins in his visage. I had remembered him as tall, taller than the others enclosed with us in that little house in Venice. He looked tall no longer, but perhaps this impression was only due to his wider girth, or to the bulk of those creaking, stiffened garments.

There was nothing here to recall the young man who had come smiling to me in his shirt, the man who broke my virgin heart. I thought of my Giuliano, so straight and true even into his fifties, his hair grey as iron but dense, his cleanly narrow body and golden skin, his long musician's fingers. This corrupted, bloated, encrusted figure was not worth his shadow; this was a man I had thought I loved but who had brought me only tears. But he was Filippo's father.

'Now you can see me, but I am not to see you. Lift your veil, if you please!'

I took hold of the corners of the thin cloth with trembling fingers and turned it back over my head. I saw the idle curiosity, the reflex reaction of the libertine to any female face, even one no longer young – and then recognition dawned. I could not resist a quiver of satisfaction. *I am not so changed, then. Not so much as he, perhaps.*

Without taking his eyes from my face, he croaked: 'Leave us!'

I gasped. All of this planning, all of my little courage bound up in this moment, only to be dismissed?

'Not you!' he hissed, and he leaned forward and momentarily took hold of my forearm, a spasm of pain crossing his face as he did so – the first time he had touched me after all those years. I remembered Vinta interrogating me as I sat there in my shift: *he was embracing me with both arms,* I'd said, and I shivered, with a distant echo of the lust I had felt in that moment. Behind me, I heard the young secretary getting to his feet and gathering together his papers.

'Wait!'

'Your Highness?'

'Bring the lady your chair.'

There was a short silence. 'My chair?'

'That's what I said, you fool!' roared the Prince.

'Forgive me...' There was a scrape of wood on the marble floor, and the chair was placed behind me. I sank into it in disbelief, as I heard the secretary knocking softly at the far door. Vincenzo's eyes did not leave my face until the door closed and the sentries crashed back into position. I wondered if the young man would wait there, not eavesdropping but listening for his master to shout out for him, to dismiss me.

'Giulia!' he said and took my hand in his distorted one. In his look of roguish surprise there was the faintest glimmer of the swagger from that enclosed bedroom, the sweat and semen on the sheets, that briny smell. *We have worked well, have we not?* he'd said to Vinta.

'I thought I should see you again, sweet orphan.'

I said nothing, for I could not understand what he meant. He smiled: he had teeth of polished wood.

'How does the world know you now?'

'As the widow of Giuliano Sperati, once musician to the court of Florence, later organist of the institute of the Pietà of the Republic of Venice,' I said.

'Whoever you say you are, you are still beautiful. The years have spared you as they did not spare my poor wife – only that she was no vision of loveliness to begin with. And now the worms have her, and will have me too before long, and she will never again be able to complain of my straying from her side.'

I inclined my head. 'I am sorry, Your Highness.'

'Ah! Well, so am I. Eleonora admirably carried out the role allotted to her. A wise counsellor – not that I listened that often, but I was glad when I did – and an irreproachable mother.' He looked me up and down. 'Tis a pity I did not love her.'

I wished he had spared me that.

'She suffered an apoplexy that did not kill her straight away, but which left half her face palsied, with her mouth drooped out of shape. I pitied her, and perhaps if I loved her at all it was when I saw her reduced like that, though she and I had not been husband and wife for the best part of fifteen years. She drooled like an idiot child and had to have a woman with her at all times to wipe her face – for half a year or more. But you—'

'My husband was granted a good end,' I said, but I didn't want to describe Giuliano's death to the Prince. It would have felt like infidelity.

'Were you happy?'

'Yes. I was the happiest of women. He was the best of men.'

'How fortunate... but I am sure,' and here the seducer's smile flickered again, 'that you never forgot the first man who loved you.'

Love, he says now!

'Never.' *Yet I learned that it is not the first who counts in the end, but the last.*

'Sir—'

'I must tell you, my little Florentine fig...'

He saw me start, and said, 'Forgive me, not the words to use with a respectable widow. *I* think of marrying again. The Duchess of Mondragone has a dowry of four hundred thousand scudi. No test, of course, will be required of me this time.'

I did not like his mocking tone.

'May I wish Your Highness well in your endeavours—'

'It is not good to live alone. One is tempted, though when I enter the lists these days I often struggle to raise my lance.'

I bowed my head. I did not dare interrupt him.

'I have asked my Chamberlain to make enquiries. The duchess is young – she might be too demanding. And my children would not welcome a full cradle. No, what I would really like is to have my Margherita by my side again, if they will let her out of her cloistered prison.'

'A nun!' I exclaimed, in spite of myself.

'My Margherita went most unwillingly to have her hair shorn. Here, poor girl, she sang like a bird in a gilded cage, and laughed, and danced, and loved to organise masques... a very fetching one, as I recall, with female warriors. There was an Atalanta of the company who was most accommodating – for my wife, of course, could not accommodate me.'

He paused, and I opened my mouth to tell him my petition, but he went on confidently: 'I shall find better surgeons. I shall breach that fortress at last – that is to say, I shall try.' He frowned. 'I still remember her screams – those bunglers! Perhaps that barrier will have atrophied with time and will crumble at a new assault. But if a breach cannot be made, then she and I will live serenely as brother and sister, and I shall slake my ardour elsewhere... what remains of it.'

I would have done anything to stop this flow of words, but I didn't know how. Then his voice hardened. 'You see an old man, Giulia, where once you had a young one. You remember, I broke three lances in you in the space of one night! I can only dream of such prowess now.'

I turned my face away, longing to pull down my veil.

'Please, sir, this is not seemly. I am not a young woman – I came only that you might hear my petition—'

'All my life I have had young women to service my every whim. This body has drooped, and aged, and become dropsical. It has made its owner cry out at the stings of gout, cry in frustration at the stiffness of joints that were once pliable, but the bodies that lay in my bed were always young. Their faces, though... they were compliant, accepting, sometimes avid for something that was not of my person – for jewels, fine clothes. I am convinced that some at least pretended to a pleasure they did not feel. You, maiden of Florence, cried out in pain but then in pleasure. Of that I am sure.'

Despairing, I sank my head to my breast, trying to hide my face.

'There! That little gesture! How could I have forgotten it?'

'I would not please you now.'

'I don't believe you. I have never forgotten the expressions that crossed your face in that room: modesty, but also desire. They told me that you wept when they said you would not see me again. But dear lady... why do you weep now? I can tell you that you would please me still. I fear that what I have become would not please you.'

I shivered, for he had gone straight to the truth.

'I didn't come here to talk of what we did, Your Highness. You must know that I had no real choice in the matter. We were both puppets on a stage that was bigger than either of us.'

'That is true.'

'I would have done anything to have escaped that orphanage.'

'And you have. And well, judging by the quality of the weeds you wear. I cannot believe you to be indigent. But if you did not come to talk of what we did – a fond memory, you must admit, for us both – then why, gentle lady, did you come?'

'I came, sir, to talk of our son.' And then I handed him Agostino's letter.

*

'Of course I will act.' Vincenzo reached for a little bell sitting on the scrivener's desk and rang it with force. It seemed as though the young man had been waiting for nothing else, from the speed with which he came through the door.

'Two letters, Silvio – no, three – all to Florence. The first to our cousin Cosimo; you know the form. Then send a copy of it to his minister – we all know it is Vinta who rules, but must observe the formalities – and another copy to our own envoy. Ready?'

'Your Highness.'

'*It has come to our notice that our natural son, begat by us in consequence of the conditions imposed on us by Grand Duke Francesco and Her Highness his consort before we entered into matrimony with our beloved and much missed Eleonora, is under arrest and languishes in an unknown prison. Recognised by his mother's husband, he goes by the name of Filippo Sperati* – that's right, isn't it?'

I nodded.

'*...and as that lady, now widowed, has led a quiet and irreproachable life we do not believe that her child's true parentage is broadly known. At the time your esteemed minister the Cavaliere Vinta handled all matters relating to the case with the greatest discretion and is personally acquainted with all its details. We do not hesitate therefore to suggest that he could again be trusted to bring this urgent matter to a conclusion satisfactory to all parties.*

'*We do not presume to enter into the merits of the case against Filippo Sperati nor to interfere in the just processes of a sovereign state, but it would be our greatest pleasure if his accusers might speedily be appeased by his banishment from the territory of the Grand Duchy of Florence, and that he be supplied with letters of safe conduct that he may live out his expulsion here in our dukedom of Mantua. We are certain, remembering our ties of blood and mutual affection, that our request will be met with a speedy response, and that Filippo Sperati be not subjected to any affliction either in body or purse. We kiss your hands...* and so forth.'

The second letter was soon underway.

Grasping his stick, Vincenzo hobbled out into the room, and banged on the door. 'You there!' he shouted at one of the soldiers. 'Tell them to saddle Eraldo and Freccia.'

'The berbers?'

'You heard me. And bring Antonio and Egidio here.'

He stumbled back to where I sat watching the scribe. 'When you've finished there, get them money – enough for the journey and so that my horses can be cared for at the first stage until my men return for them.' I saw the young man nod, but his pen didn't slacken.

The double doors opened again to a manservant carrying a tray covered with a linen cloth.

'*Out with you*,' shouted the Prince. 'Where are the men I want?'

The servant backed out without a word. The Prince looked at me as though he had forgotten I was there.

'Ah! Perhaps you are hungry.'

'No, sir, I cannot think of eating.'

I watched the young man scratch his quill across the page. Now that my goal had been achieved, and so readily, a new anxiety set in. Was I in time? Three letters had to be written, all saying the same thing... could the boy not be quicker?

Then two knights were announced, older men, one of them missing an eye. The glance of his remaining eye was proud, and he disdained to cover that horrible dark cavity. The Prince grasped his stick and motioned them to the door. I couldn't hear what he said to them save his final words: 'Do not come back until you have him.'

That was when I started to cry.

*

Wine was brought, then fruit and eggs, and the Prince urged me to eat, but I was able to sip only a little wine. We were alone – properly alone. The scribe had gone, the soldiers guarding the doors had retreated to the chamber where I and the other petitioners had waited, only hours ago though it seemed to me days. As I cradled my goblet I thought of those two knights – 'my most trusted men,' the Prince had said, 'by my shoulder on my last crusade' – riding the Prince's swiftest horses, their noses towards Tuscany. What more could I do now but follow them?

'I should leave you, sir,' I said, 'but know that you have the undying gratitude of a mother.'

'No. You must wait here until our son is returned to us.'

'I am at your command, sir – only Vinta expects me.'

'Let my letters, my knights, do their work. It pleases me that you remain here a little longer as my guest.'

'There is my son – my husband's son. I must tell him.'

'He is a musician, is he not? Was he not the subject of the petition you brought?'

I coloured at that. 'I beg your forgiveness. I only wanted to be sure I would see you.'

'And you thought you might not if you told the real reason.'

'I thought I might be prevented.'

He laughed then. 'I do believe you are as astute as our old friend the cavaliere.'

I suppressed a shudder.

'Let that petition stand, Giulia, for I am always in need of musicians. We shall have your son brought here as our guest also. Humour an old man in the meantime and let him show you something. Give me your arm.'

'Not old, sir,' I said, but I helped him up all the same. Leaning on me and grasping his stick in his other hand, he led me through the further door and deeper into his apartments. I had never seen such richness, not even in the most heavily endowed churches. Perhaps there are such places in Venice, but they have never been open to me.

He came to a halt in a bedchamber, but turned his back on the great canopied bed and led me instead into a gleaming little barrel-vaulted room that led off it – a chapel. Vincenzo released me, and genuflected slowly towards the altar, trying to suppress the groan of pain that escaped him as he rose. I dropped on one knee also, and for the first time ever the joint gave out a muffled crack.

'Did we appreciate our youth when we had it, Giulia?'

'I don't know. I only know that I have had much to be thankful for, and because of your generosity, still have. What was it you wanted to show me?'

'Here, above this prie-dieu. Our agent in Venice acquired it.'

He pointed to a tiny picture in a gilded frame that almost engulfed it. It was about the size of my hand, from the wrist to the tip of my longest finger, and no wider than a handspan.

'It is a jewel,' I said, gazing at the curly child in Our Lady's arms, at her gentle smile.

'*Oh!*' I cried, and put my hand to my mouth, for my voice was loud in that enclosed space. The Prince was at my shoulder – I could smell him now, the sweetish scent of something decaying.

'You see? You have been with me these past five years. That is what I meant when I said I had thought I should see you again.'

Our Lady's smile was my own. I remembered Filippo coming home to dine with us, his face bright with excitement and pride. *Master Jacopo said I was so good at faces that I should finish the picture. A painting on copper – work as finicky as a goldsmith's, I think, for the paint doesn't soak in and so must not be applied too dilute, lest the colours run.* He could only have been about thirteen or fourteen at most. *Unless he's painting a portrait my master's faces all look the same, you see.* Giuliano had reproved him for that.

'He did this,' I whispered. 'Filippo painted my face. I never knew.'

Vincenzo said nothing, but leaned his stick against the prie-dieu and, putting his hands on my shoulders, kissed my forehead.

'God smiles on your mission. He will bring us back our son. Now I should take you back to yours.'

Chapter Twenty-Eight

Palazzo Te

> *Non sono, ohimè, non sono*
> *quel ch'altra volta fui, ma un'ombra mesta*
> *un lacrimevol suono,*
> *una voce dolente...*

I am not, alas, that which once I was, but am now a wretched
shadow, a tearful groan, a mournful voice...

Torquato Tasso, set to music by Benedetto Pallavicino when
in the service of Vincenzo Gonzaga, translation by Iain Fenlon,
Music and Patronage in Sixteenth-century Mantua (1980)

The following morning, a carriage came to our lodgings. Dark
and plain, free of any coat of arms, it looked to me less like the
property of a prince than the vehicle of someone who did not want
to be noticed.

'We can walk,' I said, puzzled.

'The Prince wishes you to come to his summer palace,' said
the courtier.

Summer palace, I thought, *in this cold*.

To begin with, I shrank back in my seat, leaving the canvas
over the windows. Outside all was tumult, and despite the protests of the coachman, we made slow progress through what
must have been crowds, not only of humans but of livestock.
The courtier sat within, so I did not feel free to talk with my

son, instead looking at my hands in my lap, but was grateful for Tino's nearness nevertheless.

After some minutes of this, the hubbub reduced, and the horses set up a gentle canter.

'The Prince would wish you to see this,' said the courtier, leaning over to pin back the canvas.

I looked out on an avenue of trees and, at the end of it, a long, low building, shimmering in the pure winter sunshine of that morning, of rough-cut creamy stone yet massive as a fortress. I remember the echo of the horses' hooves as the carriage passed under the archway. In the courtyard within, someone opened the door. I expected another servant, but it was the Prince himself.

He greeted my son with courteous condescension, and as quickly dismissed him.

'Stay here in the guard-house, where they have instructions to look after you. We shall talk of your appointment later.'

I do not think I have ever seen such a beautiful place. Within was a mirage of colonnades, a long low creamy temple of a building reflected in bright water, its many rooms covered with paintings of such exuberance and abandon that I had to look away. I remembered then, that the Prince had spoken of such a place when I was shut in with him in Venice – but it had seemed as remote to me as the moon.

'This was my lair – my grandfather's old pleasure garden, where he kept the woman he loved. You see that nude painted up there? Olympias seduced by Jove. That's a portrait of her, they say.'

I could not suppress a gasp, for that image left nothing to the imagination. I thought of Vinta and his disgusting little statuette.

'I kept my Agnese here,' said the Prince, 'over my wife's protests. That boy you saw – the one who wrote those letters – was born here.'

'Your son?'

'Silvio, my favourite son, though you might not think it the way I abuse him. It is the pain of my knee that makes me irritable. I prefer him over those that came from my marriage bed. My heirs take after the Lady Eleonora. They have her long, mournful chin, that endless nose, her humourlessness, but none of her good sense. I trust none of them. My second son in particular – Ferdinando – has inherited my vices without my joy in them. But my wife insisted he be given to the church; she was always very pious. He's a cardinal in Rome. He's not my only cleric: Silvio's older brother is one also, and his sister a nun. So you see, Giulia, the Church benefits from my sins! I told the Holy Father himself that, after he wrote to me complaining that I led a dissolute life and set a bad example.'

Without thinking, I said, 'What does their mother say?'

'Agnese? Ah, she is too busy consoling herself for my loss with a man young enough to be her son. I found her a husband, of course, and ennobled him. Afterwards, I even provided him with heirs! It pleases me to be generous, you see.' He laughed at his own wit, while I could not even manage a polite smile, but as quickly his expression turned to a rictus of pain. 'My damned knee!'

'Will you not sit, sir? I tire you!' I pulled over a leather buttoned chair, and he creaked into it.

'What have I done to deserve this suffering?' he cried. 'A week ago, Giulia, they burned an aged Jewess for witchcraft, beneath the windows of my palace. *Her* agony is over – while I am tormented daily... I do not encourage such spectacles myself and will not watch them. She was probably only some foolish old woman who was losing her wits, and her worst sin was her ugliness, but those meddlesome friars *will* rouse the people, and the peace must be kept. It was that or burn the houses in the ghetto, and where would this noble house go for loans the next time the Holy Father or the Venetian delegation deigns to visit? I am expected to provide a splendid show, you see.'

I felt sick. I thought of that old woman's sons and daughters, unable to do anything to prevent their mother's catastrophe, in terror for their own lives. But the Prince did not notice my discomfort.

'I had to hobble off to another part of the palace,' he said. 'They were throwing bulbs of fennel into the flames to sweeten the stench of burning flesh, but that did nothing to stifle her screams... My doctors tell me that smoke quickly engulfs the lungs, rendering the victim insensible. I don't believe them. My poor knee, though, is aflame with the torments of hell, and has been so, with occasional remissions, for more than twenty years. I even had to return from a crusade because of it. I have always taken their advice – but blood-letting, mud packs, baths, tinctures, spring water brought all the way from Flanders, have done little to ease my pain. I took the waters in the Low Countries, and in Naples, yet I am sure it was not the bathing that made me feel better but the distraction to be had in those resorts. And now even those joys are harder to come by.'

'I am so sorry,' I murmured. I could not look at him, in his towering self-love.

'You remember Donati, don't you?'

'Yes!' I said, looking up in surprise.

'He was closer to me than a father. When he died, he left me all his books and engravings. Kind of him, wasn't it?'

I remembered Donati. I remembered his hands on me in Florence.

'He thought I wasn't beautiful,' I blurted.

The Prince laughed at that until his eyes streamed, and I feared he would do himself harm.

'Oh! Oh, Giulia! He told me that my Medici princess *was*! He was wrong there, too. I made a great fuss of her in public, made sure they knew I carried her portrait with me everywhere – all to cover up my dismay. Donati said he was only thinking of her capacity for childbearing. You *were* beautiful, Giulia, you still are. If Vinta had let me take you with me, you would have lived here – right here.'

'You would have tired of me too, sir.'

'Oh? Well, possibly. I'd have found you a husband, though.'

'Vinta did that.'

'Ah! Yes, of course.' He tapped his stick a few times on the floor, then changed the subject.

'This place will look better two months or so from now. They'll come to sweep it clean, and those tables will be uncovered and polished, and carriage-loads of food and wine brought, and lights, and we will have masquerades and feasting until dawn. But perhaps not, Giulia, for your poor Prince no longer has the stamina or the will for what delighted him once. No matter what gifts he makes in return for firm flesh and strong white teeth, if the fox cannot be coaxed from his lair... Oh, dear Giulia, you could have anything you wanted of me now, if you would only humour a sickly and ailing man.'

'I demand nothing of you. Our son will be free, that is all. That is everything. But my body would not please you, for it bears the signs of all the years, all my children.'

'Ha! I wouldn't see the signs, my eyes are so clouded now. If you would let me take your face in my hands I wouldn't see it as clearly as if I stood two paces from you. Sometimes, you know, I ask them to bring me the beautiful things I have bought, that I may touch them: Paduan bronzes, ivory Madonnas. My paintings I must look at from a distance if I am to see them at all. I can barely write now and prefer to be read to. I think my sons wish only that I would shuffle off before I spend any more of their inheritance.'

'I am sure, sir, that if my firstborn – our son – had not been restored to me after that first year of life in the orphanage—'

'A son of mine, in an orphanage? The scoundrels.'

I wondered then what he really had been told, or how much he had cared, but went on. 'Without him, I might have resented the presence of my other children, though I would always have loved them as a mother. Filippo, sir, is my most beautiful child, though I have never said so to him nor to his brothers. The thought that he might twist on a rope, his agony laughed at by half of Florence, his poor face all swollen—'

'Giulia, Giulia! Don't cry. He will be free by now, I am sure of it – he is on his way.' He took my hands. 'Let us walk on, for my joints grow stiff sitting here. Will you let me lean on you?'

'Gladly, sir.'

'I wish you would not speak so formally to me – if you love me at all then I should be *tu*, not sir.'

'I... yes, only it is strange in my mouth. The only man I have ever addressed familiarly was my husband – and of course my sons. I loved Giuliano. He was the best of men. I want to remain faithful to his memory.'

'You have been happier than I, sweet Giulia. I have found diversion, but never contentment. And now the light is waning, and I am afraid. Let us leave now – this place is icy. I want to show you my real home.'

'Tino?' I said.

'He has been returned to your lodgings.'

I felt the weight of him on my arm as that day he led me deep into his labyrinth. I remember a vast gallery, so long and so crowded that I could barely make out the doors at the far end. The deep windows facing to the south made a bath of sunlight reflected in the Murano mirrors opposite. We moved slowly among the petrified figures of marble and bronze, the inlaid tables, the gently swaying ivory figurines, and Vincenzo talked. I felt the eyes of his silent servant on my back. The Prince could remember everything about his treasures, how he had acquired them, from whom, how much they had cost him – dizzying sums. He talked of them, I thought, with the kind of detail some fathers remember only of their children.

'This one I love,' he said, pausing before a marble figure of a crouched, naked woman. One knee was raised, the other bent to the ground, and she looked over her shoulder in surprise as though someone had disturbed her doing something very private – bathing or admiring her own beauty in a mountain pool.

'You see,' he said, tracing a finger down the statue's spine, 'this Venus is centuries old, but she does not wither, nor does she betray. It is my fantasy that one of these days she will respond to my touch. She will rise up, all naked as she is, and come into my embrace. And that day will be the day I die, Giulia.' His hand paused, laid against the statue's left buttock, then flickered down between her legs. 'Not yet, though,' he laughed. 'She is, as ever, cold and hard and dry and unyielding.' He pulled me a little closer. 'My biggest fear,' he said, in a quieter voice – I think so that his attendant could not hear – 'is that I am no longer man enough to satisfy a woman. I have sent a young man, a Venetian chemist, across the ocean Columbus charted for us, for there in that unknown continent they say there is a worm which if applied to a man's privy parts will make him swell like a boy of seventeen. Only, he has been gone three years, and for two of those years I have had no word of him.'

His poor mother, I thought, but aloud I said, 'Oh, sir, is it not better to think not of new worlds on earth but instead the one that awaits all good men? Can you not accept the cooling of the blood as a gift?'

Vincenzo frowned. 'You're right, I know you are. But I cannot. I love life, I love your sex too dearly. And what happens here,' he let go of my arm and tapped his forehead, 'has not changed, even though here...' He grasped his codpiece with such fervour that I felt myself blush. 'This sluggard refuses to get off his mattress and serve me as he once did.' He took my arm again, wheezing. 'You think me absurd, Giulia, with my unclean face, my fiery knee, my fading eyes. I do not see you so well, but I sense your pity nevertheless.'

Later, I offered him a treasure of my own. 'As you keep our son's painting in your chapel, you might like this too. It is a simple thing.'

With trembling fingers I unlaced the leather bag and brought the picture out. To me, it is the most marvellous thing I have ever seen: not only the skill with which it has been painted (to my eye – I cannot claim to be an expert) but the spirit that imbues it.

It too is a little painting, designed for private devotion, its height no more than the length of my hand and forearm combined. It was only at the last minute that I lifted it from its hook above the prie-dieu in what was my chamber and Giuliano's, and I think I did so not with the idea of showing it to the Prince, but from faith in Our Lady's help to a mother in distress.

I heard the Prince's intake of breath as he took it in his hands. I watched him study it, holding it at arm's length, and with a fluttering of joy realised that his silence, his expression, was one of admiration. I must describe the painting to you, for I no longer possess it.

Of the room in which a young girl sits suckling her child there are few visible features, but from the left a weak light falls across the ochre background, so there must be a window there though none is shown. I think it is the evening also, because the girl's face is calm but shows signs of tiredness. The only furniture that can be seen is the edge of a plain wooden table, and her cross-framed chair, but most of that is obscured by the folds of her dress. However, I know what the chair looks like. I have sat in it many times. A goldfinch is perched on the table, as if he has hopped through the window looking for crumbs. He watches the mother and child intently. They give no indication that they have seen him, and he shows no fear of them.

Yes, she feeds him. They are enclosed in their little private world, that unique still moment where mother and child are again as one as they were when he sheltered in the womb. Did you know that world at all, Mother, or was I torn from you as Filippo was from me? In the painting, the child is wrapped in swaddling bands, but they have been loosened, and his legs kick free. The girl's brown hair is gathered beneath a plain cap, dazzling white against the sombre background. Her dress is grey, with a squared neck edged in white, and the bodice is unfastened down the front – the infant's small hand lies against the slope of her breast and a finger gently presses to encourage the milk. The faintest shadow of an indent in her flesh around the edge of the finger shows this, and is done so well that when I look at it I think I am looking at life itself. I recognise also the slippers she wears.

No, this is not a painting of me. But it is a painting of a girl of the people. She wears the uniform of the Innocenti. You know, dear Mother, though you live in a city where there are few trees for birds to build their nests in, that this is not a portrait of any girl with her baby. It is the little bird that proclaims this lowly mother the Queen of Heaven and her son the Saviour of the World, for the goldfinch feasts on thorns, and bears that crimson stain on his tiny head since that day when he flew down onto our Lord's head, so shamefully crowned as it was, and the blood that was shed for all of us dripped onto his feathers.

'This is marvellous,' murmured the Prince. 'Even with my poor eyes I can see this is worthy of the Caravaggio himself, but I do not think he has ever achieved such intimacy, such quietness. My son did this?'

'He did,' I said, and saw tears in the Prince's eyes.

'And what about this portrait, Giulia? This is me in my coronation robes.' We were standing in his apartments, beneath one of his many portraits, yet this one to me looked like no man I knew. The figure was as stiff and lifeless as a dressed-up marionette.

'They are most fine – heavy, I am sure, to wear,' I said, remembering my rejected bridal gown.

'But as an image of me?'

'I think the artist has not got such a good likeness – not as much as these others.'

'I look like a buffoon, do I not?'

'I think he has painted your robes to perfection.'

'Ha! Then I think I must find someone to repaint my face... my son must do it, though he must paint me as a young man, not the wreck I have become. You will guide him in that, will you not?'

I was about to answer but he went on without a pause. 'Oh, what a day that was! My people loved me – they had not loved my father, for he taxed them and was generous only to the Church when he should have realised that his people needed not only bread but also circuses. They got many circuses with me, and music, and theatricals, and masques. That day, I paraded through my city, my kingdom, and around me, my outriders, gentlemen of the treasury, flung fistfuls of gold and silver coins into the crowd, coins minted for the occasion, bearing the image of their new Prince.'

No, I did not ask him if he remembered the coin he had given to me.

'There was a feast, such as had never been seen in Mantua before – and I wonder if there will ever be such again. Guests from all over Italy, from Vienna, from France, from the Holy See, dining on crystal and fine porcelain, the plates taken away after each course and smashed – why do you bridle, Giulia? They had served their purpose for that unforgettable day and for no other. I couldn't eat like that now.'

'I am sorry for your suffering, sir.'

'You, though, you look as healthy as a fish.'

'I have led a quiet life. I have lost two children but my others are straight and strong. I have been loved, and had few things to trouble me, until now.'

He passed his free hand lightly across my brow; instinctively I closed my eyes.

'I lost a little boy too. But our son is free by now, I am sure of it,' he said.

'I will believe it when I can hold him again in my arms.'

'We will know very soon. And then his home will be here. Giulia – do not leave me now. Bring your other children here – not just my boy, not just Tino – and let me help them. I know that you do not approve of my profligacy, but you must know that I have made the fortunes of many talented men: artists, musicians, goldsmiths, glass-blowers, architects, alchemists. My wings might be clipped by age and infirmity but I can still shelter them, if their mother will walk with me occasionally and give me her sweet counsel. And then, who knows?'

'You do me too much honour,' I said.

I loved this man once. I thought I should die if I did not see him again and hung on every word he gave that poor little sparrow he toyed with. But Giuliano, who was the true father of all my children, is dead, and only the Prince had the power to save Filippo. I could not tell him that all I wanted, with my son restored to my arms, was to flee Mantua for Venice, and never to leave it again.

That evening, after Tino and I had finished our austere meal, a gentleman and a page called at our lodgings. The woman who kept the place and had been insolently polite with us, as is the nature of such people with foreigners they don't expect to see again, knocked on the door of our rooms and with great solemnity in her manner said that the callers had come to take us to the Ducal Palace, for we were to be guests of the Grand Duke himself. She hoped that we would not speak ill of her humble house, and in appreciation of our kindness she would be much obliged if we would take back the money we had already given her. I can only think that the gentleman himself had already made good her account.

We followed him, of course. Who would dare refuse such a summons? He led my son and I through endless corridors dazzling with beautiful things, glass and gilt and fine marbles, glittering gold plate and faience of deep blue and gold on milky white, paintings drenched with such richness of colour that just looking at them my life felt pallid. Standing in the draughty apartments assigned to us, I didn't know how we should find our way out again any more than I had done on the day of that audience, and looked at Tino only to see that he was as disorientated as I.

'I will call for you again in an hour,' said the gentleman, bowing. 'His Highness requires your presence at an entertainment.'

At last I found my voice. 'Sir,' I said, 'His Highness does me a great honour, but I fear I should shame him by the modesty of my dress.'

The man did not blink at this. 'His Highness anticipated this consideration and commanded me to tell you that your sober widow's weeds become you so much that he would not wish to see you in any finery that would dare to compete with the sweetness of your face. And your son must also present himself as he does now, with the decent restraint of one who earns his living by the talent of hand and ear. He told me to tell you, sir,' he said, turning to Tino, 'that he does not desire your presence as a courtier, for he has plenty of those, but would be most grateful for your professional opinion on this evening's entertainment – and your thoughts as to what better amusements might be organised to follow it.'

I felt sorely out of place all the same, and involuntarily hung back when we entered the theatre, with its tiers of seats seemingly reaching into the heavens, glittering in the light of what must have been a thousand tapers. The sound hit me like a buffeting storm: so many people laughing and shouting, the reddened mouths of the women in their starched ruffs, and stiffened brocade and velvet, the gems sewn onto their garments flashing in the light from the sconces. I felt the eyes of those people rest on us in amused and disdainful curiosity, and as we were led to places just below a dais in the centre of those raked rows of seats, I heard them muttering behind their hands. It was better when we sat down. I couldn't see their faces then, and only the backs of the heads of those filling the seats below us. I pulled my veil down that no one might see my burning face and put my hand in Tino's. His hands are like his father's, just as Filippo's are like the Prince's, or rather, like the hands the Prince once had. Oh, Filippo! I should have been passing the evening in prayer, not tossed into that well of flashing sound!

A trumpet blast – and then in roar and rustle hundreds got to their feet as the Prince entered, the confidence and majesty of his presence not diminished by his grip on his cane. The people parted as the waters parted for Moses, leaving the steps up to his throne on the dais free, and everyone turned and bowed before him like the sheaves of wheat that are also in the scriptures. My place was next to the steps, so that the Prince would pass directly by me, and I stood with my head bowed, wishing I was not so conspicuous in my black in the midst of all that finery. Only the presence of my son beside me gave me courage, that and my reason for being in Mantua. For Filippo, I would have walked through a pit of lions.

'Dear orphan,' I heard, and raised my head, aware of hundreds of pairs of eyes upon me. The Prince took my hand and kissed my fingers, while behind him the collective murmur rose like wind in a grove of olives. 'Do raise your veil. We would not have you miss any of the spectacle.'

I do not know how I should describe what I witnessed, whether it was music, or dance, or a play, or all of those things and being all, more. What I remember most was my distraction, the thought of those fleet horses on their way to Florence, my impatience with the darkness outside that would have halted their progress.

Yet there were moments when I lost myself in the tale played out before me. There have been many times, since I was taught to read not only Italian but also Latin, that I have opened the scriptures and found that what I read there seemed written for me – a fact that has both comforted and frightened me. Here too. Though we were indoors, I looked upon a landscape, a little temple upon a hill, trees, water, but not a landscape as one sees from a boat on a river, or when borne along by a horse and cart. No, this was more a landscape that one sees in a painting, only that the people in it moved, and danced, and sang – oh, they sang so sweetly that I wept without at first realising it, and when I did, could not and did not want to stop. A poor virgin was condemned to die – to be sacrificed to the gods – and all that could save her was the marriage of two noble people, for only this would propitiate those capricious deities and save both that girl and her sylvan paradise. Yet this man and woman did not love each other. They loved others. All was explained in a perfect recitative, by a barefoot man in peasant's garb, but with white expressive hands that had never done a peasant's work. I thought of the poor virgin I had been, and the sacrifice that was made of the only wealth I had, and that done so that two other nobles might marry. But above all I thought of the fruit of that sacrifice. I schooled myself to watch and to remember, and not only because the Prince was sure to ask me what I had thought of the spectacle; when Filippo was restored to me, I wanted to be able to tell him what his father had wanted me to see.

But in the fable unfolding before me, it was not the virgin who would save the noble couple but they her, if they only cared enough, for her, or for their duty. I thought of how I might describe the grace of the dancers, the lightness of their naked feet, the looseness of their fluttering garments revealing the whiteness of a shoulder, the slope of a breast. As the widow of a musician and the mother of another, I knew how many hours had gone into ensuring that the words they sang and the movements they made blended in absolute harmony. I heard the Prince's laughter, behind me, above me, as in one scene, the players were all blindfolded, and rushed about the stage in criss-cross patterns (I saw the slightest movement of lips and knew they counted their steps) to deliberately collide one with another and to explore each other's clothes, faces, bodies, in search of the one who was desired most… my face burned but hope fluttered in my breast. How could things of such beauty exist in the same world as the dungeon of the Stinche?

All those years ago in Venice, it was the Prince's habit to rouse the entire house at whatever hour he pleased to come to me. And it was so in that palace in Mantua.

I was lying down when I heard the knock; sleep had not come. My eyes opened on solid darkness, for the tapestried hangings on the bed made night within, even at midday, but in the silence the slightest creak of that vast building was magnified. A door closed nearby, but I could not say which one nor how close, though I felt the air shift and change in the chamber, and then heard the soft brushing of feet on the glazed floor, and saw the wavering of a candle flame through a crack in the hangings.

'Giulia!' He spoke softly.

'Sir?'

'My messenger is returned. Your son – our son – is free. He follows on, with my other man, with the post wagons, which he knows will be guarded.'

What else would a mother have done? I pushed through the hangings and just as I was, in my nightshift, and my feet bare, slipped down to the floor and put my arms around Filippo's saviour, and cried into his shirt. I felt his hand on my back.

'Dear lady, let me put down the candle.'

I pulled away from him, and he bent one knee – and yelped.

'Let me, sir!'

'My knee – you see how wretchedly decayed is your Prince...' For a moment, I remembered him as he was, pushing Vinta in the shoulder, grasping me around my waist and pulling me into his arms. A moment only. I took the candleholder from his trembling hand and laid it down, hearing it clink on the tiles. I looked up. His uplit face looked devilish, that terrible inflamed patch darker, but he reached out his hands to me.

'Dear Giulia. Embrace me again, as you did just now. It is some years since I have been shown such spontaneous affection. And those times I was, I didn't appreciate it.'

I held him without speaking, my cheek against his chest. I smelled that acid tang again, as though whatever was killing him was seeping through his skin where there had once been only a young man's healthy sweat. I felt him move against me, and held my breath, thinking of what must come next, men being the creatures that they are. Nothing. He stroked my shoulders and sighed.

'You are still beautiful, Giulia, but I can no longer pay you tribute.'

When I woke hours later, from the deepest sleep I could remember in weeks, to the knowledge that Filippo was free, it was to find his father's head with that pathetic tuft of stiffened, faded hair pillowed on my breast. All he had done, all he could do, was talk to me, though there was much I wish he had left unsaid.

'My wife was dutiful, but not happy, Giulia. She was imperious, haughty. A hundred and fifty horsemen and nearly as many mules brought her and her dowry: jewels, gold chains, silk, damask, cut velvet and of course endless shining coin.'

I thought of how just one scudo was enough to restore my child to me.

'The wretched girl didn't even blink when I told her one thousand souls dwelled in my palace, all in my service. My mother, her aunt, said this was fit for the firstborn of a Grand Duke and of an Austrian princess, and that all I had to do was make the effort to love her. But you should have seen her at the wedding feast prepared for her. All that fanfare, fireworks, music. She sat up on that dais and barely picked at her food – on plates of chased gold and silver I had commissioned for the occasion, I might add. Her dress, of course, was stiffer than a suit of armour – perhaps that was why she wouldn't eat. I know it took an eternity for them to free her of it that night, while I paced in an antechamber.'

I remembered standing at the window of that house in Florence, with Filippo seeded in me, to hear the crashing and cheering as this man came to meet his bride.

'I remember now, something about that night—' he went on.

'Sir, I think it better you don't say it.'

'No, no, you'll want to hear this! In the morning she asked me, "Who is Giulia?"'

That wounded me, even now. I saw what my life might have been, brought to this city as this man's concubine, waiting for him to come to me in that shimmering palace he had taken me to. But for how long would I have been his favourite?

'What did you say?' I whispered.

'I don't remember now.' I felt him shrug. 'I do remember the advice my mother gave her, for Eleonora repeated it to me, crying so much about it I had to go out and amuse myself elsewhere. It was to ignore my passing fancies, you know, scullery maids, innkeepers' daughters, peasant girls …'

'Orphans?'

He laughed. 'Not the ones under my mother's patronage. I wouldn't have dared. Mother did all she could to restrain me, of course. She would choose my children's wet nurses less I think for the abundance of their milk but for the plainness of their countenances; there was one, I remember, for my firstborn, whose face was like a slab of polenta. My wife liked her. But to begin with, it was not even a certainty that Eleonora would fulfil her duty. Two years passed before I had a son – my heir, for what he is worth. It was my mother's idea that my next should be given to the Church in thanksgiving, eagerly seconded by my wife, but what use he is to it I do not know, for Ferdinando is the most like myself of all my children – whether from the marriage bed or any of the others. No, what Mother told Eleonora was not to be fearful if there were many who caught my eye. She was to be anxious if there was one only, for that meant I was in love. And I was, Giulia, at different times.'

I wished he would be silent, and for a moment he was, doubt-less thinking of all those who had smiled up at him – and perhaps those who had had no choice but to yield to him. But he had another surprise for me.

'Oh, there is something else I must tell you – my wedding voyage.'

'You need not—'

'But this regards you. There was a delay of some weeks, other things needing attention. But we went to Venice, to that palace I wanted to take you to. It was sold long ago; my father said it was an unacceptable expense. I'll confess I'd already got bored of Eleonora's long face by then, so one night I got the boatman to take me to someone who would be happier to see me – the same boatman who used to bring me to you, Giulia. But first I asked to be taken to that house, just to look at it once more. You of course must have seen it many times since.'

'I never have,' I said.

I wasn't expecting the end so quickly. I was sitting waiting, as I had been instructed, in the window seat, as I did every morning. Two courtiers came out of his chamber, too engrossed in their conversation to notice me in the deep embrasure.

'He rambles. At six this morning he had all his children still in Mantua summoned to him and bade farewell to each. But he keeps talking about someone called Filippo. "Has Filippo come? Where is Filippo?" He won't be comforted.'

'It is not good. Does he know the doctors despair?'

'Yes, but he won't resign himself. Quite the opposite. We thought he did, as late last night he insisted he would put on a Franciscan habit. One was brought, and he was helped into it, and for an hour or so he was calm, but then he rallied, and asked not for a priest, but that some of his treasures might be brought to him. A troop of servants came carrying each one of his costly baubles, and he caressed every one and wept over them.'

'As well he might. This place is in debt to the ears. They will have to be sold if the dukedom has any hope of survival.'

'After that he changed his mind about the habit, complaining that it scratched him, and that his people had loved a prince, not a friar. He said he mustn't disappoint them. He bade Silvio take note, to have him embalmed in such a way that he was seated upon a throne, a sceptre in his hand, a crown upon his head, and much more...'

'Grandiloquent to the end! It's his coronation all over again.'

'It'll not happen. There's no money for it.'

'Who is that widow that's been closeted with him?'

'Her? Oh, some supplicant, come here with a musician son who needs work. One of his enthusiasms.'

'Not a lover, then...'

'Ah, no, she's far too ripened for that. Our Prince has always liked his fruit firm against the teeth. No, I expect she's like that beldam who used to pray to keep his headaches away.'

'I remember! Only she stopped praying when he forgot her monthly stipend.'

When they had stopped laughing the first one said, 'You can see that this one must have been a pretty woman, though. A clear skin still, and graceful manners – a lady, whoever she is.'

I didn't want to hear any more, so I stood up and moved into their line of vision. One of them muttered an apology, and turned away, holding the other by the elbow.

'He does not wander,' I said softly, and they looked back at me. 'I too await Filippo.'

The bells of Mantua had already tolled the death of their Prince when Filippo fell into my arms. He was thinner, his beautiful face older, but he lived. I laughed for joy as I held him, though tears rolled down my cheeks, and I touched him wherever I could, his face, his shoulders, his chest, his hands – he was whole. I dreaded, though, to think of the marks his body might bear that I couldn't see, but he gave no sign that my embrace pained him.

'He is dead, the man who sired you,' I whispered. 'But it is to him you owe your release.'

I asked them to bring food to the rooms allocated to me. It was longer in coming than it had been, and I wondered how long it would be until I was dismissed. Tino had sent letters to Venice saying that he would return soon. It was what he wanted, and in any case from the conversations he had had with the court musicians it was clear that with the Prince dead, the golden age of music and masque in Mantua would die too. Eleonora's son was expected to inherit only debts.

I looked at Filippo's hands as he ate. His nails were clean and shaped, as they had always been. I watched him walk to the table, trembling at the thought of torn tendons, feet held to the fire, but his gait was easy.

'Where did they take you?' I asked at last, as Filippo drained his glass.

'To a house, where I was held under guard.'

'A *house*?'

'Yes. I didn't see it until the day I left, for they only took the bandage off my eyes when they turned me into the chamber I was to sleep in – live in, I mean. And the shutters were nailed closed, so I knew it was day or night only by the light that seeped around the edges, and by the sounds from the street below. They gave me candles and brought me food, and water to wash with. I heard others come and go below and heard the murmurs of my guards out on the landing, but saw them only when each morning they opened the door and had me pass out my waste bucket. They were not always the same men. The house was close to the river, that I can say, for I heard the shouts of the bargemen, but I couldn't distinguish the bells well enough to say what parish I was in – though I think the bells of the Duomo were at my back.'

I felt my heart lurch. 'Describe the room,' I said. 'Describe it as minutely as you can – its aspect, its furnishings.'

He did so, and I knew it as well as he.

'I don't know how long I was there for. Weeks – I passed three Sundays in there, on my knees when I heard the bells calling the faithful to Mass, though that comfort was denied me. There was a little wooden figure of Our Lady in a hollow in the wall; she was my only company.

'It was a Monday evening when I heard voices below, men's voices – I heard women too in that place, for being high up, I was close to the kitchen, and I heard a maidservant once try to josh the soldiers, but they sent her away with hard words. Someone came upstairs, and said something to my guards, but too softly for me to make out the words. Then the door was opened, and they told me to follow them. I had longed to be released from that room but was fearful once it happened. I held out my wrists to them, thinking they would bind me again, but they shook their heads, and we went down, one before, one behind me.

'There were three men in the room they brought me to. There was an older one, bearded, who looked familiar to me – I remembered afterwards that he had once called Pocchetti down from the scaffolding where we were working together, apparently to talk about another commission. The other two I had never seen: not knights, but soldiers, I would say, with scarred faces – one of them lacked an eye – and hard hands. I learned from the one who accompanied me on the journey here that they are the Prince's most trusted men. I don't think I want to know what other business they may have done for him. I will never forget the shock of recognition on their faces when I was brought before them – men I had never seen before in my life. One of them actually laughed and said something like "blood will out".'

'You have other brothers here, Filippo.'

'Matteo is my brother, and Tino. I don't want the favour of the Mantuans. I want only to live in peace.'

He went to the door to call for more wine, but there was no servant there. That vast barn of a place was emptying slowly, as its Prince stiffened in his coffin. I saw paintings stacked against a wall that afternoon. I never saw Filippo's painting again, but he has promised he will paint me another.

Filippo came back to the table, shrugging. Then Tino asked: 'What of the charges?'

'The old man said I was to leave with those two men, for my own safety, and as a favour to the house of Mantua, given the closeness of the two Grand-Ducal houses. He asked my pardon for the way I had been guarded but told me that he had used his influence to have me brought to that house for my own protection. "If you had been consigned to one of the city prisons, who knows what might have happened?" He gave me his word that the calumny against me would be thoroughly investigated, and if, as expected, it proved groundless, then my banishment would be overturned and the perpetrators punished. "I shall try to obtain the bishop's permission to interrogate the two nuns myself," he said. "If their testimonies do not match exactly, then I expect they will be flogged for their crime," and I could have sworn from the look on his face that he would have wielded the birch himself if he could – but for the pleasure of it, not from indignation on my behalf. "As for the nun you are supposed to have violated," he said, shifting in his chair, "an examination will establish beyond doubt whether she has had carnal knowledge of a man." His eyes glittered at that, and his beard wagged. I was glad to leave his presence.

'None of this took long, for the Mantuans were keen to head north again. One of them was to ride ahead, while the other soldier and I would follow quietly with the post, to not draw attention to ourselves. When we left, the man whose unwilling guest I had been took both my hands and said he hoped he had again been of service to my family, and asked to be remembered to you, Mother, "though she has bested me this time." What could he have meant?'

'He meant, I think, that all this was an attempt to bring me back to Florence, Filippo – but we will never know that for sure. It never occurred to him that I might pass by Mantua first – yet to me it seemed the most obvious thing to do.'

'Would you have come to Florence?'

'If the Prince had not received me, of course. I would have prostrated myself before Vinta – that is the name of the man whose house you were in – and begged him for his help to find you. I would have done anything he wanted to save you. That's what he expected I would do.'

I thought that I would not hear from Vinta again. But if he had underestimated me, then I too had underestimated him.

We returned to Venice, and the first person Filippo sought out was Master Jacopo, who was overjoyed to see him. His old master had no need for Filippo's skill in the art of the fresco, for which, in the damp city I am resolved to die in, there is not much demand. But, recognising the expertise my son gained working for Pocchetti, Master Jacopo provided Filippo with letters of recommendation to the curia of Verona and of Vicenza. So my son also works on dry land at times, yet not so far from his mother's arms. I could not have borne being parted from him again otherwise.

Three months after our return I found Tommasa dead in her chair by the window, her embroidery fallen to the floor. Her face was still warm, for the sunlight fell on it through the glass, but her hands were icy. I could see she had died peacefully, without a struggle.

Chapter Twenty-Nine

Vinta, at last
October 1613

*...dolorosissima nuova della morte del Senatore Cav. Vinta
sentita da me con quel travaglio che Ella può immaginare
maggiore, havendo io perso un tanto padrone e protettore...*

...you can imagine how great was my pain at the very sad
news of the death of Senator Cavaliere Vinta, for I had lost such
a patron and protector...

Galileo Galilei, letter to Andrea Cioli

All my children save Camilla were with me at home when that
letter came. Though I at once recognised the handwriting, I could
see that it was not his usual confident script; this hand was palsied.

Your son knows who he is, wrote Vinta. *Have you never
wished for the same knowledge yourself, nor wondered why as a
child whose very existence depended on charity, you bore such an
illustrious name?* Of course I had wondered, but I thought there
was not much to tell. Some scion of that family, once the richest in
Florence but now reduced to earning their living as the rest of us
must do, had impregnated a servant girl. I didn't think that there
was love in my making.

*I hope that you realise, from the trouble I went to on Filippo's
behalf, just how high is my esteem for you,* Vinta went on. *The
two nuns who bore false witness are now imprisoned within their*

convent. I shuddered wondering what that would be like – for me, the walls of a convent alone were as impregnable as any gaol. *The bride of Christ they claimed had been debauched by your son has been examined and will go to her holy bridegroom as pure as the day she was born.* I knew what she must have undergone to prove her innocence. With that image in my head I read the remainder of Vinta's missive without paying much attention. I skimmed phrases in which he swore undying loyalty to me, recalled my courage and modesty of years ago, and hoped that I would come under his humble roof again this time as an honoured guest. But at the last sentence I cried out and dropped the letter as if it burned me. *Your mother lives. Come to Florence and you shall see her.*

Tino and Masina accompanied me on this journey – taking the road I had been carried on with Filippo growing in my womb. In Florence we slept at Agostino's house. Filippo, too, offered to come, but I begged him not to, for I didn't want him to cross again the threshold of the house that had been his prison.

I didn't want the cavaliere to see my youngest child. Just the thought of his fleshy lips on her fingers, his eyes lingering on her sweet face and form, made me quiver with revulsion. That day, she stayed safely under Agostino's roof.

How can I describe seeing my native city again? It seemed small after Venice, but cacophonous. It was bewildering to make my way through streets thronged with a tumult of horses and wagons, rather than cross bridges over canals. And then to see my tormentor again... A fisherman from whom I sometimes buy our Friday meal told me that he was once saved from drowning, and that as the water closed over his head for what he thought was the last time, he saw his life pass before him with absolute clarity: the face of his dead mother, the companions of his boyhood, a dog he had loved. I wonder, then, if I shall live long, for when I least expected it, I have gazed on those men who so shamelessly abused

my girlhood, my innocence – the Prince, and then the dead Grand
Duke's creature. Am I destined to see all these faces once more,
and then take my leave of life itself?

I also walked with face averted before the gate of the Pietà and
muttered a prayer for the girls incarcerated there. I walked up the
steps of the Innocenti, beneath the impassive eyes of those glazed
roundels of half-swaddled babes, and stared through the opening
by which so many blameless infants – yes, blameless, for what
did they do? – pass into an unknown future, while their unhappy
mothers walk quickly away into the darkness.

And then I stood in front of that house on the Arno, and trembled.

'Mother, do you really want to do this?' asked Tino softly.

'If mine lives, she will remember me. I do this for her,' I said,
and raised my hand to the chain.

So little had changed, and yet so much. The house smelled the
same, of beeswax and log fires, but it was empty, cavernous,
silent, as it had not been. I clutched Tino's arm, for I began to
shake, and felt the secret places of my body shrivel as if they
would hide themselves. We followed the felted feet of a servant
upstairs. He was a stranger – he could not have been born when
I last set foot there.

He left us standing in a room I had never entered before. It was
hung with tapestries that I could see told a story, but I didn't know
which: knights on horseback, ladies in towers, dogs, rabbits and a
carpet of flowers.

The servant returned almost immediately.

'I shall take you to the minister, my lady. The gentleman can
wait here.'

Tino opened his mouth but the man was prepared.

'The minister has some things to say to the lady which he may
not wish you to hear, sir. But your mother will be only just across
the landing – within earshot.'

'I have a voice and can use it,' I said to my son, and pressed his hand.

The light was waning and that room not well lit, but it was almost as it had been when I saw it last: the false painted hangings, the day-bed where they had made me lie in its old place against the wall. Then it had been thronged with people, bright with rich garments, gleaming teeth and talk and peering eyes. In the light of those flickering candles Vinta was still Vinta – his iron-grey hair had turned to white but was as plentiful as ever, his beard fluffy as sea spray. When he came close to me, smiling, his hands held out, I could smell him, and that room in the inn on the road back to Florence was all about me. I pulled my hands from his grasp.

'You came, dear Giulia!' I had not forgotten that voice.

I never did adopt the Venetian style of dress, with so much of the silky skin between chin and breast exposed. When I was in the orphanage I dreamed of fine clothes, and realised later that it was really a very little sin to do so, compared with the evil things men do when they believe they are right, or at any rate when they know that no one will stop them. In this house Vinta had lured me back to, they had given a poor virgin fine, if modest, clothes, because they thought it would make it easier to corrupt her, though anything they could have given me would have been beautiful in my eyes because for the first time in my life it was mine and mine only. It is the shame of what happened there – in the room in which I now stood – and what followed that has made me always want to cover myself up. Too many men looked at me, you see. And now I am a widow, nearly fifty years old. I have not turned heads for some time – not that I ever wanted to, not after the inventory that was made of me that day. I feel safe, shrouded in my widow's weeds, my hair covered, my face veiled.

'Would you let me see you, Giulia? We are not strangers, after all, and I have followed your doings all these years.'

Standing in that room before that man I thought at first I would have been better unclothed, that he might see the folds of my stomach, the silvered lines, the coarsening of my skin, my hair streaked with grey. But as he stood only a pace from me, his eyes never leaving my face, I saw they were bluish with cataract, the irises white-rimmed – those eyes did not look quite human. I realised that he could not see me clearly, and so I stood before him as the girl I had been, the one he had lusted after even as he delivered me into the Prince's embrace. Those weak eyes were creviced about now with wrinkles and hard, dry moles, but the look in them was that which I had seen when he raised the candle above us in that chamber, his other hand on my flesh. The wet, purplish mouth had a string of white rime along the lower lip, and pockets of it in the corners. But I lifted my veil.

'At last!' he said, and took a step forward.

I backed away from him. 'May I at least sit?'

'I forget myself. Here...' He bustled behind me and I heard a metallic click, the scrape of a chair, then felt his hands on my shoulders, pushing me downwards. His beard brushed my cheek, and I confess I cried out loud and put my hands up to my face to ward him off.

'I mean you no harm,' he said.

He brought another chair from where it stood against the wall and sat down facing me.

'I have had a long career, Giulia, but of all the tasks I have ever been entrusted with, I consider the Congress of Venice the most extraordinary.'

'Indeed,' I said, looking down at my folded hands.

'I do not care for surprises and have made it my business to encounter as few as possible in my professional career, by anticipating them, knowing what was going to happen before my master did. Discreet informers have always helped, of course. But even I am not privy to the talk that takes place within the curtains of the marriage bed.'

'You tried, though. With Deodata.' I wanted to spit in his beard.

'Ah, that!' he said. 'Consider that disinterested concern for your happiness, nothing more.'

'Liar.'

He went on as though I had not spoken. 'I was not thinking of *your* marriage bed, but of Grand Duke Francesco's and his Venetian whore. I have never forgotten the stubbornness in his face after his poor Austrian was interred. It was as if the widower had washed his hands clean of the dust of the vault and wiped the mother of his legal children from his memory – and from his conscience. There were many who remonstrated with him not to marry the Cappello woman. I knew better than to object, though privately I considered him a fool and a catspaw. He was free to take a mistress where he pleased, but a gentleman marries for duty. You may remember my own dear wife—'

'I shall never forget her.'

'Camilla was the niece of the man who held the most exalted office at the court of the Medici. I have held it ever since I succeeded him. Grand Duke Francesco trusted no one as much as he trusted me. I had been expecting him to call me to begin the negotiations with Mantua for the marriage of his daughter to the young Gonzaga prince. I remember vividly the morning I was called to his *studiolo* in the Palazzo Vecchio. That little room stank – it often did – because behind one of those gilded panels there was a staircase leading to one of his infernal laboratories. I have hidden behind that panel myself on occasion, when my employer wished me to overhear a conversation without betraying my presence. He spoke of the calumnies put about by Parma – that it was the groom who had failed in his duty, not the bride's body that blocked his path. "*Erectio, introductio, emissio,*" he said, "the canonical requirement for consummation of a marriage." So he told me to find a virgin, and put the Prince to the test. I said I thought it might be difficult to find a father who would agree to such a proceeding

– though in truth there was one who had consented to his daughter being kept by Francesco's widowed father. I'd handled the negotiations myself. He was ready for that objection, though. He said: "Find one who has no father." Francesco was not so wily, Giulia. Those were the Cappello woman's orders.'

'Why are you telling me this?'

'I want you to know that I was a good servant, that I followed instructions. And that I acted in the interests of Florence – and in yours.'

'Mine?'

'We were in the studiolo also on that occasion when I told him you had been delivered of a son and that he had been given up to the Innocenti. Francesco was angry, for though his son-in-law's seed was potent, his Eleonora had just lost a child. I knew that already, of course. The silly girl had insisted on travelling to Florence to flaunt her fecundity in her stepmother's face and miscarried on the journey home. After that we discussed a husband for you.'

'The only kind thing you did for me.'

'You see? Grand Duke Francesco was delighted with my choice. "A musician! In our employ?"'

'Yes, I told him. A Roman. And he has been guilty of an indiscretion, and so is more amenable to our plans.' Vinta watched me, a small smile on those purplish lips.

'I remember. With the wife of his maestro di cappella,' I said, and was gratified to see his discomfiture. I nearly said, 'We had no secrets,' but there was one Giuliano never knew.

Vinta recovered quickly, though. 'The Grand Duke laughed. "I shall hear the sweet notes he makes from afar, but never have to see the man. And a musician must always comport himself nobly, though he is so poor he does not even have tears to cry with! A foreigner too. Wise as ever, Vinta. That way, if he is not sufficiently grateful to us, he can be banished. Her too along with him." But he risked a great deal, your Giuliano, taking the Prince's child from the Innocenti. I kept that news from Francesco.'

'I must be grateful to you for that too, then.'

'I would like that, naturally. You never saw that studiolo, Giulia, but in Francesco's time it was panelled with the most exquisite paintings. Mythological scenes. You won't know the legend, of course, but there was one of Andromeda—'

'I know her story.' Vinta, of course, did not know that I had learned to read.

'Ah! Well, it depicted her bound to the rock, at the moment Perseus came to release her from her chains, but modest even though she is naked, she turns her face away from her rescuer. I must see if I cannot find that painting and bring it here. Those panels must be stored somewhere… you see, that look of hers reminds me of you, that first evening you were here under my—'

'Please stop!'

'I have always thought of myself as your Perseus, saving you—'

'Which I neither needed nor desired. My mother. You brought me here to speak of my mother. Do so, and then let me go.'

'Ah, yes, your mother.' He steepled his fingers and eyed me, but I noticed the tremor in his hands. 'She lives.'

'Where?' I whispered.

'Just beyond the city boundary. She is, you might say, a holy woman.' He laughed a little. 'A holy fool, perhaps. Of such is the kingdom of heaven, I am told.'

'Where?'

'All in good time. You do not ask me about your father.'

'Why should I care about him? He never cared for me.'

'I knew *my* father, of course,' said Vinta. 'My name has been respected in Volterra for centuries – when the Medici were mere bankers and merchants. The Albizzi too knew greatness – though their star has been on the wane for some time. They made their money in wool, and one of them rose to be Prior of this city – when it was a Republic – but another ended his life on the scaffold, yet another in exile. You have gone pale, Giulia, but I talk of events from a long time ago. It is true that of recent years your kinsmen have had to earn their bread in the way that lesser men must and ask favours of men more powerful than themselves that their sons not starve. That father I told you of, who handed his daughter over to be concubine to the widowed Grand Duke – he also was an Albizzi. I ensured he was well compensated.'

'*Pander!*'

'Ha! I have called myself that, at times,' he said, unperturbed. 'When the Grand Duke died, that woman – your kinswoman – was shut up in a convent far away in Umbria by the husband to whom she had been forcibly married, her children taken from her. You, on the other hand, have been most fortunate. You have twice said you owe me some gratitude, I think.'

I stared straight at him. 'You took payment, sir, long ago,' I said coldly.

'And I would remind you that you are a Florentine citizen, lady, and that I am the most trusted advisor of the fourth Grand Duke I have had the honour to serve.'

We sat in silence, eyes locked like cats facing each other in a yard. Mere minutes passed, but I only knew it was not longer because no bells broke the silence.

'You forget,' he said eventually, 'that your husband would have been dead in a pool of blood had I not found him that post in Venice.'

Was it really Martelli who had sent those assassins? On a musician's salary?

'I am grateful for that too. Just as I am for the gifts you sent for the births of my eldest children.'

'Gifts?'

'Money.'

'Ah... that must have been my wife. She was much given to charitable work.'

I longed to strike him. 'I loved her,' I murmured.

'An exemplary woman, I know... Giulia – Grand Dukes come and go. Their loyal servant, however, remains and manages things as he thinks fit – with an eye, of course, for the common good. I can make, or break, any man, woman or family in this city.' He paused. 'Since I saw you that first time I have thought of you every day of my life.'

Those weren't a man's eyes, but some creature's. Do they not say that the fallen angel at times takes the form of a goat?

'There was another Albizzi came to me looking for a post for his grandson,' he said. My skin prickled.

'That old man is dead, now, has been for many years, but I knew him well and respected him. I recollected there had been some scandal some years before – there is not much that I miss, as I am sure you know – a manservant who died in the poor ward at Santa Maria Nuova, of injuries sustained beneath Albizzi's roof. I was searching for you, Giulia, at the time old Albizzi called...' I saw his smile, the suggestive raising of his eyebrows; I sat rigid as marble.

'The girls I had seen in the Innocenti and the Abbandonati disappointed me... they had scabies, dull hair, grey skin.'

I thought of those beds where we were huddled together, where illness gathered us all into its foetid arms.

'I told him how the reputation of Florence was at stake, and this impoverished nobleman saw a way of solving my problem and thus ensuring a place for his boy. A sharp lad, Sebastiano, diligent – dead to smallpox many years now. Old Albizzi made no promises: "I saw the infant only briefly, as a newborn, and have had no desire to see her since, but you say that the Mantuan wants a beautiful girl – her mother was that. If the child lives, our instructions were that she went to the Pietà before she showed signs of being a woman, and from thence to the Dominican sisters so that she might expiate her mother's sin. She might be fit for your purpose, cavaliere, and it would be a great honour to serve Florence so."'

I turned my face away, for I was weeping, and loathed that he could see it.

'You see, Giulia, it was your own grandfather who gave you to the Prince. I knew as soon as you were brought into the Prioress's parlour that my quest was over. The first thing I noticed about you was the texture of your skin, your clear brow, those candid eyes... I decided then I had to have you, after the Prince had done with you.' He smiled again, and said, more loudly this time, 'It seems the Albizzi make a practice of whoring their virgins.'

'So this Sebastiano...' I said, my lips stiff.

'Your cousin. Your mother's brother's son.'

I repeated those words silently. They made no sense.

'My *father's* brother's son,' I corrected.

'Ah, poor Giulia! You are an Albizzi, but not on your *father's* side. *He* was a nobody – no family name even. Perhaps he, too, was an orphan? Many of his class are. Nobody now knows nor cares who *he* was, and where he lies is known only to God – in some pauper's pit, I expect. It was he who died in the poor ward. Your gently born mother whored herself with one of her father's servants. They were caught trying to flee.'

'You *fiend*,' I whispered. 'You and all of them.'

'Albizzi flogged the man himself, until his back was red raw and his ribs could be seen—'

'*Stop!*'

'His daughter was beating on the door, hearing her lover's screams.'

'*For pity's sake!*' I sobbed openly – how could I not? This devil spoke of my parents, of you.

'Just tell me where my mother is,' I cried, 'then let me go!'

'Don't waste your time, Giulia. She is quite mad. The Minoresses at San Matteo in Arcetri care for her, but I doubt she knows by now that she ever had a daughter. Your father died raving: his wounds turned black. He rotted to death.'

Vinta's outline was blurred by my tears. But I saw him rise and rustle towards me, a great dark bird of prey in his black mantle. Then he dropped on his knees before me, his face burrowing in my lap. I gasped, grasped handfuls of his hair and thrust him away from me.

'Giulia, have pity! Your mother is a whore and your father was a nobody, but I see only *you*. Haven't you made me wait long enough? Stay with me – this house will be yours, my name also!'

I was on my feet by then, backing away from him towards the door.

I heard footsteps, and someone rattled the doorhandle. I thought my heart would burst out of my mouth – the fiend must have locked me in when he brought me my chair.

'Mother?' called Tino.

I felt the door at my back, but Vinta threw his weight against me. His mouth was wet against my throat, his hands pawing at my breasts. I tried to push him away, but he had the strength of a madman – and most horrible of all, I felt the pressure of his desire, old and palsied as he was.

'*Mother!*' My son's fists pummelled the oak.

I flailed out my right arm, and my hand knocked over something metal, some ornament on the *credenza* near the door. I grasped it, cold and knobbly against my palm. I swung it round with all the strength I had against the back of Vinta's head.

He made some muffled noise against my throat, his wet mouth dragged on my skin, and his arms relaxed. Then his body slid down against mine in an obscene, heavy caress, his head bumping on my breasts and then against the fork of my legs. I heard a strange sound, between bubbling and blowing, and then, as he folded onto the floor, a groan such as an old pair of fire bellows makes. I pulled my feet free of his sprawled body.

There was no mistaking that utter stillness, the sudden slackness of that old face. I could smell something metallic, and saw that white hair stained red. My hands felt numb; my weapon fell and clanged on the tiles.

'*Mother!*' I could hear the babble of other voices beyond the door. I turned and flung myself against it. Something dug into my side. Only then did I see that Vinta had merely bolted the door. I could have opened it at any time and escaped into my son's arms. I fumbled at the bolt, thinking I should never make it slide. At last the door opened, and Tino caught me under the arms before I fell. Behind him was the young servant who had admitted us, and an older man.

'I've killed him, Tino!' I howled, and sagged against him.

'Oh Mother, Mother...' My son picked me up and, stepping around the dark, still mass, carried me over to the day-bed.

'*No! Not there!*'

Tino looked at me as though I was mad. Perhaps I was. I had just killed a man, the man the world would say had transformed my life, had given me freedom. I clung to Tino's shoulder, for my legs would not hold me, waiting for the servants to come over and bind me, and give me up to justice.

'Will you go for the captain of the Bargello, or will I, Giacomo?' I heard one of them say. From the temporary safety of Tino's arms, I saw them look at each other and realised their predicament. They must have been the only male servants in the household. With one of them gone, who could hold Tino and I until the captain's men came for me?

'We'll need to bind them first,' said the younger one, eyeing Tino with some apprehension.

'You will not,' said a new voice. 'They have set me free. Is it right that those who brought justice when no one else would should pay?'

The slight figure of a young woman stood in the doorway. Her sleeves were pinned back, her apron stained, her hands, which she clenched and unclenched, chafed and raw. She was the maid of all work no doubt, for I saw no other female face in that quiet house, nor heard any voice.

I saw the two men exchange glances, hesitate. My future and Tino's hung on that moment, that look. Would they be dutiful servants and have vengeance for their master's death or would they heed the words of the lowest of the household, so low that Vinta could do what he pleased with her, and clearly had?

The girl walked up to the corpse, her face working. She kicked it repeatedly, with a force I would not have thought her capable of. It juddered; I thought I would be sick, for that movement made Vinta seem alive still. Whatever my fate was to be, I feared more that he would get to his feet and speak again. Neither of the men moved to stop the girl. It was only when the effort had exhausted her and she bent over and spat on Vinta's face that the younger one put his arms around her, in a mirror of Tino's embrace of me.

'Stop, Isabella,' he said gently. 'He's gone. But you know *we* couldn't have stopped him.'

'I know, Giacomo.' She stood quietly in his arms. In that brief silence I saw his eyes meet the other servant's, over her head, and the other man's almost imperceptible nod.

Isabella twisted round in Giacomo's arms, to look at Tino.

'Did you do this?' she said.

'*I* did,' I heard myself say. 'My son had nothing to do with it.'

'That's true,' said the older servant. 'He could not have done. The door was bolted.'

'Let me go, brother,' said the girl, shaking Giacomo off. She came up to me, kissed me, and burst into tears.

'It's all right, Tino,' I said, gently disengaging myself. Then I did what any mother would do. I comforted her.

'What do we do now, Riccardo?' said Giacomo.

'We're servants, aren't we? What we always do. Clean up after our betters,' said the older man.

Obediently, Giacomo leaned over the corpse, wiping something in the folds of Vinta's cloak. When he straightened up, and replaced the object on the credenza, I saw for the first time what it was: that little bronze satyr, leering, lusting – the one Vinta had used to instruct me.

'You struck him with *that*?' asked Riccardo.

I nodded. I didn't even think to invent some defence, but to my astonishment the fellow smiled. 'It's only a little thing, so your arm must be strong.'

'But what are we going to *do* with him?' said Giacomo, his voice rising in panic. Of course, the crisis was far from over. I imagined this Giacomo put to interrogation by the same methods I had feared would be used on Filippo. I saw the risk he ran; it would be all too easy for him to be caught up in what a prosecutor could easily present as a conspiracy, in which he took part to avenge his sister. There might even be a reward for Riccardo, for four corpses dangling from the windows of the Bargello. I saw that Isabella realised all this too. Pale, with lips parted and pleading eyes, she faced him.

'I do not know for sure what wrong our master did this lady,' she said, 'but you know what he did to me. You couldn't help me then, but will you help her now?'

'I liked him no more than you did,' said Riccardo, after a pause. 'Must he go on harming after he is dead? Take that ankle, Giacomo. I'll get the other.'

Isabella held my arm; I felt her tremble but from the way she breathed out I knew she shared my relief. We watched as the two servants dragged the body towards the day-bed. Tino nudged Isabella and I out of the way, but I could not tear my eyes away from the sight of Vinta's head bumping on the floor. His terrible goat's eyes were only half-closed, grey lips peeled back on rotted teeth. The blood in his hair smeared on the tiles. Vinta looked as though he had been dead a week, not mere minutes. I'd once seen a dyer given to drink hauled from the canal near the church of the Barefoot Carmelites. His corpse, though two days in the water, had been less revolting than this one.

'He fell,' said Riccardo. 'He often falls asleep in here at night. I'll bring a goblet of wine. I will leave it by his hand, spilled. We'll come in and find him in the morning.' I watched as he and Giacomo arranged my tormentor on his side, the damaged part of his face against the cold tiles, a pale hand flung forward.

'It might not have been you,' said Riccardo, looking up at me. 'He often complained of a tightness in his chest.'

'He violated me,' I heard Isabella say, 'instead of providing a dowry and finding me a husband, as a master must. But he indentured my brother too – it was a place he desperately needed – and called it a fair exchange.'

'He made me my sister's pander,' said Giacomo, 'and expected us to be grateful. Because of him, Isabella has already consigned a child to the Innocenti.'

'A girl?' I asked, though I knew.

'Yes. A girl. A boy he said he might have kept.'

I shut my eyes for a moment. 'Merciful heaven.' So Vinta might have thought of me every day, but even if that was true, he'd sated his frustration on others. I thought of Deodata, his spy whom I'd loved. How many had there been like her, like this Isabella? Had her child gone with a token, as Filippo had done? Or had her mother seen her tormentor's face in that poor little girl's and never wanted to see her again?

Isabella started to weep once more.

'Now he is dead,' said Giacomo, 'she and I are free to go elsewhere.'

'And you, sir?' asked Tino, looking at Riccardo. It was the first time my son had spoken aloud since coming in to that terrible scene.

'I'll find something. Same as them.' He bent over his late master and closed the lids over those horrible eyes. 'Perhaps whoever takes this house next will take us too. In the meantime Giacomo and I will take what's owing to us – in kind. That half-goat thing for instance... that must be worth something – unless of course, lady, you wish to have it.'

'No!' I cried. 'It's a loathsome thing and I never wish to see it again.'

'I want it, lady,' said Isabella, 'as a memento of your courage.'

'Take your mother into the adjoining chamber, sir,' said Riccardo. 'I shall bring some wine to revive her.'

'The good wine,' said Giacomo.

When we left an hour later, Isabella embraced me again. I think of her often.

Tino said, as we walked away, 'They do not know our names.' He was warning me, as gently as he could, never to contact anyone in that house on the Arno ever again.

Vinta had visited me in my dreams over the years, but after that day, he was back, more vividly than when he lived. We are in the inn on the road to Florence, and it is there that I kill him with the little satyr. I am taken back in chains, and there is no husband, no dowry for me. I plead my belly, but know that after I have delivered, they will hang me.

It is unwise to write all this, for I am not so artless that I don't know it amounts to a confession. I had no intention of felling Vinta as I did; I wanted only to stop him. If I were to lose my life for that, I would not call it an injustice, but what would be unjust would be my fault visited on my children, the money their father laid by for them confiscated, their name associated forever with that bloody deed. And Vinta's servants would have joined me on the scaffold, punished for their presence of mind more than for their plunder.

Perhaps I should burn these pages.

Days later, Agostino played the organ at the funeral in Santa Croce, an affair of great pomp. I have this vision that the Lady

Camilla opened her eyes in her coffin as the vault was opened to admit her husband, sighed once, and shut them again. I have had Masses said for her soul. Her birthing chair is here still. My daughter, named for her, will need it soon. My grandchild will be a citizen of the Venetian Republic.

I have wondered often why Vinta did not earlier take the simplest course of action to satisfy his desires. Giuliano survived Martelli's attempt on his life (if indeed he was behind it), but why was it not repeated? Or Vinta could have bent justice to his will, had Giuliano arrested on some convenient charge and quietly strangled in the Stinche, throwing me and my children utterly on his mercy. I am forced to think, though, that Vinta, for all his sins, believed himself a just man, a good servant of Florence, concerned with upholding the common good, the stability prosperity depends upon. And he knew a just man does not commit murder. He did in the end cause false charges to be laid against my innocent son, but only because other stratagems to lure me back had failed.

Then what about Deodata, Giacomo's sister, myself? I cannot know what he said to them, or to others. But on that terrible night in the inn on the road back to Florence, he begged me to have mercy on him. He could not see his own fault. No, that was mine, a daughter of Eve who unleashed evil on the world. My face and form caused him to sin – he said as much.

I have had Masses said for his soul, as he died unshriven, attempting to commit a mortal sin. Prayers have been sung to heaven for him by childish orphan voices. But I think those Masses have really been said for me. My crime I have whispered into the ear of that kind friar. I have also told him that in that moment I didn't fear retribution for what I had done so much as dread that the heap of clothes and blood and hair lying by the day-bed might stir, and those eyes reopen.

Chapter Thirty

San Matteo in Arcetri

...frenesia si chiama propriamente quella affettione, o passione interiore, che accompagnata dalla febre acuta, porta seco una continuata dementia nel cerebro del paziente...

Frenzy is the term properly given to that effect, or internal turmoil, which along with a high fever, produces a continuous dementia in the brain of the patient.

Tommaso Garzoni, *L'hospidale dei pazzi incurabili* (1586)

I looked down at my native city, drowsing in that autumn afternoon. What a little place it seemed. Yet up there I could still hear the sound of the streets, the carts, the cobblestones, the shouts, the bells. San Miniato already lay below us, a church that had once marked the boundary of my world.

'It's not much longer now,' said Tino. 'You are pale, Mother, but at least the air up here is purer.'

'If the way did not wind so much...' I said.

'Shall we ask the carter to stop at the next fountain?'

'Please do!' I squeezed Masina's hand again.

Tino leaned forward and muttered in the driver's ear. 'Certainly, sir, for the horse sweats,' said the man.

'It's such a long way,' I said.

'That's what they intended, no doubt,' said Tino.

*

'Ours is a poor house,' said the Prioress, sitting opposite us in her cramped parlour. I had seen that it was, the moment we had alighted by the convent wall. A carving of a lamp, the light of St Clare, was the only decoration above the weathered and stained doorway. The room we were shown into by a silent, sandalled lay sister was distempered and bare except for a crudely carved crucifix and a spotted engraving of St Francis receiving the stigmata.

Tino loosened the strings of his purse.

'No,' said the Prioress, 'that is not what I meant, though we will not turn away any support. This community exists still thanks to the generosity of a few pious widows and sometimes what our brother friars give us, for our rule does not permit us to beg our bread as they may. Of course, the twenty-five florins we receive each Easter for Sister Benedetta's care are essential. She is hardly demanding, but we can keep her decently and we hope offer some comfort to her troubled soul.'

'Who pays that fee?' asked Tino.

'That I am not at liberty to say.'

'Yet it comes from the parish of San Pier Maggiore.'

The nun inclined her head gently in reply. 'By birth, Sister Benedetta is the most illustrious of our sisters, but at the same time, because of her affliction, the most lowly. The intention, I was told, was that she be sent to the Benedictine sisters, but they would not have her: her veiled kinswomen objected. So she was brought here. We are poor, but the air is cleaner here than in the city, and our diet simpler – we eat only what we can grow in our cloister garden and seldom have meat. The work is unceasing. The Grand Duke – the one who died so suddenly with his Duchess, I mean – paid for repairs here some years ago, but only on condition that we too would make over part of our convent to the production of silk.'

'We saw the mulberry trees on our way,' I said, and felt my right foot shifting involuntarily as though it rested on a treadle.

'We had hoped that the simple discipline of repetitive tasks would have helped Sister Benedetta. A routine of work and prayer and silence calms all but the most restless of spirits, but even if she were truly herself, the person she once was, I don't believe that she could have coped. She came unable to perform even some of the simplest tasks, other than putting food in her mouth, for these had always been done for her. She was not brought up to work, you see, like our other sisters. There are no other noblewomen here. We have only the daughters of artisans, of tailors, dyers, tanners, those who can afford our modest dowry. That it is not higher has tended to repel those fathers who have means, for they seek a more comfortable – a more estimable – setting for their unwed daughters. Our advantage is that for the most part, I can say that our sisters are here because they are called, not because they are surplus to the demand for young brides. The exception is, of course, Sister Benedetta. She is here because she is a prisoner, and has been from the moment that door closed on her. But she is no trouble to anyone and teaches us humility.'

'What was she called, do you know, before she was given that name?'

'She came here with it. Benedetta may even be the name she had at birth. Do you think you are ready to see her now?'

'Yes.'

'I shall have to ask your son to remain here in the parlour. Our rules also forbid you and your daughter to enter our enclosure, but for this visit, our sisters have confined themselves to the dormitory. They are sitting in silence there with their sewing as we speak. Once you have seen our poor sister, they will be set free.'

'I am most grateful.'

'There is something about you that tells me you know how to behave in a place like this. You were in a convent once, if I am not mistaken.'

'I was brought up in the Pietà.'

'I wonder now how it was I did not see it straight away,' she murmured. She opened a drawer in the desk; the scrape of warping wood was loud in that quiet place, and I jumped.

'There is no need to be fearful,' said the nun, keys in her hand. 'Your mother can harm no one, perhaps by now not even herself.'

Tino told me later that the time he spent waiting for us seemed an eternity, as he strained to hear beyond the relentless rhythm of the crickets outside the high grilled window – what? A scream? A cry? Within the convent all was muffled, so he never knew at what point I saw you – my mother, his unhappy grandmother.

The Prioress stood back to let Masina and I enter the cell.

'I shall be watching through the grille, should you need me,' she murmured, and then withdrew, softly closing the door. I wish I had thanked her for the kindness of that gesture, of leaving the three of us alone in that moment.

I saw you then, an old, old woman motionless in the corner, clean, and orderly in your dress – the habit of the Minoress, though the Prioress told me before I left that you had never been professed. Your jaws champed continuously, your face folded in on your lack of teeth, but your eyes were as bright as a bird's, and as untamed. In your arms you held a doll – I think it was once Our Lady, the kind we used to carry in processions – and it wrung my heart to see you kiss its wooden face I know not how many times in that short while we were with you. Its painted features were almost obliterated. It was dressed with a child's idea of richness, in clothes made of scraps of old habits, and bright bits of silk left over from the looms, all clean, carefully mended. The Prioress later told me that the doll had other clothes.

'Hello, Sister Benedetta,' I said. Should I have said Mother? Your face, collapsed as a lump of clay that the potter has abandoned on his wheel, was to my shame indistinguishable to me from any other old woman's. Do we all begin to look the same as each other as we are brought closer to that final levelling, or is that only what the young think? There was no sign that you recognised me – nor in me your younger self, or the man who loved you. I still do not know if I look more like you or him, and I never will.

I put my hand out to the doll, thinking you might let me touch it before I could touch you – I was afraid to lay a hand on you, Mother, because I feared what I saw in your eyes – but you turned your back on me, hiding it. I called your name softly, several times, and waited, but you gave no sign of having even heard me.

The Prioress came in then. She put a hand on my arm, but I don't know whether she meant to comfort me, or to caution me. Her eyes were wet. Masina had not spoken a word, but I heard her sniffles.

'She had that doll within weeks of coming here; she is never separated from it,' whispered the Prioress. 'Come outside.'

We followed her. The door was closed but I noticed that the Prioress didn't lock it. From within I heard you murmuring to the doll, reassuring it.

'Though the poor soul was brought here bound hand and foot, and gagged, she struggled all the same. We were told we would have the care of a madwoman, but that we would be well rewarded. I listened to her over the next few weeks and months and I believe that she is not mad, not really, only that she suffers. From odd things she has said, it is clear that she is an educated woman, but she refuses to look at books. We have a small scriptorium, and I thought she might benefit from quiet application to writing out the texts of the Books of Hours that Sister Eustocchia then illuminates, but she turned her back on the desk and the inks. She is an excellent needlewoman, or was, and I had hopes when I saw some linen handkerchiefs she had embroidered, until the morning when I went to her cell and found that she had shredded all her work with her teeth – just as a cornered animal may eat her young. I gave her the doll when I saw that she would not leave off cuddling her pillow. Apart from myself and two sisters who assist her to wash, she trusts only our chaplain. When he comes to bring her the sacraments, she puts the doll in her cot and kisses it good night. The father of one of our sisters made the cot for her, at my request.'

'She receives the sacraments?' I asked. 'I thought—'

'That those afflicted in their minds could not? So did I, but our chaplain said there are many apparently sane who should not, but who do. He said there is surely a place in heaven for one who has suffered so much.'

I asked her then if she had any visitors. The Prioress shook her head. 'You are the first. The gift that maintains her always arrives on time, carried by a servant. No one has ever asked to see if she was properly cared for – though she always has been.'

I started to cry, and the Prioress put her hands on my shoulders to comfort me. 'Come again,' she said. 'I cannot say it will make a difference, but I think you will be sorry if you do not try. I believe, though, that today has been enough for her.'

I looked one last time through the grille and saw my mother's back turned to me. She was nursing the doll. Then, very clearly, I heard the words: 'Pretty ladies.'

I have never gone back. A few days later the Prioress wrote to me at Agostino's address. I sat a long time with her letter in my hand. *Though your intention was only loving, your visit has caused her great distress. I shall spare you a description of the scenes we have witnessed. It is only that she never sees strangers – forgive me for using that term, for I know it must pain you – and was convinced you came to take her 'child' from her. Only this morning has she permitted any of us to approach her again, though we have cared for her all these years, and grown old alongside her. Continue to pray for your mother as I know you do, and for me also, and know that one day 'there shall be no more death, neither sorrow, nor crying, neither shall there be any more pain: for the former things are passed away.' If we see any change in her, be assured that I shall write to you again, at your home in Venice. Nothing is impossible to God, Giulia.*

So I sit here, Mother, and weep over this fardel, blotting the ink of words that have cost me so much. I do not know how to reach you. I believe the Prioress when she says that you are not mad, but that you have suffered much. I am the last person in the world who would wish to make you suffer further, yet it seems that is what I would do.

What is left, then? I will pray for you, and for my father too, for he loved you, and in the end died for you. I am only sorry that I thought for so long that he was merely some heartless corrupter of girls. There are quite enough of those.

Since we have returned to Venice, Masina, my youngest living child, talks only of her desire to join the Poor Clares. She is twenty-one, a little older than I was when I was given to the Prince. Her decision has caused my heart to ache, but she is as happy with it as the dear little saint of Assisi himself. The house of the Clares in the district of Santa Croce burned down not long after I was brought to Venice that first time, and since then they have lived as guests of the Benedictine sisters, but when their convent is rebuilt it promises to be more magnificent than anything that has gone before – though I suspect Masina would be happier in surroundings like those of San Matteo in Arcetri. Master Jacopo already expects commissions for the convent church, and that Filippo may produce work there to delight his sister for the rest of her days is something that pleases me.

It was I who went to Mother Gabriela to speak for my daughter. Masina is already preparing the things she will take with her beyond the grille, and sings as she does so, though my heart breaks. I wonder what will happen to her pretty hair when it is all shorn from her head – and about much else besides.

Filippo is to wed. He is also to be a father. His betrothed is a poor girl of nineteen, obliged to work as Master Jacopo's servant to support a widowed mother and two younger children. She is beautiful, this girl, and Filippo persuaded her to let him paint her lovely face as Our Lady's. To put her at her ease, he talked to her as he worked, and it was then that they fell in love.

I am cross that he went on to seduce her. It is the kind of thing the Prince would have done. But to come to me penitent, and tell me he wishes to marry, is just what Giuliano would have told him to do.

I know now that you will never read this, Mother. Even if I can only be writing for myself, I still need to think of you there. I need you to be my mother; I need to say to you things I could only tell a mother.

My courses came upon me first when I was, I think, fourteen years old, and with them came thoughts which I knew were not right for one who was meant to dedicate her life to God. Those courses held up a hand to stall the Prince when he was impatient to prove his potency. They told me by their absence whenever a new life grew within me, and by their return, when my child began to grow weary of my milk. Now their visits grow less frequent – they come like a friend who finds me asleep in my chair, a book fallen from my hand, and who gently steals away rather than disturb my rest. Dr Marinello insists I chew sage leaves daily and take the tincture he makes from the pods of that pretty yellow flower, that I not be afflicted by melancholy.

I look in the mirror and see that the oval of my face is blurred, and more than ever I like to go about with my neck well covered. I pluck the occasional dark hair from beneath my chin, where such hairs have never been before. I know this is a small sin of pride, for I do this only for myself, having no man who expects me to please him.

I work at my loom every day. It seems like a natural thing to do, to sit there, my foot in the position it has had for as long as I can remember, and follow the rhythm of the rise and fall of the heddles, the quick movement of the shuttle thrown across, the beater pulled forward once, twice, pushing the weft tightly into place. I was a good weaver – and I never really forgot those movements, though I am not as fast as I was, and when I returned to my task, here in Venice, my arms ached, my muscles sang. But this labour made them strong again, and I am proud of what I can do. I am happier to make what I use rather than pay someone else for it, and to put by some little things that Filippo's wife will need for her child. I select the wool myself, for I realise I have not forgotten either how to judge its quality. That shorn from the beast's shoulder is in my view the best. Silk I will not weave again. It shimmers, but always felt harsh to the touch, and the skeins almost sticky.

As the cloth grows, I can let my thoughts run on. I think of you, Mother, and pray that in that place where, as the Prioress wrote, 'there shall be no more death, neither sorrow, nor crying, neither shall there be any more pain', I may be as I never was, a little child at your knee, with my father's benevolent gaze on us both. Yet I am also a woman, with a woman's yearning to hold the man she loves again, and for him never to be taken from her. So most of all I consider a dream I have more and more frequently, and which has banished the images of dungeons and executioner's block. I am peeping through the curtains of the bed in that house where we lived in Florence and see Giuliano standing in the shaft of light where the shutters are open. His skin is golden. He turns to me and smiles and, remembering that he is naked, covers himself with his shirt, but I smile back and he drops it. Then he is climbing back up onto the bed, and leans over me, and when he is about to kiss me, I wake. But the night will come when I shall not wake.

Historical Note

That an orphan called Giulia was taken from the Dominican-run female orphanage of the Pietà to serve as a human test bench for Vincenzo Gonzaga's proof of virility is historical fact, attested to with explicit detail in correspondence in the Medici archive of the Archivio di Stato, Florence. The first part of the novel depends heavily on these sources, which have not been exaggerated by me; I have reproduced some phrases almost word for word. Giulia herself disappears from the correspondence completely after her plaintive question about not seeing the Prince again, so everything I have written after that episode is invention. Later diarists attribute the surname Albizzi to Giulia, and record that on returning from Venice she was married to a Roman musician called Giuliano and dowered with three thousand gold scudi (some saying after she had given birth to a child by Vincenzo; the sex of the child is never specified). One diarist records a more sombre fate, stating that Giulia was reduced to begging a crust door to door, but his account includes some obvious inaccuracies, such as that the test took place in Mantua. The correspondence in the archive does specify Francesco de' Medici's intention to dower Giulia and find her a husband, so it is to be hoped that Vinta carried out this instruction as faithfully as he clearly did all others. Vinta's assault of Giulia on the return from Venice is invented, but it is clear from the correspondence with Francesco de' Medici that the minister was attracted to Giulia and had absolute power over her.

There have been attempts to identify Giulia's husband as Giulio Caccini, the Roman musician and composer employed by the Medici (first proposed by Maria Bellonci, 1947). Apart from the fact that Giulio and Giuliano are not versions of the same name, Caccini was married twice, neither wife was named Giulia, and both wives were themselves musicians. Bellonci also stated that Giulia's child was taken to Mantua and that Giulia herself died young (presumably referring to the death of Caccini's first wife). Kate Simon (1988) repeats the story of the child, but neither provides a source. It is likely that we will never know exactly who the real Giulia was, nor her story after the Congress of Venice. I have invented a surname for her husband.

Giovan Battista Guarini's *Il Pastor Fido* was performed for Vincenzo Gonzaga in Mantua in 1598. The revival performance that Giulia witnesses is my invention, but in keeping with Vincenzo's nostalgia for lost youth.

Giulia's first home, the Ospedale degli Innocenti, built to the designs of Filippo Brunelleschi in 1419 and decorated along its façade with glazed terracotta roundels from the workshop of Andrea della Robbia of swaddled infants, still stands in Piazza Santissima Annunziata in Florence. Founded by the Silk Guild, the most powerful of the Florentine guilds, the Innocenti functioned as an orphanage into the twentieth century and still fulfils its mission of the care of children. The first administration of a smallpox vaccine in Italy took place in the Innocenti in 1756. Forty years ago, visiting the museum (where alongside works of art are to be found the unbearably moving tokens left by mothers with their infants), I looked out into the courtyard to see wandering about a number of heavily pregnant girls about the same age as I was. Today, as well as providing help to needy families and facilitating fostering arrangements, the Innocenti is the headquarters of the UNICEF Innocenti Research Centre, supporting advocacy for children and facilitating the implementation of the United Nations Convention on the Rights of the Child worldwide.

Founded in 1554, the Dominican-allied female orphanage of the Pietà moved in 1568 from its first home in Borgo Ognissanti to Via del Mandorlo (now Via Giuseppe Giusti); the building now houses the Kunsthistorisches Institut.

Selected Bibliography

Vincenzo Gonzaga:

Il Parentado fra la Principessa Eleonora de' Medici e il Principe Don Vincenzio Gonzaga, Florence, 1887 (facsimile reprint, Bologna 1967). The original correspondence regarding the 'test', held in the Archivio di Stato, Florence and the Reale Archivio, Mantua. Also reprinted in edited form as *Una prova di matrimonio*, Rome, 1961, and subsequently reissued in 1965 with the title *Una Vergine per il Principe*, to coincide with Pasquale Festa Campanile's absurd and inaccurate film of that title, which played the story for laughs.

Maria Bellonci, *A Prince of Mantua*, London, 1956. A fluent, but sometimes highly coloured and unsubstantiated, account of Vincenzo's life.

Roger Peyrefitte, *The Prince's Person*, London, 1964. Purporting to tell the story of the Congress of Venice as non-fiction. Based on original documents, but gaps are filled with invention.

Kate Simon, *A Renaissance Tapestry: the Gonzaga of Mantua*, New York, 1988. A useful and readable overview of the history of the Gonzaga family, but which repeats some of Bellonci's assertions.

Paola Venturelli and others, *Vincenzo Gonzaga – il fasto del potere*, Mantua, 2012. Exhibition catalogue with essays on Vincenzo's collecting of art and antiquities, building projects and patronage of art and music.

Valeria Finucci, *The Prince's Body*, Cambridge (Mass.), 2015. This study documents the ill health that plagued Vincenzo Gonzaga for much of his life, and his attempts at cures, as well as the medical context of the 'test' and the annulment of Vincenzo's first marriage, and Vincenzo's search for a cure for impotence.

Life in Renaissance Florence:

John K. Brackett, *Justice and Crime in Late Renaissance Florence 1537–1609*, Cambridge, 1992.

Rudolph Bell, *How to do it: Guides to Good Living for Renaissance Italians*, Chicago, 1999. An entertaining study of contemporary self-help guides covering conception, pregnancy, childbirth, childrearing, adolescence and marriage.

Nicholas Terpstra, *Lost Girls: Sex and Death in Renaissance Florence*, Baltimore, 2002. A history of the orphanage of the Pietà, which does not quite follow through with firm evidence for its rather lurid hypothesis.

Mary Rogers and Paola Tinagli, *Women in Italy, 1350–1650: Ideas and Realities*, Manchester, 2005. This is a highly useful source for the roles and status of women in the period. The authors frame the contemporary sources they quote with historical context, and then allow the protagonists to speak for themselves.

Elizabeth Currie, *Inside the Renaissance House*, London, 2006.

Tim Carter and Richard Goldthwaite, *Orpheus in the Marketplace*, Cambridge (Mass.), 2013. The life of the Florentine musician and composer Jacopo Peri, based on Peri's own papers and accounts; a thorough study of the status and career of a rather more successful musician than was the Giuliano of this novel.

Sara Orlando, 'Le fanciulle di Via del Mandorlo', thesis for the degree of Modern History, University of Florence, 2013. An examination of the demographic origins of the inmates of the Pietà, and the rules governing their lives.

Acknowledgements

I would like to thank Sarah Shaw and all the team at Fairlight Books for their faith in the story I wanted to tell and for helping me make it as good as it can be. I have dedicated this book to the memory of the art historian Paola Tinagli for her fact-check read and for telling me that she cried over her keyboard as she read Giulia's story. I am grateful too to Maria McCann for her feedback on an early draft of the novel and to my Arvon friend Claire Tansey for taking me to Dante's church, Santa Margherita dei Cerchi, where (in my book) Giulia and Giuliano marry. I thank again my agent, Annette Green, for believing in me as a writer, and of course my husband and sons for putting up with research visits masquerading as their holidays; Antonio deserves particular thanks for compiling the family trees of the Gonzaga and Medici families.

The writing of this book was supported by a residency awarded by the Irish Writers Centre to Cill Rialaig artists' village, Co. Kerry, in 2019. This would not be the book it is without the companionship and support of the 'Cill Rialaig Seven' (you know why) and of other talented writers in or of Ireland: Catherine Kullmann, Patricia O'Reilly, Fiona O'Rourke, Constance Emmett, Derville Murphy and Maybelle Wallis. Who said writing was a lonely business?

About the Author

Katherine Mezzacappa is an Irish author currently living in Carrara, northern Tuscany. She holds a BA in History of Art from UEA, an MLitt in English Literature from Durham and a Masters in Creative Writing from Canterbury Christ Church University. Her debut novel (writing as Katie Hutton), *The Gypsy Bride*, made the last fifteen in the Historical Novel Society's 2018 new novel competition. Her short fiction has been short- and longlisted in numerous competitions, and she has been awarded residencies at Cill Rialaig artists' village by the Irish Writers Centre (2019) and at Hald Hovedgaard by the Danish Centre for Writers and Translators (2022).

ALAN ROBERT CLARK

Valhalla

May of Teck, only daughter of a noble family fallen from grace, has been selected to marry the troublesome Prince Eddy, heir to the British throne. Submitting to the wishes of Queen Victoria and under pressure from her family, young May agrees. But just as a spark of love and devotion arises between the young couple, Prince Eddy dies of influenza. To her horror, May discovers she is instead to be married to the brother, Georgie, a cold and domineering man. But what can she do?

From the author of *The Prince of Mirrors* comes this gripping account of the life of Queen Mary, one of the most formidable queens of Britain.

'*Clark takes an iconic and forbidding figure and transforms her into a passionate, loving and damaged woman*'

—Simon Russell Beale

'*Atmospheric and vividly imagined.* Valhalla *brings to life a woman who had otherwise seemed frozen in history; its theme of royal duty still all too relevant*'

—Margaret Drabble

ELIZABETH MACDONALD

A Matter of Interpretation

It's thirteenth-century Europe and a young monk, Michael Scot, has been asked by the Holy Roman Emperor to translate the works of Aristotle and recover his 'lost' knowledge.

The Scot sets to his task, travelling from the Emperor's Italian court to the translation schools of Toledo and from there to the Moorish library of Córdoba. But when the Pope deems the translations heretical, the Scot refuses to desist. So begins a battle for power between Church and State – one that has shaped how we view the world today.

'*Mac Donald has succeeded in making the art of translation centre stage in a thrilling, witty, violent and mysterious debut filled with scheming characters*'

—Jen Calleja, author and translator, Shortlisted for The Man Booker International Prize

'*In lush historic prose, Elizabeth Mac Donald leads the reader on a complex journey, where all interactions are tinged with superstition and suspicion*'

—Nuala O'Connor, author of *Becoming Belle*